Dogfight,
A Love Story

Dogfight,
A Love Story

A Novel

Matt Burgess

DOUBLEDAY
New York London Toronto
Sydney Auckland

QD

· DOUBLEDAY

Copyright © 2010 by Matt Burgess

All rights reserved. Published in the United States by Doubleday, a division of Random House, Inc., New York, and in Canada by Random House of Canada Limited, Toronto.
www.doubleday.com

DOUBLEDAY and the DD colophon are registered trademarks of Random House, Inc.

Book design by Michael Collica

Library of Congress Cataloging-in-Publication Data

Burgess, Matt
Dogfight, A love story / Matt Burgess.—1st ed.
p. cm.
1. Hispanic American youth—Fiction. 2. Drug dealers—Fiction.
3. Brothers—Fiction. 4. Street life—Fiction. 5. Queens (New York, N.Y.)—Fiction. I. Title.
PS3602.U746D64 2010
813'.6—dc22
2009041885

ISBN 978-0-385-53298-3

PRINTED IN THE UNITED STATES OF AMERICA

1 3 5 7 9 10 8 6 4 2

First Edition

For Georgia Banks

When the crack of doom arrives ...

man will flee from his brother.

—The Qur'an

Contents

Acknowledgments

"I'd like to thank my mother" is something my mother's been whispering in my ear since I started this book, and so, straightaway, I'd like to thank my mother, Sandy Burgess. And my father, George Burgess, the best man I know. I'd also like to thank Charles Baxter, Julie Schumacher, and Ethan Rutherford, who all read multiple drafts of this novel and offered invaluable feedback; my friends and my siblings, without whom I wouldn't have any stories; my agent, Leigh Feldman, for her generosity, enthusiasm, and support; Andrew R., who answered countless questions about the Queens underworld (and who asked that his full name not be used); and all the wonderful people at Doubleday, especially Bill Thomas, who made this book better in innumerable ways, and Nora Reichard, who put every word of every sentence on trial for its life. Finally, I'd like to thank Georgia Banks, to whom I have dedicated this book, along with my love and my life.

Dogfight,
A Love Story

Part One

1

Little Round Pills

In the middle of Alfredo Batista's brain there is a tall gray filing cabinet, frequently opened. The drawers are deep, the folders fattened with a lifetime of regrettable moments. There is, tucked away toward the back, a list of women whose phone numbers he never asked for. There are the debts accrued. In the bottom drawer, in separate folders, there are the things he never learned to do: drive an automobile, throw a knuckleball, tie a knot in a cherry stem using only his tongue. What else? In the top drawer, there is a file recounting the evening he left the Mets game early, thinking the run deficit insurmountable. There is the why-didn't-I-wear-a-condom folder. There is—this one's surprisingly thin—the crimes-against-my-brother folder. Alfredo is only nineteen years old, and already his cabinet overflows with files, none of them collecting dust, each one routinely inspected. All it takes is a random word, a face in passing, and a memory blooms, a cabinet drawer slides open. An intracranial research librarian—Alfredo imagines him bespectacled, with frayed pant cuffs and dandruff on his shoulders—waddles over to the open drawer, plucks out the appropriate file, and passes it on to the brain's well-staffed and efficiently run Department of Regret. Here, unable to help himself, Alfredo scrutinizes the folder. He re-creates the event's sensory details. He goes over, with sick and

meticulous precision, exactly what was said and, of course, what was not said. He relinks the chain of events.

A new folder is to be added. It will be labeled with today's date, June 14, 2002, and above that, in blocky capital letters, a name: SHIFRIN, VLADIMIR.

"Who's Vladimir Shifrin?" Alfredo says.

Winston—a dark-skinned Haitian with long, delicate fingers—pulls down on the brim of his Spider-Man hat. He looks over his shoulder. Drops his voice to a conspiratorial whisper. "From what I understand," he says, "Vladimir is a drug dealer."

"This is why you call me?" Alfredo says. "Why you wake me up? Drag me over here?"

They sit close together on a wood-slatted bench in Jackson Heights' Travers Park. There are other parks in Queens—like Astoria Park or Flushing Meadows—where you can snooze under a tree or stick your nose in trumpet-shaped flowers. These parks are pastoral, as the guidebooks might say. They've got grass you can yank right out of the ground. But here in Jackson Heights, the parks, like Travers, are asphalt parks, blacktop playgrounds. There aren't any flowers or butterflies, and that keeps exactly nobody away.

It's two o'clock in the afternoon right now—it's a nice, unseasonably cool, late-spring Friday—and Travers is packed. Everyone is out. Everyone and their mother is out. There are games of soccer, handball, freeze tag, skilo, and skully. Look around. Shirtless men play netless basketball. A father snaps pictures of his little girl, while a Chinese woman dances to the water-like rhythms of tai chi, while teenagers bum cigarettes off the neighborhood schizo, while bees, drunk with pleasure, swarm the bottoms of trash cans. The swings squeak. An old Jewish man—Max Marshmallow, Alfredo's friend—checkmates another old Jewish man whose body deflates like a popped bag of potato chips. A little white boy, oddly calm, has his head stuck between the vertical bars of a fence, and Alfredo can't help but think of his own brother, the newly named Tariq, spending his last hours up at the Fishkill Correctional Facility. On Travers's softball field, Pakistanis play cricket. On a bench in the sun, the Mexicans who didn't get picked up by this morning's work truck take swigs from their brown paper bags. And in the middle of the park, over by the sprinklers, squats a giant and inexplicable stone tortoise, as if for thousands of years he's been making the

trip north from the Galápagos, and he's decided to stop here, in the middle of a park in western Queens, so much does he favor the company of little children and the intermittent splash of sprinkler water. Alfredo understands. He likes it here too. He feels a particular affinity for the father snapping pictures of his daughter. But, all things considered, Alfredo would rather be home, asleep, his face in a pillow.

"Vladimir's a drug dealer," he says. "That's great. Good for him. But hey, sorry, why do I give two shits?"

"Wow," Winston says. He scoots over on the bench, puts some extra space between them. "I guess you give two shits because you *told* me to go find a drug dealer who—"

"I asked you to find a *dog,* actually." Well, to be fair, Alfredo asked Winston to find both, a dog and a new neighborhood drug dealer, maybe even a two-for-one, a new neighborhood drug dealer walking a dog. But Alfredo is going to outlay some shit here anyway because he's tired, because his feet are blistered, because—most of all—Winston is wearing that red and blue Spider-Man hat. Alfredo keeps looking at it, his eyes narrowing. "But instead of a dog, you're talking about—"

"Vladimir."

"You're talking about Vladimir. Any chance he's a drug-dealing dog?"

"He is a drug-dealing fifteen-year-old boy. Slinging outside the Catholic school on Thirty-first Ave—"

"McClancy's?"

"Please. Don't get too interested. He slings outside McClancy's. He *attends* McClancy's. Him being a fifteen-year-old boy and all. And maybe he's holding down exactly the kind of package we need to pick up for Jose."

"Tariq," Alfredo corrects.

"Sorry. Maybe he's holding down exactly the kind of package we need to pick up for Tariq. Oops. I'm sorry. Maybe he's holding down exactly the kind of package *you* need to pick up for Tariq."

"So?"

"God damn, you're in a bitchy mood. Maybe I should just go over to Gianni's." Winston stays right where he's at. He's about to walk away like that stone tortoise is about to hop over the fence. "Do you have any idea how rude you're being right now?" he asks. "I'm telling a story here, and you're not even *trying* to listen. You're looking all over the

park. At God knows what. And I can't get into a good storytelling rhythm, you know what I mean?"

"Where's your Mets hat?" Alfredo says.

Winston looks away. "Oh."

Either due to stress or drug abuse, Winston suffers from alopecia, a condition that causes his hair to fall out in clumps. Coils on his pillowcase. A nest in the drain. Alfredo feels bad for him, genuinely sorry, and he makes all the requisite clucking noises of sympathetic friendship, but he does not downplay the problem, does not tell Winston that it ain't that bad or that it's nothing to worry about. Business is business, and Alfredo considers Winston's quilt-like scalp to be a professional liability. The poor guy—overweight, bulging eyeballs, ashy skin—is already eminently punkable, and the alopecia just makes it worse. *Shave your dome*, Alfredo argues. *You're a big black Haitian. This is a post-Jordan era.* But Winston says nah. He thinks he has dents in his skull. He thinks he got dropped too many times as a baby and he'd look ridiculous now with a completely bald head. He thinks he maybe doesn't have alopecia at all, and the patches will grow back starting tomorrow, or possibly the next day. In the meantime, he wears his red and blue web-speckled Spider-Man hat. The only problem, however, is that the superhero endorsement makes Winston no less vulnerable. The red antagonizes the Crips; the blue, the Bloods. (Winston's skin—black—does him no favors with the Latin Kings or the Vice Lords or the Netas or MS-13.) So Alfredo buys him new, more imposing, and yet more color-neutral hats. Wool knits in the winter. Baseball caps when it's warm. But within days these hats get misplaced, left behind on a rooftop somewhere, or lost under the cushions of a customer's couch. On Monday, Alfredo gave Winston one of the new black Mets hats, and now, on Friday, Spidey's back.

"I think maybe I left it on the subway last night."

"On the subway," Alfredo says. "Let me ask you something—"

"I don't know," Winston says. He picks at the splintered wood of the bench. "You buy these hats for me, and I appreciate them. Seriously. And I swear to God I'm not trying to lose them. It's just, I don't know. I don't know what's the matter with me."

On the lam from the handball courts, a Sky Bounce blue ball skips past their bench. Alfredo bends over, scoops it up. Doesn't even bobble it. He feels tempted to bring it up to his nose—he loves the sharp,

summery, rubbery smell—but that might look awfully strange, and so he tosses it back toward the courts unsniffed. The ball sails over the heads of the players, but park etiquette demands that they shout out thanks anyway.

"It was a cool hat, too," Winston says.

"It's okay," Alfredo says. "Tell me about Vladimir."

"All he sells is Ecstasy. Nothing else. No pot, no coke, no heroin. Just E. Just a straight-up E pusher. Like this is 1997 or something."

"Is that the end of the story?"

"You're mad about the hat still? Ask me how much he sells the E for."

Alfredo asks.

"Ten dollars," Winston says. He leans back on the bench, stretches his legs out in front of him. "Ten dollars for an *entire pill*. That, my friend, is what he's *selling* it for."

"Terrible," Alfredo says. "You can't even get crack for ten dollars anymore. Me and Isabel wanna go see a movie, it costs us *twice* that. A *movie*."

"Ask me who his connect is. His brother. That's who. I don't know his name, but let's call him Boris." Winston's feet tap out a happy rhythm as he talks. "This so-called Boris? He's a chemist. Boris the Chemist. You can't make this shit up. The two of them are fresh off the boat, Boris and Vladimir. Been here like three weeks. Maybe more—I don't know. Boris, from what I understand, makes the X right in the apartment. The kitchen, I guess. That's not factual, though. That's just us speculating. The rumor is that he gets in his lab coat, rocks out with his beakers, and however many hours later he's brewed up some X. Doesn't even know he's supposed to stamp it, so the pills go out logoless."

Alfredo shakes his head. He says, "They're not branding their product."

"They don't know *what* they're doing. So then Boris gives the pills to Vladimir, and little bro stands outside the school gates at three sharp every day. And he *under*sells the whole fucking neighborhood. Because what do they care?" Winston's ass is now hovering above the bench. "There's no middleman. From the kitchen to the street. Ten-dollar Ecstasy."

"You've tried this Ecstasy? It's good shits?"

Winston grimaces. "I haven't done E in a serious minute. You hear about those lab monkeys? Going brain-dead?" He picks at the cuticle around his thumb. "Matter of fact—not that I want to make a big deal or anything—but I am quitting all drugs. Including weed. Starting tomorrow."

"Starting tomorrow," Alfredo says. He watches two little Indian girls march past the bench. With their shoulders hunched forward, they clutch dollar bills in their little brown fists.

"But the preppies," Winston says, elbowing Alfredo. "Over at that Catholic school? They're buying Vladimir out. Rolling on X five, six, seven days a week."

"Those poor nuns," Alfredo says. He hears a familiar jingle coming from around the corner: the patented, crazy-making *doo-doo-dee-doo* of Mister Softee, the ice cream man. Kids run into one another, grab at their parents' wallets, snap their heads back and forth in a lactose frenzy. The ice cream truck pulls up in front of the park's entrance. The jingle is louder, the children palsied. Alfredo takes off his glasses and breathes fog onto the lenses. When he puts them back on, he grins—pleased to see those two little Indian girls at the front of the ice cream line.

"You got any of that money you owe me?" Winston says. "I could really go for a cone."

"How much of this is fact?" Alfredo says. "You know what I mean? This Vladimir kid. The kitchen. The ten-dollar E. Boris. How much do we know for sure?"

"Nothing," he says. "Never even seen the kid. These are things I've heard over at Gianni's. A couple of times. From different people. But still." He puts his hands in the air, exposes for inspection the cool whites of his palms. "This is just shit I've heard."

Alfredo turns away and looks around the park for his favorites. The picture-snapping father is gone. And the little boy—where'd he go?— has somehow slipped his head free from the metal bars. At least the ʼrtoise is still here. And Max Marshmallow over by the stone chess ʼs, harrumphing and kvetching toward another checkmate. He'll ʼas long as I will, Alfredo thinks—forever. And ah, here come ʼ supremo favorites, the little Indian girls, walking past ʼh now. They hold their ice cream cones high, the first with bounty.

"How'd you know Mister Softee was coming?" he calls out to them. "You got his schedule memorized?"

They hasten their steps. Don't talk to strangers, their mothers have warned. Don't go into vans, or pet somebody's dog, or accept candy from an outstretched hand, or discuss ice cream with strange men sitting on park benches. It disturbs Alfredo to see himself through their eyes: a menace. He fingers his mustache, wondering if it makes him look like a child molester. His jeans begin to vibrate. It's his phone, humming inside his pocket—it's either Baka, his drug connect, looking for the money he's owed, or it's Isabel, his girlfriend, calling to confirm that Alfredo will have his Boricuan ass home by four o'clock, so they can walk over to Elmhurst Hospital together. She may cap this reminder with a threat—*If you're late, expect a frying pan upside the head*—or she might hang up with some sweetness, sing him a snatch of whatever Spanish love song she just heard on Mega 97.9. Could go either way. Isabel is seven months swollen with the tentatively named Christian Louis Batista, and Alfredo, while trying to be a sensitive guy about the whole thing, is having some migraine-inducing difficulties negotiating the minefield of her moods. Pregnant! Third trimester! Alfredo wants to chase those Indian girls down and shove his phone in their faces. You see this? This is my girlfriend calling. My baby's mama. A woman who loves me. See? I'm not some scary chester. I am a Puerto Rican, an American citizen, a father-to-be. But Alfredo also understands that chasing two little girls in a city park is not the best way to prove one's own innocent intentions. He stays on his bench and lets the phone vibrate. If Isabel needs him home by four, then he doesn't have time to be taking calls. He doesn't have time to hear about frying pans or Enrique's "Experiencia Religiosa" or little Christian karate kicking the walls of her uterus or the latest shit Alfredo's mother pulled. Alfredo's got work to do.

"Look at you," Winston says. "You're deliberating on this Vladimir situation. You're saying, 'Hey—*hey*.' You're going, 'My man came through with some info that's not too shabby this time.' "

"This kid. He's going to have much drugs on him?"

"You know what today is? Today is the last day of school for all the private-school kids. Get out a week early so they can beat the traffic out to the Poconos. Remember when we was in high school? Last day before summer vacation? Kids *lining up* for drugs. Dealers coming correct."

"And Vl—"

"And our man Vladimir is gonna have his pockets full of pills. Make his money for the long summer ahead. Know what I mean?"

Alfredo stands up and feels dizzy. "Okay," he says. He punches his timecard, clocks in for the day. "Let's go rob him."

Back in the day, when Alfredo and Winston were little shits and new friends, they chanced upon the Alleyway. Too narrow for a car, but wide enough to accommodate a couple of teenaged boys, the Alleyway succeeded an earlier discovery—marijuana—and provided an ideal venue for the smoking of those first, poorly rolled blunts. No police, no old ladies, no moochers asking for a real quick hit. Nobody but the two of them. The Alleyway is T-shaped, and Alfredo and Winston got blazed at the bottom of that T, behind a gate door closed to the street. On either side of them they had stores—a Laundromat and a nail salon—both of which produce their own olfactory, marijuana-masking chemicals. At the top of the T are two- and three-family homes, far enough away that crinkle-nosed neighbors rarely called the cops; close enough that when they did, Winston and Alfredo ran right at the houses, choosing among multiple escapes, this one's driveway or that one's backyard, and slipping safely to the street with the ease of THC coursing through capillaries. This went on for years. Winston and Alfredo would duck into the Alleyway and come out fifteen minutes later, giggling and red-eyed, a cloud of smoke blooming behind them.

When Tariq went to prison, all that stopped. Because when Tariq went to prison, Winston and Alfredo went to work, using the Alleyway now as their base of operations. What made it so well suited to recreational purposes—low exposure, multiple exits—made it equally well suited for professional ones. But no more smoking, Alfredo said. Can't shit where we eat. Can't toke where we sling. It was one of many rules, and today he's allowing it to be broken.

"Fifteen years old?" Winston says. Pinched between his fingers he holds what was supposed to be a courage-fortifying blunt. "I mean that's just a little kid. You know?"

Alfredo sits on the ground, his back against the wall, his hand on his chest. He counts his heartbeats. The big dark pillow hasn't materialized yet to smother his face, but he knows that it's coming.

"And it's the middle of the day," Winston says. "And it's like a really nice day, too. Hey, Jesus. Do you need like a paper bag to breathe into?"

Alfredo shakes his head.

"Well, let me know," Winston says. A glass bottle lies on the ground, and Winston kicks it, sends it clattering, helicoptering down toward the other end of the Alleyway. "The kid's gonna be outside a *school*," he says. "That's what worries me. They've got cops in schools nowadays. Right? Aren't there like cops in the *hall*ways?"

"I don't know about cops," Alfredo says. "There might be some nuns." Winston extends the blunt toward Alfredo, and Alfredo waves it away. He's already taken two, three hits, hoping to dilute the panic filling his chest. It hasn't worked. He leans forward, away from the wall, and puts his head between his knees.

"Why don't we just go over to Gianni's," Winston says. "Cop a few slices. Chill out a bit." As he inhales another lungful of weed, the cherry at the tip of his blunt glows red. He passes it back toward Alfredo, but again Alfredo waves it away. "You serious?" Winston says. Confused, he looks down at his hand, as if to make sure this is still a blunt he's offering, that it hasn't turned into something else entirely, a cup of tea maybe, or a big brass tuba. "You don't want any *more* of this?"

"It's all yours," Alfredo says. Keeping Winston smoking keeps Winston quiet. As long as he's got that blunt bopping between his lips, he can't prattle on about everything he's worried about, and he can't, in turn, sharpen Alfredo's own secret fears. God knows Alfredo's not above breaking the law, but he hates to steal. He wishes he were more like the recently deceased John Gotti, a gangster who saw the pleasures in thieving, who'd hijack a truck full of fur coats just for the thrill of getting away with it. But that's not Alfredo. To talk about it, sure. To sit on a park bench and scheme. But to be in an alleyway about to go do the thing—that, for Alfredo, is a chest-seizing nightmare. He closes his eyes and carefully, carefully breathes in through his mouth. It was more than two years ago, while sitting next to his older brother in the backseat of a Camaro at three thirty in the morning, that the hairs on Alfredo's arms stood up, and he discovered he was a hyperventilator.

Earlier that night, Virgil's Catering Hall in East Elmhurst had hosted the sweet sixteen birthday party of a Miss Rashida Katabi. There had been a DJ spinning records, shawarma in warm buffet trays,

an elaborate cake-cutting ceremony. The privilege of using Virgil's for this special occasion had cost Rashida's father, a walleyed Lebanese man, $2,800, which sum he paid in cash. How did Alfredo know all this? Because his brother told him. And his brother knew because the guys in the front seat of the Camaro—Gio and Conrad—told him, and *they* knew because they worked at Virgil's and had closed down the catering hall only a couple hours previous. They were driving back now, still wearing their polyester uniforms, with friends in the backseat, with intentions: they were going to break in and rob the place. The plan had been formulated weeks in advance over late-night bottles of Corona. Keys had been copied, combinations scribbled down. They'd just been waiting for someone like Mr. Katabi to walk into Virgil's with an envelope stuffed full of cash.

Alfredo had begged his way into the car and now he was asking to get out. Bent over on the sidewalk, his skinny legs quivering like a dog's, Alfredo could take deep breaths but he couldn't breathe any of it out. December's cold air poured down his lungs. His fingertips felt numb. A hive's worth of bees seemed to buzz in his ears. In his haste to get out of the car he left the back door open, and the Camaro's internal system beeped and dinged. The ceiling light glowed above his conspirators' heads. Alfredo watched them watch him. Outside, exposed in the street, choking on air, certain he was going to die, Alfredo felt that it was the tears falling out of his eyes, more than anything else, that disqualified him as a criminal badass. With shouted apologies from the front seat, the car drove away, left him behind. They drove toward Virgil's Catering Hall, and—although they didn't know this at the time—they also drove toward their eventual arrests, toward court dates and public defenders and years-long imprisonments.

That first panic attack, and the ones he's had since, the palpitations he feels now, might have something to do with the sacred prohibition against stealing. Alfredo wonders if he's crazy to credit his breathing difficulties to a fear of supernatural retribution. And yet it *is* a commandment, number seven, *Thou shalt not steal*, right after don't kill nobody or commit adultery. And while he doesn't go to Mass anymore on Sunday mornings, or melt the paper-tasting wafer onto his tongue—it has been five years since his last confession—he still walks the streets afraid. He peeks up at the clouds, fearful of somehow giving offense. He has rules: he won't take the Lord's name in vain, he says a

quick grace before dinner, he can't pass a church without making the sign of the cross. Sometimes before he falls asleep, he'll send God a silent prayer in which he offers a general thanks for the life he's been allowed to create for himself and asks only that God do nothing to snatch the pleasures of that life away (Isabel mainly, and now Christian Louis too). Alfredo respectfully prays for noninterference. No lightning bolts, okay? Please don't burn down New York. You leave me alone, I'll leave You alone.

Alfredo stands up off the ground, but that only seems to make it worse. His arms are goose-pimpled, his tongue coated with anxiety. All this trouble, and he won't even get to keep the pills for himself. He intends to give them to Tariq, who returns home tomorrow after an absence of two and a half years. A drug package being the standard reentry-day gift. Alfredo hoping to impress upon his brother that he is a weight-slinging gangster with resources to spare. *Well, that changes everything,* his lungs say. *If you're not going to keep the pills for yourself . . .* Yeah, right. Stealing is stealing. He can ask for Vladimir's E, he can put in a request—what is religious scholarship if not the prying open of loopholes?—but if Vladimir says no, nah, nyet, go fuck yourself, then Alfredo, the weight-slinging gangster, knows he won't be able to just reach out and take it, hit this stranger, this ninth grader, right in the mouth.

Winston, who's never thrown a punch outside the world of two-dimensional video games, blows a gray stream of sticky-smelling smoke into the sky. The smoke rises, drifts toward the two- and three-family homes, toward a clothesline with pinned-up jeans and T-shirts and orphan socks. It curlicues into an open pant leg. Alfredo expects the smoke, now hidden, to ascend even farther up the jeans and come out the waist, maybe in the shape of a man's chest, and this thought is quickly replaced by another: two, three hits of that blunt and I'm already blazed, waiting on some gray-skinned savior to come out of the sky.

"What's the matter?" Winston says. "What you looking at?"

"Maybe for this Vladimir thing," Alfredo says, and, as always, talking relaxes him: better to be pushing words out of his mouth than drawing air in. "I'm saying if it'll make you feel better. Stop your crying. Maybe we can call the Alphabet Brothers."

"Why? So they can rob Vladimir while we stand in the background and cheer them on?"

"So *you* can stand in the back. So *I* can stop hearing you bitch."

"Sure," Winston says. Having smoked the blunt down to roach size, he stubs it out on the brick wall of the Alleyway. There was still some pot left, the best part actually, but Winston doesn't do roaches. He doesn't like burning his valuable fingers. "Whatever. Do your thing. Call up the Alphabet Brothers."

The Alphabet Brothers—Alex, Bam-Bam, and Curtis Hughes—are a trio of tough black guys from Corona, Queens: Jackson Heights' neighboring neighborhood. The brothers don't look too tough, though. Each of them is over six feet tall, but not one of them weighs more than 145 pounds. (Their mother, Mrs. Hughes, calls them a bunch of skinny belinks.) They've got the long lean bodies of blacktop basketball players, and if you saw them out on the court you'd think they were pure shooters, the guys who spot up behind the arc and put up J's, who are squeamish about running through screens, who don't like to bang in the post for rebounds. The Alphabet Brothers, however, don't do any of that. Sports aren't really their thing. Their thing is punching people in the face.

It starts in the hands. Due to some genetic quirk, the Alphabet Brothers have arthritic-looking fists, with bony knuckles as big and as round as walnut shells. If Vladimir refuses to hand over his goods, the brothers will act. Each one punches from the shoulder and hits like a mule.

But, unfortunately for Alfredo, the Alphabet Brothers don't work for free. The negative aspect to their involvement is the negative of any merger, corporate or piratical: splitting the spoils. But like the Comcast/AT&T merger recently announced in the papers—Alfredo's a proud reader of the *New York Post*—without the collaboration, there ain't no profits. The two parties need each other. Alfredo provides the information; the lump-fisted brothers, the violence. The brothers, God bless 'em, do the actual stealing. They also cover Alfredo's ass retribution-wise. If the young and inexperienced Vladimir cops a postrobbery, pride-stung hard-on, if he gets all horny for revenge, then he'll have to come after two separate crews, and—seeing as how the poor kid's unaffiliated—he'll have to come after crew one (Alfredo and Winston) and crew two (Alex, Bam-Bam, and Curtis) all on his

own. "And to make moves like that," Winston suggested, "guy would have to be drunk on some mad vodka."

But as is Alfredo's wont, he worries still. The concern isn't that the Alphabet Brothers will, after robbing Vladimir, turn around and rob Winston and Alfredo, too. They've got too much history together, too much mutual business: they've got a dogfight going off tomorrow night in Max Marshmallow's basement. But what if the Alphabet Brothers try to press their man advantage? Intimidation artists, they might lean over Alfredo with their cumulative height advantage of twenty-one inches (Alfredo's five foot six and a half) and loudly insist the spoils be split according to man, and not crew, thereby giving the brothers the majority of Vladimir's E and cash. What if they gang up and . . . oh, never mind. Alex and Bam-Bam's cell phones go directly to voice mail. Only Curtis answers Alfredo's call.

A good thing, too. Pulling the string on one Alphabet Brother is easier than marionetting all three, even if that one is Curtis Hughes, seventeen years old, the youngest of the trio and the most belligerent, which is a little like ranking last in a leper colony beauty contest.

"You're not serious," Curtis says when he arrives. "*That* is your drug dealer? The little white boy across the street? With his hands in his fucking *pockets*?" Curtis hocks up a loogie and spits it onto the sidewalk, just far enough away from Alfredo's Timberland boot. "Tell me that the real boss hog is round the corner. Slinging X by the fistful. Tell me, Alfredo, that you're fucking with me."

Alfredo and Winston had Curtis meet them here, on the sidewalk across from the Catholic school, and he's shown up scowling. He climbs off his bike, a twenty-four-inch Schwinn built for children. Face doused, shirt stuck to his chest, Curtis, despite the cool weather, is sweating like Patrick Ewing at the foul line. Little bikes are his preferred mode of transportation—they advertise to the world that he's an original gangster, not above taking a bicycle away from a child—but it isn't easy for a grown man to ride a boy's bike, it's especially hard on the knees, and Curtis agreed to pedal the twenty blocks over here because he thought he was robbing a drug dealer. Not some wannabe, his thumb up his ass.

"Because I don't need to come all the way out here to rob white people. I can do that at home."

15

"Don't worry," Winston says. He pops a piece of General Tso's chicken into his mouth. On the way over here, Winston, his eyes red and his stomach grumbling, stopped in the Wok 'n' Roll on Seventy-third for some Chinese takeout. He eats the chicken straight from the container, pork fried rice sticking to his chin. "Trust me," he says.

Curtis stares, his face contorted as if somebody just smeared a dollop of fecal matter under his nose. "Now I know I'm a fucking idiot," he says. "I know there's nothing I can do about being so obviously stupid. But over in Corona, the drug dealers? They look like me. And the kids that look like *that*? Over there, across the street? Those are the wiggers playing dress-up for Halloween. Punk bitches just trying to look hard. And nobody gets fooled, starts thinking these kids are for real, worth anybody's time, except, you know, the jerk-offs. But hey. That's Corona."

"We wanna know if he's a drug dealer," Alfredo says. "Let's go ask him."

They make their way across the street. Monsignor McClancy High School is a graffitiless, freshly painted three-story building, with large windows and grass lawns and big, shadow-casting trees. This could've been Alfredo's school. Without his father's accident, without the subsequent loss of Jose Sr.'s store and the soaring costs of his medical bills, Alfredo might have ended up here, carrying books and notebooks through McClancy's heavy doors. He went to grammar school at the nearby Our Lady of Fatima and the all-boys McClancy would have been the next logical parochial step. Oh well. Alfredo went from Fatima to I.S. 145 to Newtown High, where he lasted a little under two years before dropping out. Had things broke differently—had lightning bolts not been tossed—Alfredo might've found himself in McClancy's smaller classrooms, learning from ear-yanking nuns who don't take any shit. Who knows? He might have gotten that cap and gown after all. Might've been in seminary school by now, on his way to wafer-dropping, thurible-swinging priesthood.

As a preemptive measure, Alfredo takes off his glasses and stashes them in his pocket, next to his baggie of Internet-purchased prescription pills. The edges of trees, windows, people—it all goes fuzzy. He squints. What else can he do? These glasses are his only pair and he

doesn't need Vladimir landing a lucky punch and cracking a lens. Although a battle royal seems increasingly unlikely. Alfredo wants to believe Winston's story, but Curtis's doubts match his own. There's no question the kid they're walking toward is Vladimir—his is the only Slavic face in a sea of Hispanics—but is this Vladimir a drug dealer holding down weight? He's certainly trying to *look* like a drug dealer. Over his McClancy-mandated shirt and tie, he wears a purple and gold retro Lakers jersey. On his head he's got on a straight-billed black baseball cap, turned around backward. His pants are baggy and slung low. But the problem is that the kid's trying too hard. It's as if Moscow's version of MTV just recently started playing Snoop Dogg and Dr. Dre videos, and Vladimir—anticipating his own American debut—took notes. He's even got an old-school pager clipped to the waist of his wool pants. And it's all wrong anyway. Not only does the hip-hop outfit clash with Vladimir's pale skin and above-the-lip peach fuzz, but it's a pusherman ensemble from a different time and place: the early nineties, the West Coast. There is, however, one cause for hope. A group of kids float around Vladimir. A promising sign—split the nucleus of a teenaged atom and you'll often find drugs—but in the five minutes Alfredo and Winston were across the street, waiting for Curtis, they didn't see one hand-to-hand. Not a single money-for-pills exchange. Either the kids have already copped, or they're waiting to cop, or—Alfredo hates to even think it—this little Russian's got nothing to sell.

"Hey, Vladimir," Alfredo shouts as he gets closer. "What's good with X? Let's talk about some E."

Vladimir's face goes blank. His pink lips don't twist or curl or bend; his mouth is a dumb slot set into the bottom of his face. His eyes move from left to right, scan his interrogators: one black guy; another black guy, heavier and shorter than the first; and a Hispanic, the one who's talking, and the shortest of the three. Vladimir's eyes move without fear or excitement or confusion, as if he were a third grader reading a quadratic equation. As if he were staring at a pile of bricks. He blinks often.

"You speak English?" Alfredo whispers.

"Jesus Christ," Curtis says.

"Ecstasy," Alfredo says. For Vladimir's benefit, Alfredo pantomimes

dropping a little round pill onto the tip of his tongue. He makes his eyes go wide, smiles with all his teeth. "You eat them and dance to techno? Start feeling fantastic? No? Doesn't ring a bell?"

Curtis punches Vladimir in the chest. He falls backward into the chain-link fence. The metal squeaks and strains as the fence flexes to keep Vladimir upright. His mouth hangs open. The air has jumped from his body.

"Those are Air Jordans?" Alfredo says, pointing to Vladimir's shoes. "I haven't seen those in a while. What year are they?"

Vladimir rubs his chest, chews on the air around him. Winston, Alfredo, and Curtis are circled around him, and around that circle a larger one has formed: the onlookers, the Catholic schoolboys with leather bookbags slung over their shoulders. These kids watch in profile, their bodies half turned in case they suddenly need to run for their lives.

Curtis drags his tongue across his upper row of teeth. He leans in close to Vladimir and breathes softly onto his face. "Run your shit," he says.

Vladimir moves as if submerged in honey. From his pocket he takes out a money clip—a thin wad of tens tucked into the fold—and hands it to Curtis. Vladimir reaches back in, roots around, and pulls the pocket inside out. A white tongue outside his pants, the tip flecked with fuzz. That's all he's got: a money clip and some lint.

"This jersey expensive?" Alfredo says. He pinches the fabric between his fingers. "You get it off eBay? How much those Air Jordans cost?"

"Take off your shoes," Curtis says.

To untie his sneakers, Vladimir crouches down into a catcher's stance. Blond hairs uncurl from the bottom of his hat. The back of his neck needs a shave, Alfredo thinks. He grabs the kid's shirt and eases him back up. Poor Vladimir. It's his first ball, and he doesn't know whom to listen to, when to sit down and when to stand up.

"I'll get my own sneakers," Alfredo whispers. "But the Ecstasy. Can you please give one of these black guys your Ecstasy?"

Vladimir turns his other pocket inside out. A set of house keys—attached to a dirt-smudged rabbit's foot—falls to the ground. Toppling out after them is a silver-and-black cell phone, and some loose change, too. The coins jangle as they hit the sidewalk. Vladimir looks

down at the ground. He smells faintly and sweetly metallic, like a can of soda opened and left out overnight. His hands are steady, but his eyes have gone moist.

"Oh jeez," Winston says.

Curtis throws a left hook, punches Vladimir in the ribs. There's a dull *phttht,* the sound of a bowling ball getting dropped in the sand. Vladimir falls to his knees. Hunched over, his forehead kissing the sidewalk, he holds the side of his rib cage with one hand, and with the other hand he slaps at the pavement beneath him.

"Come on," Winston says. "Maybe we should go." In a circular, unconscious movement, he rubs his chest, inadvertently wiping chicken grease all over his shirt. "Maybe we should just get out of here."

"Shut up," Curtis says. He sticks his hands in Vladimir's back pockets. He looks in his hat, and, finding nothing, tosses it into the street. He bends over and crooks a finger into Vladimir's socks, feeling around the kid's ankles and heels. The futility of the search, not to mention its intimacy, its skin-on-skin contact, seems to embarrass Curtis. As he straightens up, he gives Vladimir's shoulder a shove. "Take off your pants," Curtis says. "And squat."

"Come on," Alfredo says. "It's not up his ass."

Curtis smiles. "See? I'm so incredibly stupid. I don't know these things. Tell me, Alfredo. Please. Where's the E at?"

They look around. While nobody was paying attention, the high school rubberneckers have vanished. Those kids have money, they've got parents who can spend six thousand a year on tuition, but they are still an urban crowd—they knew how long they could watch and they knew when to slink away. Only a matter of time before the skinny black kid with the all-bone fists turned his interrogation toward them, and so they took off. Maybe to go get the wheezing Vladimir some help.

"Hey, Winston," Curtis says, still smiling. "Where's this E at?"

Alfredo considers putting his glasses back on, but it doesn't seem necessary. He squints and sees nothing. This long stretch of sidewalk is wide open, without sharp corners or alleyways. And because it's outside a school, in front of a tow-away zone, there aren't any parked cars nearby. No tires or front bumpers where a supply of X might be stashed. If Vladimir doesn't have the drugs on him, then he doesn't have any drugs at all. Alfredo rubs his overstrained eyes.

"I think we should get out of here," Winston says.

Again, inside Alfredo's pocket, his phone begins to hum. "What time is it?" he asks no one in particular, and perhaps accordingly, no one answers him. It's gotta be pretty close to four, he thinks. He could check his phone for the time, find out for sure, but he doesn't want to see his home number flashing and chastising, Isabel on the other end of the line, her knuckles turning white. *Incoming . . .* a frying pan to the head. He reaches for Vladimir's waist and unclips the kid's pager. Vladimir recoils, collapses his body inward.

"Don't worry," Alfredo says. "Hey, listen. Tilt your head back. Breathe in through your nose." Alfredo holds the pager up to his eyes. He puts his glasses back on, checks again, and sees that the pager is off, the LCD screen dim, blank save for the ghost outline of digital eights.

"What time is it?" Winston says.

"Three twenty-seven," Alfredo says. Vladimir begins to push himself up off the sidewalk. He opens his mouth, and Alfredo kicks him right in the neck.

The last time Alfredo's *tias* visited from Puerto Rico, they reached in for a cheek pinch and then stopped. Straightening their backs, they eyed his mustache with suspicion. It can't be, they said. This is Alfredito? The third grader who used to memorize license plates? He had changed beyond recognition. Sometimes he can't even recognize himself. There are old family photographs in shoeboxes, in albums, in frames on the walls of the Batista house, and when he sees the kid in these photographs—the little boy with the bow tie, standing with his nursery-school classmates; the little boy who's got his arm around his brother's shoulders at Coney Island; the little boy holding a stuffed duck or a baseball, or sitting on the kitchen table eating cake with his hands—when he sees this kid in unremembered clothes in unremembered rooms, playing with unremembered train sets, he can't quite believe that the picture person is him, one and the same, Alfredo Batista.

It awes him to see Vladimir gag. On all fours, red-faced, Vladimir crawls on the sidewalk, away from Alfredo. He doesn't get far.

Curtis hooks his hands under Vladimir's armpits. He yanks him up, braces him against the chain-link fence. Vladimir's eyes are open and white. His feet pad at the ground as if slipping on ice. Close to his face,

Curtis pants with an almost sexual excitement. He's been taken off his leash. He snaps his hips, deals from the shoulder, and hits Vladimir in the mouth. Vladimir's head smacks the fence. Perhaps because of that head-on-metal clang, no one hears the soft tear of his lower lip. His eyes are closed. A tooth—a lower canine, yellow rimmed—punctures the lip and pops clean through to the outside of his face. Around that tip-filled hole, blood swells, drips down his smooth white chin.

Winston walks away. Alfredo, seeing his friend leave, gives pursuit.

"Hey," Curtis says. "Where you guys going?"

"Keep the money clip," Alfredo says without turning around. "It's all yours."

"But hey. Hold on. Are we still doing that thing tomorrow?" He's a little boy whose pals have just gone home for supper and taken their ball with them. "We're still doing that dogfight, yeah?"

Alfredo doesn't answer. Winston, elbows out, is hustling down the block, and Alfredo needs to jog to keep pace. "Hold up," he says. His boots aren't made for running; they pound preexisting blisters. "Slow down, wouldya?"

"I gotta go home." Winston, like Alfredo before him, does not turn around to answer. He rounds the corner, putting Curtis and the boy out of sight.

"Winston."

"I've gotta go home, okay?"

Alfredo grabs him by the elbow and turns him around. "Would you just hold on, please?"

Winston won't look at him. Half his forehead is streaked with sweat; the other half, dry. A preexisting condition. When hot or anxious, the right side of his face perspires; when eating samosas or Sammy's halal or KFC spicy chicken or pizza slices overflaked with red pepper, the left side beads up. Alfredo blames the drug abuse. The pot, the coke, the E, the everything else—somewhere along the way a switch got flipped, Winston's glands derailed.

"Please," Alfredo says. He pulls Winston by the elbow, steers him toward the pay phone on Seventy-second Street. They have a history with this particular phone. When Alfredo and Winston were ten years old they used it to make prank calls; at eleven they tagged the side of it with a black Magic Marker, "Yap" for Alfredo, "Sagat" for Winston; at

21

thirteen, and working off the instructions of Jose Batista, Sr., they cottonballed the phone and others in the neighborhood; and now, at nineteen years old, Alfredo picks up the receiver and dials 911. When asked what his emergency is, Alfredo looks at Winston and tells the operator a little kid has been hurt, knocked out on Seventy-first Street, between Thirty-first and Thirty-second avenues. He's surprised by the evenness of his own voice. He didn't expect to be so calm, to ask for an ambulance in the same easy tone he'd use to order a gypsy cab or a pepperoni pizza. The operator asks for Alfredo's name, and he answers by hanging up. He sticks his finger in the coin return slot, just to make sure.

"All those kids saw us," Winston says. "They saw our faces."

A red and yellow bodega squats at the end of the block. Signs advertise the store's wares, but for whatever reason the plurals have been lopped off. The bodega promises its customers cigarette, magazine, sandwich, bus ticket to Atlantic City. Alfredo points his chin at the place. He tells Winston, "Come in here with me. I want to show you something."

Bells clatter as Winston and Alfredo push through the door. Behind the cash register, the Pakistani proprietor jabbers Urdu into his headset, talking to some long-distance relative in Islamabad or Peshawar or someplace Alfredo's never heard of. The man smiles at them as they walk past his counter. They pass the coconut ices, the ramen noodles, the mousetraps and ant traps, the single rolls of toilet paper, the dusty packages of Indian rice, and they keep going till they reach the back of the bodega, where giant refrigerators rise up out of the ground. Behind the frosted-glass doors sit six-packs of Budweiser and forties of malt liquor, each can and bottle individually priced.

"We're gonna get drunk?" Winston says.

Alfredo reaches into his pocket and pulls out Vladimir's pager. With his thumbs, he pushes the top off the plastic case. He slides it carefully along its grooves. Inside the pager, where one might expect wires or microchips or triple-A batteries, are little round pills of Ecstasy. Neatly stacked in three rows of—the numbers burst in Alfredo's head—nineteen pills each, minus five that Vladimir must have already sold that afternoon. Fifty-two pills in a hollowed-out pager.

"Abracadabra."

Winston looks at the pills. "I told you," he says, but there's no swagger in his voice.

"How tough was that kid?" Alfredo says. "Took a beating and wouldn't give it up. Know what I mean? I tell ya, I'd like that kid to work for *me*."

"You don't pay enough."

I don't *make* enough, Alfredo thinks. But right now, in his hand, he holds fifty-two pills, with a street value of $25 apiece. Talking about— Alfredo's math is immediate—$1,300. That's Christian Louis money. That's money that could help pay for cribs, cradles, high chairs, humidifiers, mobiles, titanium strollers, diapers, plush giraffes, breast pumps for Mama, clothes the baby will grow out of, and the endless parade of pediatrician visits. Of course $1,300 can't cover all that. All by itself a crib with a waterproof mattress can cost close to a G. But $1,300 would help. At the very least it could buy more drugs, which could be converted into more cash for more drugs for more cash for more drugs and on and on and on. But this package ain't for me, Alfredo reminds himself. It ain't mine, it ain't mine.

Winston licks the tip of his finger and plucks out a pill. Instead of swallowing it whole, he chews on it, so the MDMA can zip into his bloodstream.

"You gonna give my brother twenty-five bucks for that?" Alfredo asks.

"Take it out of what you owe me," Winston says.

Again, Alfredo's phone hums, and he feels the tug of its telecommunicative leash. Time to go. He fits the cap back onto the E-beeper and slides it into his pocket. It's got to be close to four o'clock, if not later, and Alfredo is nine blocks from home. He and Winston make moves toward the front of the bodega. The Pakistani behind the counter cups his hand over his headset's mouthpiece. He wants to know if he can help them find anything they need. Oh sure. Alfredo needs a time machine, stronger lungs, a pit bull, a healthy baby, a Lotto ticket for his father, a more mentally balanced brother. Actually what Alfredo really needs right now is one of them Ecstasy pills. After watching Curtis punch a hole in Vladimir's mouth, Alfredo would love to swing open a neurological floodgate and get a brainful of serotonin howling through his body. He could take just one pill, he tells himself, and give

Tariq the remaining fifty, a nice round number. Outside the bodega, the sun is shining.

"I don't hear any ambulance sirens," Winston says. "Where's the whoop-whoop?"

Alfredo decides to keep the E in his pocket. He doesn't need the guilt. He doesn't need another file for the cabinet: *Ecstasy, June 14, 2002, afternoon, another drug I shouldn't have taken.* Besides, Alfredo has a long day ahead of him. He can't show up at the hospital with his pupils all dilated, his teeth grinding. Isabel would be pissed. Or worse—she'd be disappointed in him.

2

The Incredible Floating Fetus

The denizens of the clumsily named Elmhurst Hospital Emergency Room Waiting Room—the wounded, the pregnant, the hypochondriacs, the sneezers and coughers and terminally ill, the insured and uninsured, the kids who need stitches, the careless bagel cutters who gashed open their hands—they all sit on the edges of their chairs, their ears cocked toward the nurses' station, waiting for their names to be called. Not Isabel Guerrero. Alone among these waiting room waiters, Isabel is happy to wait. Happy to lean back in her shit-brown metal folding chair and put down roots.

On the inside of her eyelids, Christian Louis floats. He's in a diaper. He's got a wine-splashed birthmark on his cheek. In a voice that's somewhere between a baby's and a man's, he tells Isabel he has spina bifida. Where does he learn such words! Yesterday he told her, smiling, that he had Down syndrome. The day before, cystic fibrosis. There are hundreds of birth defects, diseases where the nervous system shuts down and kidneys collapse, where babies get hooked up to machines and never come off—and with her unborn child whispering these diseases in her ear, Isabel is shook. She believes Christian Louis. She knows Jose's—sorry, *Tariq's*—return is a bad omen, a black crow on the health of her child. Leave this waiting room? No thanks. Isabel stays right where she's at, undiagnosed.

Not that she's comfortable or anything. I'm sweating like a pig, she thinks—and she doesn't even know if pigs sweat. Babe? That animated oinker in *Charlotte's Web*? They seemed pretty dry. She thinks of the pigs she's seen in real life, like the ones over at the churrascaria on Northern Boulevard, but they were all dead. So, okay, she has no idea if pigs sweat or not, but goddamn, she's sweating, that's for sure. And it's not even hot outside. And they didn't even walk here. Alfredo had said his feet hurt, and Isabel took a step back and spread out her arms. Twenty-nine weeks pregnant. One hundred and sixty-two pounds. With breasts that were already big but have gotten bigger, more tender, sensitive it seems to changes in weather, and hanging off her like sacks of potatoes. Isabel said, "*Your* feet hurt? You gotta be kidding." He wasn't. He insisted they take the Q32. From that air-conditioned bus to this air-conditioned waiting room, Isabel hasn't even had a chance to work up a sweat. And yet . . . she sweats. Like (maybe) a pig. She pretends to scratch the back of her neck and gives her armpit a covert sniff. Nothing horrible. Fabric softener, salt, a little something earthy. On the inside of her eyelids, Christian Louis drifts by, doing the backstroke. He says, *Hey Mama. Maybe this anxiety you're feeling has less to do with my potential spina bifida and more to do with . . . oh I don't know . . . Uncle Tariq? Let's talk about that!*

Isabel says, *Nah. Let's talk about how hot I am.* She wishes she were the kind of woman who could just peel off her sweaty shirt and stuff it in a garbage can. Imagine? Not giving a shit like that? That's a Sigourney Weaver in *Aliens* move. That's some *Thelma and Louise* action. Imagine Alfredo coming back—from the bathroom, the parking lot, the water fountain, the operating room, from wherever the fuck he's at—and finding you here, in the front row of the waiting room, wearing only your sneakers, your sweatpants (elastic waistbands!), your bra, and that's it, nothing else, just your big tata pregnant breastesses swinging in this AC-generated breeze.

She turns to look at the people directly behind her: a white couple in their thirties. The woman, like Isabel, is pregnant. (The other day Alfredo showed her an article in the *Post* about the boom in babies, nine months after September 11. *I guess Osama sets the mood,* she'd said.) But unlike Isabel, the woman is probably not here for her prenatal checkup. They're here, Isabel assumes, for the man, who's got a bloody towel pressed to the back of his head. They pay Isabel no atten-

tion. It is, she thinks, one of the better things about hospital waiting rooms. Invisible, she hears no hey mama, no teeth sucking, no hiss hiss hiss. Waiting rooms are, for her, the next best thing to movie theaters. This one is even set up like a movie theater: long rows of chairs all face the same direction, and the people in them stare straight ahead at the TVs bolted prison style to the top corners of the wall. The television on the right plays national news (priests going to jail, Enron cronies on trial), while the one on the left shows telenovelas (gemelos malos, pelea entre hermanos). No one talks to anyone else. Thank God. Usually she'd be up in the OB-GYN section of the hospital, but a burst water pipe kicked her down here, to the ER waiting room, where Isabel worried there'd be more men, more maniacs, more ogling catcallers, but so far, so good. Everyone adheres to the subway contract. Keep your eyes glassy. Build up your own protective bubble of thoughts.

Isabel leans forward in her chair. She puts her hands behind her back and folds up an inch of her shirt. The skin is hot. With the bottom of her shirt hiked up, she presses the exposed small of her back to the cool metal of her chair. Jesus Cristo! Santa Maria! She angles herself in the chair to feel as much of the metal as possible. All ball busting aside, Isabel's feet don't hurt that bad. She expected her calves and ankles to cankle; she expected her feet to swell up and feel as tender as her boobs. But they've been all right. (A hereditary thing, maybe. Her mother the puta always had strong legs and feet, and Isabel should know—she's absorbed many a kick.) So the feet are fine, no problem at all, but her back? Particularly her lower back? Forget about it. There's some Boy Scouts and sailors in there, tying up knots. Lately, at the Manhattan video store where she's worked part-time since she was fifteen years old, Isabel has had nightmare days restocking tapes onto the bottom shelves. She's started stashing them on the top, hiding *The Warriors* behind *The Bad News Bears, Youngblood* behind *Anaconda*. She'd work at the cash register, but she has to pee every ten minutes. Run to the employees-only toilet, squat over the bowl, squeeze out a pathetic trickle. Then go back to work and bend over so some jerk will be able to find *Xanadu* when he wants to rent it. Fuck the whales, Isabel thinks. Forget about the manatees and the troops in Afghanistan. Save my back! Put me on one of those wooden boards like Hannibal Lecter and wheel my ass around.

But this metal chair cooling her off? Beautiful. Let other people go

see doctors. Hear about Tay-Sachs and Huntington's chorea. Isabel is fine right here. She's recently decided to build her happiness out of things just like this: buttered popcorn, the click of a movie projector, Alfredo's mother leaving the house, putting on underwear straight from the dryer, getting into a bathtub surrounded by candles (Isabel's never actually done this, but she will, as soon as she and Alfredo get their own apartment), the smell of Magic Markers, riding the subway into Manhattan, the monkeys at the Central Park Zoo, the café at the Museum of Natural History, the increasingly rare delight of taking a good and solid shit, and, just now added to the list, cold metal on hot skin.

Alfredo plops down into the seat next to hers. "We're next," he says. He wiggles the eyebrows. "I've been schmoozing the nurses. Bribing them with Starbursts." He slips a pink one into her hand. "I told them, 'Listen. We've been here an hour and a half. I work for Channel Seven news, and I'm gonna come in here with a camera crew, expose everyone in this dump of a hospital.' They didn't buy it. I get Starbursts from the vending machine. I tell the nurses, 'Listen. What can you do for us? Here's some candy.' I said, 'But not the pink ones. The pink ones are for mi amor.' " He slips another one into her hand. " 'They're her favorites.' "

"Are you crazy?" Isabel says. "You think just because you give the nurses some"—In the movie version of her life, it would be at this exact moment that a nurse would lean into a microphone and call out Isabel's name. "*Ms. Guerrero. The doctors can see you now.*" Cut to Alfredo grinning. Cut to Isabel with her mouth open. But for maybe the first time ever, she is glad this isn't the movie version of her life. A nurse doesn't call out her name. Isabel gets to finish her sentence and stay in the waiting room—"candy, that we're gonna be next in line or something?"

For another hour she and Alfredo wait in their chairs. Alfredo gets up once to buy more Starbursts. He brings the whole package back to Isabel this time, not only the pinks, but also the reds, yellows, and oranges. He slides the candy into her palm one by one, as if he were bribing a maître d'.

"What do you think he's gonna say?" Alfredo asks. "When he sees you?"

She doesn't know if he means Tariq or the doctor. She takes his

hands. They're smooth and uncalloused. With his fingernails bitten down to the quick, raw and sensitive skin is exposed. She kisses a knuckle. More items for the list! Put it down between Magic Markers and candlelit baths: the pleasures of unwrapping a Starburst, the softness of her boyfriend's hands.

When she was fourteen years old Isabel got her arm broken, and she sat in this waiting room for over three hours. She was more than eager to see a doctor that time. Prior to that she'd been to this hospital only once, to escape from her mother's womb, and after her arm broke, she didn't come back until she was pregnant herself and had to pee in a cup and apply for Medicaid and schedule prenatal appointments like the one today. Just once! Her arm got broke, and her mother called a cab and took her to the hospital. Her only visit between ages zero and nineteen. But did she have more than that one opportunity to come to the hospital? Could she have benefited from consistent medical attention? Would it have been helpful to talk to a staff psychologist, or a sympathetic social worker? *Oh boy!*

She was twelve years old when she lost her virginity. She was pulling back the shower curtain—the one with the map of the world—and she already had one foot out of the tub, when her mother's boyfriend came into the bathroom. His name was Raul Diaz. With his hand covering his mouth, so that his words came out muffled, he told Isabel she was beautiful. He stepped into the bathtub with her. The room smelled like soap. Water dripped off her body. His belt buckle clattered against the wall of the tub. Afterward, when she saw the blood on the tiles, she wondered if this was her first period, and if the rest of her menstruating would always be this bloody and painful. Raul wouldn't look at her. He whispered, *Lo siento. Lo siento.* He helped her clean up the blood. They used paper towels.

Raul was a Cubano. He wore a gold watch too big for his wrist. In the mornings he read *El Diario* with his feet up on the kitchen table, but he never looked comfortable doing it, probably because his legs were too short. He started coming into her bedroom at night. *Isabel? You awake?*

One afternoon, with Raul out of the house, Isabel's mother whipped her with a surge protector. She called Isabel a whore. She held

the outlet end of the surge protector, with its empty, unsmiling faces, and she hit Isabel with the cord, attacking from close range. Snake-like welts rose to the surface of her back. They were bulbous-headed, with slithering, three-pronged tongues.

Like a cartographer she drew borders in her bed. A third of the mattress, the part right next to the wall, was hers. This was her safe zone. When Raul snuck into her room, she moved over into the other two-thirds. When Raul left, she moved back. Columbus returning to the New World! She'd press her body against the wall and go back to sleep.

Urinary tract infection: the diagnosis at thirteen. The school nurse told her she was going to have to start peeing right after sex. Isabel imagined this, getting up when Raul got up, following him out of the bedroom. Later that day, the nurse called Isabel back into her office and gave her a bottle of cranberry juice she'd picked up on her lunch break. *Cranberry juice is good for UTIs,* she explained. She told Isabel she was also going to have to get herself some antibiotics. *And don't let any of these boys peer-pressure you into being sexually active,* she said. She waited for Isabel to nod, and so Isabel nodded. *Is everything okay at home?* the nurse asked. Isabel scratched the side of her nose. *Everything's fine,* she said. *Thank you very much for the cranberry juice.*

Sometimes, when Raul climbed on top of her, she pretended to be asleep. She became an expert at pretending to be asleep. Sometimes, when Raul climbed on top of her, she got out of bed and watched from across the room. Or she'd watch from the ceiling, see things from up high the way people can do right after they've been struck by lightning. She'd watch that man, Raul, rape that girl, Isabel. She'd see his hand jammed into the pillow, next to that poor girl's face. Sometimes, however, Isabel couldn't make the leap out of her body. Sometimes, for whatever reason, she'd be stuck in that bed, listening to the *tick-tock* of his enormous gold watch. He always smelled and tasted like mouthwash.

When she was fourteen years old, Raul moved out. Isabel's mother slammed a door on her arm. Then she called a cab, took her to the hospital.

Frankie, her mother's new boyfriend, moved in. He moved out. New guys moved in, moved out, moved in. Isabel slept in her safe zone and waited for these men to tiptoe into her bedroom, but they never did. Not one of these men raped her. But unfortunately no one from

the future ever traveled back in time to tell her that, and so she was always afraid. If Frankie didn't grab her in the kitchen today, he'd get her tomorrow. If one boyfriend moved out without touching her, the next boyfriend would. She could take quicker showers and get dressed in the bathroom and wear two pairs of pants to bed and not clean her privates and try to avoid the apartment on lazy weekend days, but in the end—Raul taught her this—if they wanted to get her, they would. While she waited for it to happen, she took a serrated knife and cut up her arms.

While her mother was between boyfriends, she and Isabel ate tons of spaghetti with butter and parmesan cheese. They played a game where they'd pretend it was pesto gnocchi, baked ziti, fettuccine Alfredo. Her mother would ask what she wanted for dinner, and Isabel would say, *Linguine with clam sauce.* And her mother would say, *Excellent! Just what I planned on making!* Sometimes, on her way home, Isabel stopped to look at the menus of Italian restaurants, so that she could bring new, more exotic pasta names into the apartment. Penne puttanesca, rigatoni carbonara. Her mother would ask her to explain what they were. Carbonara: pancetta, scallions, black pepper, and egg. *Coming right up,* she'd say. And then she'd serve Isabel a steaming bowl of spaghetti with butter and parmesan cheese. *Bravo, Mama! Perfecto!*

A new boyfriend moved in. Isabel waited. She cut her legs. Blood wriggled into her socks.

Daring escape! At fifteen years old Isabel got a part-time job after school at a video store in Manhattan. She showed up early, left late, covered other people's shifts. The manager praised her work ethic. Isabel went to school less often. In her free time, with the money she made at work, she hit up the movie theaters. Always alone, always in the back row, where no one could see her. She'd unzip her purse, take out a can of soda, and cough loudly as she popped open the tab. In the movie version of her life she didn't work at a video store and she didn't see so many movies, unless the movie version of her life was *Clerks* or *Cinema Paradiso* or *The Purple Rose of Cairo.*

One day at the store she put on *Casablanca.* It was her first time seeing it. At the end of the movie, when Rick and that lady are hugging at the airport, Isabel stood behind the counter, ringing up a customer, staring at the TV screen, and she actually said out loud, *What are you doing, girl? Get on that fucking plane.*

"That's us!" Alfredo says. They're calling Isabel's name, and Alfredo hurries toward the nurses' station, moving through people as if this were a deli and he's got a ticketed number in his fist, his right to roast beef. "That's us," he says again. "Excuse me. Perdón, señora. We're coming! Hold on!"

Up at the front desk, he turns and waves Isabel over. She is not moving fast enough apparently, and so his waving intensifies. She is an airplane, and he is the man on the runway with the orange wands, his hands chopping through the air. Alfredo says something to the nurse. He holds up one finger. He takes a few cautious steps away from the desk before spinning around and dashing over to Isabel.

"You okay?" he says.

An old white man sits in a chair, his hands folded over his cane. Isabel accidentally clips him, bangs his ear with her hip. She steps on a woman's foot. The floor tilts away from her. The bottoms of her shoes have been replaced by ball bearings. She has the sensation of going down stairs and expecting there to be one more step than there actually is. Again and again, Isabel steps through that phantom step and has to catch herself. She leans against the backrest of an empty chair.

"What's the matter?" Alfredo says.

A blue-scrubbed nurse pushes an empty wheelchair toward Isabel. Miraculously, in a city-run hospital of God knows how many employees, the nurse is the same one who met with Isabel and Alfredo on their first visit. She helped them fill out the forms, enroll in PCAP and Medicaid. She counseled Isabel on HIV protection and the benefits of a nutritionally balanced prenatal diet. The nurse has, as she did then, a long braid of black hair snaked over her shoulder. It has been six months since Isabel has seen this woman, and her reappearance now feels ominous. As if the hospital already knows about the diseases baby Christian's been whispering in her ear. As if the hospital can tell just by seeing her bang into chairs that there is something wrong wrong wrong. So they send the O.N.—the Original Nurse—and tell her to bring a wheelchair. The nurse tilts her head toward the chair. Her thin lips smile.

"I can walk," Isabel says.

"Yeah, but why? If you don't have to?"

"This is a nice ride," Alfredo says, running his hand over the arm-rest. He expertly depresses the wheel brakes and flips open the metal footrests. Holding Isabel's arm, he eases her into the chair. "Let me at those handlebars," he tells the nurse.

Two large doors wheeze open, and Isabel is pushed into a new area of the hospital where the lights are brighter and the sounds noisier. Sneakers squeak as nurses and doctors hustle from the ruptured appendix in 104 to the stabbing victim down the hall. The smell of the place—rotting skin and pink antibacterial soap—lingers like a punch in the neck. Worst of all: while Isabel is wheeled around corners and down corridors, through this Elmhurst bazaar, the nurse straggles behind, walking in step with Alfredo. This is not an ideal position for Isabel, who always sits in the back of movie theaters and sleeps pressed against the wall and insists on taking whatever seat faces the door in restaurants. When people loom unseen over her shoulder, when voices float behind her head, Isabel's scalp tingles and her arms tighten. The nurse offers Alfredo directions: go there, make a left here. Maybe she tilts her chin. Maybe she points. Maybe, when a turn approaches, she touches the small of Alfredo's back.

"I'm coming from a job interview," he says. He isn't talking to Isabel. "I think it went okay. The interview. I felt like I asked some good questions. I was on point, I think. Thing is, I'm hoping to make some professional breakthroughs. But who knows, right?"

He must remember the nurse from that first PCAP visit—which doesn't surprise Isabel; he misses little—and he is trying, for reasons Isabel only vaguely understands, to atone for something. Six months ago on the Q32 bus coming back from the hospital, Alfredo complained about having to pretend he was unemployed. He had looked down at the clipboard in the nurse's hand and said he was temporarily between jobs. Spitting the words out like they were curdled milk. As if he expected the Medicaid enrollment form to have an employment status box marked "Drug Dealer." "Do you know how hard I work?" he asked Isabel. "How I'm out there every day? Busting my ass like a dog?" He went on. He complained about how sick he felt, how miserable, how low that hospital experience had dragged him. Until Isabel, in an attempt to put things in perspective, said, "*Your* hospital experience? I had a hand shoved up my vagina." On the bus a surprisingly high number of people (three) turned around to look at them. For the rest

of the trip home Alfredo said nothing. He stared out the window, watching as Elmhurst gave way to Jackson Heights.

"I forget," Isabel says. "What kind of job were you interviewing for?"

"Sales," he says. "Cell phones and pagers. That kind of thing."

Isabel smiles, not knowing where he gets this shit from. If he anticipates the questions and plans what to say ahead of time, or if he just digs right in and pulls it straight out of his ass.

"Well, I think you'll probably get that job," the nurse says. "You seem *very* personable." The chair stops in front of an empty examination room. Despite being small and windowless, a considerable draft blows out of the room, prickling Isabel's legs. The nurse comes around to the front of the chair and bends forward at the waist. "You think maybe you'll be able to stand up now?"

"I never needed to sit down."

The nurse smiles in Alfredo's direction. Isabel has one ally in this world—when Christian Louis is born, she'll have two—but until then, it is Alfredo, and Alfredo only. Do not, you blue-scrubbed bitch, try to turn him against me. In the movie version of Isabel's life, she steps to this nurse and scratches her face.

Isabel walks into the examination room. She is greeted by a sink, a blood pressure cuff, a computer monitor, and a box of rubber gloves with five rubber fingers sticking out of the top as if waving hello. The metal scale, the metal cabinets, and the metal footstool all seem to have been waiting for her. The only grouchy holdout is the examination table, with its unwelcoming strip of white paper. And the nurse, of course. She sticks a small cup in Isabel's hands and asks her to leave.

"The bathroom is next door," the nurse says. She winks. "You probably have to tinkle anyway, am I right?"

With both hands wrapped tight around the cup, Isabel walks out of the room, leaving Alfredo and the nurse behind. The nurse takes her ponytail and drapes it over her other shoulder. She tells Alfredo to sit tight and make himself comfortable. She says the doctor should be with them shortly. And then, like Isabel before her, she walks out of the room.

Abandoned, Alfredo fiddles with the sink. Turns it on and off. He taps on the door to the metal cabinet, which makes a solidly tinny sound, like rain on a rooftop. He wonders if there are some prescription pills inside this cabinet. Some painkillers maybe. He taps on the

metal again, as if expecting any Percocets or Vicodins to tap back. With a steady hand, he fingers the handle to the cabinet door. His breathing is disconcertingly calm.

Maybe he's been cured. Maybe now that he stole that E-beeper and got away with it, he will never again hyperventilate. Maybe—oh Lord—maybe he should've kicked the air out of someone else's throat a long time ago. He doesn't like thinking about it. He'd felt like one of Winston's video game street fighters: somebody hit a button, and Alfredo's foot flew forward. It was something his brother might have done—hurt a stranger on instinct, like an animal—and Alfredo long ago promised that his brother's methods would never be his own. He sold coke, so Alfredo sells weed. He made deliveries, so Alfredo stands on a corner, lets the duff buyers come to him. He got pinched robbing a catering hall, so Alfredo doesn't even walk past catering halls. He treated Isabel poorly, so Alfredo treats her—or at least tries to—in the way she deserves. But what about Vladimir? The kid's eyes were bulging. His face flushed red. He may have swallowed his own tongue. He may . . . oh fuck this. Alfredo can stand in this examination room by himself and feel guilty, or he can open the cabinet door, add some prescription pills to the clear plastic baggie of scrips he already has in his pocket, get caught by Isabel, get caught by the doctor, and then watch the Medicaid form get torn in half, forcing Isabel to give birth on a wood-slatted bench in Travers Park, Santeria priestesses easing Christian Louis's head from her womb. Or Alfredo can follow Isabel and the nurse and bounce on up out of here. Go looking for a rest-room of his own.

The first bathroom door he finds is locked. Maybe he didn't give the knob a good-enough turn. Maybe if he just—nope, it's locked. Because he doesn't want to just stand outside the door and wait, his arms folded in front of his chest; because he does enough of that at work, on the corner; because the whole idea right now is to keep moving and stop thinking—Alfredo goes in search of another restroom.

Doctors zip past him. Nurses, too. Everyone wears sneakers, and everyone, it seems, gives Alfredo a look. It's not quite a disapproving look, but it's close, and Alfredo gets the message: *You know, son, you can't just wander around a hospital, and* (clutching clipboard to chest) *if I weren't so busy . . .* Maybe they're right. Alfredo in the wrong place at the wrong time might cause mortal damage. Say he trips over a plug

to one of those *beep-beep* machines, or bumps into a perfectly cali-brated microscope. But give me a break, Alfredo thinks. Not like he's going to slip on a banana peel and send high-priced hospital equip-ment toppling down one after another like so many dominoes. No, what really worries Alfredo is making a left at the end of this corridor and witnessing someone's private misery. A woman's mastectomy consultation. A little girl shiny pink with third-degree burns. Because what Alfredo sees now is more than enough. Patients in gurneys, exposed, pushing away turkey sandwiches, crying, calling out for help. Alfredo hastens his steps. If he weren't so far gone already, he'd go back to Isabel—if he even knew how to get back. He has arrived at this point in the hospital by making end-of-corridor turns indiscrimi-nately, without reason to his lefts and rights, and while he won't exactly admit he's lost, he's as close as a man can get. Ah, but what's that? He passes a ladies' restroom, and the feminized glyph on the door gives hope. She's all dolled up in her triangle skirt, and so her stick-figured boyfriend must be close by. And here he is, the old pimp. End of the hall.

Intragender modesty has little virtue in a place with bedpans and sponge baths, with male doctors asking female patients to disrobe and nurses sliding catheters into the heads of penises. Alfredo walks into one of the hospital's few men's rooms, one of the few lavatories with multiple stalls and multiple urinals. A guy stands hunched over the sink and washes his hands. Alfredo hurries past him, unzipping as he goes. His bladder—which had been considerate enough to keep quiet on the long journey over here—now belts out an aria. He takes aim at a little blue urinal cake. It is not as much fun as pissing into a urinal full of ice cubes, but at least Alfredo has the gratifying pleasure of see-ing his pee turn green. He gives himself a couple of perfunctory shakes, flushes the lever with his elbow, and makes his way back to the sink where that guy is still—still!—scrubbing away.

"Oh man, I hate this fucking place," the guy says. "The diseases? You kidding me? I'm not OCD or anything, but I must've come in here five times already. Just to wash my hands. You know how many germs are floating around here?"

No, but Alfredo does know that men shouldn't talk to other men in the men's room. The two of them stand at the sink, which is a more acceptable conversational district than the urinals or (God forbid) the

stalls, but *still*. This is the *bathroom*. Alfredo wouldn't talk to his father in the bathroom. Maybe it's a hospital thing—they have a way of breaking down people's boundaries. And actually, Alfredo feels a little desperate to talk to someone himself. He points to the sign above the sink and reads the words aloud. " 'Washing hands saves lives,' " he says. "Well there you go. You're doing a service."

"I been here ten minutes. I should get a fucking Medal of Honor."

"You wanna hear something? My girlfriend—she's eight months pregnant, okay?" She is, of course, only seven months pregnant, but Alfredo tells meaningless lies to stay in practice. "She's got these monthly prenatal checkups. I don't have to come, but I come. Nothing for me to do except hold her hand. Which is fine. I love her. But I gotta take off time from work to get down here. And I really need to be at work right now, know what I mean? Because, like everyone else, I've taken a big financial hit since nine-eleven and when this fucking baby comes, God bless him, you know how much it's gonna cost me? For diapers alone? You know how much I'm paying *already* for things? You know how much I'm gonna *have* to pay?"

"Everyone pays," the guy says. He splashes water on his face. He is in his mid- to late twenties. An obvious fake tanner enthusiast, he has turned his white skin orange, probably thinking it makes him look healthier, more vivacious, and maybe it does, but not today. Today his head sags. On his face he carries a day's worth of beard—a cluster of hair on each artificially tanned cheek, shadows on the chin and upper lip. Worst of all, an arrowhead of stubble pokes out from the center of his hairline. Alfredo guesses the guy is the reluctant owner of a widow's peak, and part of his daily routine is shaving it off with a razor. Just one more thing he didn't get to do today. Alfredo knows tired, and this dude is *tired*. The guy looks in the mirror and scowls. "Insurance, no insurance. Kids, no kids. Doesn't matter. Everyone pays. Right out the ass."

Alfredo pulls out his bag of prescription pills. He leaves it on the edge of the sink, while he goes to the paper towel dispenser. He needs to dry his hands thoroughly before touching the pills. He can't have the greens of OxyContin mixing with the blues of Viagra.

"Well," the guy says, looking at the bag.

"So what are we thinking here? Insomnia? Pain? Depression?" Alfredo looks from the inside of the bag to the guy in front of him,

going back and forth as if one will tell him about the other. As if Alfredo is a used car salesman, trying to size up this mark as a Vette guy or a Cadillac gent. Inside the bag, Alfredo's fingers pinch a Xanax. "Anxiety?" he says. "Is that what we're talking about?"

"Here I am. Complaining about hospitals. And you're a fucking pharmacist."

"Well, I left my prescription pad at home."

The guy turns off the faucet and the bathroom goes quiet. He smiles. Alfredo expected to catch him off-balance, to pressure him into a quick, one-pill sale. The way Alfredo imagined it, the guy gives him twenty bucks for a Xanax because Alfredo convinces him he actually needed it, or because the guy convinces himself twenty bucks ain't a bad deal to get away from an aggressive Puerto Rican pusher. Now, however, Alfredo's starting to think he imagined this all wrong.

"Stress," the guy says. He grins like a wolf sniffing at a rabbit hole. "What have you got for stress?"

Alfredo thinks one thing: *cop*. It'd explain the cynicism, the condescending grin, the nonchalant appraisal of drugs. And if he were a shield-chaser, late twenties would put him at just the right age for the NYPD's narcotics squad. Here's Alfredo about to get locked up over twenty measly dollars. With Isabel waiting for him on the other side of the hospital! He looks for bulges on the guy's hips, by his ankles. He looks for cheap shoes, skin puffy with alcohol, coffee-stained teeth, powdered sugar around the mouth, a wristband with the color of the day, a palpable and nauseating air of superiority. Alfredo goes back through their conversation—did the guy laugh at his own jokes? Is he here visiting his partner, winged in some Elmhurst shootout? Does he use fake tanner because he never sees the sun, because he walks a beat all night and sleeps all day? Alfredo zips up the bag. He says, "Sorry, but I don't have anything for stress."

"Sure you do. I saw some Zoloft in there. White oval pill? Looked like you had the hundred millis."

"No, no, no, no, no." Alfredo puts the bag in his pocket. "That was something else."

The guy smiles like he washes his hands: for way too long. "Don't worry about it," he says. "Stress can be a positive thing. Keep you sharp. Alert."

"Maybe I should join the army then," Alfredo says. "Go over to Iraq

like they're talking about. Take down Saddam. Plenty of stress there, I bet."

"Ha ha. Get that Medal of Honor, huh?" He rips a paper towel out of the dispenser. "You don't have any Zoloft? That's cool. What I really want—hey, stick around for a second. What I'm really looking for is some Ecstasy. You got any X, my friend?"

Holding a cup of her own warm pee, Isabel hurries into the examination room. She finds it empty. She walks back out, checks the room number above the door, looks both ways down the hall. Feeling embarrassed, exposed—her pee is shockingly yellow—she goes right back into the room and sits on the examination table. The strip of paper crinkles under her ass. Her feet dangle. Is it possible for a grown adult human being to sit with her feet kicking at air and not feel ridiculous? In the movie version of her life—Isabel knows this one's a stretch—her pee would not be so yellow. She'd be better hydrated. Inside that cup, Isabel imagines, it smells like the Port Authority bus terminal. She eases herself off the table and goes to the sink. She bends her head to the nozzle, drinks cold water straight from the tap.

"Just last week I look out my window and see my wife in the backyard. Gardening. She doesn't know I'm watching. And I catch her taking a long drink from the hose, and I'm thinking how lucky am I? How incredibly beautiful is this wife of mine?"

He is a big-bellied Indian man, with receding hair and one large eyebrow stretched out across his forehead. If his wife is beautiful, or even moderately attractive, then this is one lucky man indeed. Consider the eyebrow alone. Exceptionally bushy, it threatens to sprout tentacles, threatens to grab the stethoscope off his shoulders, to pass him scalpels whenever he needs them. More hair shoots out of his nostrils and from the cuffs of his lab coat. This is Isabel's sixth prenatal exam and her sixth doctor.

He takes her cup of pee. He looks down and away, clucking his tongue.

"But I didn't get *you* anything," he says.

Isabel stares at this Indian man, at his big belly and fleshy nose, and she wonders—briefly, insanely—if this is Alfredo in disguise. She used to have thoughts like these when she was a kid, when she imagined

her white, elderly third-grade teacher, Mrs. Rosenstock, was really her mother dressed up in a wig and rubber mask. At school, Isabel would whisper words in Spanish while looking into Mrs. Rosenstock's eyes for some glint of understanding. At home, she would raise her hand at the kitchen table, hoping to catch her mother unawares. Ridiculous? Of course. But never were Mrs. Rosenstock and Isabel's mother spotted in the same place at the same time!

"Have you seen my boyfriend?" she asks the doctor. "He was in here like a minute ago."

"Afraid not." With his thumb, he flips the cap off the cup of her urine. A white stick appears in his hand, and he jabs it into the cup. He stirs, as if mixing café con leche. This is normally the lab tech's job, but the doctor gives the impression that he must keep his expert hands occupied. Isabel imagines that when he goes home to India, if he goes home to India, he spends his vacation administering physicals to the entire population, checking every pulse, asking every man, woman, and child to open up and say *aaaaaaaaah.* "Please, my dear. Sit down."

She has questions about the health of her baby, but the doctor, breathless, runs her through tests as if trying to outpace her anxieties. He makes little eye contact. He takes her blood pressure, squeezes her hands and ankles, puts her on the scale, asks about varicose vein developments, pulls the stick out of her urine cup, draws blood from her arm—and all the while, Isabel feels like she's not even in the room. But when he lifts the bottom of her shirt, she goes stiff. She lies on the table, smelling the lemon tea on the doctor's breath. She closes her eyes. Because she is all alone, she summons Christian Louis. She hopes not to hear the names of new diseases, but rather his kind, soothing words: *Is okay, Mama. Relax.*

But Isabel's ears are stuffed. She hears nothing and the doctor's hands are cold. Checking for fetal size and position, he palpates the uterus, prods at the baby's head and shoulders. Isabel's fists are clenched, her body rigid. Despite his mama's summons, Christian Louis does not appear on the inside of her eyelids. All she sees is darkness. But Isabel keeps the hope. Her eyes stay shut, and in the middle of darkness blooms a crimson ring. It is only the imprint of the fluorescent light above her head, penetrating the thin skin of her eyelid. But to Isabel, whose eyes are still closed, it is a small red world, on fire.

She sat in Travers Park and watched the handball games. It was 1998. She was fifteen years old. She'd gone down to the park because at home her mother's new boyfriend was moving in, carrying his boxes into the apartment and plopping them down in the living room. Out on the handball court one man in particular caught her attention. Wearing a wife-beater, banging into the other players, he hammered the ball, swung through it as if it owed him money. After the game, while the other guys reclined against the fence or doused their heads in water, the man stood alone in the middle of the court. Isabel moved toward him. She was frightened but she sounded strong and calm when she told him he was very sweaty and if he wanted to cool off he ought to take her to the movies. His cheek twitched. *You smell good,* he said. With an almost snarl he told her his name, as if daring her to be unimpressed. Jose Batista Jr. looked down at the hand she extended toward him. He laughed.

He fingered her on the floor of the movie theater. This was before stadium seating. The two of them were lying down between rows of seats. Isabel kept her head off the floor, so she wouldn't get any spilled soda in her hair.

When he drove her home, she asked him to come upstairs and meet her mother's new boyfriend.

That night, trying to fall asleep, Isabel decided she won't go to any more movie theaters with Jose. Can't shit where you eat, as the expression goes. She established new rules. Kissing and hand-holding were fine. If necessary, he may feel her up and/or she may give him a hand-job. But there will be no bj's. There will be no more fingering. There will be absolutely no sex. Underline that one. Put it in bold.

Forget the subway. Forget about taking the R train from Roosevelt Avenue to Woodhaven Boulevard. Jose had a van. He drove her to the Queens Center Mall, where he bought her jewelry from Claire's. Junky bracelets, that kind of thing. They shared a plate of nachos from the food court, and afterward he asked her if he had any gunk in his teeth. On the drive home, he showed her the van's hiding spots. Behind interior panels and underneath seats, he kept bags of coke and weed, vials of crack, things Isabel had never seen before.

He said if they're not going to have sex, then there wasn't no point

to kissing. It was all signs of affection, right? He stopped holding her hand. He asked if she'd ever heard of blue balls. He told her his friends thought she was immature, that he could do a lot better.

Her first experience with consensual sex: the Costco parking lot, in the back of Jose's van, where silver duct tape covered the rips in the seat cushions. A cardboard lemon tree dangled from the rearview mirror.

She said she had her period. She said she had to go to work. She said she had to write an essay on John Adams for school. She said, cough cough, that she was sick. She said she got her period again. He told her he could do much better. He told her he had girls lined up. Once she found a used condom in the back of his van, and when she confronted him about it, he said, *Promise you won't laugh? I come back here sometimes and masturbate into rubbers.* She believed him.

Sometimes when they were having sex, she'd step outside of her body and sit in the front seat and do something real cool and casual-like. File her nails, for instance. Or flip through a magazine.

He never hit her. He told her he loved her. When he drove her home and her mother's boyfriend was smoking a cigarette on the stoop, Jose escorted her to the front door, let her hang off his powerful arm.

You're a bad fuck. You just lie there. You don't like trying new positions. You don't ever say anything. You're dry. You can't come and there's something wrong with you. What else did he tell her? Oh, yeah. He said he could do a lot better, but she knew that already.

To become initiated into the Latin Queens a woman needs to allow three Kings to fuck her at the same time. Or she can let them beat her for thirty seconds apiece. Forget it.

They swapped stories from childhood, and here's one of his: His father used to take him and his little brother onto subways to panhandle. The father told people on the train that his daughter had recently passed away. He showed a picture of the little girl and a photocopy of the obituary. He offered to give people the name and number of the funeral home, in case anyone wanted to check up on his story. He owed the home $1,700. Every dollar, quarter, dime, nickel, and prayer helped. He sent his sons down the car to collect money in their hats, and Jose's little brother always got more because he'd blubber like a baby. Even between the cars where no one could see him. Snot coming out of his nose. *Oh my God,* Isabel said. *I'm so sorry.* She asked how his

sister passed away, and Jose told her she didn't understand. There was no sister. The picture was of his cousin Angelique, who grew up and lives in Jersey and works in a dental office. When he saw Isabel's face, his eyes went wide and she could tell he regretted telling her this. *But my father's a cripple now*, he said. *That's a sad story that's true.*

She loved him. She talked about him all the time at the kitchen table. She talked about the gun he bought off a Chinese guy from Flushing.

After the Virgil's robbery, after the police arrested Jose, after he spent a couple days in lockup, the Batistas sprung him out on bail. So there was that at least. For a little while, until the trial, she would be able to hold on to him. They spent New Year's Eve together, driving around Queens and Manhattan, making coke deliveries. At midnight, while Jose was up in a Forest Hills apartment, selling an eightball, Isabel sat alone in the van, listening to the ball drop on the radio. This was 1999 becoming 2000. The tabloids anticipated a Y2K computer Armageddon of reset clocks and erased debts and falling airplanes and a whole world plunged into darkness. But when Isabel looked up she saw lights still burning in dozens of windows. She imagined champagne-flushed faces pressed to the glass. She checked to make sure the doors were locked. She turned down the volume on the radio. She switched seats, got behind the wheel, and wished she knew how to drive. This was it, she thought. For the next two to three years, maybe more, depending on the judge, this was going to be her life. Sitting alone. Waiting for Jose to come back.

The doctor tucks Isabel's shirt under her breasts. From what looks like a tube of toothpaste, he squeezes a clear sticky substance onto her stomach. Gelatinous lumps swim in the goo. Isabel's belly button—recently outied—glistens. She feels cold. When the doctor leans over her body, she pinches her thighs together.

"Have you been having any strange symptoms?" he asks, as if making small talk.

"Strange symptoms?" she says. Her nipples are darker, her back hurts, she passes gas through the night. All normal, pregnancy-related symptoms, apparently, but what about the white discharge that sometimes leaks from her vagina? What about the bleeding? She gets nose-

bleeds; she wipes her ass and there's blood on the toilet paper; she pulls her toothbrush out of her mouth and the bristles are tinged pink. What about absentmindedness? After making scrambled eggs the other day, she came back into the kitchen two hours later to find the stove still on, its blue flame tickling the bottom of the pan. In the last four months, she's lost her house keys twice. She sometimes forgets what day of the week it is. Normal, pregnancy-related absentmindedness? Or not-fit-to-raise-a-child absentmindedness? Isabel has difficulty sleeping, but she's always had difficulty sleeping. She feels faint, dizzy, itchy, and constipated. Her legs cramp up something terrible, her face swells, and sometimes she can't breathe. If she could get any information at all in this hospital—for instance, what vitamins she should be taking, how much weight she should have gained, how much anxiety is too much anxiety, where the fuck have they taken her boyfriend—then maybe she'd be better able to answer this doctor's question, better able to separate the strange symptoms from the normal ones. She says, "I feel like my head is underwater."

"Stuffy ears," the doctor says. "That happens. That's okay." He taps her nose. "And I bet a little nasal congestion, too?"

Alfredo opens the door. For a moment he hovers in the doorway, his hand on the knob. He squints, and when he decides he likes what he sees he bursts into the room with apologies. Got lost going to the bathroom, he explains. Got lost coming back. His voice booms. He takes the bottom of Isabel's shirt and is about to roll it down over her stomach, cover her up, when he sees the gunk spread all over her belly. He scoops some of it up, rubs it between thumb and index finger. When the doctor comes nears him, Alfredo starts pumping his hand. "Nice to meet you," Alfredo says. "A real pleasure." Still shaking the doctor's hand, Alfredo hooks a thumb toward Isabel's belly. "I'm the father. Hey, listen, sorry I'm late."

"Better late than never," the doctor says. "Lots of fathers don't come to these checkups at all."

"Lost going to the bathroom?" Isabel says. "What else happen? You fall in the bowl?"

Like a little boy, Alfredo shrugs. As if Isabel asked him if he ate all the cookies or finger-painted on the walls. She grabs his waistband and pulls him close. She wants to shove her nose in his chest. She

wants him up on this table next to her, so she can whisper in his ear, *Don't you ever leave me alone again.*

While Alfredo squeezes Isabel's hand, the doctor waves his magic wand over her slime-slicked belly. Presto zesto! The computer monitor's speaker vibrates with the *thump-thump* of Christian Louis's heart.

"My God," Isabel says. "Listen to that."

The doctor nods approvingly. "All the tests look great. Healthy baby, healthy mama."

"Good work," Alfredo says. He gives her a thumbs-up. Disaster averted for one more day. With a healthy baby and a healthy baby mama, Alfredo starts bopping his head. "That's a pretty ill beat, don't you think? Thump-thump. Yeah. That's what I'm talking about. Little man's gone be a *rapper.* Thump-thump." Alfredo taps his toe. "Thump-thump. *Mama carrying a strong-hearted baby / Gonna be pimping gold chains and Mercedes.* Thump-thump. Turn that joint up, Doctor!"

The doctor taps his lips, as if deciding how best to proceed. He puts the wand in Isabel's hand so that she can hold it over Christian Louis herself. Free now of all medical responsibilities, the doctor gets up off his stool. He snaps his fingers. Puts some wiggle in his hips and shoulders.

"My man!" Alfredo says. "That's some Calcutta shit, right there! Thump-thump. *Our baby's the ultimate MC / Gonna buy us a house with some cable TV.*"

Alfredo freestyles while the good doctor waves his arms. The men are grooving. Alfredo gets louder, more pumped. The doctor's belly jiggles. Sweat streams into his eyebrow. He's getting tired—the stethoscope doesn't bounce as high off his shoulders as it did just a few moments ago. Soon he'll wipe his brow, button his lab coat, and move on to the next patient. Maybe later tonight at dinner, while uncorking a bottle of wine, he'll tell his beautiful wife about the little jig he did with a Latino couple.

Alfredo stomps his feet, bends his knees, rolls his shoulders, dips his hips—tries, all by himself, to keep this dance party going.

Christian Louis Batista says, *Thump-thump!*

Isabel puts her hands in the air.

3

A Brief Interlude on
the Art of Talking Shit

The streets started murmuring a couple of years ago, after the Virgil's robbery. Gio, Conrad, and Jose Jr. stole over twenty-five hundred dollars from the catering hall, and a mere two days later detectives showed up at their homes. Spiral-bound notebooks in their hands, cuffs in their pockets. *That's some awfully quick police work,* the neighborhood shit-talkers said. *And what a coincidence Alfredo happened to step out of that car.* Alfredo's defenders—principally Winston—argued that coincidences happen every day. That people were just trying to stir up trouble for the sake of stirring up trouble. That they were looking for conspiracy where none existed. That Alfredo caught a lucky break, that's all. No big deal. End of story.

This became a slightly harder position to maintain after Jose went to prison and Alfredo took over his business. Buying trees directly from Baka, Junior's old connect. Raising eyebrows all over the neighborhood. *Well, there you go,* the shit-talkers said. *There's your motive. Greed. Second oldest story there is.* Alfredo's dwindling supporters found this laughable. *Jose's in prison! His little brother can't make a few bucks? Maybe Jose put Baka and Alfredo in touch himself. Ever think of that?* (Voices rising, voices cracking.) *Jesus, man—that shit happens every day of the week.*

This became an almost impossible position to maintain after Alfredo was caught—in Manhattan, at South Street Seaport—sucking

46

face with Isabel Guerrero, as in Isabel Guerrero, Jose's girlfriend Isabel Guerrero.

Damn, said Alfredo's defenders.

Love, the shit-talkers said, rubbing their hands together. *Oldest story there is.*

And then—like a gift from the gossip gods—Izzy got pregnant, and the streets went buck wild. Some of the chattiest shit-talkers must've gone to bed with their gums bleeding, with ice packs pressed to their overworked jaws. Must've spent their days recuperating with herbal tea, straight from the pot. Thanks to their efforts, the gossip grew legs, left the neighborhood, spread out to the borders of Queens, and then, eventually, farther north, upstate. How could it not? People got arrested and some of them were sent out to Woodbourne and Sing Sing and Attica and Otisville and Bedford Hills, but a small number rode the bus up to Fishkill, and of that number, all of them—Alfredo was sure of this—all of them found his brother as soon as their feet hit the ground. Big grins on their stupid fucking faces.

You heard, man? You heard?

Alfredo wondered how often his brother found himself on the other end of that news. And man oh man, what fun the other inmates must have had. When Tariq walked through the mess hall with a brown-lettuced hamburger on his tray did the other tables grow suddenly quiet? Or did they burst into laughter? Did the guards find out? Did they use it to taunt him? When Alfredo couldn't sleep—which was every night—he asked himself these questions, and they always led him to the same place, the überworry, the mother of all questions: What's Tariq gonna do when he comes home?

Yeah, well, join the club, Dito. That's what everyone else wants to know, too. While chalking up cues at the pool hall, while bending slices at Gianni's, while getting haircuts at Headz Ain't Ready, while waiting on the platform for the 7 train, while tagging up streetlamps, while splitting open blunts, while sitting on bar stools and milk crates and beach chairs and apartment stoops, the shit-talkers speculated as to what the Batista brothers have planned for their upcoming reunion. They couldn't ask Tariq, for obvious reasons. But they could always find Alfredo outside the Alleyway and tap him on the shoulder, put the question to him directly. But they won't. It seemed somehow less rude—and definitely more fun—to talk about Alfredo behind his

back. Everyone wanted to know what he had planned, but no one was willing to come right out and ask him.

Except for Max Marshmallow. Rude questions? Please. He was seventy-two years old. Asking rude questions was one of his specialties.

Last Sunday, with street-corner business slow to nonexistent, Alfredo walked into a late-night bodega to rifle through its magazine rack. This was days before Alfredo had ever even heard of Vladimir Shifrin. Max Marshmallow, the bodega's owner, sat behind the counter, reading four different newspapers—his nightly research for a book he'd always been planning to write, *A Comprehensive History of New York Schemes*. In one hand he held a yellow highlighter, in the other, a red-handled pair of scissors. He put both away as soon as Alfredo walked in.

"How's that beautiful mother of yours?" Max asked.

"Come on," Alfredo said. He stood staring at the magazines, his back to the counter. "Why you wanna know?"

"It's called making conversation," Max said.

"She's fine."

"And your father?"

"He says hello, actually."

"Really?"

"No, not really. It's just something people say. It's called being polite."

"And the gorgeous Isabel?" Max said. "Who—I hope you don't mind me saying—puts blood in my penis. How is she? Seven months along now, if I'm not mistaken."

"Six," Alfredo lied.

"Great, great," Max said. He leaned forward on his stool, his elbows on the counter, and got to the good stuff. "So what you gonna do when your brother gets home?"

Alfredo groaned. "You're as bad as the rest of them."

"I'm worse," Max said. He grinned, his false teeth gleaming. They were bright white, these teeth, and while most fogies opt for at least some slight discoloration—chompers artificially stained by artificial packs of cigarettes and artificial cups of coffee—Max went with the ivories. A smile that dazzles. He said he couldn't figure out why anyone would choose—would pay!—to look old. The teeth shared tenancy

with a perpetually refreshed set of marshmallows, always two, one in each cheek. They started as a punishment, quickly became a trademark, and now, all these years later, they were one more boyish affectation. He claimed that his mother used to stuff his mouth full of marshmallows to keep him from talking, but, clearly, it never worked. "Humor me," he told Alfredo. "Soon as you see your brother—what do you do? What you got planned?"

"Noisemakers," Alfredo said. "Pointy hats. A piñata maybe, although I don't know if I wanna put a bat in his hands."

"Probably not."

"No," Alfredo said. "Probably not." He scanned the titles in the magazine rack, looking for the latest issue of *GamePro*, the video game monthly. He wasn't looking for himself—if he was going to read a magazine, it'd be *Baseball Weekly* or the *Source*—he was looking for Winston, across the street in the Alleyway, guarding the stash. "Tell you the truth," Alfredo said, "I don't really have a plan. Drugs. I'm trying to find a package of drugs for him. Winston thinks it's a nice gesture." He couldn't keep himself from shrugging, from keeping the self-pity out of his voice. "Beyond that, I don't know. I'm trying not to think about it too much."

"Maybe you should start," Max said.

"Maybe you should mind your own business."

"I would," Max said, sweeping his arm out, gesturing to the unplugged deli-meat slicer, the unsold roach hotels, the unsold squeeze bottles of Fox's U-bet Chocolate Syrup, the unsold naan next to the unsold hot dog buns, "but my business isn't as interesting as yours."

Separated by age and ethnicity, Max and Alfredo are unlikely friends, but both men love to talk, and gabbers will always find each other. The Batista family used to own this store, used to live in the little railroad apartment set up in back. (You couldn't beat the commute.) But after Jose Sr.'s accident, they sold the place to Max, who reversed a neighborhood trend and became the first non-Arab, non-Korean, non-Latino to purchase a bodega in over twenty years. Not that he called it a bodega. He insisted instead on the anachronistic "candy store," the term connoting for him a bygone borough of egg creams, pitched pennies, Koosman's Mets, and the '64 World's Fair. When Alfredo started peddling reefer on the sidewalk, it must have challenged Max's sepia vision of The Way Things Were—but as a

functioning New Yorker, he quickly adapted to The Way Things Is. It helped of course that they enjoyed each other's company. Max liked coming up with schemes, and Alfredo liked shooting them down.

"This is what you do," Max said.

"Great," Alfredo said. He found the issue of *GamePro* and plucked it out of the rack. "Let's hear it. Lay it on me. Tell me what to do."

"Poker," Max said. He folded his arms triumphantly across his chest.

"Poker," Alfredo said.

"You tell Jose—"

"Tariq," Alfredo corrected.

"You tell Tariq you're throwing him a welcome home party. These meshuggener types? They're easily flattered. Trust me, I know. You tell him you're throwing a party in his honor, but not the kind of party with noisemakers and pointy hats. A poker game, okay? We do it under the store, in the basement. Move some boxes around. Get a nice green felt table from Costco. Yeah? We'll invite over some of your friends, invite over some of his friends. Crack open some beers. It'll be beautiful."

"And then what?" Alfredo said. "We charge all the players fifty bucks a head? House keeps ten percent of all winnings?"

"Ten percent seems a little high, if you ask me."

Above their heads Max's idea spread its wings, and Alfredo took aim.

"I don't know about poker," Alfredo said. He thought his friends would actually love to participate in an underground poker game, but he wanted to punish Max for sticking that schnoz of his where it didn't belong. "Guys I know? If they play cards, they're doing it on the Internet."

"That's not the same," Max cried. A marshmallow quivered on the tip of his tongue. "Where's the camaraderie on the Internet? Where's the bullshitting?"

As Alfredo moved toward the door, he held up the *GamePro*. "I'm taking this," he said.

"It defeats the whole purpose, the Internet. There's no *stories*."

"Sorry, Max. The poker's a dud."

"It's a better idea than your piñata," he said with the fat, lower-lipped petulance of a child.

"The piñata was a maybe," Alfredo said. "It was always up in the air."

He laughed at his own joke, as he had a tendency to do.

"Where you going with that magazine?" Max asked him, but he'd already escaped. The door slammed shut behind him.

An hour later, Max walked out onto the sidewalk, the candy store's awning glowing yellow and red behind him, his seventy-two-year-old face pink and exhilarated. Alfredo, who handled the money transactions, stood on one side of the street, and Winston, who handled the drugs, stood on the other. When he looked up from his magazine, Winston smiled and waved, and Max, with equal vigor, waved back. It was three o'clock in the morning.

"My man, Fredo!" Max said. Arms swinging, pelvis out, he strutted over to where Alfredo was standing. If not for the marshmallows, he might've whistled. "What's poppin, homeboy? What's crack-a-lackin?"

"If you're here to buy prostate shrinkers," Alfredo said, "I don't have any."

They stood shoulder to shoulder, both men staring into the street as if waiting for a bus. "You know why you didn't like the poker idea?" Max said.

"Why didn't I like the poker idea?"

"Because it was boring," Max said. He grabbed hold of his crotch and gave it a squeeze. "It didn't have any balls."

"I'm thinking—I can't be sure about this—but I'm thinking you got a new plan, yeah?"

"I know you're real busy," Max whispered, looking both ways down the deserted sidewalk. "But I'd like to show you something."

He turned on his heel and strolled away toward the candy store, walking with the air of a man who fully expected to be followed. Winston, apparently, expected the same. He stuck a finger in his magazine, marking his place, and hollered out a request for a diet soda. Anyone else? Any other requests for the errand boy? Sure! Perched under an AC, a pigeon lifted its groggy wing and asked for a five a.m. wake-up call. The streetlamps wanted new bulbs. The tires of parked cars, more air. And if Alfredo wasn't too busy, would he mind emptying out the wastebaskets on the corner? It never ends. When he closed his eyes, he saw spots, little novas of light. In the last hour and a half, he had made exactly one drug sale, a dime bag sold to a teenager named

AIDS. Alfredo wanted to go home, pour himself into bed with Isabel, wrestle with the twin icebergs she called her feet. But instead, like a good boy, he followed Max Marshmallow into the candy store.

On the counter a newspaper sat primed for Alfredo's inspection.

"Check this out," Max said. He pointed to an AP-credited photo of a sweaty-faced black guy, his hands wrapped tight around a microphone. "You know who this is?" Max asked, and didn't wait for an answer. "DMX. That's what it says right here. Dark Man X. You listen to his music?"

"Not really," Alfredo said. "He's from Yonkers. I don't listen to rappers from Yonkers."

"I don't know anything about that," Max said. "But it says right here"—he looked down at his finger, as if to make sure it was still under the photo and hadn't wandered over to the lingerie ad on the other side of the page—"it says right here that there's some controversy over his lyrics. I don't give a shit about any of that, but it gave me an idea. Every great idea—I ever tell you this?—every great idea you're ever going to get is going to hit you while you're reading the paper. I read four papers a day. The *Post, Newsday,* the *Daily News,* and the *New York Times.* The *Times* is the best. If I spoke Spanish, I'd read your *El Diario.*"

"Max," Alfredo said.

"So I'm looking at this DMX guy, and I get to thinking, right? I have all that space under the store. I want to get some gambling going, there's big money in gambling, but you tell me we need something your friends can't find on the Internet. So Alfredo, let me ask you— what do you know about dogfighting?"

"Dogfighting?"

"Dogfighting," Max said.

"I don't know anything about dogfighting," Alfredo said. "I don't know anyone who's ever even *been* to a dogfight."

"Yeah, but think about it for a second. Imagine the effect it would have on Jose."

"Tariq," Alfredo corrected.

"Okay, imagine the effect it would have on Tariq."

Alfredo imagined it. He imagined Tariq walking down into the basement on Saturday night, the night he comes home, the dogs nipping at air, Alfredo standing between them, arms raised, a wad of cash

in his fist. Huh. A thing like that might actually impress Tariq, a man who respects only power and violence. He'd see that Alfredo ain't the greasy-faced seventeen-year-old he left behind. Little brother was all grown up. A neighborhood player. A dogfighting entrepreneur who will not be easily intimidated.

"I don't know," Alfredo said. "I think maybe it's not a bad idea."

A small current of panic jolted Max's face. "Really?"

"You're serious about this, right?" Alfredo said. "I don't want to make moves on this unless you're for real."

Max bit into a marshmallow, and for a brief moment Alfredo felt sorry for this old man, who spent his days and nights dreaming up credit card schemes and calling card schemes and bail bond schemes and sweetheart schemes and underground gambling schemes without ever intending to follow through on any of them. Just another shit-talker. A cash-register jockey trying to protect himself from the sharp teeth of boredom.

"Are *you* serious?" Max asked.

"I'm not sure," Alfredo said. "I think so."

"Then I think so too," Max said. "Why not, right?" He rolled back his shoulders. "Let's do it."

Things moved quickly after that.

Alfredo went out onto the sidewalk and phoned the Alphabet Brothers, the only guys he knew who owned a pit bull. He asked them if they might be interested in some dogfighting, preferably on this upcoming Saturday night. Violence and mayhem? Of course they were interested. One slight hang-up: they didn't own a pit bull, they owned a German shepherd. Was that gonna be a problem? Not at all! It was even better, matter of fact. A pit bull brawling a German shepherd would be a more unexpected matchup and therefore, to Alfredo's thinking, a more authentic dogfighting experience.

"What's the dog's name?" he asked, wanting to know for publicity purposes. When they told him, he said, "You're kidding."

The next day he went to the shit-talkers. It was like the Mets reaching out to the Yankees, like Piazza canoodling with Clemens. Alfredo visited the neighborhood gossips outside their bodegas and barbershops, their pizzerias and pool halls, and he whispered in their ears, asking that they please not tell anyone, thereby ensuring they would. Within hours, the word was on the wire.

Now all Alfredo needed to do was find himself a dog. On Tuesday, he took the R train to the Animal Care and Control center in Rego Park, only to find out that they're not open on Tuesdays—not that it mattered since according to the sign in the window they don't even offer any animals up for adoption. They just take them in. Well great. On to Plan B. If he couldn't adopt a pit bull, he'd steal one. On Wednesday, Alfredo (taking shallow breaths) and Winston (smoking blunts) walked through what seemed like every last alleyway in the neighborhood, including the Alleyway, looking in people's backyards for a chained-up, left-alone pit bull. They found a thousand dandelions, nine deflated soccer balls, dozens of white plastic patio chairs with pockets of week-old rainwater in the seats, a little Filipino girl fiddling with matches (they told her to stop), a tireless car propped up on cement blocks, abandoned baby diapers, busted TVs, cigarette butts, countless planes above their heads roaring into LaGuardia Airport, a pair of sneakers tied together and hung from a telephone pole (the sight of which made Alfredo's blister-clad feet squirm in their Timberlands), nice old ladies, mean old ladies, basketball hoops, barbecue grills, and hundreds of American flags, draped over balconies and stuck in the ground, big flags and little flags, all of which had been purchased in the last nine months. What Alfredo and Winston did not find, however, was a pit bull. On Thursday, exhausted, they loitered outside 7-Eleven and waited for a Slurpee-craving dog walker to leave his pit tied to a parking meter. It didn't happen. By late evening, with only forty-eight hours to go, Winston and Alfredo started thinking beyond pit bulls: they would have settled for another German shepherd, a rottweiler, an obese rat, a rabid squirrel, a piranha in a fishbowl. Any animal, really, with a cantankerous disposition. On Friday, after coming back from Elmhurst Hospital with Isabel, Alfredo called Winston and told him all the prenatal tests came back strong. Healthy baby, healthy mama. Disaster averted for one more day. Alfredo had a good feeling. This is the night, he told Winston. This is the night, this is the night. We gonna get ourselves a dog.

4

The Heist, Part One

When Alfredo walks into Gianni's Pizzeria, he finds Winston exactly where he expects to find Winston: by the front door, hunched over the *Street Fighter II* machine. Surrounded by Asian onlookers, he hammers the keypad and throttles the joystick. When his on-screen avatar leaps, Winston goes up on his tiptoes. When the character moves left, Winston leans with her; when she moves right, Winston bangs into his opponent, a Chinese teenager with liberally gelled hair. Like most experienced gamers, the Chinese kid plays with his back straight and his fingers loose, an even-tempered maestro conducting an orchestra. Alfredo can see, however, that the kid's shoulders have started to slump.

In a video game there are a certain number of frames per second, layered sequentially so as to give the impression of continuous movement. Just like a movie. What Winston can do is see *between* those frames.

Whatever the hell that means. When he tries to explain it, Alfredo usually zones out and starts thinking about something else: the Mets, Isabel, a folder in the cabinet. As far as Alfredo can tell, Winston plays defensively. He waits for his opponent to make an aggressive move, reacts before the next frame pops up, and then beats the virtual shit out of him. For instance:

In one fluid motion, the Chinese kid taps his buttons and crooks his joystick, and his on-screen character, the ninja Ryu, shoots a pixilated fireball from his pixilated fingertips. But Winston sees between the frames. His character, the ninety-eight-pound Chun-Li, has already leapt over Ryu. She crouches behind him, her chest heaving. While the fireball moves into empty space, Chun-Li takes out Ryu's legs with a low roundhouse kick. As he falls, she catches him with an uppercut; while he's in the air, she finishes him off with a series of punches and kicks: low, medium, and high. An eight-hit combo. The fireball spirals off the screen, exits stage left and into the wings. Game over.

The boys in the crowd turn to look at one another. Almost all of them, Alfredo imagines, made the trip out here from Flushing, riding the 7 train from Main Street to Eighty-second for the opportunity to challenge Winston in a game that's almost as old as they are. Those who have never seen Winston play before allow their eyes to widen.

It is a cutthroat world, the world of high-level competitive gaming. The participants are almost universally the socially abused—the stutterers, the BO challenged, the acne pocked, the alopecia afflicted, the kids who collected Magic cards and lurked in the back of the gym during dodgeball. Whupping somebody's ass in *Street Fighter II* is their chance to stand tall, to get in an opponent's face and talk some shit. But that's not Winston's style. He gives the Chinese kid a slight bow, then turns to the crowd and quietly asks, "Who's next?"

No one jumps forward. Reluctant to embarrass themselves, the onlookers drift toward Gianni's counter for some slices and garlic knots; others, the ones with particularly delicate egos, leave the pizzeria entirely and head for Flushing, running away from Winston as if he were a fire-breathing Godzilla. *That's my best friend*, Alfredo wants to tell them. *How do you like that?*

Outside the pizzeria, Alfredo launches into his usual post-Gianni's spiel: how Winston's getting exploited like a circus bear, how he's bringing in like 90 percent of Gianni's business, how that fat dago probably wakes up on Saturday mornings to push a wheelbarrow full of quarters to the bank, how Alfredo knows Winston gets his free slices and his unlimited Mountain Dews but maybe he should be getting

paid like the business partner he is—which is to say, maybe Winston should be getting paid cash money.

"Get your hands in the wheelbarrow, if you know what I mean."

Winston looks straight ahead, stares out of an empty face. His eyes are dilated, his pupils eclipsed. "What's good with that X?" he says. Behind him, two white kids circle each other, slap boxing. Winston pays them no mind. "You wanna go halfsies on a pill?" he asks.

"That shit's for my brother," Alfredo says.

"No, definitely. I'm really just talking about half a pill though."

The older of the two white kids—he must be around twelve—catches the younger upside the head with an open-hand stinger. Alfredo wants to tell them to stop, but he hasn't had much luck talking to kids today, and besides, he ain't in the business of parenting other people's children.

Winston says, "You think one pill's gonna make a difference to your brother?"

Because in addition to being a video game prodigy, Winston is also a skilled and insistent needler, and because Alfredo owes him money, and because Winston might still be shaken up over the Vladimir incident, and because it's supposedly his last night of doing drugs (and even if Alfredo wants to roll his eyes every time he hears that bullshit, friendship requires that he act like he believes him), and because, really, what's one more pill, because fifty is a nice round number, because Tariq will never know, because a crashing Winston is a foot-dragging Winston, because even if it goes against everything Alfredo believes in, sometimes it's just easier to give in—Alfredo decides to hand over a pill. He brings Winston around the corner where no one can see them. And where it smells like some seriously stank-ass shit. Damn! The fruit and vegetable grocers must have illegally dumped their overripe produce down the gutter, and now the smell of rot wafts up from beneath the sidewalk. Alfredo would pinch his nostrils together but he needs both hands to pull the top off the E-beeper. Like any magic trick performed twice, it's lost much of its pizzazz. He grabs a pill out of the beeper, but before he drops it into Winston's cupped palms, he first takes a peek. He brings the X close to his face for inspection, and his forehead runs cold. He feels an urge—it both frightens and exhilarates—to bash in Winston's skull.

What Alfredo sees in the middle of the pill, etched into its chalky surface, is this:

∞

A logo. A brand. A tattoo shared by all the other pills in the beeper. Meaning Winston's intelligence report was faulty. The pills *do* hit the streets with logos, and, even worse, it's a logo Alfredo recognizes, an infinity sign, which emblazons not only all of Vladimir's E, but Baka's as well. Meaning either Boris gets in his lab coat, brews up some pills, and stamps them with a copyright-infringing logo, or there is no Boris the Chemist. If one thing is inaccurate in Winston's report, why can't all of it be inaccurate? Maybe Vladimir buys his pills from Baka, or from the pusherman *above* Baka. And maybe—the thought tightens like a knot—that superthug won't be too happy about his boy getting kicked in the throat.

Of the five boroughs, Queens has the most efficiently run drug industry. From Jamaica to Astoria, the crack, coke, and H game goes through a small number of corporations, each one tightly structured. Records are kept. Codes are scribbled into ledgers. There is a hierarchy with easily replaceable five-oh lookouts kicking it up to corner boys kicking it up to enforcers and treasurers and runners, who are all kicking it up to local gang leaders who themselves are kicking it up to a dozen boss hogs. With their drug money, these top-of-the-triangle gangsters open up travel agencies and antique shops and any other business with easily fudged books, and they smoke Cubans and dream of hip-hop stardom, and then, after three, four, or maybe even five years, the federal indictments come hammering down and these gangsters go straight to jail. The twenty-five-year-olds on the rung below move up and become the new boss hogs. And then in three, four, or maybe even five years . . .

Alfredo ain't interested. He sticks to weed, buying a little at a time off Baka and marketing it creatively. Selling it, for instance, not in miniature Ziploc baggies but in clear plastic vials, the kind hospitals use. The rubber stopper at the top of the plastic tube gives the impression the weed was stuffed in an airtight container; the curved shape magnifies the amount of product inside, allowing Alfredo to skim a bit

off the top; and the vials' glassy smoothness suggests to consumers that these tubes have recently been plucked from the unfortunate anuses of Colombian drug mules. Freshness, therefore, is guaranteed. If he were keeping this Ecstasy, as opposed to giving it to his brother tomorrow, Alfredo would market it in a couples package, selling two pills at a time—one for your pleasure, one for hers—with a discounted Viagra thrown in to counteract E's dick-softening effects.

Not that Alfredo's *all* about the marketing. He also looks for income outside the corporate pyramid. Buying scrips off the Internet. Running dogfights in Max's basement. It was always Alfredo's brother who wanted to climb up the triangle, to push the real shit—yak, crack, and China—at the real weight, but Alfredo is happy to stay a free agent. Less money equals less jail time and fewer bullets in the ass. But Alfredo's survival as a free agent requires that he stay quiet, that he not shatter the wrong guy's jaw.

Disgusted, Alfredo throws the infinity-branded pill to the ground. While he rattles the E-beeper and explains the situation, Winston gets down on his hands and knees. He slips his fingers into the cracks between sidewalk panels. He takes out his cell, hoping to make use of its green glow, but the phone is off or the battery's dead—Winston having probably neglected to charge it. Alfredo's harangue is smoke, and Winston crawls underneath it. He brings his face close to the sidewalk, close to the subterranean smells of rotten fruits and rotten vegetables, until he finally finds his pill. Only a couple of inches away this whole time. And within striking distance of Alfredo's boot.

If candy and the fat man have the five second rule, then drugs and the drug addict have five years. Winston brushes the pill against his shirt and throws it down the hatch.

"What's the problem?" he says. As he chews the pill, his face sours, comes alive. "So the X got logos? That's beautiful, far as I see it. Saves us the trouble of branding it ourselves."

"You told me—"

"I was wrong. I guess that's my bad. But maybe—just hold on— maybe there's no reason to get our panties in a bunch. Maybe these logos will turn out to be a positive factor in our overall plans. Because like I'm saying—"

"Please," Alfredo says. Blood hammers his temples. He raises his

hand—for what? to bunch Winston's shirt in his fist?—and ends up just patting him on the chest, as if Winston were the one who needs soothing. "Just . . . okay? Just not right now."

"All I'm saying—"

"You're pushing me."

"Jesus," Winston says. "I'm not pushing anybody. All I'm saying is—"

"All you're saying should be nothing right now. Right now you should be keeping your fucking mouth shut."

Winston takes off his Spider-Man cap and flexes the bill. He and Alfredo do not speak to each other this way. Sure, they bicker. They know each other's limits, and sometimes—as if that knowledge is too much to bear—they test those limits. But bickering ain't fighting. Alfredo and Winston aren't supposed to raise their voices or bark at each other or curse each other out. Pain shoots across Alfredo's forehead. A cabinet drawer slides open.

Winston stares into the empty shell of his hat, as if it concealed some secret message, a cryptic code, a sun-bleached map. He says, "I just thought of where we might be able to find a dog."

He'd been clueless all week, but he gets yelled at and cursed at, and all of a sudden—how convenient!—he has an idea regarding the whereabouts of a pit bull. Okay, Alfredo thinks. That's fine. Alfredo's pulled this shit himself. In sixth and seventh grade, he'd hide his decent report cards in his book bag, saving them for when he got into trouble. He never had to wait long. He'd break a vase playing Wiffle ball in the house with Jose Jr., or he'd get lippy with his mother at the kitchen table, and then it'd be all *hijo de Diablo,* you're grounded, no TV for a month. After about an hour, Alfredo would slink out of his room and say, "Sorry, Papi—but I need you to sign my report card." And Jose Sr. would see A— in Language Arts, B in Social Studies, B— in Science, A+ in Math, and how could he stay mad at him after that, particularly when he probably didn't want to be mad at him in the first place. So it goes with Winston. He'd kept this dog info under his Spider-Man cap as a kind of collateral. Divulge in Case of Emergency. Or maybe not. Maybe Winston thought of it right when he said he thought of it. Doesn't matter to Alfredo. He's just happy for the distraction, happy to think about something other than his anxiety marquee: *The Return of Tariq,* and below that, just now added to the signboard, *Infinity-Branded X.*

"I figure we just been waiting to get lucky this whole time," Winston says. "Going through people's backyards. Waiting outside Seven-Eleven. We're like sitting around, expecting a dog to drop out of the sky."

"Okay," Alfredo says. "I like where your head's at."

Winston closes his eyes, as if he just misplaced the thread of his argument. "But what if . . . okay, hold on . . . what if we went to a place we *know* has dogs. Yeah? What if we went looking for an intimidating dog where dog owners need to intimidate?" Winston spreads his arms out wide and suggests a place they've passed thousands of times before, a place where at this time of night there'd be some scary motherfucking dogs just waiting to get took: the Queens County Savings Bank.

"A bank?" Alfredo says. "There ain't any dogs in banks."

"Sure there is. At night and shit. To guard the money. I've seen them, I think."

"Like you thought Vladimir's pills didn't have logos?" When Winston looks away, Alfredo says, "Even if Queens County had pit bulls—so what? How we supposed to rob a bank of its dogs?"

"I guess it's a dumb idea."

Alfredo wonders if it's an intentionally dumb idea. Is Winston playing stupid to be annoying, as payback for Alfredo's outburst earlier? In the end, it seems irrelevant—Winston's dumb idea sparkplugs a better one.

"What about the used car lots?" Alfredo says.

Because car lots in Queens, like little old ladies, all seem to huddle together, Winston and Alfredo are able to limit their reconnaissance to a ten-block radius. At the first lot they visit, Alfredo rattles the fence while Winston mimics *woof-woofs*. A cat darts under a fender. At the second lot they think they see some kind of dog crouching in the shadows, but it turns out to be a tire. At the third lot, at the fourth lot, at the fifth lot, more of the same, and so—who can blame them?—they approach the sixth lot with diminished hopes.

Northern Boulevard's redundantly named Allouez Preowned Used Cars Supercenter is protected by a twenty-foot-high fence. Razor wire slithers across the top, each coil evenly spaced as if a giant snake had

come here to molt. Behind the fence glint Caravans and Cherokees and Honda Odysseys, their respective prices scribbled onto their respective windshields in bright white soap.

$3800.	$5295.
120,000 miles.	94,000 miles.
One owner.	Runs like new.

"What's that?" Winston says, pointing toward the back of the lot.

Alfredo squints. "What's what?"

"You don't see that? Between the cars? Way back there? What *is* that?"

Alfredo cleans his glasses against the hem of his shirt. Once he's respectacled, he thinks he sees something, a blur maybe—yes, yes, he *definitely* sees it, a black blurry creature dancing between cars, spinning and leaping.

"I think it's a cat," Winston says. Disappointment floods his voice. "Yeah, that's a cat for sure."

Alfredo kicks the bottom of the fence. The chain links' quivering shoots reverberations through the asphalt toward the back of the lot and tickles the bottoms of paws. The blurry black creature lifts its blurry black head. Slowly, as if annoyed, it squares its shoulders and begins to gallop toward them, revealing itself in long-legged strides.

"Doberman," Alfredo says, as the dog gets closer.

"Is that a fighting dog?"

"I wouldn't want to fight one."

It is possible—no, rather it is likely—that somewhere along the trip out west Lewis turned to Clark and told him to shut his fucking mouth. Perhaps they walked on for hours or even days in awkward silence, but all was surely forgiven when at last they passed Mount Hood and saw for the first time the shimmering Pacific. *Mission accomplished!* Grinning, Winston and Alfredo slap palms. For here, finally, is their own prize: a dog, and a mean-looking one too. Just inches away, close enough to tap on the nose. Close enough for Alfredo to feel its hot breath on his knuckles. The Doberman steps forward, darkly displeased.

In a threatening situation, a dog will often look toward its owner for cues on how to behave. Rounded eyes, open mouth, tense arms, shal-

low breaths: if a dog sees these in its guardian, it knows to attack. But the Doberman's owner is not here. The Doberman's owner—Mr. Allouez of Allouez Preowned Used Cars Supercenter—is probably at home on Long Island, watching Letterman throw pencils at the camera. Without Mr. Allouez's nonverbal input, the Doberman must make decisions on its own.

"Do not," Alfredo whispers, "look into its eyes."

The dog lunges. Up on its hind legs, it gnashes its jaws and claws at metal. Saliva, thick and heavy, spills across the fence. The blessed fence. The Doberman turns its head sideways and insinuates its long snout into a diamond-shaped chain link. Lips curl upward, expose sharp yellow teeth.

"Jesus Christ," Alfredo says, and immediately—to atone for the blasphemy—makes the sign of the cross. Both he and Winston take generous steps away from the fence. Their heels hang over the lip of the curb. "You looked in its eyes," Alfredo says.

"I looked in its eyes," Winston says. His hand covers his heart. "And while I'm admitting things let me admit something else. I ain't going *near* that dog."

Well that's too bad, Alfredo thinks. Because I ain't going near that fucking dog either. And that's just the start of their trouble. Not only is this Doberman snarling, but it is snarling within a well-lit compound, circumscribed by a twenty-foot-high fence. Alfredo closes his eyes. Think of it as a math equation with a complex string of integers, plus and minus signs, parenthetical asides. You need to break the problem down into smaller problems and isolate its component difficulties. Solving part one, Alfredo hopes, will help unlock part two.

He reaches into his baggie of prescription pills and pulls out a Valium. The pill—ten milligrams, the smallest dose he sells—costs about fifteen dollars on the street. It hurts to be throwing money away, but that's the cost of doing business. Gotta spend cash to make cash. Pill in hand, Alfredo rears back and goes into his windup.

One of the great frustrations of Alfredo's childhood was his excommunication from the green-grassed world of Little League baseball. The Elmjack baseball fields were four miles away from Alfredo's house, and after Jose Sr.'s accident, and after the cars were sold, and after Lizette went to work at Remmelts Oculists, there wasn't anyone around who could escort the eleven-year-old Alfredo to games. Those

four miles loomed large, and Alfredo, like Pete Rose before him, found himself banned from organized baseball. The prohibition may have elicited less door slamming in the Batista household if Alfredo's brother had not gotten his full Little League allotment. Or if people weren't always talking about how good Alfredo's brother was. *The line drives he smashed! The backpedaling catches he made!* Had Alfredo been allowed to stay in Little League all the way up to the Babe Ruth division, who's to say he wouldn't have matched, or maybe even surpassed, Jose Jr.'s talents? Given the extra Elmjack years, the extra games and practices, the tutelage of coaches and assistant coaches, the years-long encouragement of his mother in the bleachers, doing her cross-word puzzles between innings—given all that, Alfredo's arm might have finally bloomed and it could be him they talk about now when they talk about baseball. They'd say, *Remember that time Alfredito threw out that kid at home plate? Ball didn't even bounce.* But that never happened. Alfredo never threw anyone out at home plate, and so, understandably, nobody talks about it. All because Alfredo was born too late. When he came into adolescence, the party was already over. The plastic cups had been stacked high, the radio unplugged, the ash-trays all dumped out.

Alfredo's arm comes forward. Teeth gritted, he throws the Valium. A strike is the back of the dog's gullet, but, of course, the story of Alfredo's baseball-tossing career: impressive velocity, unfortunate aim. The pill bounces off a link in the fence and lands on the sidewalk outside the car lot. In the worst possible place. The fence prevents the Dober-man from getting at the Valium, which lies on the sidewalk so close to the dog's snapping jaws that Alfredo feels reluctant to go pick it up. Unreasonable? Alfredo admits the fence looks perfectly adequate, but stranger things have happened than a dog chewing through metal to chase a young Puerto Rican down the street.

"Do me a favor," Alfredo says, pointing at the pill. "Go get that for me?"

Without taking a step forward, Winston says, "Sure. No problem. I'll do that right away."

Alfredo pulls out another Valium. He adjusts his trajectory, aims far and high. This time when he throws, he feels an icy tingling shoot down his shoulder all the way to his fingertips. The pill soars over the dog's head. Impressive velocity—if it were a Frisbee and not a Valium,

the dog might give pursuit. Instead, he gets low to the ground and growls.

"My turn," Winston says.

"One more."

"One more is going to turn into ten more. I want a throw while there's still some pills left. And to be honest I feel like maybe you owe me."

Alfredo wonders if in fifty years he and Winston will be sitting on a bench in Travers Park, fighting with liver-spotted hands over which one of them gets to toss Wonder bread to the pigeons. "If there's an aspirin in there," he says, handing Winston the bag, "save it for me."

Winston's fingers close around a Valium of his own. In an uncharacteristic display of self-confidence—as if to say *I will need only one pill to perform this feat*—he seals the plastic baggie and sticks it in his pocket. He tugs down on the bill of his Spider-Man cap. He adjusts his crotch. He'd probably spit too, if the Ecstasy hadn't dried out his mouth. Winston takes a deep breath and a step forward and—apparently unconcerned with the pretenses of machismo—pitches the pill underhand. The Valium arcs. It spins. It squirts through an opening in the fence and hits the dog square on the snout.

On the people side of the fence, there is much cheering. Alfredo goes for a high five and Winston comes in for a hug and any potential awkwardness is bulldozed by the glory of the moment, like when Gary Carter leapt into Jesse Orosco's arms. Somehow Winston and Alfredo do all things at once: hug, bump fists, high-five, slap each other's backs.

On the dog side of the fence, the Doberman bends to the pill, which is rattling on the ground like a dropped dime. A tentative paw clamps down on top of the Valium. Everything is quiet. The dog lifts its paw and gives the pill a deep and solicitous sniff. *Blecch.* Disgusted by the pill, bored with Winston and Alfredo and everything else, the dog saunters toward the back of the lot, disappointed perhaps that it didn't get to chew on somebody's jugular, but eager, surely, to resume dancing.

"This shit ain't meant to be," Winston says sadly. "We're gonna have to call people soon. I mean if this dogfight ain't gonna happen, we're gonna have to let everybody know. We've got heads coming out here from *Staten Island*."

"Nobody's canceling anything," Alfredo says.

"Whatever happened to simple parties?" Winston says. "Whatever happened to getting somebody an ice cream cake?"

If only it were that easy. Go down to Carvel, cop a Cookie Puss cake or a Fudgie the Whale, and let Tariq blow out the candles. Punch him lightly on the shoulder and say, "Hey big bro, sorry I knocked up your girl." *Fuck that.* Alfredo ain't sorry. Alfredo, who feels guilty about everything, refuses to apologize for falling in love with Isabel. In the intracranial filing cabinet, the Winston folder from this night alone is thicker than the Tariq folder. Fuck that maniac. And even if Alfredo were sorry—which he ain't, but even if he were—apologizing would make as big a difference as handshakes and ice cream. Power and violence. That's the way it's gonna have to be. Alfredo needs this dogfight, needs it to advertise his gangsterism. *I have gotten too big to be slapped around without repercussions.* It's the LoJack sticker in the window of a sports car, the horns protruding from a bull's head, the logo branded onto the surface of Ecstasy.

"Unless we going to all this trouble," Winston says, "so you and Izzy can have a guard dog. That's some shit I'd understand."

With the Doberman dancing at the back of the lot, Winston apparently feels brave enough to approach the fence. He scoops up a pill of Valium, the only one he can reach, and slips it into his back pocket. He's rolling on a double dose of X and God knows what else—a sleeping pill should come in handy at around six a.m., when he's under the covers, grinding his teeth and staring up at the ceiling. Unlike the Doberman, Winston won't hesitate to swallow the pill.

It occurs to Alfredo that the Doberman might not have been so eager to walk from the Valium if it had smelled like bacon. Or better yet, if it had tasted like bacon. "I've got an idea," he says.

"I'm sure you do."

"You wanna go for a ride?"

Winston laughs. "The ghetto car?"

The ghetto car is not an automobile of shabby or suspect value, a lemon with a busted window or broken carburetor. It has never coughed out foul smoke or dragged its muffler through the streets of

Queens, because, strictly speaking, it doesn't exist. It is, from bumper to bumper, an imaginary car.

Because of the hours Winston and Alfredo keep, their bellies rumble at inopportune times, when the only economical dining option is McDonald's. But McDonald's, late at night, locks all its doors for security reasons, keeping open only its drive-thru window. And to get food from this drive-thru window you absolutely, no exceptions, had to be in a car.

"No car. No food."

Because Alfredo can't afford a real automobile, used or otherwise, and because he doesn't even know how to drive, all he's got is the ghetto car.

Speaking into the McDonald's intercom and disguising his voice, Alfredo orders a couple of McChickens for himself, a bottle of water for Winston, a Happy Meal for Christian Louis (Alfredo is collecting the toys), and a bacon cheeseburger for the Doberman pinscher at Allouez Preowned Used Cars Supercenter. A garbled intercom voice instructs him to drive forward. And so, as he did last night, and the night before that, and all the nights before that, Alfredo pulls up to the pickup window in a squatting position, arms extended and firmly locked in front of him, hands clutching an imaginary steering wheel. He rolls down the imaginary window. He asks Winston, sitting shotgun, to scavenge under the imaginary seats and look for imaginary change.

The acne-scarred attendant closes her eyes.

"You guys need to get a life," she says.

"I'm sorry," Alfredo says. He turns down the knob on the ghetto car's radio. "I didn't catch that. What'd you say?"

"No car," she says. "No food."

"I ask you for a one-time exception," Alfredo says. "Give us this food tonight and we will never bother you again."

"Rules," the girl says.

"Rules?" Alfredo asks Winston. Winston shrugs. Alfredo turns to the girl and shakes his head: never heard of 'em, not familiar. But the girl doesn't smirk or roll her eyes or even frown. She stands in her balcony and stares. "Please," Alfredo says. "If nothing else, then just the bacon cheeseburger. I can see it back there. It's already been made. You're just going to throw it out."

"No car. No food."

It was perhaps foolish of Alfredo to think this night would be different from any other night. Foolish to think he could somehow charm a sack of greasy food from this acne-scarred gorgon. Behind Alfredo and Winston, a car, a real one, honks its horn. Alfredo wishes he could drive this ghetto car down the streets of Jackson Heights, drop Winston off on Northern Boulevard near the Doberman—here, you figure it out—and then keep going, all the way home. He's tired. It's been a night full of setbacks, and Alfredo wants to go home, wash his face, smear on his anti-zit creams, rub Isabel's belly, and, if he wakes her up, play their I Wish game. Like everyone else, she'll probably want to talk about Tariq. She'll want to know Alfredo's plan of attack, but he will insist they play the game. *I wish the baby gets your chin,* he'll say. *I wish he has your elbows,* she'll say, and Alfredo will contest that one. Whispering, they will argue under their sheet on the sofa bed, debating which one of them has the superior elbows.

The car hits its horn again. It isn't a polite *beep-beep* as before; this honk's got teeth. Normally Alfredo would maintain the charade. Still squatting, feeling the burn in his quads, Alfredo would hook an arm behind the passenger seat's imaginary headrest and back the ghetto car out of the drive-thru and into the parking lot. Tonight, however, he stands up—his knees popping—and walks away.

"Wait up!" Winston says. With his height advantage and longer legs, he catches up to Alfredo easily. "What a bitch, huh? That McDonald's girl?"

"I'm sorry about earlier," Alfredo says.

"About what?" Winston says. They match each other step for step, the two of them moving quickly down Northern Boulevard, their boots slapping the pavement.

"About saying what I said. I'm sorry."

"Thank you," Winston says. His hand flutters at his side, as if he was about to clap Alfredo's shoulder, but he apparently thinks better of it. "I'm sorry too."

They stop at the intersection so that traffic may pass. It is Friday night and there are plenty of cars, Camrys and Civics and Corollas, yellow cabs and gypsy cabs, drunks returning home from the bars and clubs in Manhattan, drivers escorting escorts to johns, janitors and doormen and security guards coming off their shifts—all of them

stream by while the light says go. Impatient, eager to get moving again, Alfredo hits the green button on the corner. He knows it won't do anything. These buttons—To Cross Street, Push Button, Wait for Walk Signal—were all disconnected years ago when the Department of Transportation switched to computer-controlled traffic signals. The only reason they remain scattered on street corners throughout the outer boroughs is because it'd be too expensive to remove them all. Mayor Bloomberg and Giuliani before him and Dinkins before him and Koch before him, they all figured, *Fuck it. So we've got some buttons in Queens that don't work. They'll act as placebos, as decoration. At the very least, they'll fool the tourists.* But Alfredo isn't fooled. This is his home. He knows this push button doesn't work, and yet . . . he pushes it anyway.

The light changes from Don't Walk to Walk.

Nothing to get all excited about. Alfredo pushed a nonfunctioning button and the cars stopped and a traffic light switched in his favor. Someone like Isabel might consider this an omen. She would take this blinking Walk sign as an indication that the universe is going to start tilting in his direction, that the infinity logos will turn out to be no big deal, that the bacon cheeseburger will prove unnecessary, that the Doberman is going to happily lick the Valium straight out of Alfredo's palm and a few minutes later the dog will yawn and his thin legs will tremble and he'll eventually pass out and then Alfredo will—will do what? Go get wire cutters from some twenty-four-hour hardware store. Open up a hole in the fence like the one near the handball courts at Travers Park. Breathing naturally, Alfredo will lift up the dog and take it to Max's basement and—because the push button worked—the next day the cops and Mr. Allouez will find a hole in the fence and the cars untouched and the dog gone and they'll perfectly misunderstand it. The headline in the *Post* will read "World's Smartest Doberman Escapes Confinement! Lock Up Your T-Bones!" And then Winston will quit drugs for real and the Mets will beat the Yankees in tomorrow's game and the dogfight will go off beautifully and Alfredo will make lots of money and an impressed and intimidated Tariq will leave Isabel alone and—a little further along in this favorable future—Isabel and Alfredo and their healthy-hearted baby boy will move out of his parents' apartment and into a place of their own, where Isabel will take bubble baths surrounded by candles. Someone else might think all

that, but Alfredo doesn't. He doesn't believe in omens. He doesn't think that in Queens white doves settle down onto the prows of arks. And even if for a tantalizing moment Alfredo allowed himself to believe in all that good-times-are-a-gonna-be-rolling bullshit, there is, five blocks away, a navy blue 1997 Chevy Impala that says otherwise.

"DT," Alfredo says.

"You sure?" Winston says.

Alfredo's authority in these matters should not be challenged. He has difficulty seeing something twenty feet in front of his face, but for whatever reason—call it experience, vigilance, paranoia—Alfredo can stand on the corner of Fifty-ninth Street and Northern Boulevard and spot a DT cruising down Arthur Avenue in the Bronx. A DT coming right at him, four, no wait, three blocks away? Forget about it.

Because he and Winston elicit more suspicion as a twosome than they do individually, Alfredo says, "I'll see you in a couple of minutes. Get in touch with you on your cell."

They don't slap palms or shake hands, because they don't want to give the impression they're completing some kind of transaction. Instead, they bump fists. Just a couple of law-abiding buddies saying good-bye. Winston walks up Fifty-ninth Street; Alfredo goes down Northern Boulevard to where the Impala waits. Best to walk toward it, to not look suspicious. The Impala has pulled up in front of a fire hydrant and sits there patiently, its engine humming, its hazards off. Rising up out of the trunk, a cluster of antennae stand at attention. Alfredo looks at the car for a full second, just as he would if a gorilla was eyeballing him on the sidewalk. A one-Mississippi beat. Not long enough to issue a challenge, not short enough to invite one. After the second passes, he looks forward again. Like his big brother taught him, he walks at a relaxed, regular pace. He keeps his head up, his shoulders straight. But, of course, it doesn't matter.

A tinted window rolls down. The driver, a fat-faced white guy, sticks his head out and says, "Help you with something?"

"Nope," Alfredo says. The driver waits for more answers as if more questions were asked. He wears a Jets jersey, the kind with the numbers ironed on instead of sewed, a cheap and flimsy thing. Alfredo can't see the name on the back, but he's sure it reads "Chrebet," the Jets' second-string wide receiver, a white guy playing a black position. Below the jersey's sleeve, the driver sports a green armband. Even

though Alfredo can't see anyone else, he knows there are three more guys in the car, one sitting shotgun, two more in back. Like the driver, all three of these guys will have green sweatbands wrapped around their biceps. Alfredo's sure of it. At roll call—which started almost seven hours ago—sleep-deprived sergeants across the city must've announced green as the color of the day, helping the uniformed cops identify their plainclothes brothers. Chevy Impalas, tinted windows, extra antennae, phosphorescent clothing accessories: Alfredo wonders why they just don't wear nametags that say NYPD Undercover. "Thank you, sir," Alfredo tells the driver. "But I don't need any help at all."

"Who's the big black guy you said good-bye to? That your boyfriend?"

The cop sitting shotgun leans forward. "Hey, drug dealer," he says. He wears a green armband and an Islanders jersey. Even undercover, these guys can't stop wearing uniforms. "Let's see some of those drugs you got on you."

This is how they talk. They assume you're breaking the law and try to trick you into agreeing. "No drugs," Alfredo says.

"That don't make no sense. You're a neighborhood drug dealer. What about a dime bag? You gotta have a dime bag."

"How about your gun?" the driver says. "Maybe we can get a lookit at the gun in the waistband of your jeans."

If he were standing outside Max's candy store, Alfredo might have given these guys some mouth. What's a dime bag, Officer? Selling drugs is against the law, Officer. Out in front of Max's store, Alfredo could get lippy because he wouldn't have too much to sweat over. His stash would be off his person, across the street, behind a loose brick. Outside Max's candy store, Alfredo could give these four DTs his Alfred E. Neuman what-me-worry. Because outside Max's candy store, Alfredo wasn't a fucking idiot. He didn't have a bag of prescription pills in one pocket, fifty hits of Ecstasy in the other.

He shows the cops his open palms. "No drugs, sir. No guns."

"Your legs are shaking," the driver says.

"No they're not."

"Okay." The driver sticks his finger in his mouth and picks at something between his teeth. His face is contorted in concentration. "You don't have any drugs. You don't have a gun. Your legs aren't shaking. Lookit. Your palms are empty." Whatever was between his teeth

now rests in a wet clump on the tip of his finger. He flicks it into the street. "You're clean," the driver tells Alfredo. "You're a credit to the community."

"I should be getting home," Alfredo says. Stupid idiot that he is, he starts to walk away.

All four doors open at once, a navy blue insect spreading its wings. Alfredo can't run. His feet burst raw with blisters. And besides, these cops would love to stretch their legs and chase Alfredo just for the pleasure of beating the shit out of him. *And he resisted arrest, Your Honor.* They come toward him, wearing a Jets jersey, an Islanders jersey, a Mets jersey, and a Hawaiian shirt. They are white, white, Dominican, and Guyanese. Badges swing from chains around their necks. They push Alfredo against a wall. All day the bricks of this wall have been baking in the June sun, and they feel warm now against Alfredo's cheek. His glasses slip off his nose. There are fingers in his hair. Hands grab his ankles, pat down his legs, run up the bars of his rib cage. His feet are kicked apart. A cop bends Alfredo forward at the waist and credit-cards him, swipes the side of his hand up through Alfredo's ass crack. They are looking for intent to sell. For a weapon, a felony charge, some overtime. Fingers pinch the wetness under Alfredo's armpits.

"You nervous about something?" The cop's breath is warm and moist and smells like peppermint, like red and white candies in cellophane wrappers. "What you nervous about? You got drugs in your pocket?"

"Lookit those legs shaking!"

"They are not," Alfredo says, but the words snag on something as they leave his mouth.

"They are not," a cop says in a high, girlish voice.

Pressed up against the wall, Alfredo feels hands plumbing his pockets. The right and the left. His eyes burn. Alfredo has never spent a single night in lockup. Imagine the irony. Going to jail the day before Tariq comes home. Through the thin cloth of his pocket, a stranger's fingertips press into Alfredo's thigh. They brush up against his balls and his body tightens. He goes up onto his toes, and then suddenly—with these desperate hands clutching his body—Alfredo remembers he doesn't have the baggie of prescription pills because Winston took it away from him, nearly half an hour ago. He's going to be okay. The

Holy Ghost swirls around his feet, swells him with buoyancy. When Alfredo gets home, he will recite the Our Father. On Sunday, he will go to Mass and kneel down, eyes closed, head dipped to his chest, palms pressed together.

"What's this?" says the Dominican cop, the one who struggles to grow a mustache. He holds up Alfredo's beeper. "What have we got here?"

"Let me see," says the Islanders jersey. "Looks like a drug dealer's pager. Pager? Beeper? Is there a difference?"

"Ask the drug dealer," the driver says.

"Is there a difference, drug dealer, between a pager and a beeper?"

"It's just a beeper," Alfredo says.

"You get your drug pages on this it's-just-a-beeper?" the cop asks. "Call them back and say, 'What you need?' We're talking big weight, right? Selling over in Corona. I know all about it. Selling the good shit in Corona." He tosses the beeper at Alfredo.

In his shortened Little League career, Alfredo tended to overthink things in the field—the ball is rolling toward me, I should charge it, throw it to first—and was prone, therefore, to the occasional error. The beeper bounces off his chest, scuttles through his fingers, and hits the ground hard. But it does not split open. The top does not pop off. The Holy Ghost has Its fingers wrapped around the beeper, squeezing it tight.

The Guyanese cop picks it up off the sidewalk. He rubs his thumb over a corner of the beeper, where the plastic has been smoothed and flattened, scuffed by the fall. He is the cop with the Hawaiian shirt, the cop who apparently does not care for sports. Frowning, he presses buttons on the top of the beeper. "I think it's broke," he says. "It's not turning back on."

"Oh, I'm sorry," says the cop in the Islanders jersey. "How you gonna get your drug pages now?"

The Guyanese cop turns over the beeper. Alfredo stares at it, thinking of all the other things these guys could be doing. On Roosevelt Avenue, underneath the elevated 7 train, there are drag queens selling blowjobs. There are Wall Street CEOs whose doors could be getting kicked in. Without a doubt, a block away in any direction, some drunk guy is whaling on his wife or molesting his stepdaughter. Why don't the cops go do something about that? Why don't they keep their hands

out of my pockets and go find Osama fucking bin Laden? The Guyanese cop brings the beeper to Alfredo and clips it to the collar of his T-shirt. The beeper weighs heavy. It causes the shirt to droop downward, exposing the root of Alfredo's throat.

"Tell us about your boy Curtis Hughes," the cop says.

"You knew him," the driver says. "You both being drug dealers and all."

"No," Alfredo says.

"No, what?"

"No, I don't know him," Alfredo says. He isn't worried. These cops aren't investigators. Ninety percent of them aren't even detectives. DT is just something they're called on the street. These cops—to the left of Alfredo, to the right, sitting on the hood of the car, clipping beepers to his chest—are from the NYPD's Anti-Crime Unit. They are patrolmen who get to wear sports jerseys. They are bloodhounds, good for sniffing out drugs and guns, and that's about all. They don't know who Alfredo is. Anti-Crime comes heavy, assumes everything, knows nothing. If they were genuinely suspicious of Alfredo, they'd be acting like his best friend. There'd be polite questions in soft voices. So they mentioned Curtis Hughes? So what? Alfredo's curious, but unworried. Curtis Hughes is a name that falls out of policemen's mouths often. "He's a drug dealer?" Alfredo asks. "Does he live around here?"

"Stop jerking us off," the Dominican says, unsure of himself. "We know you know about him getting merked. Come on, hombre. We know you know about your boy Curtis getting beat to death."

"That's not right," Alfredo says.

"What's not right?"

"That's not right," Alfredo says again.

"I thought you didn't know him."

"Beat to death?" Alfredo leans against the wall. "I went out to get a cheeseburger and I couldn't because I don't have a car and I'm just walking along and you guys stop me and accuse me of having drugs and guns and you get out of the car and you push me around and . . ." Alfredo continues to detail the events of the last few minutes. Speaking in a monotone—it is the only voice available to him—he lists his grievances, the things that have happened to him, the things for which he is not responsible. There is a scratch in the lens of his glasses, he tells them. Caused by their hands pushing him against the wall. There

is a scrape on his cheek from the bricks. Alfredo talks because it keeps him from confronting the death of Curtis Hughes and he talks because he knows it bores the police officers. Look at them. The Dominican dips his head to his armband and wipes the sweat from his eyes. This was a mistake, they think. If this little Puerto Rican knew anything worth knowing, he wouldn't talk so fucking much. They stopped him looking for overtime, for drugs and guns at the bottom of his pockets, and when they didn't find anything they took a shot on this Curtis Hughes kid, the latest African American male DOA. Best-case scenario, they break open a homicide case. Worst-case scenario, they make a kid piss his pants a bit and they've got a funny story for later tonight. Something to talk about over vodka tonics at Legends Bar. But instead, four plainclothes officers near the end of their shift are listening to some spic drone on about—what's he blabbing about now?—some dog who dances to songs no one else can hear.

"Go home," the driver snaps. He looks like a man who's found mold on a peach he'd already bit into. "I don't want to see your face on these streets ever again," he says. It is the standard DT good-bye. "You understand? Comprende? Go home to your boyfriend. It isn't safe for you out here." The cops get into their 1997 Chevy Impala and speed away, leaving Alfredo behind, alone, slumped against a brick wall.

5

Ricochet

Late at night, Jose Sr. rolls his wheelchair across the Batistas' parrot-infested living room. The TV plays what sounds like an infomercial—the standard get-rich-quick scheme, how to make thousands before breakfast—but Isabel can't see the television, nor can she see Jose Sr.'s sweaty face hovering above hers, because she has her eyes screwed shut. She's a real pro. The Meryl Streep of simulated sleep. The sofa bed's metal bar burrows into her hip, but she gives no indication it bothers her. When Jose Sr. asks her if she's awake, she answers with a little snore action: breathes deeply through the nose, lets the air whistle through a nostril. She drools and twitches. Her eyeballs ricochet behind their lids, mimicking REM palpitations.

Wow, this is heavier than it looks. I'd like to thank the Academy, my agent, my fellow nominees, my boyfriend Alfredo, my baby Christian Louis . . .

"Hey, Isabel," Jose whispers. She can smell his aftershave. She can hear him chewing his nightly cherries, spitting the pits into a bowl. "Izzy?"

While he watches her, the room's parrots watch him. They are Lizette's bewitchment: wooden parrots, plush parrots, porcelain parrots, suspended from the ceiling by thin wires, perched menacingly on end tables. Alfredo's mother gives them a weekly dusting; no strange

thing, Isabel reasons, since everything around here is dusted weekly, or vacuumed weekly, or scrubbed or laundered or Windexed weekly. This is a fastidiously maintained apartment with as many rules as church—*thou shalt not eat in the living room*—and Jose bucks these rules as soon as his wife shuffles off to bed. Each cherry is a protest, each protest cataloged by the room's ever-watchful birds.

"Can you hear me? You awake, girl?"

Of course she can hear him! Of course she is awake! To fall asleep tonight would be conceding defeat to tomorrow, and Isabel needs to delay Saturday's arrival for as long as she can. The parrot with the clock in its belly argues that since it's way past midnight, Saturday's already here, but Isabel refuses to acknowledge such narrow-minded nitpickery. As far as she's concerned, if she never goes to sleep, Saturday never dawns, and if Saturday never dawns, then Tariq never shows up, and if Tariq never shows up, then everything gets to stay the same. Simple as that. In the movie version of Isabel's life, today is her Groundhog Day. With some obvious differences: the Hollywood version of Jose Sr. would've conked out by now, so that she could spend these precious hours in the kitchen, left alone, standing over the stove and preparing the Big Surprise for Alfredo.

"You fall asleep already?" Jose whispers. "You can't hear me at all?"

When she doesn't answer, he turns up the volume on his infomercial. Some extra decibels on the TV—that's all he was after. He wasn't looking to climb into bed with her, rub his feet against hers. How could he? His legs don't work. For something like eight years now, he's been paralyzed below the waist.

If Jose Sr. looked it up in the dictionary, he'd find the following bull-shit:

ric•o•chet (rik′e-sha′, -shet′)—*n.* A method of firing by which the projectile is made to glance or skip along a surface with a rebound or series of rebounds.

A *method* of firing? You serious? A definition like that doesn't acknowledge just how random, just how accidental firearm violence can be—it's as if the OED were sponsored by the NRA. Because you

can ask anyone in western Queens, or in Brownsville or Shaolin or even the Boogie Down Bronx, and they will tell you a ricochet is a mistake. Scan an article in your local newspaper and you'll find "ricochet" coupled with "innocent bystander." Whoops! Ricochets are why the NYPD is instructed to aim always for center mass, for the solar plexus, to shoot to kill. Because when you try to wing the bad guy and shoot him in the leg, you either miss or the bullet enters the thigh muscle and exits clean out the other side, and then—whiz, bang—you've got yourself a ricochet. The word in Spanish is *rebote.*

Jose Sr. had been working behind the counter. It was late at night. While his family slept in the apartment behind the store, Jose listened to sports talk radio at a very low volume. Bored, he grabbed a porno from the magazine rack (*Club International*) and took it out of its plastic wrapping. Who's gonna tell? It was his store, his inventory. He spread the magazine open on the counter. Yawning into his fist, he flipped through the pages, stopping every now and again to bring his face close to the magazine and scrutinize a nipple.

A young kid walked into the store. The first customer in over an hour, he carried a brown paper bag, the crinkly kind one slips around a sweaty can of Modelo Especial. The boy—a Latino, maybe even a Puerto Rican, a boy who could've been Jose's own son—stuck that crinkly bag in Jose's face and told him, in a man's voice, to hand over the fucking money.

You can hear this story from anybody. Lizette knows it. Alfredo and Tariq know it. Even Isabel knows it well enough to tell it. But nobody talks about it with as much eagerness, with as much hand-waving flair, as Jose himself.

He didn't beg for his life. He'd had a gun shoved in his face before, and while that's not something one could ever get used to, he was at least able to maintain some composure. No tears. No quivering lips. With his words jamming together, he talked about his family, his wife and their two sons. He didn't tell the boy that they were all asleep behind an employees-only door. Of course not. Instead he talked about random things, silly things, hoping to appear calm so that the boy might be calm. *My youngest son is right around your age,* he said, even though it wasn't true. *Hey, maybe you two even go to school together.* For reasons he doesn't understand, he told the boy about how

Alfredo can multiply giant numbers in his head, how he can memorize all sorts of license plates. He didn't know what else to say.

The bag caught fire. People have told him that's impossible. A bullet punches right through a paper bag, no problemo. But Jose swears he saw a little curl of flame, there and then not there. The light on the ceiling above his head flickered, and he remembers thinking, That's something I need to do. Change that bulb.

Later, in the hospital, Lizette told Jose it was a miracle. Shot point-blank in the face and the bullet misses him? Doesn't happen. He should be dead. According to the cops, the bullet ricocheted off the wall behind him. According to the doctors, it entered the T12 region of his spinal cord. *It's a miracle you're not dead,* she told Jose. She talked about a higher power. *Higher power?* Jose asked. He wanted to know who caused the ricochet. Who put the bullet in his back? God do that, too? *That's right,* Lizette said, and blew cool air into her coffee cup.

Jose smelled the firecrackers smell, but he never heard the pistol's report. Not when it happened, not afterward. He saw a tongue of flame lick away the edges of the paper bag (maybe), and then he was on his back behind the counter, and then he was in a hospital room with a ponytailed nurse squeezing his shoulder, and then they were moving into this new apartment, Jose no help at all, unable to lift even a box.

He wonders why the boy pulled the trigger. Because Jose didn't move fast enough, or because he moved too fast, or because it was simply too hot in the store, or because the wrong commercial came on over the radio? Or maybe there isn't always a causal relationship with these kinds of things. Jose doesn't know. He thinks he never heard the gunshot because his eardrums ruptured. To this day he has trouble hearing, although Lizette thinks it's a ruse, her husband faking deafness so he doesn't have to wheel himself toward her when she calls for him.

But Isabel believes him. She figures he's gotta be deaf. Why else would he be turning up the volume on his infomercial? He doesn't know she's secretly awake. He thinks he's got no audience in this room, and without an audience there's no reason to fake it. Where's the angle? If Jose weren't sitting in that chair, she certainly wouldn't be pretending to sleep. She'd be up, boiling water for the Big Surprise. But

as it is—with Isabel under observation—there's nothing she can do but wait. She hopes Christian Louis will float by on the inside of her eyelids. She hopes he'll be riding a series of numbered, hurdle-jumping sheep. Maybe he'll be bent forward at the waist like a jockey, making *yip yip* noises, with his fierce infant fists buried knuckle-deep in wool. She tries to will the image onto the back of her eyelids, but all she sees is darkness. She's faking sleep, and Christian Louis doesn't stop by when Mama's being duplicitous. Fair enough, Isabel thinks. She waits. She schemes.

Alfredo turns over each deadbolt with a whisper. He cracks open the front door a couple of inches—push it any farther, it starts creaking—and he tiptoes into the living room. These late-night stratagems aren't for the benefit of his mother, who passes out shortly after sundown like a hummingbird, exhausted from the all-day effort of flapping her wings. Impossible to wake up, she sleeps at the back of the apartment with the extraneous aid of a slumber mask, a box fan, earplugs, and two Tylenol PMs. Forget about her. Forget about Papi too, who is snoring loudly only a few feet away, a lumber mill crammed into a wheelchair. Jose's a lighter sleeper than his wife, but Alfredo's gonna have to wake him up soon anyway. No, all these stealth moves— Alfredo feels like he's been walking on his toes ever since he slipped into the apartment—are for Isabel's benefit alone.

Then it's all for nothing, because she ain't even here. The sofa bed's thin mattress bears only the imprint of her body. He assumes she's either stuck on the bowl, battling pregnancy-related constipation, or she's in the kitchen, asleep on her feet and snacking on cookies. Lately, in the middle of the night, she's been staggering into the kitchen to pour herself a glass of milk and twist off some Oreos. The next day she claims no recollection. With chocolate mashed in her teeth, she denies all accusations. Sometimes Alfredo will open the freezer and find a pint of ice cream with the lid off and a spoon sticking straight out of the top. Isabel will say, *Nah, wasn't me, I don't even like pistachio.* Alfredo will say, *Okay.* He thinks those Kansas farmers who wake up with crop circles in their backyard should stop squinting up past the sky and look instead across the breakfast table, check the wife's housecoat for tractor keys.

Of course it's always possible Isabel's being framed. Stranger things have happened around here. But Alfredo knows he isn't doing the framing, and his father couldn't plant a spoon in a freezer he isn't able to reach, and Alfredo's mother—admittedly the most likely suspect—would never sully her own kitchen. One morning he caught her dragging a finger over the countertop, scooping up Oreo crumbs. Her lips were drawn back in panic, as if the chocolate were anthrax.

"Parrot droppings?" Alfredo had said.

"Your girlfriend, she's going to give us mice."

"Actually it was me. I had the midnight munchies." Not that she believed him. Lizette had been lied to so often in her life that she'd built up an immunity. Bullshit clanged off her. She wiped down the countertop and stuck the milk-coated glass into the dishwasher.

"We'll be infested," she said. "More so than we already are."

"I won't do it again." Lying to his mother, Alfredo felt like a boy playing chopsticks for a woman used to the symphony, and yet it pleased him to have covered for Isabel, even ineffectively. He felt taller somehow, taking responsibility for a thing he did not do.

Meanwhile, outside this apartment, Curtis Hughes is dead. Alfredo double-checks the deadbolts, makes sure to fasten all the door chains. He imagines Curtis lying in the back of an ambulance with the lights flashing and the sirens turned off. Something cold and dark like seawater takes hold of Alfredo's throat. It drops whispers into his ear. If Curtis's beating is linked to this Vladimir/infinity-logo disaster, then "C. Hughes" is merely one name at the top of a list that includes "A. Batista," and "Winston," too.

Winston. After the police left Alfredo, he called Winston six times, and six times the phone went straight to voice mail. *Hey, uh, leave a message?* Alfredo pictured Winston holding the phone to his ear as an aluminum bat caught him from behind, smashing the bones in his hand, breaking the phone into bits. Alfredo searched the streets for the Spider-Man hat, looking near gutters and under parked cars, before he spooked himself and ran all the way home.

For the seventh time in the last twenty minutes, he dials Winston's number. He knocks his knuckles against the beak of a wooden parrot, hoping—praying really—that this time the call will be answered. Just give me a ring. Tell me the phone is *on,* at least.

Hey, uh, leave a message?

The TV flickers light onto Papi's sleeping face. Jose watches, or rather he was watching, at an unreasonable volume, the Home Shopping Network. He doesn't buy anything, not anymore at least, not since Lizette canceled his credit card. About a year after the accident, an HSN package arrived every other day: candleholders, digital cameras, vacuum cleaners, cologne, a sauna belt, dual drills, lint rollers, magic blenders, suction cup hooks, Space Bags, a knife sharpener called the Samurai Shark, Dr. Ho's neck massager, the Lauren Hutton Face Disc. These brown-boxed parcels became for Jose one of the few ways he communicated with a world outside this two-bedroom apartment. The collapsible ladders and magical mops were his street gossip, his walk to the mall.

Alfredo turns off the television. In the sudden silence Jose's head tilts back and he snores more deeply than before. His face shines with sweat. It's hot in this room—hotter even than it is outside—and every degree seems to glaze Jose's cheeks and neck. Even his glasses look damp. Alfredo knows that tomorrow morning Tariq will come home from prison and he will see this face—the liver spots, the mustache dappled gray—and he will think their father has aged decades. But that's all wrong, Alfredo thinks. Couldn't be wronger! Look at the button-down shirt Jose wears. Look at his hair slicked back with gel. These aren't the signs of a shriveled enfeeblement, but rather the bulwarks erected against it. Granted, one sideburn extends lower than the other, but you try shaving in a wheelchair, your eye line below the mirror. Isn't it enough, big brother, that Papi shaves at all? How could a man be old if his cheeks still smell of Aqua Velva? If his lips are stained with cherry juice?

Of course, unlike Tariq, Alfredo never went away for two and a half years. He knows what it's like to see his father transformed—from walker to sitter, from upright to broken—but he doesn't know, and he can't appreciate, what it's like to see the man suddenly grow old. Their only significant separation dates back to when Alfredo was in the third grade and Jose lived with a white woman for four days in Rego Park. Four days—that's it, the longest amount of time father and son have spent away from each other. Alfredo never enrolled in college or joined the merchant marines. He never even went to summer camp. In the living room, in the dark, Alfredo approaches his father's wheelchair, stepping around the empty sofa bed, head brushing against a low-

hanging parrot, and he wonders if now is not the time to get the hell out. Leave this room, this apartment, this neighborhood, this borough, this city of New York. His brother comes home in a few hours. A guy is out on the street murdering drug dealers, avenging Vladimir. Maybe. So maybe what Alfredo needs to do is pack a bag, buy a bus ticket for him and his pregnant girlfriend, and head . . . like west or something. Alfredo catches his lips moving. It's a stupid idea. What would you tell Isabel? *We need to get out of Jackson Heights for a little while. Nothing to worry about. Plenty of women go into labor at the back of a Greyhound.* Moving through the dark, he accidentally kicks over a bowl. Cherry pits and cherry stems skip across the floor. The bowl goes *clatter clatter.*

"Nice going," Jose says. Behind the lens of his glasses, his eyes stare down at the ground. Bright red cherry flesh clings to some of the pits; the juice bleeds onto Lizette's carpet.

"You're not supposed to eat in here," Alfredo says.

"You're not supposed to kick my bowl."

Too tired to argue, Alfredo moves behind the wheelchair. His feet hurt. Since Thursday morning he's gotten four hours of sleep. Alfredo hopes that this—getting wheels to roll forward in a room with wall-to-wall carpeting—will be the last difficult job in a day full of difficult jobs. He lifts the handlebars, digs in, and pushes hard. The wheels tangle with the carpet, but after a little time and with a little effort, the Batista boys get rolling. They cruise toward the bedrooms at the back of the apartment.

"You pick up our investment?" Jose asks. By which he means, *Did you get me my Lotto tickets?* He's an every-day player, a purist who never lets the machine Quick Pick his numbers, but instead chooses himself, playing his sons' birthdays or his Social Security number or particular license plates or—if a bad streak gets bad enough—the date he got shot, Jose hoping the Lotto gods appreciate irony. The morning after a drawing, he spreads his pink tickets across the table and opens up his *Newsday* and checks his numbers against the winning numbers, Jose circling matches, crossing out misses. Lotto, Take 5, Mega, Win 4, the Numbers—he'll play them all. But he won't do scratch-offs. They're low class, he explains. A sucker's game. But the real reason, Alfredo knows, is that the scratch-offs provide too instant a gratification, too immediate a disappointment. Where's the suspense? After

closing his *Newsday* and after finishing his buttered bialy and café con leche, Jose methodically balls up the loser Lotto tickets and tosses them in the trash. Then he re-ups. He'll give Alfredo five or ten or fifteen dollars and tell him to go buy more—*and make sure you play these exact numbers.* He sends Alfredo out into the world on his behalf so that the father can be, once again, for the next twenty-four hours, a possible millionaire. Their agreement is Jose keeps 90 percent of all winnings and Alfredo pockets the rest. A little scratch for doing the legwork, so to speak. For picking up the tickets. Except tonight— understandably—Alfredo forgot. "I saw this set of knives on HSN I'd like to buy with our earnings," Jose says. "These knives, I swear to God, they'd cut off a finger."

"Well," Alfredo says. He speaks into the heartbreakingly boyish swirl of hair at the back of his father's head. "The thing is . . ."

Jose's hands flare out as if he's going to clutch the wheels and arrest their progress. These hands hover in the air for a moment before drifting back into his lap. He crosses one muscular arm over the other. "That's not like you," he says. "To forget like that. What if those numbers hit, Dito?"

"Then I owe you a million dollars."

"Am I gonna have to partner up with your brother when he comes home? Hire him to pick up my tickets?"

"He can't," Alfredo says. "He can't gamble. He'd violate his parole."

"Oh please. What, are they staking out bodegas now? Junior can just go straight downstairs—"

"Tariq," Alfredo says. "Not Junior. *Tariq.*" With his fists choking the handlebars, he shoves Jose out of the living room. The chair's wheels jump the lip of the carpet and hit the smooth linoleum of the kitchen floor. Ordinarily, this tactile transition is Alfredo's favorite part of the journey. He doesn't know how to drive, but when he hits the linoleum Alfredo usually imagines that this is what it must be like to catch a string of green lights, or to punch the gas on a blacktopped highway. Tonight, however, Alfredo finds no satisfaction in the creamy smoothness of rubber wheels on a kitchen floor. "Even if Tariq could pick up your tickets, he wouldn't. It's against his new *religion.*"

Isabel stands at the range, her face hovering above a giant pot. The kitchen is as dark as pitch, save for a few purple fingers of fire. Alfredo doesn't know if the fire comes from the stove or from Isabel her-

self, doesn't know which one of them is illuminating and which one is the illuminated. She wears his old Our Lady of Fatima gym shorts. With her third-trimester belly swelling her tank top, she looks beautiful and monstrous and strange.

She turns to them but doesn't say anything. Water sizzles, the refrigerator hums. Is she sleepwalking? Has she graduated from late-night Oreos and ice cream to some serious stovetop cooking? Alfredo doesn't know what's in the pot but he imagines it can be anything—a box of linguine, the head of a pig—and just as he's about to ask, she brings her finger to her lips as if to say *Shhhhhhhh.* Fire crawls up the side of the pot. It occurs to Alfredo that he has possibly steered his father's wheelchair into some kind of dream.

Someone—in the apartment above or below or around them—turns on a faucet, and the pipes in the Batistas' walls begin to moan. A neighbor getting a late-night drink of water perhaps. Someone who has been asleep all night and will be able to go right back to bed. Alfredo wonders what the hell they've got to be so thirsty about.

"I just hope those numbers don't hit," Jose whispers. "That'd be just the thing."

Alfredo pushes the wheelchair down the hall to an open door, his father's bedroom. A queen-sized mattress dominates the room. Scattered across the bed lie a dozen pillows, each one autographed by Jose's signature hair grease. Lizette visits the Laundromat as frequently as she visits church—the entire bedroom smells freshly laundered—but Jose's grease stains are just that, stains, impossible to get out. Lizette keeps trying, however. She hasn't lost faith in the redemptive powers of a good scrubbing. Her dresser and Jose's dresser face each other on opposite walls, as if locked in an interminable staring contest. Alfredo parks his father at the foot of the bed and turns on the light.

Lizette doesn't yank the sheets over her head or roll over or throw an arm across her eyes because Lizette sleeps next door in the boys' old room. She made the move a few months ago, on the same night Isabel showed up at the front door with a duffel bag and a DVD player and with bruises on her neck. Lizette went into Alfredo's room; Alfredo and his guest were deported to the living room sofa bed. *It's your father's late hours,* Lizette said. *He's always waking me up.* Now where Tariq will sleep—with both bedrooms and the sofa bed occupied—is yet to be determined. Alfredo considers asking his father but it's

unlikely he's got any idea. Papi's not on the wire, not in this house, not anymore.

Alfredo depresses the wheel brakes and locks the chair in place. Both men share the same warped, nervous smile. Alfredo hooks his arms under his father's damp armpits. With a grunt, he scoops him clean out of the chair. They stagger backward. He and his father are chest to chest, one body, and while Jose isn't particularly heavy, it is all dead, helpless weight. His legs dangle. His hands scramble to touch each other behind Alfredo's back. When his father starts slipping, Alfredo shoves his face into his neck, which feels smooth and smells of Aqua Velva. Together, father and son spin around, dancing dangerously, until the backs of Jose's knees kiss the edge of the bed. Alfredo eases him onto the mattress. Both men breathe with their mouths open. They gorge themselves on great big gulps of air.

"Tomorrow night," Jose says, "we'll get Junior to help." He unbuttons his pants slowly, his hands shaking. "Unless it's against his religion."

Alfredo pulls at the cuffs, wiggles the pants off his father. His legs are spidery, thin and awkward, and in the move from chair to bed, fresh capillaries have burst. Purple splotches speckle his thighs. Hugging his waist is a pair of underwear that's as old as Alfredo. They are white cotton and damp in the middle.

"I guess I had an accident," Jose says. He sits up on his elbows, to stare into Alfredo's face. "Can you take them with you? The underwear? Can you hide them or throw them out or something? I don't want your mother to know."

With his head turned to the side, Alfredo pulls off the underwear. The smell of urine is released into the room. As is Jose's penis, which is sizably serpentine, thick and substantial. Impressed, as he always is whenever he sees this penis, Alfredo is careful not to smile. He is also careful not to hold the underwear at arm's length or daintily pinch the elastic waistband; instead, he lets the damp undies hang from his fingertips casually, so as to show Jose how little this bothers him, how pleased and honored he feels to be able to do this thing for his father.

"You gonna change the diapers for your son?" Jose asks.

Alfredo props pillows around his father's legs. "You want the covers on you?"

"No," Jose says. "I want your mother to come in here in the morning and catch me with a raging hard-on."

"Good night, Papi."

"We'll play those same numbers tomorrow? In the Lotto? Or we can run with some new numbers. If you want. Maybe Isabel's birthday?"

"Yeah," Alfredo says. "I better get out there before she sets the kitchen on fire."

"You see any license plates tonight?"

"A few." Alfredo knows his father doesn't want him to leave. "I saw an unmarked police car."

"They stop you?"

"Plate number 3AT649."

Jose asks him what's all that multiplied together, three times six times four times nine, and Alfredo tells him instantly. Jose asks him what's that number times four (Jose's lucky number), and the answer takes Alfredo as long as it takes him to close his eyes and see the digits—green-and-purple-hued—fall against a black backdrop and lock into place: 2,592.

Jose lets loose a low whistle. "Good man, Dito. Good man."

Now it's Alfredo who doesn't want to leave. He leans into the door-frame, lingers inside his father's benediction. Above the bed's head-board floats the ghost outline of a giant crucifix. When Lizette switched rooms she took only the alarm clock off her dresser and the cross off the wall. But it's still there, sort of. Alfredo can see a T where the cross used to hang; the paint on that part of the wall seems fresher. He wants to know if this pseudocrucifix might still work, if it might still impart a sliver of divine protection for his father's unbelieving soul. And if so, Alfredo wonders, might there be any juice left for a good man like me?

Isabel and Alfredo lie in bed, careful not to touch each other. Out on the street, below their open window, rubber-gloved men from Staten Island toss bags of garbage into the jagged maw of a sanitation truck. Pizza boxes, expired milk, cleaned-out cans, discarded magazines, uneaten rice, shredded bills—it all gets gnashed up and digested. With a release of hydraulic pressure, a noise somewhere between a belch

and a sigh, the truck moves on to the next apartment building. Isabel and Alfredo listen to it *beep-beep-beep* away.

Alfredo laces his hands behind his head, so that his elbows jut out, twin antennae trying to pick up a signal. His armpits reek. *Talk about garbage!* He must feel guilty—he *should* feel guilty, Isabel thinks—otherwise his BO wouldn't be so brolic. It's as if something inside of him has curdled. She can smell his pits even with her back to him. She lies on her side, faces the parrot with the clock embedded in its belly. It is 3:47 a.m. It is 3:48 a.m., and Isabel is a kiddie pool. Because he knows something is wrong, Christian Louis swims laps. He crashes into his mama's uterine wall, turns, crashes into her bladder. He swims freestyle. He swims the butterfly and backstroke. He churns his fetal arms, kicks his fetal legs. Isabel wants to roll over and lie on her other side, but she can't, because if she rolls over, she will have to face Alfredo, and if she faces Alfredo, she will have to claw out his eyeballs.

The Big Surprise did not go as well as she'd hoped.

Things *had* been going just fine. Just as they were supposed to go. When the water began to simmer, Isabel turned off the gas. Step two: she put on some oven mitts. She experienced a minor hiccup when she had to carry the pot into the bathroom. Not only was the pot heavy, but the floor felt tilted at an angle. And not only did the floor feel tilted, but her foot had fallen asleep. (Increased clumsiness, pins and needles in her extremities—add it to the list of things she forgot to ask the doctor.) On her way to the bathroom, Isabel banged into the kitchen table. Inside the pot, hot water swished.

Don't spill that shit on your belly, Christian Louis said. When Isabel told him not to curse, he said, *I've got Tourette's! I'm autistic! I've got a rotten case of thalassemia!*

Isabel set the pot down on a bath mat. She can't be sure if she heard a sizzle. She was too busy running back into the kitchen, tossing off oven mitts. She was too busy reaching under the sofa bed, grabbing the box of Epsom salts she'd bought earlier in the day. The box rattled—maraca-like—as she ran with it into the bathroom. She dumped columns of salt into the pot. The water swirled gray with clouds.

"What are you doing?" Alfredo said. In his hand he held what looked like a pair of droopy tighty-whities, definitely not the pair of silk boxers she'd given him for Christmas. "Are you sleepwalking?" he said. "Is it dangerous to wake you?"

Isabel stood up, her back screaming. With a majestic sweep of her arm, she beckoned her boyfriend to the toilet seat. "Welcome," she said, feeling suddenly silly, "to Spa de Batista."

Because Alfredo walks all night from one end of Queens to the other, and because—for God knows what reason—he insists on wearing those heavy Timberland boots, his feet break out in calluses. His heels coarsen, his soles blister, his dogs get to barking. So Isabel—stunning girlfriend that she is—set up this foot massage with the idea that Alfredo would sit on his throne, kick off his boots, and plunge his maltreated feet into the salty water. He would feel like a sultan, fanned by the giant feathers of a mystical bird. Isabel put all this together so that later tonight in bed she could look for some indication in the outward signs of his sleep—some hint in his fluttering eyelids or twitching fingertips—that he was dreaming about her, a woman who loves him, who knows when his feet ache and who does something about it. A woman, in other words, worth fighting for.

"Baby," Alfredo said. He pressed his palms to his forehead. "I'm tired."

"Exactly," she said.

"I'm not really in the mood."

"I set this all up," Isabel said.

"Okay, but I'm just trying to go to sleep. You know what I'm saying? I'm just trying to get to *bed*."

"Exactly," Isabel said. "This will relax you. Get rid of your aches and pains. See? It's a foot massager."

"You want me to stick my fucking foot in there?" Needless to say, in the movie version of her life Alfredo does not say this. "Don't be stupid, baby. That's a pot. That's a pot my mama uses to cook rice."

Isabel let him know that if they had more money then maybe she could afford a *real* foot massager, and maybe she could get some other things too, like a crib or an OB-GYN or a crisscross support sling for her back, or maybe even their very own apartment (!), where Isabel could take baths surrounded by candles. But you know, that's if they *had* money, which is a ridiculous idea—like all her ideas, of course, since she's so stupid, right?—because as we all know there ain't no foot massager money and there ain't no moving out money coming around here either.

Alfredo sat down on the toilet. He tossed the underwear into the

tub. He untied his boots and neatly placed them to the side. From his pockets he removed a beeper Isabel had never seen before, and holding it with both hands he slid it into the open mouth of his boot. He took out his cell phone, dialed a number with his eyes closed, and when what sounded like a message clicked on, he hung up the phone. She didn't ask. She watched him peel off his socks. From the bottom of one of those socks he pulled out a small wad of cash, no more than three or four bills, and threw it at Isabel's bare feet. They stared at each other, Isabel and Alfredo did, with this pathetic sum of crumpled money on the floor between them—it was maybe thirty-five dollars, maybe less—and then Alfredo thrust his foot into the water.

His head snapped back, banged against the wall behind him. His foot came out of the water looking pinkish-white and soft.

"Is it too hot? Are you okay?"

"Are you kidding me, Isabel?"

"Please don't yell."

"Who's yelling?"

She clamped her hands onto the sides of her belly, as if to cover Christian Louis's underdeveloped ears. "What if you wake up your mother?" They both knew that'd be impossible. "Please," Isabel said. "Please don't yell."

"Who, Isabel, is yelling?"

"I was just trying to do something nice. I was just trying to take care of you."

"Everyone needs to stop trying to help me. Please." Alfredo wrapped a towel around his foot. He lifted the pot and peeked underneath it. "You know the rug is completely burnt. Because you are *retarded*. Because you are a *child*. My mother's bath mat now has a big black circle right in the middle of it."

The water got dumped down the drain. Lizette's scorched bath mat got balled up and stashed under the sofa bed, along with the Epsom salts and damp underwear. And now Isabel stares at the parrot clock. She's halfway convinced it will take off and fly shrieking into her face.

The garbage truck turns the corner. It is 3:49 a.m. With the truck gone, Isabel and Alfredo listen to nothing. Soon the paper guys will come. The *New York Times*, the *Daily News*, the *Post*, *Newsday*, *El Diario*. No prepubescent boys in this neighborhood, pedaling down maple-shaded streets, tossing the morning edition over rose bushes

and onto welcome mats. Here the papers get delivered by men, immigrants from Ecuador, Colombia, Pakistan, Korea. They drive cars through all of Queens, stopping at the buildings on their list and leaving the engine running while they run out and drop thick stacks of plastic-bagged newspapers onto stoops. They will be here soon, these men. And when they arrive, there will be no denying a new day has begun. The midnight transition from p.m. to a.m., the sunrise, the beeping garbage trucks, the morning papers—Isabel can fool herself no longer. Extra, extra! Saturday's coming, whether she likes it or not. She and Alfredo lie in bed, waiting. The silence sits on their chests.

"You got any new songs?" he says.

She scoots closer to the edge of the bed.

"Not for me, of course," he says. "Don't sing for me. I don't deserve to hear a new song. But the baby. It's not fair the baby doesn't get—"

"You were mean. I was just trying to do something nice. I made a mistake. I'm sorry. But you were *mean*."

"I'm a bad person," Alfredo says. He reaches toward her. He taps her recently outied belly button. "This is your microphone. This belly button right here. Sing into that. You want, I'll close my ears. I'll stick a pillow over my head."

Isabel is a wealth of lullabies. Alfredo assumes she's carried them with her from childhood. He assumes they were passed down from Isabel's mother to her. But that's not the case at all. Isabel grew up in a tuneless home and she's had to work hard for her lullabies. Secretly, without anyone knowing but Christian Louis, she goes down to the public library, logs on to their computers, and searches the Web for cradlesongs. She writes down the lyrics, commits them to memory. Never having heard any of these songs, she needs to work out the proper beats and cadences—and so at night she practices. She rehearses.

Alfredo rests a hand on her stomach. "Little man's had a rough day," he says. "The hospital and shit. Listening to us fight. He only wants a little lullaby. Half a lullaby, even."

She just learned a new one, too. It's about three little bears who roll over in bed and fall crashing to the ground. Alfredo's right—a song would be just the thing to get Christian Louis to chill out, to balm his thrashing legs—but there ain't no way she's singing. She'd rather suffer.

"Don't make me break out some Nas," Alfredo says.

"You think if you ignore something long enough it'll just go away."

"She speaks!"

"Where's he gonna sleep? What happens the first time you leave me alone with him?" When he doesn't answer, she says, "He's going to try to kill you."

"He'll have to get in line. Right behind you, yeah?" Alfredo laughs and rattles her elbow. He tries to keep his voice bright, but she knows better. "I'll tell you what we're gonna do," he says. "This'll pick you up. You listening? It's about tomorrow. Hey, you listening? First things first, we tell my mother I was smoking a giant cigar and I put it out on her bath mat. I'll take the blame. No? Okay, then we'll tell her I was taking a shit, drinking the world's largest cup of coffee and I couldn't find a big enough coaster. Or how about this? Hey, listen up. We run away. From the road we send her a check for a new bath mat."

Isabel rolls over. With the living room dark, she sees only the outline of Alfredo's face. "We run away?" she asks.

"You'd be cool with that? Packing up? Leaving here?" Alfredo kicks the sheets off of him, plants his feet on the ground. "Ask the baby. Find out what the baby says about leaving on up out of here."

She doesn't need to ask. Christian Louis is curled up inside her ear, a megaphone pressed to his tiny lips. "The baby wants us to run," she says. "The baby says, 'Go. Right now. Run away.' "

Above Isabel and Alfredo's heads the parrots eye one another nervously. Their beaks are closed, their wings tucked tight to their chests. Outside a car passes and the room fills with light.

Part Two

6

From the New York State Department of Correctional Services

STATE OF NEW YORK—EXECUTIVE DEPARTMENT—DIVISION OF PAROLE
INMATE STATUS REPORT FOR PAROLE BOARD APPEARANCE

PAROLE SUMMARY—RELEASE APPLICANT
(May, 2002)

PART 1

Name: BATISTA JR, Jose	CR: 2-0 ME: 4-0	PE: 1/12/04
NYSID: 7153902J	DIN: 92G0192	DOB: 7/12/81
Rec'd Date: 1/12/00	PVNT: NO	Time on Parole: —

Crime, (felony class), sentence & date p(lea) or v(erdict);

1) BURGLARY 3rd (D)   2-0/4-0 12/5/99   PLEA

Guideline Range: 12–48 Months;
          28 Mos. Total Time Served at Time of Review

EEC—   Granted   Denied   Non-Certified
          If Denied or Non-Certified, are reasons in file:

Special Programs: WR/   from   to
        Furloughs: ;   Day Reporting from   to
        Program Violations:

Mand. SPP: Y ; Citizen: Y ; INS Warrant: N ; Other Warrants: N
Comments:

Official Statements: Judge N   ; DA N   ; Def. Atty N   ;

Certificate of Relief: _____ Eligible

Co-Defendant:	Name & NYSID		Status
HALL, Conrad	2465190Z	92A1088	BURGLARY 3rd (D) 2-0/4-0 Altona CF 1/03 I
DUPRE, Giovanni	3599201R	92H4537	BURGLARY 3rd (D) 2-0/4-0 Otisville CF 1/03 I

INMATE STATUS REPORT FOR PAROLE BOARD APPEARANCE
Page 2

NAME: BATISTA JR, Jose   NYSID: 7153902J   DIN: 92G0192

Present Offense:

The description of the Instant Offense was derived from the Presentence Investigation. On December 5, 1999, the subject, Jose Batista Jr., along with his co-defendants, Conrad Hall and Giovanni Dupre, did unlawfully enter the commercial premise, Virgil Caterers at 75-01 31st Avenue, East Elmhurst, NY, and did unlawfully remove from the above premises $5000 cash US currency belonging to the victim/complainant, Virgil Barbaretto.

The subject was identified via surveillance tapes delivered to the NYPD by Barbaretto, and via the affidavits of co-defendants Hall and Dupre. The subject was summarily arrested at his place of residence, 79-09 34th Ave, Jackson Heights, NY, on 12/7/99.

CRIMINAL RECORD

Arrest Date	Arrest Charges	Place	Disposition
INSTANT OFFENSE :			
12/7/99	BURGLARY 3rd (D)	Queens Cty. Crt. 1/10/2000	Conv. upon plea BURGLARY 2-0/4-0

PAROLE INTERVIEW

INMATE'S STATEMENT:

The subject was interviewed on 5/22/02 at Fishkill C.F. Regarding the I.O., subject admits participation. He continues to state the I.O. was his first offense, and, indeed, he has no prior criminal record.

Subject states his motivation for this act was for quick monetary gain. Subject states at the time of the I.O. he was unemployed and living in his parents' residence. In contradiction to the testimonies of his co-defendants, subject states he never received any of the money that was removed from Virgil Caterers; and, indeed, at the occasion of his arrest he only had $7.00 in his possession.

INMATE STATUS REPORT FOR PAROLE BOARD APPEARANCE
Page 3

NAME: BATISTA JR, Jose   NYSID: 7153902J   DIN: 92G0192

Subject states he is guilty for the I.O. Subject states he "has learned his lesson."

INSTITUTIONAL ADJUSTMENT:

Subject has had difficulty making custodial adjustment. During the first nine months of his institutional incarceration, subject incurred numerous

disciplinary infractions. Disciplinary infractions include failures to report, failure to maintain acceptable living area, and, most frequently, violently aggressive behavior toward both C.O.s and other inmates.

Subject's custodial adjustment has improved. He has not incurred any disciplinary actions since September 2000. Subject credits improvement to a "spiritual awakening."

Subject continues his educational pursuits, obtaining his G.E.D. in February 2002. He is currently enrolled in the College Bound program working toward his Associate's Degree.

PROPOSED RESIDENCE:

The subject proposed to reside with his parents, Jose Batista Sr. and Lizette Batista, at the following address:

>   79-09 34th Ave
>   Apt. 52
>   Jackson Heights, NY 11372
>   (718) 424-9131

PROPOSED EMPLOYMENT:
  To be developed.

INMATE STATUS REPORT FOR PAROLE BOARD APPEARANCE
Page 4

NAME: BATISTA JR, Jose   NYSID: 7153902J   DIN: 92G0192

INMATE'S PLANS:

The subject proposes to go back to school to finish his education and to be reunited with his family. He is seeking assistance through the Prisoner Reentry Institute.

SUPERVISION NEEDS:
1. Vocational training.

SPECIAL CONDITIONS RECOMMENDED:
1. Anger management therapy.
2. Substance abuse counseling with periodic drug testing.
3. Curfew.

Prepared by: Approved by:
FPO I, D.N. Landry   FPO II, L.R. Flory
Date: 5/22/02   Date: 5/22/02

Facility: Fishkill C.F.
DBT:rw

Ticket:: ticket

STATE OF NEW YORK
EXECUTIVE DEPARTMENT—DIVISION OF PAROLE
CERTIFICATE OF RELEASE TO PAROLE SUPERVISION
DETERMINATE—POST-RELEASE SUPERVISION

SENTENCE: 2-0/4-0   NYSID NO. 7153902J

BATISTA JR., JOSE , now confined in Fishkill CF who was convicted of
BURGLARY 3rd (D) and sentenced in the county of Queens at a term of the
County Court, Judge Richard J. Oh presiding on the 10th day of January
2000, for the term of 2-0/4-0 the maximum term of such sentence expires
on the 10th day of January 2004, has agreed to abide by the conditions to
which he has signed his name below, and is hereby released by virtue of the
authority conferred by New York State Law.

Jose Batista Jr. is additionally subject to a period of 2 (two) years Post-
Release Supervision, which will commence on the release date of June 15,

2002 and he will be under the legal jurisdiction of the Division of Parole until the Post-Release Supervision maximum expiration date of <u>June 15, 2004</u>.

Date of Release: <u>6/15/2002</u>
Post-Release Supervision Period: <u>2 (two) years</u>
Post-Release Supervision Maximum Expiration Date: <u>6/15/2004</u>
Residence: 79-09 34th Ave
Apt. 52
Jackson Hts, NY, 11372
718-424-9131
I, Jose Batista Jr. 92G0192, voluntarily accept Parole Post-Release Supervision. I fully understand that my person, residence and property are subject to search and inspection. I understand that Parole Post-Release Supervision is defined by these Conditions of Release and all other conditions that may be imposed upon me by the Board of Parole or its representatives. I understand that my violation of these conditions may result in the revocation of my release.

CONDITIONS OF RELEASE

1. I will proceed directly to the area to which I have been released, and, within twenty-four hours of my release, make my arrival report to the Office of the Division of Parole unless other instructions are designated on my release agreement. Report to: **P.O. Dimmick, SPO Hebert, Queens I Area Office 1010 Hazen St., East Elmhurst, NY 11370 718-546-5891**
2. I will make office and/or written reports as directed.
3. I will not leave the State of New York or any other State to which I am released or transferred, or any area defined in writing by my Parole Officer without permission.
4. I will permit my Parole Officer to visit me at my residence and/or place of employment and I will permit the search and inspection of my person, residence and property. I will discuss any proposed changes in my residence, employment or program status with my Parole Officer. I understand that I have an immediate and continuing duty to notify my Parole Officer of any changes in my residence, employment or program status when circumstances beyond my control make prior discussion impossible.

5. I will reply promptly, fully, and truthfully to any inquiry of, or communication by, my Parole Officer or other representative of the Division of Parole.

6. I will notify my Parole Officer immediately any time I am in contact with, or arrested by, any law enforcement agency. I understand that I have a continuing duty to notify my Parole Officer of such contact or arrest.

7. I will not be in the company of, or fraternize with, any person I know to have a criminal record or whom I know to have been adjudicated a Youthful Offender, except for accidental encounters in public places, work, school, or in any other instance with the permission of my Parole Officer.

8. I will not behave in such manner as to violate the provisions of any law to which I am subject, which provide for a penalty of imprisonment, nor will my behavior threaten the safety or well-being of myself or others.

9. I will not own, possess, or purchase any shotgun, rifle, or firearm of any type without the written permission of my Parole Officer. I will not own, possess, or purchase any deadly weapon as defined in the Penal Law or any dangerous knife, dirk, razor, stiletto, or imitation pistol. In addition, I will not own, possess, or purchase any instrument readily capable of causing physical injury without a satisfactory explanation for ownership, possession, or purchase.

10. In the event that I leave the jurisdiction of the State of New York, I hereby waive my right to resist extradition to the State of New York from any state in the Union and from any territory or country outside the United States. This waiver shall be in full force and effect until I am discharged from Parole or Conditional Release. I fully understand that I have the right under the Constitution of the United States and under law to contest any effort to extradite me from another state and return me to New York, and I freely and knowingly waive this right as a condition of my Parole or Conditional Release.

11. I will not use or possess any drug paraphernalia or use or possess any controlled substance without proper medical authorization.

12. Special Conditions:
    I will seek, obtain, and maintain employment and/or an
        academic/vocational program.
    I will submit to substance abuse testing as directed by the P.O.

I will participate in a substance abuse treatment program as directed by the P.O.

I will participate in an anger management program as directed by the P.O.

I will abide by a curfew established by the P.O.

I will cooperate with a mental health evaluation referral, and follow-up treatment as directed by the P.O.

I will not associate in any way or communicate by any means with (associates Conrad Hall and Giovanni Dupre) without the permission of the P.O.

I will cooperate with all medical referrals and treatment recommendations.

13. I will fully comply with the instructions of my Parole Officer and obey such special additional written conditions as he or she, a member of the Board of Parole, or an authorized representative of the Division of Parole, may impose.

I hereby certify that I have read and that I understand the foregoing conditions of my release and that I have received a copy of this Certificate of Release.

Signed this <u>15th</u> day of <u>June</u> 20 <u>02</u>

Releasee Tariq Batista

Tariq Batista

Witness J. Beardsley

J. Beardsley

3010PRS (12/00)

COPY TO INMATE

7

Reentry

Isabel sits in the front seat of a car, her painted toes wiggling out the window. On the dashboard, the vents are probably tilted upward so that the AC blasts up her skirt, cools off her crotch. Isabel stands on the corner, eating an arepa. Her chin shines with grease, which she doesn't wipe off, which is not like her at all. Isabel sits in the back of a cab. Isabel climbs the stairs to the 7 train. Isabel pushes a baby carriage—but no, no, no, no, that's impossible, it's too soon. The rear doors of a van swing open and Isabel steps out, leaps to the street. The van advertises Carpet Cleaning Services, but Isabel holds no vacuum, no broom or mop. Isabel walks out of one of the jewelry stores on Seventy-fourth Street. She carries a little bag probably stuffed with gold chains, but wait a second, never mind, that woman is obviously not Isabel. That lady's Indian, which Isabel is not, and she's wearing high heels, which Isabel never wears. Isabel crosses the street at the intersection. Isabel jaywalks, gliding between moving cars. Stuck at the light, Isabel foolishly presses the green button on the corner. Isabel comes out of a pool hall, Isabel walks into a bank, Isabel sits behind a large plate-glass window while a Chinese lady files her nails, Isabel trips over her own feet and falls to the sidewalk, and when Tariq reaches out to grab her elbow and help her up, she pulls away from him and hustles down the street.

As he watches her run away, he feels something he's been feeling all morning, something like a lump of ice caught in his throat. The woman's handbag bounces as she motors down the block. The struts in her neck tighten. Tariq knows she wants to turn around and give him a look, but she won't—he sees this in her neck—because he frightens her.

Isabel walks toward him, gives him a wide berth so that they don't bump shoulders. He has been seeing Isabels all morning: at the Beacon train station; on the 6:50 a.m. to Grand Central; in the subway; out the windows of the elevated 7 train, many feet below the tracks, where Isabel was a lonely dot on the pavement. But there had been just one or two Isabel sightings at a time. Now that he's off that train and in Jackson Heights, he sees the slight upward tilt of her nose on every woman's face, her curly hair and copper skin, her mouth passing him on the right, the lips thick and full of blood. Everywhere he looks, he sees Isabel, and every time he sees Isabel, the ice in his throat turns to water.

But oh man this Isabel walking toward him, with her features all fuzzy . . . Tariq can't be sure. Incarceration weakened his eyesight. Too early every evening, all the Fishkill lights would click off, except for a small bulb at the end of the corridor, by the CO station, and this bulb shot a golden sliver into his cell. He'd get out of bed and sit on the floor and bring the Book into this sliver. With his face pressed against the bars, he'd read and reread, his eyes straining in the dark. And so now the Isabel coming toward him looks all fuzzy, but she walks *exactly* like the real Isabel walks, with her head down and her soft hands scrunched into fists. Get ready, Tariq. This Isabel might actually be her.

He throws himself into the nearest store, where he crouches down low and peeks out the window. Lights flicker off the glass, red lights and yellow lights and white lights, all of them flashing from inside the store. Motors whir, machines beep. Along one wall, a counter stretches toward the back of the store, and behind that counter are cameras, phones, TV sets, DVD players, answering machines, pagers, antennae, and, with his hands tugging at his beard, an Arab man in a loose-fitting cream-colored robe. Along the other wall: more electronics, another counter, another Arab man. It takes Tariq a moment to understand that these men are not twins. Only one man and only one counter exists. The store's other half is a mirror.

Tariq puts his hand flat against the window. He knows he's not afraid to see Isabel. Not at all. *Absolutely* not. No, the reason he ran into this store is because he's afraid she might see him. Before that can happen, certain moves need to be made.

From the Arab man, Tariq buys himself a wristwatch, which happens to be the very first item on his agenda. Coincidence? Is it some kind of accident that of all the stores on Roosevelt Avenue, he ducked into this one, an electronics joint he didn't even know existed? Of course not. There are no accidents, happy or otherwise. Tariq has been put on a straight path.

In addition to the clothes he's wearing (plain white T-shirt; natty, rubber-soled Converses; a pair of prisoner-made jeans that taper to an end just above his ankles), and in addition to the train ticket to Grand Central Station and the green sheet with parole stipulations and the nineteen Steri-Strips in his cheek, the Fishkill Correctional Facility gave Tariq upon his release two twenty-dollar bills. Gratis. For time served. Thanks for the memories. Earlier today, he used one of these twenties to buy a MetroCard, and the machine spat out his change, eighteen gold dollar coins that he'd never seen before in his life. He goes away and they change the currency? Seriously? Instead of Washington or Lincoln, the coin shows a young girl, with a baby asleep on her shoulder. Even she, this moonfaced girl, reminds him of Isabel. With her coins he pays for his watch.

It is a Casio F-91W, a water-resistant model (not quite the same as waterproof, but so what?) with an alarm, stopwatch, digital numbers, and a light rubber wristband. At a cost of twelve dollars, it is the only watch he can afford. He presses a button on the side, which should cause the time to illuminate. *Don't worry,* the Arab man tells him. *That particular function will work better at night.* After paying for the watch, Tariq turns away from the counter, embarrassed by the width of his grin.

When exactly did the lights click off at the Fishkill Correctional Facility? Tariq doesn't know. It never mattered. Calendars, sure, to mark the passing of days—but wristwatches? Hours? Minutes? What use could they have in a place of controlled movement, where there was always someone telling you when to line up for head counts and contraband checks and cafeteria meals of overcooked beef as leathery as a dragon's tongue. But it's a brand-new morning, Tariq. Today

marks the first day in two and a half years that he has had a reason to know the time. As the Book says:

> It is He who gave the sun its radiance, the moon its lustre, and appointed its stations so that you may compute years and numbers. God did not create them but with deliberation. He distinctly explains His signs for those who can understand.

Tariq takes his Casio F-91W digital watch outside the store, where it looks flimsier under the sun's natural light. The wristband feels greasy, as if it's already been worn. He searches the watch's face for scratches. Obviously what's happened here is that the Arab man saw Tariq come into the store with his busted sneakers and his prisoner-made jeans, and he sized him up as some kind of punk. Sold him a cheap, used, worn-out, greasy Casio. Tariq moves the watch up and down on his wrist. If he were to go back into the store . . . although, of course, he won't. No way to *prove* the watch is used. And, more important, Tariq has his agenda to consider. But what if? What if he went back into the store and smashed this watch against the man's face? His nose would shatter, of course. And probably his lips and teeth and jaw. And the watch? Would that break, too? Tariq suspects that it would.

Reentry day, baby. First day home. First day of freedom. In the early months of his incarceration he made lists of things he wanted to do on this day: go straight home and take a three-hour shower, drink beers at Budd's Bar, shoot pool, go bowling, sit in a recliner, walk down to Travers Park and dominate the handball courts, hit up Sammy's Halal, sleep in a bed with three dozen pillows, go to a Mets game, smoke a dub, go to Numbers, Records, & Tapes and buy the new Nas, the new Noreaga, the new Mobb Deep, visit his old grammar school, Our Lady of Fatima, and apologize to all the nuns, snort lines off a CD case, tear up some black and white and Asian and Latina pussy.

But things changed. He changed. Things he never imagined came to pass. Difficult things? Sure. Some of them. But one must adapt, right? That is, as the expression goes, the name of the game. Tariq's new and improved reentry day to-do list:

1. ~~Buy a watch.~~
2. Buy chocolates.
3. Get a haircut.
4. Pick up a more impressive, more stylish pair of jeans.
5. Remove Steri-Strips.
6. Buy and eat two delicious slices from Gianni's Pizzeria.
7. Be home by 1:10 for the start of the Mets-Yankees game, when everyone will be together, sitting in the living room.

He checks his Casio F-91W. Time to make moves.

From a bodega on Roosevelt Avenue he buys Kit Kat bars, Snickers bars, Charleston Chews (his favorite), Mr. Goodbars, and two fistfuls of Hershey's Kisses. Not only does it cost him all six of his remaining Isabel coins, but he also has to dip into his last twenty.

"Hope you got a good dentist," says the bodega man.

Tariq stuffs the candy into all four of his pockets, really jamming it in there. Outside he walks on the sunny side of the street, partly because it's so nice out, and partly because he wants the chocolate to get warm.

Everyone inside Jackson Heights' Headz Ain't Ready barbershop—the barbers, the men getting their hair cut, the men waiting for their turn, the men flipping through issues of *Source* magazine and *Sports Illustrated*, the men who, with felt-tip pens and management's permission, scrawl their graffiti tags onto the walls—they all turn to look at Tariq when he walks through the door. No one stops what they're doing. The clippers still clip and the buzzers still buzz and the boom box still blasts an Eminem song Tariq's never heard before. But just because the men in here don't stop what they're doing doesn't mean they're not eyeballing him. As Tariq knows, there's always time for that. Even the photographs tucked into the mirrors. Even the two-dimensional hair models—their glossy head shots pasted to the walls—even they seem to give him the once-over. *Look at the new guy in his Casio watch and his too-short jeans.* One kid in particular, a broom sweeper, a skinny little

bitch with sharp elbows and a pubic hair mustache—he can't *stop* looking at Tariq. The kid runs his hand over his mouth, hiding his toothy smile.

The Book says:

Do not disagree among yourselves or you will be unmanned and lose courage. Persevere, for God is with those who endure.

In an uncomfortable wooden chair, Tariq waits for his turn. The men around him talk about the upcoming Mets-Yankees game. With Roger Clemens coming to Shea and with the DH rule not in effect, everyone wants to know if the Mets will plunk Clemens for what he did to Piazza two years ago. No one asks Tariq for his opinion. When they've exhausted the Mets game, they talk about the Nas/Jay-Z feud and they talk about the molestation scandal in the Catholic Church and they talk about a young black kid who got himself killed last night in Corona. Tariq tries to read the *Queens Gazette,* but the words keep running together. He feels certain the broom sweeper is watching him.

"You up," the barber finally says, and Tariq takes a seat in one of Headz Ain't Ready's high leather chairs. The barber circles behind him. "Damn," he says. "Look at all these gray hairs! My man, you can't be older than twenty-two years old, am I right?"

"Shave it all off," Tariq says.

Through the mirror he sees the barber frown, as if he'd much rather give Tariq a shape-up or an ill fade, as if simply shaving a man bald is a waste of his talents. "You sure?" he says. "I can take it off, but I can't put it back on."

"Get rid of it."

"You the boss," he says. Around Tariq's neck, he ties a hair-catching smock. His breath smells like coffee, his fingers like Barbasol. As he buzzes off a sideburn, he says, making conversation, "That's a real beaut you got there. Fresh. Recent."

Tariq assumes he's referring to the two-and-a-half-inch gash in his face. The barber wants to know the story, but he clearly doesn't have the balls to come out and ask for it.

What is there to say? He was out in the yard, playing cards. With his Spades partner shooting for nil, Tariq had to cover the high cards and pick up as many books as possible, and that's exactly what he was

doing, scooping up his partner's queen with an ace, when he heard what sounded like the teeth of a zipper coming undone.

The other Spades players jumped up from the table. Tariq's hand came away from his face slick with blood. He was impressed—this was before the pain arrived—by how bright red his blood looked, almost like cartoon blood, a sign, he thought, of a healthy body. Then the pulse in his cheek jumped. He closed one eye—the left one, on the untouched side of his face—to make sure he could still see out of the other eye. While he held his cheek together, blood rolled down his arm, dripped off the tip of his elbow. He tried not to get any on the playing cards.

Arturo Sanchez rang him up with a toothbrush, buck-fifty'd him with intent to blind. Tariq doesn't know if he used a blade—he never got a chance to ask him—but if Arturo didn't use a blade, then he must've spent two or three nights sharpening the handle of his toothbrush against the walls of his cell. If he did use a blade—and it certainly felt like he used a blade—then he probably snapped the plastic safety off his disposable razor, pushed out the banger, and melted it onto the toothbrush with a Bic lighter, stopping every now and again to blow on the tips of his fingers.

He cut Tariq against the grain. The toothbrush entered the cheek just above his mouth, got yanked upward, tore through facial muscles, took a banana route around the orbital bone, and came out, the toothbrush did, a half inch shy of his ear. Arturo walked away, his hunter green pants spotted with blood. He let the toothbrush drop from his fingers. An against-the-grain buck fifty is deep, although inaccurate, and while Arturo must've been pleased to see the blood squirt out of Tariq's face in long, satisfying arcs, he must've also been disappointed to have missed the soft jelly of his eye. Not to mention how pissed Arturo must've felt later that night, forced to brush his teeth with his finger.

Tariq imagined that if he were a corrections officer, he would've been lounging in the back of an ambulance, on his way to the Beacon ER for reconstructive surgery. But instead he got tossed into the inhouse medical unit, where he saw, for the very first time, his new, gashed-open face. He thought of his mother's disappointment. He thought of Isabel, and how much harder everything would be now. His cheek puckered open like the mouth of a fish.

But because he tries to strive in the way of Allah with a service worthy of Him, Tariq received the blessing of the FHS's most skilled doctor: a short, no-nonsense Korean with fingerprint smudges all over his glasses. A man respected throughout Fishkill, by both COs and inmates. As the doctor worked on the cheek, Tariq told him about Isabel and how important it was—how necessary, really—that the doctor fix him up right, that he get Tariq back to his old handsome self.

"Stop talking," the doctor said.

He didn't sit there with a needle and thread like in the old days, sewing Tariq's face back together with 150 stitches. Instead he compressed the gash, cleaned it, dried it, and reunited the cheek's two halves with something he called Steri-Strips. Tariq thought they looked like bones a dog might gnaw on. Except tiny of course, and sticky on one side. When the doctor finished applying the Steri-Strips, he jammed a tetanus needle into Tariq's arm, slapped a clear plastic Band-Aid on his face, and said, "Don't mess with it. Keep it clean. Keep it dry. The Steri-Strips should fall off on their own within seven days. That's their genius. Don't pull them off yourself before it's time. You'll get infected. And please—don't bother asking me for painkillers. Come back on Tuesday and I'll give you another Band-Aid."

"I can't," Tariq said proudly. "I'm moving out. Saturday morning, I'm going home."

The doctor grabbed Tariq's chin and tilted his head toward the light, just as Lizette used to do when she checked her son's ears for wax. The doctor inspected the left side—the clean side—of his face.

"Keep telling those psychopaths you're getting released," he said, "and I'll be seeing you in here tomorrow. Bleeding out the one good cheek you got left."

Tariq says none of this to the Headz Ain't Ready barber. He is told he's got a real beaut, fresh, recent—and all he says in response is *uh-huh*. He fidgets in the chair so as to better smush the chocolate in his pockets. The barber finishes the haircut in silence. When he's done, he holds a mirror behind Tariq's head, giving him a 360-degree view of his new, shaved, vulnerable-looking dome. Perfect. Tariq imagines he looks as bald and as clean as the day he was born. With a small brush the barber wipes the hair off Tariq's face, careful to avoid his cheek.

At the cash register, the skinny little broom sweeper rings him up. As he stares at Tariq's cheek, he passes his hand over his mouth, just below his pubic hair mustache. The haircut costs thirteen dollars, and when Tariq has to take the Kit Kats and Snickers bars out of his pocket to get at his money, the kid laughs, *hahahahaha,* and sticks his hand in a jar full of lollipops next to the register.

"Sweet tooth?" he says. "Here. Take some. You want a purple one, too? Go ahead. Take as many as you like."

Fight those in the way of Allah who fight you, but do not be aggressive: God does not like aggressors.

The broom sweeper actually grabs hold of Tariq's hand. He uncurls the fingers, shoves lollipops into his palm.

"Do you enjoy what you do?" Tariq asks.

"What?"

"I said, Do you enjoy what you do?"

"What do you mean? Do I like working in the barbershop?"

"No. That's *not* what I mean. I didn't ask, Do you like working in the barbershop? I asked, Do you *enjoy* what you *do*?"

The broom sweeper smiles. He doesn't try to hide it. His hands stay down at his hips. "I don't know," he says. "I guess I don't know what you mean. What do I . . . what am I doing?"

"Don't you know? Surely, my brother, you must know what you do. The broom? Yes? The hair on the floor? You sweep it up. You sweep it up into tidy piles and then you take it away. *That* is what you do. The question, my brother, is do you enjoy it?"

"Well," he says. He hits a button on the cash register and the drawer slides open, kisses his belly. Looking not at Tariq, looking down at the money in the drawer, he says, "I don't know. Why? What is this about?"

"What is this *about*?" Tariq puts his money on the counter. He counts out the bills. One two three four five six seven eight nine ten eleven twelve thirteen fourteen fifteen, which leaves him with exactly three dollars, just enough for a couple of pizza slices from Gianni's. "That's thirteen dollars right there," he tells the broom sweeper. "There's thirteen dollars on the counter, plus an extra two. That two dollars is for you. That's yours. You want to know why? Don't answer. I know you're not good at questions. That two dollars is me saying

thank you. For sweeping my hair off the floor. Because you seemed to *enjoy* yourself so much, I'm giving you two dollars of my money. What do you say? You say, *Thank you.* What do I say? Look at me. Don't look inside that cash register. There's nothing in there for you. Look at me. You say, *Thank you,* and I say, *No, no, no. Thank* you, *brother. You did a* very *good job.*"

1. ~~Buy a watch.~~
2. ~~Buy chocolates.~~
3. ~~Get a haircut.~~
4. Pick up a more impressive, more stylish pair of jeans.
5. Remove Steri-Strips.
6. Buy and eat two delicious slices from Gianni's Pizzeria.
7. Be home by 1:10 for the start of the Mets-Yankees game, when everyone will be together, sitting in the living room.

How fast does news travel from the streets to the prisons? You read letters. You make phone calls (collect; monitored; fifteen-minute max). You have dreams and nightmares. You stand on line at the commissary, waiting to buy another can of instant soup, and you look up and see a guy from the neighborhood, a guy you went to sixth grade with, a guy who used to steal Slurpees from little kids, and you say, *Hey! What's going on? When'd you get here? What's poppin back at home?*

And he says, *Haven't you heard?*

How fast does news travel from the cells to the streets, from Fishkill to Queens? It don't. Nobody cares ... *Yeah yeah. Boo-fucking-hoo.*

Of all the shops in the Queens Center Mall, the Macy's department store has the most merchandise, the most men's and ladies' wear, the most jewelry, the most street-level exits, the most gifts-with-purchase, the most cashiers, the most security guards, the most women with the most makeup spritzing the most perfume onto the inside wrists of passersby, the most cameras, the most shoppers, the most crying babies, the most Isabels, the most cosmetic specialists, the most everything, and it is here, inside this mall-dominating superstore, that Tariq grabs off the shelf a pair of Rocawear jeans ($68) and carries them into one of Macy's many dressing rooms.

A young, pasty, pink-haired girl guards the entrance to the rooms. She folds one button-down shirt after another. A metal hoop pierces her lip, hangs from her mouth like the knocker to a door. The age and ethnicity work, Tariq thinks, to his advantage. He's not as sure about the pink hair or the lip ring. He worries she's the kind of young woman who lives to be unimpressed, who watches scary movies with her chin on her fist, who opens birthday presents with a snap of her gum and a roll of her eyes. That's not what he needs. His plans do not call for *under*whelmed reactions. Having finished with the shirts, the girl moves on to a series of khaki pants, folding them, matching hem to hem. This is her job. She folds the clothes people tried on and discarded, the clothes nobody wants. Then somebody else—not even her—takes them away and puts them back on the shelves. When Tariq approaches her folding table, the pink-haired girl hands him a card with a 1 on it (for the number of items he's trying on), and she points him toward a dressing room in back.

"Thank you," he says, because one should always be polite.

Inside the dressing room, he gets down on his knees facing east. Or at least facing what he hopes is east. For only the second time today, he prays. Allah has a plan and Tariq has a plan, and the trick for Tariq will be keeping those plans from a battle royal. Of course, as it is written, *the best of planners is Allah,* but what Tariq needs to do is sandwich his plan to His plan, so that they become plans *within* plans.

He tries on the Rocawear jeans, the bottoms of which cover the tops of his sneakers, just as they should. In an ideal world the jeans wouldn't fit so tightly, but in an ideal world the Fishkill Correctional Facility would've given him a belt. He peeps himself in the mirror, turning this way and that to admire his ass. Looking good, he thinks— and a good thing too, since that's a part of his physique Isabel's always appreciated.

He slips out of his dressing room and enters the one next door, which looks exactly the same: same mirror, same carpeted floor, same bench with wooden slats, same vanilla-colored walls. He looks up at the light fixture above his head. He wonders if it conceals a security camera, if there's a sun-deprived man in a tiny room jammed full of closed-circuit televisions, staring at the top of Tariq's head. Oh well. As the saying goes, *No reward without risk.*

He unwraps the Snickers, Kit Kats, Goodbars, Charleston Chews,

and Kisses. The chocolates—sun-battered, pocket-pressurized—have softened nicely. They smell sweet, strongly sweet, sickly sweet, and for a moment he feels dizzy. Because he can't help himself, he eats one of the Charleston Chews. The rest he smears onto the dressing room walls. Carefully, so as not to mess up his new Rocawear jeans, he shakes a soft, dripping Snickers bar over the bench, splattering its wooden slats. He streaks the mirror with Goodbars, leaves crescent moons of chocolate on the glass. While mashing Kit Kats into the carpet, he notices a feather in the corner of the dressing room. It lies on the floor, its two ends curled upward. Another crescent moon! Somebody must have been trying on a down jacket in here, and the feather popped out of a sleeve. Has it been here since winter? Tariq can't even imagine. He leaves it alone, rubs chocolate Kisses onto the dressing room's door-knob.

Not since Little League have his hands been so filthy. Not since he slid into second base on a mud-covered infield. He turns them over, these sticky, chocolate-smeared hands. The Hershey Kisses' wrappers—those thin, metallic sheets—have rubbed off on him, and now his palms and fingers sparkle with glitter. Time to clean up. He does the best he can with his hands by rubbing them against the rough insides of his Fishkill jeans. He sucks chocolate out from under his fingernails. The candy wrappers, the three dollars of pizza money, the parole paperwork—all of this he shoves into his new Rocawear pockets. With the old pants balled up in his fist and with his head held high, he leaves the dressing room and strides over to the pink-haired girl at the folding table.

"Who you been letting around back here?" he says.

"Excuse me?" She folds a plaid shirt against her chest. She keeps the collar tucked under her chin, making it easier for her to work, to finish this shirt and move on to the next one. "I'm sorry. I didn't hear you."

"I asked who you was letting around back here. Crackheads?"

"Excuse me?"

"Excuse *me,* but I'm just trying to figure out what's going on around here when you've got dressing rooms covered in shit."

She lifts her head to look at him, and the shirt falls out from under her chin.

"Feces," he says. "I'm talking about somebody's feces up on them

walls." He throws the Fishkill jeans down onto her table. He leans forward, closes the space between her body and his. "I'm walking around back there, I look into a dressing room and I see it's got shit all over it. Right back there. Hello? You hearing me? Somebody did diarrhea up on them walls. Understand? And I'm telling you so you can get somebody down here and clean it up." He pulls his head back, a natural-looking recoil. "Unless you already know about it," he says. "Unless you already *been* knowing about it and it's cool with you to work all day in a crack den, a place where the walls get themselves shat on."

"No," she says softly. She chews on her lower lip, her teeth clicking against the metal piercing. "I don't know nothing about this."

"Well that, at least, is some *good* news."

From the waist of her pants, the pink-haired girl unclips a walkie-talkie. But she doesn't speak into it. With the walkie-talkie in hand, she wiggles out from behind her folding table and heads toward the dressing rooms at the end of the hall. She walks slowly, toe to heel. The door to the dressing room yawns open, and when the pink-haired girl gets to it and peers inside she might scream or she might run away or she might drop her walkie-talkie or she might rip off her Macy's name tag and throw it to the floor. Tariq doesn't know. He doesn't know what she says or what she does because he's already gone.

In his stiff-legged designer jeans he walks through the menswear section and the handbag section and the unmentionables section. Two security guard fat-bodies in navy blue blazers run toward him. As they get closer, they split apart, passing him on either side. Walkie-talkies are pressed to their ears, giant grins plastered across their broad honest faces.

Who's chocolate going to fool? Nobody. Particularly if you get close enough to it. But who's going to get close enough? Who's going to bring their nose right up to those brown, nut-filled smears on the wall?

But that's not even the thing. Tariq knows that these kids—the pink-haired girl, the thick-necked security guards, every last one of the embittered employees of the Macy's department store, trapped in here on a beautiful late spring Saturday morning, working the complaints department, staring at doors, breaking penny rolls into cash registers, folding the pants and shirts nobody wants—they all absolutely *need* to believe in a dressing room smeared with shit. So that later tonight, after they've clocked out, these boys and girls can go

home and drink a beer out on the stoop or smoke a dub in Astoria Park or just drive in circles around Francis Lewis Boulevard, and they can turn to their friends and say, *Guess what, just guess, what the fuck happened at work today.*

A black guy with a Big Brown Bag heads toward the exit, and Tariq times it so that they push through the doors at the exact same moment. The alarm trips and beeps. Red lights flash. The black guy stops. Tariq doesn't.

Because the haircut has left him with brown and gray hairs all over his face, and because in the sweaty walk to and from the mall these hairs began to feel like so many swarming, mandible-snapping fire ants, and because he can't show up at home like that, looking like a face-scratching bum, Tariq goes down to Travers Park and sticks his head in the sprinklers. Around him, kids are leaping and prancing through the water, but Tariq stands still, cleans himself off for Isabel. His body temperature cools. Water sprays into his eyes, fills his open mouth.

Doused, he sits on a bench in the sun—what a beautiful day!—and yanks the Steri-Strips off of his face. Every time he tugs on one, his cheek tugs back. He rolls the strips into a gooey ball on his finger and flicks them away, as if he were airmailing boogers.

Two little white boys watch him. They don't run through the sprinklers or kick a ball or play saloogie with some smaller kid's cap. Faces blank, they just stand there, seemingly content to watch this bald man tear sutures from his face.

He pays them little attention. Instead, he stares across the park at a Guyanese man sitting on a bench just like his own. Actually he doesn't so much watch the man as he watches the dog at the man's feet, a beautiful brown pit bull, its face spotted with white freckles. The dog leans into its collar. Its tongue hangs out, as crooked as a question mark. When a ball rolls by, when a tennis ball or a softball or a soccer ball or a Sky Bounce blue handball gets away from some kid and rolls near the bench, the pit bull lunges after it. And because in parks balls don't roll by without kids close behind, chasing them with out-stretched fingers, every time the dog lunges at a soccer ball, the dog also, in effect, lunges at a child. The Guyanese guy pulls up hard on the

leash. The pit bull snaps its teeth. And the children run away laughing and squealing. No one, Tariq thinks, seems to appreciate the danger. Except for himself. And the dog of course, whose legs strain forward with coiled bloodlust.

Tariq stands up off the bench, and the ground tilts. He throws his hands out in front of him. Light dances in his eyes. He feels a spirit of dizziness poured into his ear. No wonder! It is close to one and his stomach is growling.

Get this: the booths inside Gianni's Pizzeria are no longer booths. They are tables. Covered in red and white checkered *cloths.* The floors have been mopped. A sign on the door says Now Serving Iced Coffee! And the old movie posters on the walls—Stallone's *Nighthawks;* Stallone's *Rocky IV;* Stallone's arm-wrestling picture, *Over the Top*—have all been replaced by tastefully framed photographs of Italian hills and wooden gondolas and old ladies smelling luminous eggplants. Tariq grips the back of a chair, as if to make sure it actually exists. He never expected time to wait for him, to freeze in place, but he also didn't expect the skyline to look so very different, or the currency, or the inside of Gianni's Pizzeria. He never expected so much to have fucking *changed.* At least the ancient *Street Fighter II* machine still stands in the corner, where a crowd of Asian kids have collected around it to watch one of their own, a spiky-haired Korean, battle a heavyset black kid. And, most comforting of all, Gianni himself is still here. He stands sentinel behind the counter, kneading dough with his fists.

Tariq orders two slices, extra hot. He hoped to elicit a *Hey, where you been?* Or a *Nice to have you back!* Tariq wonders if Gianni can't recognize him because of the gash in his cheek and with his head shaved bald—or maybe, he tells himself, expecting hospitality from Gianni is expecting a little too much. While the slices bubble in the oven, Gianni preps a tray, covering it with wax paper, placing three napkins off to the side. Another comfort, another thing that hasn't changed. There are no napkin dispensers on any of the tables. Gianni, cheap bastard that he is, doles out all napkins himself in an effort to prevent paper overdrafts. You get three—if you're lucky—and if you want more you gotta go ask Gianni and deal with his harrumphs.

Tariq gets his money ready as the slices come out of the oven. The

crust has charred and bubbled beautifully. Here's the plan: Tariq will fold the crust down the middle and flip the tip back into the slice, so as to trap the oil. He will blow on the cheese once, maybe twice. Then he will bite in, burning the roof of his mouth so badly that for the next twenty-four hours he will regretfully prod the skin with his tongue. Oh well. What are you gonna do? Gianni throws the slices onto the tray and Tariq's cheeks fill with water.

"Four dollars even," Gianni says.

"I don't want a Coke."

"No Coke. Four dollars for the slices. You *want* a Coke?"

"Four dollars?" Tariq says. "For *two* slices?"

"Four dollars for two slices," Gianni says.

"My entire life it's been one fifty a slice."

"What do you want me to tell you? You want one slice?"

"You don't understand. I've been eating pizza bagels. Catsup and rubber cheese on a toasted bagel. On an English *muffin*." Tariq looks into his face. "I don't want one slice. One slice doesn't *mean* anything to me. I want two slices, please. For three dollars, please."

"Two dollars a slice. Two slices, four dollars. You want a calculator?"

"No thank you. I want two slices for three dollars, please."

The redness starts in Gianni's neck and rises past his chin and mustache and doughy nose all the way up to the crown of his head. He brushes his flour-covered hands against his apron.

"Hey!" someone says. When Tariq turns around he sees that the voice belongs to the heavyset black kid, the one who was playing *Street Fighter II*. The kid comes over and *throws his arm over Tariq's shoulders.* He says, "Hey, Gianni, cut this guy a break. He's a friend of mine."

Gianni points a wooden roller at Tariq's chest. "He needs to learn some manners."

"Ha ha," the black kid says. He tightens his grip around Tariq's shoulder, hugs him even closer. "Like I say, you gotta cut him some slack. He just got out of prison."

If Tariq turned to look at the kid, their faces would be touching. The kid would be able to breathe *into Tariq's mouth.*

"Figures," Gianni says. He talks to the black kid but looks only at Tariq, their heads floating on opposite sides of the counter. "You need to remind your friend here he ain't in prison no more. He's gotta get

rid of his joint mentality. You know what I'm saying? Out here there's something called etiquette."

"Ha ha," the kid says. "I'll tell him. I'll let him know."

So that Tariq may be guided out of his own darkness, he reaches, arms straining, toward the Book:

Hasten for the pardon of your Lord, and for Paradise extending over the heavens and the earth, laid out for those who take heed for themselves and fear God, who expend both in joy and tribulation, who suppress their anger and pardon their fellowmen.

"Excuse me," Tariq says, shaking the kid's arm off his shoulders. He walks away, leaves the slices untouched on the counter.

Outside, the dizziness returns. It drips down his ear, into his throat. Miniature suns float across his retinas. They burst, these suns; they burst and blood surges behind his eyes. He'd sit down if he could, if the streets didn't stink of piss and rotten fruit, if the sidewalks weren't clogged with garbage. Everywhere he looks: garbage. Garbage in the gutters, on the street, spilling out of corner wastebaskets, stacked high on the curb in black-bagged pyramids. One of these overstuffed bags has a tear in its side. Flies buzz around the hole. Brown liquid oozes out onto the sidewalk. Tariq stares at this hole in this bag, and he half expects a baby to fall out, its belly clawed open by pink-eyed rats.

The black kid has followed Tariq outside and he wants to know if everything is okay, if there's anything he can do.

"Go away," Tariq says.

"Don't you remember me?"

"Go *away.*"

The kid takes a step backward and shows himself to Tariq. He spreads his hands out wide, causing the flesh under his arms to jiggle. He is man-sized—he is XXL-sized—and yet Tariq could drop him to the ground so easily. Knock that stupid Spider-Man hat off his head and push in his eye, smash his head against the sidewalk. He wears— loosely, and yet the outlines of his breasts remain visible—a stylish Rocawear T-shirt, which Tariq thinks would nicely complement his own Rocawear jeans. He wonders what Isabel might think of this shirt.

"You don't recognize me at all?" the kid says. He takes off his Spider-

Man hat and shows Tariq the top of his head, where the hair grows only in patches.

"Winston?" Tariq says. The kid smiles and quickly puts his hat back on. "You've gotten huge," Tariq tells him.

"I got fat. But you—you're ripped. I don't want to know what happened to the guy who opened up your face."

"Where'd you get that shirt?"

"You like it?" He pulls down on the hem, so that they can both get a better look at it. The shirt tightens, making Winston's breasts even more visible. "Alfredo bought it for me a while ago," he says. "Hey, have you seen Alfredo yet? Have you even been *home* yet?"

"Give me the shirt."

"It's nice, right?"

"Give it to me."

"What?" he says. He tries to smile. Half his face looks dry, but the other half sweats. Big beady drops roll down his cheek. He dips his head to his shoulder, wipes his face dry with the sleeve of his shirt. When he looks back up at Tariq, Winston's smile widens and brightens into the genuine thing. "You got me. For a hot second, you got me good. *Give me the shirt,* he says. Ha ha. You're hilario, Jose. Sorry, sorry. Tariq. You're hilario, *Tariq.*" Still smiling, Winston shakes his head and looks around at no one in particular, like a sitcom straight man gesturing to the TV audience, as if to say *Get a load of this guy.* His eyes suddenly widen. "Holy shitballs," he says, pointing behind Tariq. "Would you look at that!"

Tariq suspects a lame schoolyard trick. Asked to give up his shirt, Winston points at the unseen world and says *Look at that!* and when Tariq does, Winston will take off running. But that's not what happens at all. Winston doesn't take off running. He actually comes closer, throws his arm once again over Tariq's bulked-up shoulders. He turns Tariq around and points across the street where a white Camaro plays HOT 97 out of its open windows, and where two halter-topped Isabels dance on the sidewalk, melting the ice in Tariq's throat, and where, behind a furniture store's plate-glass window, a sofa stares out at the street with an empty-cushioned, heartbreaking loneliness, and where the Mister Softee ice cream truck drives by and momentarily blots out Tariq's view, and where a black kid pushes a bicycle with two deflated tires, and where a young Isabel bites into a Jamaican beef patty, the

steam softening her face, and where—if Tariq follows Winston's extended index finger precisely—the Guyanese man from the park is walking down the block, his beautiful brown pit bull at his side.

"That's your dog," Winston says. Reeking of pot smoke, he squeezes Tariq tightly. "You talked to Alfredo yet? We been trying to find a dog for you all week. Like a present kind of? For the dogfight tonight? The welcome back party? You talk to Alfredo yet or what? I'm telling you, we been looking for a dog *just like* that one. And now, *poof*. Yabba-dabba-doo, man. You know what I'm saying? A pit bull. Right across the street."

The Guyanese guy holds his dog on a short leash. The pit bull doesn't trot or scamper beside him. The dog walks. He walks with his head held high, just as a man would walk. Between his legs swing an impressive pair of bright-red balls.

"It's like a sign from God," Winston whispers. He takes a plastic bag of pills out of his pocket. He reaches into the bag—without even looking at what he's grabbing—and pulls out a small white pill, which he drops onto the tip of his tongue. "You want one?" he asks, but before Tariq can say no, Winston has already sealed the bag and put it back in his pocket. "I'm quitting drugs," he says. "Starting tomorrow." He closes his eyes, pinches the bridge of his nose. "Here I am, standing right here with you for crying out loud, and a pit bull, *your* pit bull, walks across the street. Do you know me and Alfredo been looking for a dog like that all week? We found a nice one last night, a Doberman, but it was behind a fence and we couldn't get at it. All week. No luck. And now here I am with you, twelve hours from the dogfight, and . . ." He shakes his head. "It's like the gods be smiling. It's like the universe is on our side. You know what I mean?"

Tariq knows exactly what he means. Across the street, the dog and the man are walking away, nearing the intersection. They pause for the light, let the cars drive by, and then they move on, walking quickly down Northern Boulevard. From a distance of one full outer-borough block, Winston and Tariq follow.

"Stare at his shoes," Tariq says.

"Stare at his shoes," Winston repeats.

"You don't want to look at the back of his head. People can feel that

kind of thing. It tingles the scalp, don't ask me how. But if this guy feels eyes on the back of his head, then he's gonna turn around, and if he turns around—"

"Then we're sunk," Winston says. They walk in step, not faster or slower than the man and dog a block ahead of them. "So what we want to do," Winston says, "is stare at the shoes. Got it."

"Ain't no one ever felt eyes on the back of their shoes."

"And this guy ain't going nowhere without taking his feet with him."

"Exactly!" Tariq says, smiling. He feels good. He feels better than he has all day. "It's just a little trick, sure. But I'm telling you, Winston— it's little tricks that keep you ahead of the game."

"You pick it up in prison?" Winston asks.

Tariq shakes his head. He never had to follow anybody in prison because he already knew where everyone was going: the same place he was. No, shadowing people without getting caught was something he learned out here, in Queens, long before he ever got incarcerated. On Friday nights he'd meet up with Gio and Conrad—currently serving out their prison sentences at Otisville and Altona, respectively— and the three of them would follow the construction workers who stumbled off the 7 train, their jeans splattered with paint, their pockets jammed with payday cash, their blood Budweiser-thinned. *Stare at the shoes,* he'd tell Gio and Conrad. Amazing, ain't it? Years later, and he's saying the same shit.

The man and his dog turn the corner, disappear from sight for the very first time. Winston starts to hurry after them, but Tariq grabs at his shirt. He counsels patience. He explains that the guy might've stopped right around the corner, to chat with a neighbor or to scoop poop off the curb, and if Tariq and Winston were rushing they'd bump right into the guy, or they'd have to walk past him, lose their advantage, become the pursued rather than the pursuers.

"*Relax,*" Tariq says. He gestures to the Isabels passing them on their left and right. He points to the base of a maple tree, where pigeons peck at dried crusts of bread. "Take it easy, brother. Enjoy all this scenery."

When they eventually do turn the corner, they see the man and the dog halfway down the block. The guy has slackened his grip on the leash. In his free hand, he jangles a set of house keys. The dog makes a

sharp left toward a stand-alone, one-family house, a Queens residential specialty, and the man follows. They go through a fence—it is waist-high, with a latch door—and they head, the man and the dog, toward the backyard.

Winston and Tariq don't stop. They pass the house without looking at it. They go all the way around the block, taking their time, practicing their lines. When they get back to the house, they make the same sharp left the dog made. Tariq lifts the latch on the fence door as if he's been lifting it every day of his life. And what if the man hasn't gone inside the house yet? What if he's still in the backyard, sunning himself on a lounge chair, zinc oxide smeared on his nose? We're here for the party, they'll say. Told to come straight out back. You know. For the barbecue, the cookout for the Mets-Yankees game. Weiners and hamburgers? This is Rosario's, right? Tell me we've got the right house. This is Eighty-third Street, right?

Tariq holds the latch door open for Winston, who leads the way into the yard. Surprisingly calm, Winston walks right in without any apparent fear, and Tariq is impressed. More than impressed: Tariq is *proud*. He expected the kid to be shitting in his socks by now, but then—with unexpected and considerable disappointment—Tariq remembers that Winston's on drugs. Anti-anxieties, probably. Xanax, or something like it. See, that's the problem with these kids. Anxiety can be useful. Slowing down can be effective. Pay attention. Take your time.

The yard is a couple hundred square feet, small for a backyard, but a good deal bigger than a prison cell. The grass—like the hair on Winston's head—grows only in patches. Soil is exposed. Chipped clay pots line the perimeter of the yard. Nothing grows out of the pots except for the white plastic tags that indicate what *should* be growing out of them. Geraniums. Marigolds. Petunias. Rosemary. There's no lounge chair, no squeezed-out bottle of sunscreen. In one corner slumps a barbecue grill, covered in a tarp. In another corner a kiddie pool, which doesn't seem to be used for recreational purposes. Kids don't jump in the water or splash one another's faces. Instead, the pool seems to be for drinking. It serves as a big dish of water for the yard's only tenant, the pit bull. A metal chain connects the dog's collar to a steel rod buried deep in the ground, and this chain is just long enough to reach the lip of the pool. But the dog isn't drinking

any water. He's sitting in the patchy grass, watching Tariq and Winston with his jaws clamped shut and with his ears pinned to the top of his head.

Stone steps lead from the backyard into the house, where a door has been propped open to let in some air. TV noises spill out of the house. Tariq can hear it as easily as if he were in the living room with the Guyanese guy, sitting on his couch, their feet stretched out on the coffee table. It's the Mets-Yankees pregame show, and the announcers debate only one thing: whether or not Clemens will get beaned when he comes up to bat.

Next door, in the neighbor's yard, four tires stand in a rubber column, stacked one on top of the other. A sign hangs on the fence that separates that yard from this yard. The sign reads Parking for Millionaires Only.

The dog lifts his head to look over at Winston, who's got his hand balled into a fist, his arm reared back, one eye closed to the sun. Before he can complete the windup, Tariq grabs his arm. He pries open Winston's fingers and finds in his palm a tiny blue pill.

"What's this?"

"Sleeping pill," Winston whispers, as if afraid the man in the house—or maybe even the dog—will hear him.

"You're going to give the dog a sleeping pill?"

"No, I'm going to *throw* the dog a sleeping pill. I wouldn't *give* that dog the fucking time. I throw the pill, he licks it up. If he don't, we go cop some burgers and put the pill—"

"And then the dog falls asleep?" Tariq says, with his hand still gripped tight around Winston's wrist. "Yeah? Have I got that right? The dog licks up the pill and then passes out?"

"Correct," Winston whispers.

"Then what? We wait for it to fall asleep? To hit the hay? Then what? You gonna *carry* the dog back to my house? And after you've fed this sixty-pound dog a sleeping pill designed for adult human beings, who's gonna bring it back to life? Once it falls asleep, how's it ever going to wake up?"

"So don't throw the pill?" he says. Tariq stares at Winston, at his ashy skin, at the flecks of white spittle caught at the corners of his lips. "Tariq," Winston says. "You're hurting my wrist."

The Book says:

O you who believe, do not enter other houses except yours without first taking permission and saluting the inmates. This is better for you.

Which seems fairly clear-cut, sure. But Tariq knows a backyard ain't a house. A backyard is a backyard. Religious loophole? No way, this is New York State law. A backyard equals trespassing; a house equals burglary. This is a significant distinction that operates on both sides of the law: a search warrant that provides access to a residence does not necessarily provide access to the property around that residence, e.g. a garage, an alleyway, a run-down backyard.

Tariq walks toward the dog. He keeps his hand out in front of him, palm up, fingers spread apart. Under his feet, pavement gives way to patches of grass and dry soil. The dog sits up off the ground and leans forward on his two front legs. Both ears stand straight up in the air. Because the leash is tethered to the metal pole in the ground, there is a section of this yard in which the dog cannot reach Tariq. Keeping his back straight, Tariq walks out of that section. The dog watches him approach. Inside the house, the TV turns off, and the voices of the baseball announcers are replaced by the jingle of a Mister Softee truck a few blocks away. The dog's back legs flex. He exposes the small black pupils of his eyes. He smells greasy, which reminds Tariq of his father's hair gel, and the way it always stains both sides of the pillowcases. Tariq listens for footsteps padding toward the back door. He bends forward at the waist and the dog's mouth swings open. A yellowish string of saliva connects a top fang to a sharp lower fang. The dog growls, deep and low in his throat. Eyes closed, Tariq slides his hand into the dog's mouth. It feels dark and warm and moist. Teeth pinch his knuckles. A rough tongue slides across the meat of his palm. The dog jerks his head back and, eyes straining, greedily licks the tips of Tariq's fingers. Laps at his wrist. Tariq puts his other hand in the dog's mouth. If any chocolate remained in the spaces between his fingers, it's gone. The dog gnaws on the rubber wristband of the Casio watch. Good boy, good boy. He shoves his head under Tariq's hand, allows himself to be scratched behind the ears.

The hook connecting the leash to the metal pole unlatches easily. When Tariq pulls on the leash, the metal spikes on the pinch collar insinuate themselves into the dog's neck. So Tariq doesn't pull on the leash.

Winston is hugging himself. Watching Tariq and the pit bull approach, he massages his arms, squeezes himself so tightly that blood vessels rise in his knuckles. Tariq takes a quick peek back at the house. No one appears in the door. No one comes charging down the steps. When he turns back around, the dog—as if waiting for Tariq's attention—lunges at Winston. The leash hums in Tariq's hand. Winston backs into a corner, and the dog follows, pulling Tariq with him. Eyes bulging, ears pitched forward, he snaps at Winston's waist.

"Get it away from me," Winston hisses. He goes up on his tiptoes. His eyes are white and moist.

It occurs to Tariq that he needs to give this dog a name.

In the lobby of the Batistas' apartment building a sign on the elevator door says Out of Order—Fuera de Servicio. Underneath that, someone has written in pencil *Then fucking fix it!* Winston optimistically pushes the elevator button anyway. When it doesn't work, he curses under his breath, betrayed. He clearly doesn't want to be here, but Tariq made him come. He likes the idea of Winston entering the apartment before him, announcing his arrival.

They take the stairs, with Winston, like a good herald, going up first. Tariq tries to think of a time when he had the privilege of following Isabel up a flight of stairs, but he comes up with nothing, not one single time. Her ass would've been eye level, swinging from right to left, stretching the cloth of some tight-fitting jeans. One more thing he missed out on. Following Winston, however, offers its own pleasures. Nonsexual pleasures of course. With his shoulders as tense and as high as his ears, Winston takes the steps two at a time until Tariq snaps at him to slow down. The pit bull lurks unseen behind him. The dog nips at air, inches from Winston's meaty thighs. Winston's shoulders rise even higher. But he doesn't say anything, doesn't complain. He knows—how could he not?—that at any time Tariq can let go of the leash.

8

Batista Bros., Inc.

No, no, no, no, no," Lizette says. "Please. It's fine. I don't need any help."

Cookware crowds her stovetop: a pot of her famous habichuelas guisadas simmers in the back; a frying pan waits for tostones, a slab of butter islanded in its cast-iron center; and the signature dish—spicy chicken and rice—cooks in one large pot, a pot Lizette mysteriously found under the sink, when she damn well knows she left it in the cupboard. Evil spirits are rearranging her kitchen, up to no good, testing her sanity.

Isabel lifts the lid off the chicken and rice. As an added layer of protection, heavy-duty aluminum foil covers the pot. Isabel goes to work on unwrapping it. When she peels back a corner of the foil, she allows heat to escape from the pot. Puffs of steam swirl around the bulb on the ceiling. "If you want," she says, "I can stir the rice."

"No, no, no, no," Lizette says. She snatches the spoon out of Isabel's hand. "You stir the rice too much and it goes all amogollao. Yeah? It gets all *sticky.*"

"I like sticky rice," Isabel says. Actually she doesn't like sticky rice, but she's willing to start. She's willing to rejigger all her grain-related preferences, just to be contrarian. "I think it tastes better that way."

"No you don't," Lizette says. "Nobody likes sticky rice. The Chinese maybe. But even them, I'm not so sure."

She rewraps the foil around the lid, traps the steam in the pot so the rice grains will pop evenly. Normally Lizette wouldn't bother with the foil—Trade Fair is selling it for $2.99 *apiece*—but the arroz has gotta slide right off the fork tines. The chicken, the tostones, the red bean stew, the sofrito, the meal, the seating, the day—it all has to be perfect. Earlier this morning, she ran down to the Indian girls on Thirty-seventh Avenue and got her eyebrows threaded. Then she jaywalked across the street to the Korean nail salon for a ten-dollar pedicure. While they worked on her feet, she read the *Post,* the ink coming off on her fingers. Rescue workers finally stopped searching for bodies at Ground Zero. Iraq might have links to the 9/11 attacks. Pakistan and India are staring at each other over the tips of nuclear warheads, a Utah teenager got herself kidnapped, some rapper named Nas called Jay-Z "Gay-Z." An editorial made the argument that because of 9/11, intracity race relations are better than ever. *Okay,* Lizette thought. She read all the articles on the Catholic Church scandal, saw something about repressed memories, and wondered if her altar-boy sons ever got . . . oh Lord, don't even go there. In culture: MOMA's Queens opening was just two weeks away, and modern art lovers are griping about the temporary outer-borough location—even Picasso, it seems, can't drag the snooty into Queens. In sports: the Mets lost to the Yankees (4–2), but they'll go at it again today, game two of their three-game series. And in the Irrelevancy Department: the stock market took a hit. Lizette read these articles and others—or if she didn't read a particular article, she at least scanned the punny headline—but nowhere in the paper's hundred-plus pages did she see anything about the day's real story. Not that she expected tabloid coverage, of course. But the omission cast a pall over the paper's other, supposedly more important news items. Who cares about Enron? Who cares about the possible smoking ban? The *Post*—and every other paper in this city—failed to report what was in Lizette's personal edition the extra-extra, read-all-about-it, front-page splash: the return of her son, her eldest baby boy, Jose Batista Jr.

If he ever got here. The clock on the kitchen wall reads a couple of minutes past one. Lizette started cooking early because Junior's letter

said he'd be released in the morning. Plus, she's got to go to work soon. She works full-time—thank you very much—at an eyeglass shop, and while Dr. Remmelts, the optometrist, gave her the morning off, he needs her to come in for the afternoon. His wife is nine months pregnant or some such thing, and because apparently for pregnant people the whole world and everyone in it has to come to a goddamn screeching halt . . . forgive her! Forgive her the blasphemy! *The Father, the Son, and the Holy Spirit,* Lizette mutters under her breath. She's stressed, that's all. He should've been here hours ago, and now, who knows? Forget the expense, forget the inconvenience—Lizette should've taken a train up to Fishkill and picked him up. And now, because she didn't, Junior has probably kicked a hack guard in the ear and gotten himself tossed right back behind bars. Lizette knows the rate of recidivism. She reads the paper. She knows the ex in ex-con is only temporary, Indian-given; she knows the prisons have cells on the inside and revolving doors on the outside. The only thing that will keep her baby out of that spinning vortex is good old-fashioned Family Values: unified parents, Junior's favorite foods, a clean kitchen, fresh towels, cloth napkins that smell like fabric softener. Given its importance, she wishes this first meal was a Batistas-only affair. Not to be mean or anything, but Lizette wishes Isabel would suck it up and move back in with her mother. For a little while. At least till the baby is born. Is that so horrible? Does that make her a bad person? Maybe, but Lizette is more concerned with being a good mother. With Junior's personality, with the state of incarceration, well, it's going to be hard enough keeping this family together, repairing the boys' relationship, without Isabel coming in and out of the shower, walking all pregnant through the hallways.

Lizette turns down the heat on the habichuelas guisadas. In five minutes—oh why did she start cooking so early?—the chicken will be done. Lizette will take it off the burner, of course, but if she lets it sit too long the rice will get mushy, or worse: cold.

"You need the sofrito?" Isabel asks. The girl opens the freezer and pulls out an ice cube tray. Lizette makes all the sofrito herself in a food processor—nothing comes out of a jar in this kitchen—and she keeps the green peppery sauce in ice cube trays. Sure it makes the freezer stink of onion and garlic, but what are you gonna do? Lizette needs easy access to her sofrito. She doesn't cook anything without it.

Isabel turns the ice cube tray over onto the counter, so that its blocky plastic asses stick straight up in the air. She's about to bang out all the little green cubes when Lizette seizes her by the wrist.

"Someone cleans these counters, you know." Lizette turns the tray over, right side up. "Just flex it, see? Just a little pressure and the cubes slide right out. No mess, see?"

"How many cubes you want?"

"Oh, I already did the sofrito, sweetie. I used two cubes to sauté the jamón. Twenty minutes ago." Lizette inhales deeply. "You smell it?"

Because Isabel—of course—left the freezer door open, the cranky, ill-tempered refrigerator begins to hum, announcing its neglect.

"Put this away," Lizette says as she hands her the ice cube tray. "You know, dear, this kitchen's awfully small for two people."

Isabel pulls her shirt down over her belly. The poor thing's got no maternity clothes. She wears one of Dito's old Our Lady of Fatima T-shirts, and the bottom keeps riding up on her stomach, exposing a small sliver of skin. A pair of dirt-stained sweatpants have been cinched tightly around her waist. She wears no makeup or jewelry. Her hair is pulled back into a severe, face-tightening ponytail.

"You don't like what I'm wearing?" Isabel says.

Lizette smiles, upset that her thoughts have been so easily penetrated. "You look fine," she says brightly.

"I woulda wore my Versace," Isabel says, "but it's still at the cleaners."

"I think you look *perfectly fine.*"

Alfredo comes into the kitchen from the living room, where he'd been watching the Mets-Yankees pregame show with his father. Alfredo didn't even know he was walking toward the kitchen until he got here. His legs and nose had apparently brokered some kind of side deal, arranged all by themselves to carry the rest of his body into Mama's kitchen, where red beans stew in a thick, fragrant paste of olive oil, garlic, and cilantro, where chicken falls off the bone. And now that Alfredo's here, he sees he's got some work to do.

The two women lean slightly forward at the waist, moving toward each other by millimeters, like a pair of tectonic plates. *Got here just in time,* Alfredo thinks. In his mother's smile and in his girlfriend's clenching hands, Alfredo reads—quickly, accurately—that Isabel's trying to help and Mama's having none of it. So Alfredo will give Isabel something to do. So that she feels useful, wanted. So that she may keep

herself momentarily busy. So that her hands will unclench, he will ask her to do something for *him*. Give to her what his mother has denied.

"Hey, baby? Can you pour me a glass of water?"

"Your legs broken?" Isabel says.

"I'm just trying to—"

"You want water," Lizette says, "get it yourself."

"Wow," Alfredo says. "Forget it. I'm not even thirsty."

Isabel tilts her head, thinking that if she changes her angle on Alfredo, he might change as well. She could murder him. In the movie version of her life, Isabel's not in this kitchen. She's on a Greyhound bus, a balled-up sweatshirt between her head and the window. *Come on*, Christian Louis says. *Has it come to this? That even in your fantasies, you can't afford a pillow? Fuck that noise!* In the movie version of her life—and we're talking Hollywood now, no Sundance independent camcorder bullshit—in the big budget, wide release movie version of Isabel's life she's not in this garlic-reeked kitchen because she's on an airplane to Paris, up in first class, sipping on a fountain Coke, and while Alfredo is with her—he's gotta be—he's all the way back in coach, in a middle seat, between the two fattest air travelers of all time. These wide-bottomed men eat blue cheese sandwiches and sneeze into their armpits.

If only. She and Alfredo had their chance to leave last night. But Alfredo rolled over on the sofa bed and explained that he could leave Jackson Heights like Captain Britain can leave the UK. Which is to say not at all. Alfredo grew up here, he's never left here, his family's here, his friends are here, his business is here, he's written his name in the wet cement of these sidewalks. Isabel asked who the fuck Captain Britain's supposed to be. *A comic book character*, Alfredo said, and Isabel stopped listening.

"You guys want to do something useful?" Lizette says.

"Not really," Alfredo says.

"Move the table—pick it up so you don't leave streaks on the floor—and place it, gently, in the middle of the kitchen."

That's not right, Alfredo thinks. The table—flimsy, rectangle shaped, propped up on four thin metal legs—hugs the kitchen wall. That's where it *lives*. When the family eats dinner together—which is every night, work schedules permitting—they sit on only three sides of the table, Lizette and Jose Sr. on opposite ends, Alfredo and Isabel

next to each other. To move the table now is to change everything, is to block Jose's access to the bathroom and bedrooms. But Isabel has already picked up her end, and Alfredo can't have his seven months pregnant girlfriend schlepping furniture all by herself. Together, they wobble the table into the middle of the kitchen. Open on all four sides now, the table stands exposed. It seems to float. An island in the sky. Alfredo feels like he's been dropped into some other family's kitchen. Near the wall, on the linoleum floor, four clean little squares—where the table's legs used to stand—stare up at him. "Is this permanent?" he asks.

Lizette reaches into the hallway closet for the second time today. Earlier this morning she went in here to get a bath mat, to replace the one that had mysteriously gone missing. ("What bath mat?" Isabel had said under questioning.) This time, Lizette pulls out a gray metal folding chair.

Jose Sr. wheels himself into the kitchen. He'd come in here to tell Alfredo the game's about to start, but when he sees the obstruction in the middle of the kitchen he stops. "Whoa," he says. He runs his hand along one end of this new, four-sided kitchen table. "What's going on? Is this permanent?"

Lizette sets the table, muttering to herself. She puts out the good forks, knives, and plates. Instead of the usual paper towels, she gets her nice cloth napkins, recently laundered.

"We're eating dinner *now*?" Jose says. "It's one o'clock in the afternoon. The game's starting."

"The chicken's almost done," Lizette says. "When the chicken's done, we eat."

"But Junior—"

"Tariq," Alfredo corrects.

"He's not even here yet," Jose tells Lizette.

"Then we eat without him," she says, and she has to keep her hands from flying to her hair. "Does anyone know where he is? Because I haven't the faintest. And the tostones. I haven't even *started* the tostones."

Isabel grins. "I can fry them."

"You know," Lizette says. Her hands fold in prayer under her chin. "This is an awfully small kitchen."

The doorbell rings. Jose spins his chair around, and Lizette shoots

past him into the living room. Almost immediately, however, she comes back and does something Alfredo hasn't seen her do in a long time, months maybe, possibly even years: she gets behind her husband's wheelchair and pushes it. Jose rolls, she steers, and the two of them move, together, toward the living room. The doorbell rings again.

Isabel pulls her shirt down over her belly.

"You ready?" Alfredo says.

"It's not too late."

"Oh no?" He moves closer, gives her a bright, brilliant smile. "Have I got anything stuck between my teeth?"

"Is my breath bad enough?" she asks. Alfredo sticks the tip of his nose into her mouth. He sniffs her lips, and then, a rabbit in a lettuce patch, he canvasses her entire face, trying to get her to laugh, sniff-sniff-sniffing her cheeks, her forehead, her eyeballs. "Maybe I should suck on one of your mother's sofrito cubes," Isabel says. "Get my breath ass flavored."

"It's not your fault you're beautiful."

"There's always the fire escape in your father's room."

Alfredo smiles again, a less brilliant smile, a smile without teeth. He grabs Isabel's hand, which feels surprisingly warm. Heat flows out of her body and into his. He leans toward the living room, dragging Isabel with him, and he wants to say something cool and reassuring, something confidence inspiring, but he doesn't say anything. He gets distracted. His mother is screaming.

"Don't worry!" Tariq says. A dog—a pit bull!—lunges at Alfredo's mother. Elbows out, Jose Sr. wheels away and bangs into the coffee table, upsetting a small vase of lilies. Stalks spill onto the floor. Again the pit bull lunges, and Tariq yanks on the leash. The dog's front legs come up off the carpet. They flail at nothing, these legs, as if the dog were storming up a flight of invisible stairs. Lizette doesn't step away because, it seems, it hasn't yet occurred to her that she should. Her hands stick straight up in the air, her fingers splayed, her face bemused—a law-abiding citizen who finds herself suddenly, inexplicably, under arrest. Isabel holds her belly. In the corner of the living room, behind the front door, Winston—*Winston?*—looks down at the

133

ground. He is hugging himself. Vase water drips onto the carpet. The dog growls at Lizette.

"Put your hands down," Tariq tells his mother. "You're making him nervous."

Alfredo grabs a plush parrot off an end table and tosses it underhand—Winston style—into the rumpus. Like an overeager infielder, the dog tries to snatch it out of the air, but he closes his jaws too soon and misses. The parrot bounces off his freckled snout and skips across the floor. The dog chases after it, traps the bird's beaked face under his paw. He dips his head over the parrot's body, as if in mourning, and tears open its stomach. White bits of stuffing explode into the air.

"You're going to teach him bad habits," Tariq tells Alfredo. The dog chews on the parrot, and when Tariq tries to pull it away, a wing comes off in his hand.

"My God," Lizette says. Her face is red, her forehead shines. She looks up, past the parrots on wires, at her cracked ceiling, where a tea-colored bubble of plaster sags down.

Tariq gets down on the ground and wrestles the parrot away from the pit bull. The dog's wet nose is matted with cottony stuffing. He licks Tariq's face. Tariq pulls him close, blows air into his eyes, scratches him behind the ears. With the dog squirming, playfully nipping at earlobes, Tariq ties his leash to a leg of the sofa. They both seem to be laughing, sharing some private joke.

"Hi, Winston," Alfredo says.

"Hello."

"I was worried you might be dead."

"No," Winston says, sounding almost sorry to disappoint. "Hey—but my phone's dead." He reaches for the cell in his pocket—as if to prove his claim, as if he were presenting evidence before a judge—but Alfredo waves him off. No time for nonsense. The living room pulsates with noise, and Alfredo strains to hear everything at once: the dog growling, the Mets game blaring, Jose telling Tariq that their mama doesn't care for dogs in the house, and Isabel—where's Isabel?—hovering in the kitchen doorway, silent, speaking to no one.

Lizette seizes Tariq's chin. Her fingers flexed like a claw, she leads him away from both Jose and the dog. "Baby, what happened to your face?" she asks, sounding less concerned than annoyed, as if her son's face were not his own but rather something she let him borrow,

and now, years later—would you look at this?—he returns it with a deep scratch right down the middle. "That dog mangle your face, baby?"

Tariq puts his arms around her. For a moment her head pulls away from the hug—fighting, straining to get a good look at her baby's cheek—but eventually she slackens. She has waited too long for this. She rests her head against his chest.

Over his mother's shoulder, Tariq watches Isabel, who continues to hang suspended in the doorway, halfway between the kitchen and the living room. With his eyes on her she feels conscious of her feet, her hands, her awkward elbows. She presses her knees together. She wishes she didn't *have* knees. She wishes she'd worn a long-sleeved shirt. She wishes the hair on her arms were darker, and more plentiful. She wishes . . . *shhhhh*. Curled up in Isabel's ear, Christian Louis—God bless him—hums a cradlesong. The Internet taught her the lullaby, and she passed it on. Between stanzas, he says, *At least, Mama, your feet are covered.* Earlier this morning, Isabel put on socks with holes in them and then immediately changed into new ones, thinking ahead, knowing that in this moment, this first encounter, she would not want a toe exposed.

With a final squeeze, Tariq releases his mother and moves toward Isabel. He comes at her as a gorilla might, sideways, in profile, showing her only one half—the clean half—of his face.

Alfredo steps in front of him. He extends his hand, and Tariq slaps it away. Hard. He is smiling. He throws his arms around Alfredo's body and holds him close—no handshakes here, no stiff, one-armed back-slapping. Not knowing how to react, Alfredo allows himself to be hugged, his arms frozen at his sides. Tariq smells like Papi, like sweat and Barbasol and peanuts and tattered old newspapers. In Alfredo's ear, he makes low grunts of pleasure. *Been a long time,* he murmurs. Is that right? *Been a long time? Been too long?* Something like that. If Alfredo had gotten more sleep last night, then he might have heard what his brother said, and he might have zinged back with an appro-priate reply. Tariq pulls him closer, tightens his grip, and when Alfredo feels the acceleration of his brother's heartbeat, it occurs to him that if Tariq's eyes are open, then he's staring directly at Isabel.

"All right," Alfredo says, squirming to free himself. "Come on."

Tariq releases Alfredo and swims past him toward Isabel. She leans into the doorway and tries to look brave. Both Alfredo and his mother

are rushing over. They flank Tariq as he stands in front of Isabel, his body listing to one side, his thumbs hooked through his belt loops in what seems to be a forced attempt to look casual. He stares down at her and she gamely stares back for as long as she can, but eventually her back stiffens and her eyes drop to the floor. He wets his lips before speaking.

"You're further along than I thought you'd be."

"Oh yeah?"

"*Yeah*," he says, using her word, spitting it back at her. He reaches out and puts his hands on her stomach.

Instinctively, Alfredo slaps them away. He feels the sting on his fingertips. In the far corner of the living room, the dog starts barking. Tariq turns to look at his brother.

"Listen," Alfredo says. He's prepared no speech, no explanation. "Listen to me."

"I'm listening," Tariq says.

"Jose?" Lizette says. She pulls on the sleeve of his shirt. "Where'd this dog come from? What're we going to do about this *dog*?"

He ignores her. Still looking at Alfredo, he reaches out, places his hands back on Isabel's stomach. "My nephew's in here," he says. "Or is it my niece? Let me tell you something. It *feels* like a boy, the way it's kicking the shit out of my hands."

"It's a boy," Alfredo says.

"Good work," he says. "And what's this boy's name?"

Alfredo shakes his head. He refuses to say the name out loud, afraid Tariq might somehow pollute it. "We don't know."

"You don't know?" Tariq says. "You gotta have a list of possibles at least. How about Alfredo Junior?"

"We'll consider it," Isabel says. She takes his hands and forces them down to his sides. She backs away into the kitchen, and as she goes she pulls her shirt over her stomach. Tariq is beaming, almost panting. He takes a step forward to follow her, and Alfredo, who has to say something, says, "What happened to your face?"

Tariq turns to him. Alfredo has a hard time maintaining eye contact and so he stares at the knot of Tariq's Adam's apple, at the little hairs encircling the collar of his shirt. Tariq says, "What do you *think* happened to my face?"

"I don't know," Alfredo says. "You cut yourself shaving?"

"Bingo," Tariq says. "You got it. On the very first try. I cut myself shaving."

Lizette goes up on her tiptoes and kisses Tariq's shoulder. "Are you hungry, baby? I made my rice."

"What do I win?" Alfredo says. "For guessing—on my very first try—about your mangled, fucked-up face?"

"*Alfredo*," Lizette hisses.

"What do you want?" Tariq says. He tilts his chin toward the pit bull. "You want the dog? You want him, he's yours. My gift to you."

Jose Sr. says, "Your mother doesn't want dogs in the house."

"Oh would you lay off that already!" Lizette says.

Alfredo steals a peek at his brother's pit bull. Leashed to the sofa, the dog lies down with his stomach flat on the carpet. Alfredo is afraid of many things. He's afraid of eating chocolate because he's afraid of getting zits. He's afraid of moving away from home. Every day, as he slips on his Timberlands, he's afraid a mouse will be camped out at the bottom of one of his boots. He's afraid of starting the crossword in the *Daily News* because he's afraid he won't be able to finish it. He's afraid of not knowing. He doesn't know what his best friend is doing here with his ex-con brother and a pit bull terrier, and he is afraid of asking for details and advertising his ignorance. He's afraid he enables Winston's drug addiction. He's afraid of awkward silences and poisonous snakes and another terrorist attack in New York—but who isn't afraid of those things? He's afraid of his brother. He's afraid of cars. He's afraid of farms, in particular being trapped inside a silo with grain pouring down his throat—although he's never actually seen a silo in person, or even been to a farm. Isabel takes three to four shits a day, and Alfredo contributes two dumps himself, and in all DNA likelihood Christian Louis will inherit this defecatory gene, and Alfredo worries he won't be able to afford enough disposable diapers. He's afraid he'll be a cold, inattentive father, although Isabel assures him that the very fear guarantees he won't be. He's afraid he works too hard for too little gain. He's afraid of being a nine-to-five schlub, a regular guy with modest dreams. He's afraid of miscarriages. He won't even say the word out loud. When separated from Isabel, he's afraid of the sobbing sirens of ambulances. He's afraid his father's body—like the bodies of so many paraplegics—will confuse below-the-waist immobility for end-of-the-line mortality and just give out. When Alfredo

thinks of the way he kicked Vladimir in the neck, Alfredo is afraid of himself. He's afraid Vladimir—or someone Vladimir knows—killed Curtis Hughes. He's afraid the bone-knuckled Alphabet Brothers—Alex and Bam-Bam—will blame him. He's afraid of the head-tilted look Isabel gives him when he's disappointed her. He might be afraid of the dark; it's hard to tell around here, in a city where lights are constantly burning. He's afraid that Isabel—and he knows he's a fucking idiot for even thinking this—he's afraid that Isabel will leave him for Tariq. He's afraid of cats. Well, not all cats. Just one in particular, a soot-backed calico who stalks the alleyways at night, wherever Alfredo and Winston are getting stoned. Alfredo worries—in his paranoid, THC-addled state—that this cat might actually be Lizette, metamorphosed via some Santeria witchcraft for the purposes of keeping an emerald eye on her pot-smoking, misbehaving son. And dogs. Alfredo is afraid of dogs, especially this one. His eyes look like a man's eyes, with plenty of white around the pupils. That's what's so scary. These eyes bulge in their sockets, as if they want out, as if they want to return to the human face from which they came.

Wake up, Alfredo. This isn't the time.

While he was midreverie, his family agreed to make a mass movement toward the kitchen. Isabel's already in there. Lizette drags a protesting Winston by the wrist, and Jose wheels behind them, complaining about supper's ludicrous start time. Excluding the pit bull, only Tariq and Alfredo are left behind in the living room. They stand on opposite ends of the kitchen threshold, where the carpet gives way to linoleum.

"After you," Tariq says.

Alfredo reaches down and pulls a long clear plastic strip off the back of Tariq's jeans. The strip says *Rocawear* with the numbered measurements—*34 × 30*—repeating themselves all the way down to the bottom. Blue denim fuzzies float on the sticky side of the strip.

"Oh," Alfredo says. "Did you want to keep this on there?"

"See, I didn't know." His face softens, goes peaceful—an expression Alfredo recognizes as dangerous. Tariq reaches out and gives his brother's shoulder a squeeze. "Case you haven't heard, I've been away for a while. I don't know nothing. I thought keeping tags on the jeans might be the new style."

"No," Alfredo says. "It ain't."

With considerable disappointment, Lizette realizes she's going to have to skip the tostones and serve regular old bananas instead. She picked up some nice ripe ones at the store yesterday. She'll peel them and leave them exposed on the perimeter of everyone's plate. The tostones would've added a nice crispy texture to a meal full of mushies, but what're you gonna do? She doesn't have the *time* for tostones. She'd have to defrock the plantains, slice them, fry them, dip them, fry them again, blot them dry on paper towels, and sprinkle them with salt. If she made the tostones, she'd be up at the stove for whole minutes at a time, her back to her family like a substitute teacher writing the multiplication table on a blackboard, worried about the unseen class behind her, worried about spitballs and note passing and hell-raising young boys. Lizette peels ripe bananas instead of plantains, and she knows that already her meal has been tarnished. Already, things have begun to unravel.

"This is where the table lives now?" Tariq says. "In the middle of the kitchen?"

Jose wheels himself to the head of the table. To his right sits Isabel, and to her right sits Alfredo, both of them in their usual seats, where they can, if necessary, covertly hold hands. Winston sits opposite Alfredo. He plops down into the seat heavily, as if exhausted from a full day's work of drug taking and *Street Fighter II*. With the spot at the table's other end reserved for Mama, there's only one chair left. Without complaint, Tariq sits down to the left of his father and across the table from Isabel.

Lizette finishes the final preparations. She pours the red bean stew into the chicken and rice pot, and with a large wooden spoon she turns everything over. It pleases her to mix it all up, to acquaint the different food items with one another before they make the long dark journey through her family's digestive tracts. She sets the pot down in the middle of the table, on top of the *Post*. The pot's heat and moisture warp the paper's cover photograph: the swollen, guilty, apologetic mug of New York's Catholic archbishop. His Excellency might not object to this sizzling pot on his face if he were actually in this kitchen, if he could smell the oregano and chopped cilantro and puffs of paprika. Much to Lizette's satisfaction, the people around her table take deep,

appreciative sniffs. No one speaks. Taking turns, they all help themselves to food, except for the perpetually sedentary Jose, whose plate is prepared by Alfredo and passed down.

"Hey, Isabel," Jose whispers. "You interested in this baseball game?"

"Are you kidding?"

"Well, what I'm saying is, if you're not interested one way or the other, how about we switch seats. Cause look—you got a view where you can see straight into the living room."

Lizette, whose hearing is uncanny, particularly when Jose whispers, says, "This isn't a bar, you know. You don't sit down and watch a game on TV. You sit down and eat dinner."

As if to demonstrate, Winston shoves a forkful of food into his face. Rice—a consistent problem for him—dribbles out of his mouth and gets stuck to his chin. His jaw seems to be working independently from the rest of his face.

"First of all," Jose says, turning away from the boy, "people don't eat dinner at one o'clock in the afternoon. Okay? Second, I'm not trying to watch a game. I'm trying to watch an *at-bat*."

A couple of years ago, during a subway series game, the Yankees' ace pitcher, Roger Clemens, beaned the Mets' superstar slugger, Mike Piazza, right in the melon. Piazza is Italian and good-looking and wildly popular in Queens, and Mets fans claimed the beaning was intentional, Piazza having had significant statistical success against Clemens. Yankee fans called Mets fans overdramatic crybabies. The debate intensified in game two of the 2000 World Series, Mets vs. Yankees, under the lights in the Bronx, with Clemens facing Piazza again. Clemens threw an inside fastball, and Piazza swung, making poor contact. His bat broke—no big deal, happens all the time, but a chunk of wood made its way toward the mound, and in a fit of teeth-gritted rage, Clemens picked up the shard and threw it at Piazza. An on-the-field confrontation ensued, which is rare in World Series play, but then again so is bat throwing. Clemens pointed menacingly at Piazza, who had to be restrained by his teammates. Mets fans lost their perpetually aggrieved minds; their team lost the game, and then, unfairly, the series. The injustice of it all!

But now. Now Clemens is coming to Shea. And in a National League ballpark, without the protection of the designated hitter rule, Clemens will have to slither into the batter's box and hit for himself.

Many in Queens expect a tit-for-tat head beaning; more than one Mets fan hopes Clemens will be killed.

Jose Sr. doesn't hold an intense, personal grudge against Clemens, but he does know that the Mets season—and in effect the satisfaction he might wring out of the upcoming summer months—all rides on this one at-bat. Whether or not the Mets plunk Clemens, whether or not he goes down to the dirt with a baseball-sized bruise on his ample rear end, will determine whether or not the Mets return to the play-offs. Simple as that. And so Jose doesn't want to hear about this at-bat secondhand, as it seems he must experience so much else in his life. He needs to *see* the at-bat live, as it happens. If his legs still worked, he'd be at the ballpark, just to avoid the televisual delay. He'd buy a ticket in the upper deck and he'd sneak down to the blue seats in later innings. He'd be part of a crowd. He'd stand for the wave. When it came time to cheer *Let's . . . go . . . Mets,* Jose would be stomping his feet.

"So, if you don't mind switching," he asks Isabel.

"You want my seat?" Alfredo says.

"From where you're at, you can see into the living room, but you can't see the TV. I scoped it already. All you can see is parrots, and what do I need to look at parrots for? Listen," he tells Lizette, who grips the edges of her plate. "I don't *need* to switch seats with Isabel. I could always ask her for updates every couple of minutes. Who's pitching? Who's up? What inning is it? Where's Piazza? Where's Clemens? Of course I'll have to give her a physical description of Clemens so she'll know who I'm talking about. But if I could just sit there, my dear, if I could just move two feet to the right, I won't have to bother nobody, not my lovely daughter-in-law, not my lovely wife. I could keep one eye on the game, one eye on this fine-smelling chicken you prepared, and who knows—every now and again I might drop in a line of sparkling, dazzling conversation."

"You know," Lizette says, half admiringly, "you're a real piece of work."

Jose and Isabel switch places. Alfredo watches her get up and drag her chair to the head of the table, next to Tariq. As if suddenly shy, Tariq won't even look at her. He fiddles with the wristband of his watch.

Inside Alfredo's pocket, his phone begins to ring. He'd turned the volume up last night, when he thought Winston might call, or the

police somehow, with news of Winston's murder, and Alfredo forgot, this morning, to set it back to vibrate. It rings now like a bell clapper, sounding the alarm of his anxiety. With Winston and Isabel already here at the table, the most likely caller is Baka, Alfredo's connect—and if this is Baka, he's probably calling about the money Alfredo owes him, or the infinity-branded X he may have sold Vladimir Shifrin, or (*brrrrrring, brrrrrring*) he might be calling with the intent to lure Alfredo out of the house, as he may have lured Curtis Hughes last night. Alfredo wishes he could talk to the fat fuck. Not over the phone, but in person, to look him in the eye and get the info he needs.

"Your phone," Lizette says. "It's ringing. At the *dinner table.*"

"Sorry," he says as he silences the phone in his pocket. Of course there's a pit bull in the living room, devouring parrots—but so what? That's fun. That's hilarious. But Alfredo's phone ringing at the dinner table? God forbid! And God forbid Isabel gets to sit where she wants to sit. She stares at her plate of food. Although she shows no outward signs—her jaw stays rigid, her cheeks don't pucker—Alfredo knows she is grinding her teeth. "It's business," Alfredo says. "The call, I mean."

"Can we get this show on the road?" Jose says. Except for Winston, who's got a mouthful of chicken, no one has eaten anything yet. "Who's the youngest here?"

"I am," Alfredo says. Two months younger than Winston, a full year younger than Isabel. And so, the responsibility falls to him. "Bless us, O Lord, and these Thy gifts which through Thy bounty we are about to receive." Usually, when giving grace, Alfredo stuccos the words together like an auctioneer. But today he enunciates. He watches Isabel, who could not be farther away, and he watches his Muslim brother, whose eyes are closed and whose head is politely bowed. "Through Christ our Lord," Alfredo says. "Amen."

Winston swallows heavily. All around him forks and knives meet plates. They get together, say *clackety-clack*. Winston, however, puts down his utensils. He's mortified. Is this what families do? They say grace before dinner? In 2002, for fuck's sake? It never even *occurred* to Winston that he should wait. At home it's just him and his ma dukes; they never eat together, and they most definitely do not pray together. Oh shit—just thinking about it makes his throat go tight. He takes a sip of water, but it's lukewarm, and so all of a sudden he's up at the

freezer, searching for ice cubes. As the cold air blasts his face, it occurs to Winston that this too is rude, rooting in someone else's freezer without asking permission. He mixed ketamine and coke earlier today, and now his heart is trying to sneak out of the house, shoulder its way through the bars of Winston's rib cage and leap clean out of his chest. Winston's got to give the bag of scrips in his pocket back to Alfredo. He's got to quit drugs tomorrow. The uppers and downers have jumbled his brain, stolen his appetite. Maybe Winston has even taken drugs he doesn't remember taking, some hallucinogens perhaps, some magic mushrooms. *I must be trippin' balls*, he thinks, because as he sits back down in his seat he realizes his water, with the ice cubes floating in it, has fucking turned green.

Lizette turns away from Winston, shaking her head. Best to ignore it. "I was going to make an avocado salad," she announces to the table. "But the Koreans are charging three dollars apiece. Has anyone heard of such a thing? Three dollars for an avocado?"

Tariq hasn't eaten anything yet. He moves his fork around his plate, flipping over grains of yellow rice, a forty-niner prospector separating silt from gold. He spears an oil-rimmed brown square of meat and lifts it up to his eyes. "Mama, what's in this rice?"

"It's my rice," she says.

"Yeah, but is there any pork in it?"

"A little ham. For flavor."

"Oh," Tariq says.

"Oh," Lizette says, suddenly understanding. "Oh, *honey.* Can't you pick around it?"

Tariq pushes the plate away from him. He closes his eyes and little vertical lines form between the brows. Little frustrated folds of skin. His face flushes, and it looks to Alfredo as if Tariq is holding his breath, counting down from one thousand.

"It's delicious, Mama," Alfredo says. He talks with his mouth full of chicken and rice and red bean stew. "You don't know what you're missing, big brother. Right, Dad? Right? *Papi.*"

"Huh?" Jose says. He looks around the table, unsure of whom to address. He settles on Winston, the guest, the only one not staring his way, the only one who doesn't seem to *expect* anything from him. "Bottom of the second," Jose says. "One out. We're getting close."

"The food," Alfredo says. "What do you think of the food?"

Jose leans back in his wheelchair and pats the sides of his stomach. "Best meal of my life." He says this every night. "A new standard, Ma."

"That's what I'm saying," Alfredo tells his brother. "You sure you don't wanna try it? I'm telling you, you can't even *taste* the ham."

Tariq stands. He seems to lose his balance for a moment and has to brace his hand flat against the table. He smiles, as if to communicate to everyone that there's no cause for alarm. *Keep moving,* he seems to tell them. *Go about your business. Nothing to see here.* He scrapes the food off his plate and dumps it back into the communal pot. A chicken leg plops down heavily, causing red sauce to splash out of the pot and onto Lizette's floral-patterned tablecloth. Tariq doesn't seem to notice. He drags his fork over the plate long after it seems necessary, and it makes a terrible sound, a nasal squeak, as if one of them, either the fork or the plate, were crying out in pain.

"You want my banana?" Alfredo says. "It hasn't even touched the ham. I swear."

Tariq sits down. He crosses his fork and knife over his plate, making an X, and he pushes the whole thing away with the palm of his hand. "That's nice of you to offer," he says. "But no thank you."

Lizette asks if she can fix something else for him. A tuna fish sandwich maybe. Or a plate of macaroni. He doesn't answer. He sits in his seat, his lips moving silently, as if he were casting a spell or chanting a prayer. Lizette tries asking why it took him so long to come home this morning. Did he see some people he knows? Drop in on some old friends?

"What friends?" Alfredo says.

"Did you see, uhm . . . ," Lizette trails off. She wants to keep the table talk impersonal. She wants to keep long-harbored grievances out of the air, and so, in an attempt at conversational misdirection, she tries to get everyone to talk about the people they know, the friends they all have in common. She wants to give and receive benign updates on mutual acquaintances. *Is so-and-so still living at home? Did his mother ever get that kitchen repainted?* The problem, however, is the Batistas don't have any mutual acquaintances. Alfredo's right. What friends does Junior have? And it's not just him. Jose doesn't leave the house, Isabel's a veritable orphan, and Lizette's coworkers don't run in the same circles as Alfredo's deadbeat cronies. But wait!

"Did you see Ear Man," Lizette says suddenly, happily. "When you were walking up the block, did you see his new shirt?"

Of course! The neighborhood crazies! Everyone knows them, right? Lizette performs for her son, fills in the gaps of his knowledge. They took away the bench in front of the post office, she explains, and so now all the bums have scattered like pigeons. Popeye—remember him?—he smokes his Parliaments now out of a hole in his neck. The legless alky and the teenaged Rasta who panhandles while listening to a Discman have switched spots, panhandling in front of Baskin-Robbins and the Jewish Center, respectively. And the Flying Nun? Surely Junior must remember her. That woman who painted her face white and screamed at all the children? Well, she all but disappeared. Got knocked up, Lizette explains. Raped in one of the Woodside homeless shelters.

"Who'd wanna rape her?" Tariq asks.

"How's Gio and Conrad?" Alfredo asks. "You talk to them at all?"

"Far as I know," Tariq says, "they're still incarcerated."

Above the table floats a heavy cloud of familial silence. For a few long moments, no one speaks. Isabel takes wolfish bites of her chicken, some of which is for her, some of which is for Christian Louis. She's never met Conrad or Gio, but she's heard the rumors. Not at the beauty parlor or in the stalls of the girls' bathroom, but on the streets. *Dropped a dime on his brother,* people said. *Just to get at a girl.* Isabel's never asked Alfredo if the rumors are true, because she knows he wouldn't lie to her, and she hasn't yet decided which answer she'd rather hear.

On top of the table Tariq's hand lies close to hers. The dinner conversation has fragmented: Alfredo and Winston are talking about someone they both know, while Lizette asks Jose what he wants for Father's Day. No one sees Tariq's hand moving closer. No one bears witness. Isabel forgot how big his hand is, how heavily it used to weigh on her own. Dark wires of hairs uncurl from his knuckles. She thinks that if all he wants is her hand, then she'll give it to him. No problem. She'll grab her knife and saw her arm off at the wrist.

"It's bad, I know," he whispers. He turns his cheek to her. The skin around the gash is puffed up, a pair of pink ropes knotted at the ends. "But I've heard that some women like scars."

Under the table his other hand moves between her legs. He prods the fabric of her sweatpants, the cotton of her underwear. She looks across the length of the table at Alfredo, who appears distracted, still talking to Winston. Just turn your head, Alfredo. Just turn your head and see what's happening, but of course he doesn't notice because no one ever notices, no one ever notices anything. She stares at the network of flowers printed on the tablecloth. She knows that if she stays here and deals with it and lets Tariq paw her, then eventually it'll be over. He tugs on her pubic hair, and a breathless Isabel jumps out of her body. She sits up on the counter, next to the stove. Legs dangling, she watches her body, that girl Isabel, at the head of the table. The body goes completely still. The body drops a fork, which clatters against her plate, but no one bothers to care. The body grabs hold of Jose Sr.'s arm (oh good for you, girl) and shakes it. In a voice that sounds like Isabel's but is somehow calmer, stronger, the body says, "The game, Papi. The game, the game."

"The game!" Jose says. He squints into the living room. "Clemens—he's on deck!"

Alfredo stands and so does Isabel. She shoots out of her seat so suddenly that her chair tips over and crashes to the floor.

"Be careful!" Lizette shouts, and Winston's head snaps forward as if he's just been jolted awake. In the living room, the dog starts barking.

"He's on deck!" Jose says. Alfredo races to the back of his father's wheelchair, as if he wants to stake his claim as the favorite son. They slide out of the kitchen, Jose grinning, Alfredo hunched over, his head bobbing, looking like a jockey on a horse. Behind them, Winston stomps his heavy feet and Tariq trails, as if he were stalking the three men in front of him. On his way out of the kitchen, he loses his balance and bangs into the doorframe.

Left alone in the kitchen, Isabel and Lizette stare at each other across the length of the table. In the living room, the dog continues to bark. The television plays at a riotous volume.

"What do you think he wants?" Lizette says.

Before Isabel can ask what she means, the downstairs neighbor, Mr. Pettolina, starts banging on his ceiling with a wooden broom handle. *Bang, bang, bang, bang.* He's complaining about the shouting, the barking, Winston's heavy footsteps, the toppled-over chair, the ubiquitous smell of sofrito in the hallways, his shitty court stenographer job,

the wife who left him seven years ago. He raps at the ceiling, his small white teeth presumably gritted.

"Oh for fuck's sake," Lizette says.

Bang bang, says the broom handle.

"Shut up!" Lizette screams. She grabs the table for leverage and kicks down at the floor with the heel of her foot. Her hair flies. Her leg goes up and down. When the banging continues, when it becomes obvious there's no way to stop it, she collapses into her chair. Her chest heaves. She looks miserable. "I should've made the tostones," she tells Isabel. "You think he wants a sandwich?"

Isabel grabs the sides of her stomach to remind Christian Louis that his mama's still here. The broom's vibrations rise up out of the floor and tingle the bottoms of her feet. Mr. Pettolina must be really mad. She imagines him down there. He hits the ceiling so hard the plaster must be coming loose. White dust drifts down onto his face, into his hair, coats the tips of his long, delicate eyelashes.

Meanwhile, Roger Clemens enters the batter's box. In Corona, Elmhurst, East Elmhurst, Jackson Heights, Cambria Heights, Astoria, Hollis, Glendale, LeFrak, Queensbridge, Jamaica, Rockaway, Fresh Meadows, Kew Gardens, Malba, Maspeth, Ditmars, Douglaston, Howard Beach, Beechhurst, Bellerose, Rosedale, Richmond Hill, Forest Hills, Floral Park, Ozone Park, Rego Park, College Point, Hunters Point, Willets Point, Breezy Point, Bay Terrace, Bayside, Sunnyside, Woodside, Woodhaven, Ravenswood, and Ridgewood, revenge-mongers lean forward in their seats. Beat cops on Thirty-seventh Avenue stare at a TV through the window of the Headz Ain't Ready barbershop. In Whitestone, at a bowling alley, Baka watches the TV set up behind the bar; in Corona, Alex and Bam-Bam Hughes sit on their couch, an empty space between them; and in Elmhurst, the game plays on a television suspended above Vladimir Shifrin's hospital bed. It ain't all TVs, of course. There are the radio listeners: drivers stuck on the BQE and Grand Central Parkway, Con Ed employees, dishwashers and doormen working in Manhattan, a little boy on a sticky tar roof, Max Marshmallow behind the counter of his candy store. And at Shea Stadium? The hot dog vendors and peanut slingers do what they've explicitly been instructed not to do: they turn around and face the

field. The fans have all been standing since the top of the third inning. They cheer the Mets and boo Clemens, but they're holding back, these fans. They're keeping a little something in their pockets, waiting for the release, the consummation of long-anticipated violence.

The Mets pitcher throws at Clemens and misses. It happens that fast. The ball sails three feet behind him, lands in the dirt, and rolls to the backstop. That was it—their one chance. Piazza hangs his head while the umpire issues warnings. Clemens smirks. He tips his helmet at the pitcher, and an entire borough deflates.

"Season's over," Jose says. "We're done."

"It's June," Alfredo says. "There's like a hundred games left."

"We're *done*," Jose says. The next pitch is a fastball right down the middle, which Clemens fouls off. "You see?" Jose says. He waves a disgusted hand at the television. "You *see*? We missed him, now we pitch to him, and the season's all gone straight down the drain. You need confidence to play this game and we've lost all confidence. Aw Christ, Dito," he says, as if Alfredo's naïveté was not only obvious but blameworthy, responsible for the long stretch of winless baseball games in front of him. "Don't you understand?"

"Seasons don't end in June, Papi, just because we missed hitting a pitcher in the ass."

"*Don't you understand, Dito?*" Tariq says, perfectly mimicking their father's Nuyorican accent. He scratches his dog behind the ears and smiles at Alfredo, who doesn't know if his balls are getting busted here or if Tariq is winking at him over their father's head. "*You need confidence to play this game,*" Tariq says.

Jose squeezes Tariq's hand and looks up into his face. "Here's the problem," he says, his voice dropping, and it seems to Alfredo that Jose is suddenly addressing Tariq not as a father addresses a son, but as if they were peers, two guys from the neighborhood, sitting across from each other at a dominos table, sipping on cans of Modelo and bullshitting about cars and sports and women and the perpetual disappointment of children. "The problem is Dito doesn't know because he never actually played baseball."

"I played!" Alfredo says.

"Yeah, but your wrists were always too thin," Jose says.

"What the hell does that mean? My *wrists*?" With every word, Alfredo's voice rises, and he hates himself for it. At least Winston gives

no indication that he's seen or heard any of this. He lies in the recliner—
at a safe remove from the dog—with his legs up, eyes closed, and mouth
open, like a patient in traction. He snores loudly, crashing after a two-
day-long drug binge. So as not to wake him up, Alfredo lowers his
voice. "You're ridiculous," he tells his father. "You don't know what
you're talking about."

"What are you getting so upset for?" Jose says. "Not everyone's
gonna be a top-dog ballplayer. You're good at other stuff. What's fifteen times seventy-three?"

"How about this number?" Alfredo says. "Zero. The number of
times you've seen me play baseball in your entire life. How many?
Zero."

"What's he getting so upset about?" Jose asks Tariq.

"He was pretty good," Tariq shrugs.

"Thank you," Alfredo says.

"Sure," Tariq says. Alfredo knows his brother has never actually seen
him play an organized game of hardball either, but the two boys, when
left alone in the house, used to play Wiffle ball. And that kinda counts,
right? With a pillow on the sofa serving as the strike zone, big brother
batted and pitched left handed, just to give little brother a chance. One
time Alfredo hit a hanging curveball so hard he knocked three parrots
off the ceiling.

"He had a strong arm," Tariq tells Jose. "And he could run, that's for
sure."

"*Thank* you," Alfredo says.

"You were no superstar either," Jose tells Tariq. "You had the tools,
sure. My genes. But not the work ethic. I'm sorry, but am I wrong? You
weren't lazy. I won't say you were lazy, but you never really tried." He
holds his hand above his head, as if he were measuring off the height
of baseball stardom. "You never pushed yourself hard enough to get to
that next level."

"See," Tariq says, "all these years, I didn't know you was a baseball
scout."

"And he knows all this—have you noticed?—without ever having
seen us actually play in a game. Not one fucking time."

"No cursing," Jose says. "It's a sign of ignorance." The two prime-of-
life boys stand close to Jose, crowd him, look down on him in his
wheelchair. On the television, Clemens has just gone down swinging.

149

Still smirking, he struts back to the safety of the dugout. "Go get a bat," Jose tells his sons. "You two think you're so smart. Go get a bat and I'll show you what's what. I'll strike out the both of you. Three pitches for Dito. And for you, my oldest, maybe four pitches. Maybe you foul one off. You understand? I'll show you. Go get a bat."

If there was a bat in this apartment, Alfredo tells his father, Mama would've brained him with it a long time ago. Tariq starts laughing.

"Go downstairs," Jose says. "Go downstairs and grab that broom out of Pettolina's fucking—excuse me—out of Pettolina's hands, and bring it up here, and swing *that*. Okay? Swing and strike out with that. A broom handle. Because that's what I had. I had a broom handle for a bat and a piece of cardboard for a glove, and I was a *player*. I walked the field with confidence."

"How about this?" Alfredo says. "How about we all go outside? Have a base-running contest."

"Ho shit!" Tariq says. He reaches out, laughing, and he and Alfredo slap palms.

It's been some time since Alfredo's had an ally against the Axis of His Parents. There's Isabel, of course, but she is by necessity a silent ally. She's an outsider, an exile living abroad in this tyrannical nation-state, and while she can use the tools of cunning and subversion, she cannot outwardly criticize. Not without fear of having her visa revoked. But Tariq, on the other hand. Tariq is a sibling—check the DNA!—and siblings, like war vets, share the common ground of fox-hole experience. He can fight back, strap on a helmet, get dirty. Over their father's head, Tariq smiles at Alfredo, and Alfredo, with a jolt, realizes that a secret part of him has desperately missed having his big brother around.

From the kitchen doorway, Isabel watches. She looks down to find her arms folded in front of her chest.

"Papi, are they teasing you?" Lizette says. She squeezes past Isabel and comes into the living room. "Are you boys teasing him? Don't you know it's Father's Day tomorrow? Tell them what you want, Jose. Tell them what you were telling me, you old pervert. Look at him. He won't even acknowledge me. Your father, for Father's Day, wants, as a gift, a sex machine. This is what he tells me. He wants a machine for sex, a strap-on penis."

"Not a strap-on," Jose says sourly. "A machine that straps *onto* your penis."

"Onto *my* penis?" Lizette says in mock horror.

"How much it cost?" Tariq asks.

"Thirty-nine ninety-nine," Lizette says. "Or so he tells me. There's an installment plan. They take all major credit cards."

"We'll buy you two," Alfredo says. "Case you wear out the first."

"My man goes, 'We'll buy two,' " Tariq says, laughing. "In case he wears out the first!"

Again the boys slap palms, but this time they do it the way they used to: two quick pats, then a fist bump.

"You got a name for that dog yet?" Alfredo says, but before Tariq can answer, Alfredo's phone starts ringing. Baka's number flashes across the screen. Not his name, just his number—Alfredo's too paranoid to save a business contact to his phone book. What if the DEA were to get ahold of his cell?

"Little brother's been big pimpin' since I was away!" Tariq says. "You blowing up, Dito. Another business call?"

"Yeah," Alfredo smiles. "I guess."

Tariq claps his brother on the shoulder. "You were always mad smart, Dito. I'd be telling people how my brother's gonna be *running* shit one day. I'm serious. Don't look over there. Look at me. You're pulling down mad weight, am I right?"

"I'm doing okay," Alfredo says.

"You wanna know something? I used to tell people that I'd be working for you one day. I'm being serious here. Man, look at me. You gotta bring me back into the fold, Dito. I wouldn't even know where to start."

Tariq's eyes are shining, set deep in a face with two mouths, the one he uses to smile at Alfredo, and the other mouth, the crueler one, sliced into his cheek. He has changed in these last couple of years. There is the scar of course, but also the bald head, hard as a razor, and the city of muscles under his shirt. This, Alfredo thinks, is a body capable of terrible power.

Alfredo fiddles with the phone in his hands. He thinks of how differently things might've been had Curtis gone out last night with big brothers Alex and Bam-Bam.

"You feel like coming with me somewhere?" he says. "I'd ask this guy"—he gestures to Winston snoring lightly in the recliner—"but . . . well, you know."

"Absolutely," Tariq says. "Where we going?"

"There's dessert," Lizette says nervously. "There's ice cream in the freezer."

"Is it pork flavored?" Alfredo asks.

"You've got some fucking mouth on you," Tariq says, still smiling.

"No cursing," Jose says.

"Chocolate," Lizette says. "Chocolate ice cream. Your favorite. Right in the freezer. Come on."

Tariq punches Alfredo hard in the chest and then punches his own, creating an invisible cord between them. "Sorry, Mama," he says. "We got moves to make."

Christian Louis has fashioned a knife out of something, some contraband he's smuggled into Isabel's body, and either he's stabbing her uterine walls with the knife or the knife keeps slipping out of his teeny hands, but either way it hurts. She runs to the bathroom, locking the door behind her. She sits her bone-wearied body down on the toilet seat, and then jumps back up, as if something in the water leapt out and bit her. She rattles the doorknob. To be positive. To make sure. To double-check. But don't worry, Isabel. It's locked. Okay? The door is locked.

9

The Many Loves of
Vladimir Shifrin

She taught preschool in the city of Novorossiysk, right off the Black Sea, in the last-gasp days of the Soviet Union. She had long blond hair and played the acoustic guitar. Vladimir doesn't remember her name, but she was, and always will be, the first.

In the pictures he finger-painted of the two of them, they'd be holding each other's stick-figured hands, or sitting behind the large bay window of a house, or standing on a yellow sun in insulated boots. While the other children napped, he feigned sleep on a mat near her desk. At snack time, he offered her sips from his milk cartons, which she politely declined, citing germs, citing the necessity of calcium for the building of healthy bones, but she always commended his willingness to share.

One day Vladimir decided they should live together. As he got ready for school, he doused his hair with tomato juice. With his mother's eye shadow, he painted a bold black circle around his eye. Mama didn't ask. She lay perpetually in bed around this time, her body a battleground for poisons, chemo vs. cancer.

Vladimir's brother, Misha, a ninth grader, walked him to school that morning. Like Mama, Misha didn't question the eye shadow or the tomato juice. Vladimir was a *choknutiy*—the familial odd duck destined, Misha thought, for great things. When they reached the pre-

school, Misha reluctantly let go of his little brother's hand. He kissed him on the forehead. Asked him to please stay out of trouble.

Vladimir went straightaway to the pretty blond teacher and told her he was being abused at home. Lookit. A black eye. Blood in my hair. Vladimir, whose theatrical skills were precociously pronounced, could cry on command, but he held back this time, thinking restraint would play better than hamming. Besides, he didn't want his eye shadow to run.

The teacher pressed his small body against hers. Vladimir thought she smelled like ripe tomatoes (although, more likely, he smelled like ripe tomatoes). She brought him into her office and sat him down in her chair. Her hands were shaking. She gave him construction paper and crayons. She told him to sit tight. She told him she needed to think. She needed to think this whole thing through.

One shudders to imagine that her figurative blindness here—eye shadow and tomato juice, lady!—might be explained by the possibility that she herself had been abused as a child, and as a grown-up had dedicated her life to protecting the innocent bodies of children.

"I'm afraid to go home," Vladimir said.

"Oh, you poor sweet thing."

Things were going well.

After she left the office—she needed to think; she needed to make some calls—Vladimir drew pictures of the rainbow house they'd live in together. He'd miss his parents, obviously, but love requires certain sacrifices. He wouldn't miss his brother, however, because—in Vladimir's master plan—his brother was coming with him. Vladimir drew an extension off of the side of the house for Misha to sleep in.

An hour later, the teacher (what was her *name*?) tiptoed back into the room, as if it were Vladimir's office and not her own. A man trailed behind her, wearing dark pants and a flannel shirt. He looked like a carpenter, but he had the thick-bristled mustache of police inspectors around the world. The teacher put a hand on his chest, afraid, perhaps, that he might bolt at Vladimir and scoop him away.

"Here he is, honey," she said. "The boy."

Honey came forward, cracking his knuckles. He licked his thumb and rubbed a streak of eye shadow off of Vladimir's face. He bent his nose to Vladimir's hair.

"Vegetables?" the man said. He smiled at the child and then smiled

even wider at the teacher, with the easy condescension of a boyfriend. "I think what we have here is a young boy who likes to tell tales."

"Vladimir?" the teacher said.

He had one card left to play. "My mom," he said. "She's sick."

Years and years later, well into the future—when Vladimir Shifrin is a paunch-bellied assistant professor of Slavic languages and literature at a small midwestern college—he will tell this anecdote in his lecture on Anton Pavlovich Chekhov's short story "The Kiss," using his own experience with early disillusioned love to segue to the end of Chekhov's story:

> And the whole world—life itself seemed to Riabovich an inscrutable, aimless mystification . . . Raising his eyes from the stream and gazing at the sky, he recalled how Fate in the shape of an unknown woman had once caressed him; he recalled his summer fantasies and images—and his whole life seemed to him unnaturally thin and colorless and wretched . . .

But this will be a bit of pedagogical exaggeration on the part of Assistant Professor Shifrin, a lie, another tale told. Because when the pretty blond teacher sent him out of her office, he did not become unnaturally thin or colorless or wretched. He did not, as Riabovich did, cast himself upon his bed, wroth with his evil fate. No, Vladimir grew only hungrier for love. Not for the love of the teacher—with the short-term memory of children and romantics, he had moved on from her almost immediately. Instead Vladimir grew hungrier for the love of women he had never met, women whose faces he had never seen and whose names he did not yet know.

Names like Jessica Yoffe and Tonya Valit and Marina Duvenskaya. Girls who lived in the apartment next door, who sat in front of him at school with little blond hairs on the backs of their necks. In the fourth grade, Vladimir had a crush on a girl named Elena, but Andrei (Vladimir's best friend) also had a crush on her so Vladimir redirected his amorous energies toward Svetlana, but then Sergei (the class's monstrous bully) laid claim to Svetlana, and so Vladimir was forced to back off. A love poem he'd written her (well, plagiarized actually) lan-

guished in his desk till the end of the school year, when a janitor threw it away, unread. In the fifth grade he asked Olga Guseva to the end-of-the-year dance. She accepted, which precipitated a burst of elation, followed by the sharp stabs of anxiety, for this would be Vladimir's first date and he did not yet know how to dance. Then the blonder, more popular Anastasia Domani broke up with her boyfriend, and things really got complicated. An on-the-rebound Anastasia had her friends indicate to Vladimir's friends—through a series of cryptic notes and whispered hints—that a Vladimir-Anastasia merger might be possible, and when the stock proved solid, he broke up with Olga and started dating Anastasia. Within days, however, Anastasia broke it off. When Vladimir re-asked Olga to the dance, she told him to get down on his knees and beg for it in front of the entire school. With his classmates watching him, jeering him, he dropped down to the ground, hands clasped in front of him. Oh where had his confidence gone!

And he still didn't know how to dance. If his mother were alive, she could have put on a record and taught him. *Hold my hand. Here, like this. Don't look at your feet. Here, Vladimir. Like this. Yes, beautiful. Now move your feet. Wonderful. Oh, my wonderful little man.* But all Vladimir had was Misha. He didn't teach him how to dance, but he did buy Vladimir a corsage. He even showed him how to tie it to Olga's pale thin wrist.

That summer, the summer before he and Misha boarded a plane to John F. Kennedy International Airport, Vladimir got himself ready by watching subtitled American movies. None of them made any sense at all. It was like homework, except thankfully with beautiful Hollywood actresses. At the end of one these movies a blond-haired woman jumped out of an American automobile and ran into the dark mouth of an American forest, and Vladimir, watching from home, felt a strong compulsion to chase after her.

"Who's that?" he asked his brother, who knew everything.

"Why?" Misha laughed. "Do you *like* her?"

Nooooooooooooo.

Her name was Mariel Hemingway, Misha explained. The granddaughter of a famous American author.

Vladimir loved Jessica, Marina, Olga (well, not so much her anymore), Tonya, Elena, Svetlana, the unnamed teacher, and Anastasia—but he loved them in a purely nonsexual way. He wanted to be around

them, pick them lilies, stare at them through the frosted window of his apartment, but he did not want to kiss them. At most he wanted to be the kind of person who *used* to kiss girls, who had a long history of smooching and could therefore treat the subject with nonchalance. But Mariel Hemingway, this American blonde? Vladimir wanted to do things to her. He wanted to run his thumbs over her thick dark eyebrows.

America! Misha and Vladimir took a cab from JFK to their new studio apartment in Manhattan. The Big Apple! The City That Never Sleeps! Within weeks, Misha had Vladimir enrolled in a nearby public school. Misha bought him pens, folders, and three-subject notebooks for his first day of sixth grade. But this American school was not what Vladimir had expected. With its giant asphalt yard and clock tower and fence-lined perimeter and uniformed guards and metal detectors and no-talking zones and cafeteria slop and lineups and mandatory periods of exercise and with its explosive undercurrent of tension, the school felt less like an enlightened educational institution and more like a Soviet penal colony. On the morning of his first day, a girl twice Vladimir's size pushed him up against the classroom wall and grabbed his balls through his pants. In the afternoon, he watched an eighth grader drive a pair of scissors into a sixth grader's skull, using his lunchbox as a hammer, the scissors as a nail. Vladimir came home with his teeth chattering.

Misha pulled him out of classes right away and decided to send him to Catholic school. They picked one in Queens, where the price tags were lower—Misha, through his connections, was making good money, but not yet Manhattan tuition money. Besides, he reasoned, Queens probably had fewer black people and more immigrants, and a school with an immigrant-heavy population might be more accepting of a pole-thin Russian boy with middling (although quickly improving) English skills. And indeed the teachers were nicer and the classmates friendlier and Vladimir's Manhattan residence gave him a certain amount of cachet, but there was one demerit, a problem almost as serious as steel-tipped scissors puncturing one's cranium: Vladimir's new school was *all boys*.

They smelled like he did, like sweat, like feet, like poorly deodorized

armpits. They didn't carry a soft down of blond hair on the backs of their necks. Some of them didn't even *have* necks. In class, Vladimir stared at the blackboard.

At lunch he name-dropped Mariel Hemingway, but his new friends looked at him as if he were an alien from the interstellar Kingdom of Herbs. Vladimir learned new names: Alyssa Milano, Yasmine Bleeth, Jennifer Love Hewitt. "What about blondes?" he asked. You want blondes? Rebecca Romijn, Donna D'Errico, Gena Lee Nolin, Pamela Anderson. Yes, Vladimir wanted to say, but what about real blondes? Do you guys, like, know any actual girls? Do you have sisters, cousins, particularly horny housecleaners? The *Baywatch* babes are nice and all, don't get me wrong, but I can't exactly smell their Coppertone.

One time, a cluster of girls were smoking in Astoria Park, and Vladimir and his friends—at Vladimir's urging—approached them, asking to bum a cigarette or two. One of the girls slipped a Camel between his fingers and proffered her lighter, but when he saw the chipped nail polish on her fingers and when he smelled the smoke on her wet mouth and when he remembered the touch of her hand on his, he felt a stiffening in his too-tight parochial pants, and then Vladimir became very nervous indeed, and that's probably why he stuck the wrong end of the cigarette in his mouth, and tried, unsuccessfully, to light its mentholated filter. Which everyone—the boys, the girls—thought was absolutely fucking hilarious. *The filter! You were gonna light the* filter? *Oh my God! Har har har!*

"This is how we smoke in Russia," he said miserably.

It was not one of his better lies. Worse, for the next few months, it gave his friends' taunts an organizing principle. Vladimir answered a question wrong in math class? *Hey, is that how you find the radius of a circle in Russia?* ("Russia" always receiving a heavy, Boris-and-Natasha inflection.) Vladimir shot an air ball in gym class? *Does that count as a three-pointer in Russia?* Vladimir mispronounced "subsequent"? Vladimir mixed up "orgy" for "orgasm"? Vladimir neglected to super-size his Extra Value Meal? *Is that how you order fast food in Mother Russia?*

"That doesn't even make sense, twat-face."

"Do you even know what a twat is?"

"Do you?"

"Do *you*?"

They were his friends. They were mean to him. That's okay. He was mean to them, too. *Do you have HBO at home? Hindu Body Odor? Har har har!* They were eighth graders.

At home, while eating Chinese takeout, Vladimir said, "They want to know what you do for a living."

"Who does?" Misha said.

"The kids at school."

Misha looked relieved. "Tell them to mind their own business." There were rules, Misha had explained. Don't talk about what I do. Don't talk about anything that has to do with the family. "You know who talks?" he asked. "Blacks, that's who. They run their mouths and don't shut up and that's why they're always getting arrested."

"Can I tell them about Mama?"

"What about her?"

"Can I tell them about Dad?"

"Yeah, tell them he's drunk in a snowbank somewhere. Oh, come on. Don't make that face. I'm sorry. Hey, stop it. I'm *sorry.* Tell them whatever you want about Dad."

"Can I say he's in the KGB? That'd be phat."

"Don't say 'phat.' "

"What do I say about you?"

"Vladimir. You say nothing about me."

"You don't understand! This is how you make friends." It felt perverse—and strangely empowering—to instruct his brother on something. "They ask you questions, you tell them stories."

"Tell them I'm a student."

"You're too old."

"Vladimir," Misha warned.

"Well, you are."

"Tell them I'm a grad student."

"In what?"

"Perestan' bit dabayobom!"

"All I'm saying is if they ask, I want to have my story straight. Jeez. What if they tell their parents and then the parents meet you at, like, a PTA meeting or something, and they're, like, 'Hey, how's the grad life going? You're studying blankety-blank, right?' I want you to be pre-

pared, that's all. I want you to know what's coming. Maybe you're in graduate school for business? Huh? Chemistry, maybe?"

"Are you being a wise guy?"

"No! I swear!"

"Tell them I'm studying literature," Misha said. He liked the sound of it. He imagined a life of quiet study, term papers, sitting between the wings of a library carrel, hunched over old-smelling books, his nose in Gogol's "Nose." "Tell them I'm studying Russian literature."

"That's wack."

"Don't say 'wack.' You know who says 'wack'?"

Yeah, Vladimir thought. *I know.*

For high school he went to McClancy's in East Elmhurst, another Catholic all-boys school. He could've gone to school in Manhattan—his brother, at this point, was making enough bank to afford two tuitions, but some of Vladimir's friends were going to McClancy's, and so he wanted to go there too. He didn't want to start over. He was tired, he told Misha, of starting over.

New school, still no girls. The only women walking McClancy's halls were the nuns, and while Vladimir considered himself an atheist, unafraid of divine retribution, there were boundaries even he could respect. The sticky-seated porno theater of his mind screened practically everything and anything, but nun flicks stayed in their titanium canisters, unwatched. Fair game, however, were the women on the subway. And at night, before his brother came home, Vladimir spent long hours humping the bed, fantasizing about Jess Yoffe and Tonya Valit and Marina Duvenskaya. Like an FBI supercomputer, he age-advanced their faces and bodies, approximating how they might look in 2002. He even entertained fantasies of the girl from his Manhattan school, the giantess who pushed him up against the wall and grabbed hold of his privates. At least she showed interest!

It wasn't all sex, however. He thought he'd be a good boyfriend—a great boyfriend. He'd open doors and pay for things. He'd tell her he loved her. He wouldn't flinch or joke when she complained of menstrual symptoms. He'd kiss her shoulders. He'd sit with her in comfortable silence, sharing sections of the newspaper in a breakfast nook with sunlight streaming through the window (not that Vladimir had a

breakfast nook or ever read the paper). But man oh man, what he really wanted was someone to confide in. He'd tell his girlfriend he doesn't remember what his mother looked like. Unless he was looking directly at a photograph, he had to think of moms from TV and super-impose their faces onto a generic, housecoat-wearing body. It's a shameful secret that he's never told Misha, but when he gets a girl-friend and when the time feels right, he'll tell her. *If* he gets a girlfriend.

His clothes didn't help. Five days a week he wore wool pants, poly-ester shirts, snot-green ties one step above clip-ons. Talk about the Kingdom of Herbs! With his ample allowance, Vladimir invested in a new look. He bought black baseball caps at the Queens Center Mall and 1980s basketball jerseys off eBay. He scoured vintage shops in the Village looking for the same type of baggy jeans Dr. Dre wore when *The Chronic* came out. Like the names on the basketball jerseys—Barkley, Drexler—Vladimir's fashion sense was about twenty years out of date. Which is exactly why it's cool, he thought. Wearing the clothes under his Catholic uniform, Vladimir received a negligible boost in popularity and a zero percent increase in attractiveness to females. So like a home-born American, Vladimir doubled down. He reinvested. He soothed his frustrations with the ointment of more spending, more shopping.

Someone on eBay was selling a pair of the super-hard-to-get series III Air Jordans, mint condition, for only $245.

"No way," said Misha, who himself had a closet of wildly expensive shoes. But his objection to the Air Jordans wasn't the price, but rather their status as signifiers. "What are you, *black*?" Misha asked. "Pick up your pants, bro. Air Jordans are for eggplants."

So what? Vladimir wanted to say. His favorite all-time athlete was Dominique Wilkins; his favorite movie star, Will Smith. He burned Nas CDs off his friends and kept them in jewel cases labeled "Van Halen." So black people wear Air Jordans? So what? Vladimir *wanted* them. They were *cool.* If need be, he'd pay for them himself.

He stole a beeper full of Ecstasy from his brother. His brother only had, like, tons of them. Misha gave them to dealers, who used the beepers to sneak E past bouncers at Webster Hall and Club Exit. Vladimir brought it to school, where he sold the X at a price he hoped wasn't too high. Ten dollars a pill.

Vladimir's popularity skyrocketed, as did the general mood of the

Monsignor McClancy Memorial High School. He bought the Jordans and kept them in his locker. He started hanging out with juniors and seniors. He pinched a couple more pills off his brother. He'd have to be careful here. He couldn't get greedy. He bought an Orlando Magic Bo Outlaw jersey off the Internet.

In the spring, with the pheromones poppin' and the birds a-tweet-tweet-tweetin', Vladimir met a girl. Let that sink in for a while. Her name was Vicki Rodriguez and she was the little sister of one of Vladimir's new upperclassmen friends, George Rodriguez, McClancy's starting point guard and a tenacious defender who had a habit of barking at opposing players. Vladimir had gone over to George's apartment to sell him three pills of E and to play his new Xbox, and he met Vicki in the hallway, the two of them converging on the apartment's only bathroom.

"Are you going to be long?" he asked her.

"It's my fucking house," she said.

Vladimir grinned. When she came out of the bathroom he pestered her with questions—What school did she go to? Did she have to take the train there? What sorts of music did she like?—and Vicki, flattered by the attention and moderately intrigued by the accent, provided dutiful answers. Eventually, however, he ran out of things to ask. His bladder, so close to the bathroom, was throwing a tantrum, which made it difficult to concentrate. He and Vicki looked at each other and then looked away. Smiling politely, she started to slip past him, and Vladimir—confused as to why anyone would want to leave so perfect a hallway—asked her where she was going. To the mall, she said. To get a new wallet. Her old one, a pleather facsimile of the Dominican flag, had fallen apart at the seams, literally.

"I can walk with you," he said. "Over to the mall. If you want."

"Do you have any idea how fucking awkward that'd be?"

"We could brainstorm names for our children. I'm thinking Victor, Vincent, uh, Vance maybe, Viggo. Fairly unusual names for a girl, I know, but . . ." If he'd had his tie on, he would've fiddled with the knot.

At the mall, Vladimir tried to pay for her new wallet, but she wouldn't let him. She did, however, allow him to buy her a cinnamon pretzel from the food court. As they walked through the mall, people stared—or at least Vladimir felt as if they stared—at their racial incongruity, the clash of their pigmentation. So what? A Dominican girl, Vicki had

dark dark skin, as dark as skin gets outside of Africa, and while that certainly must have appealed to Vladimir, while it must have sated some unrecognized fratricidal craving, he felt attracted to this girl for reasons beyond that. She smelled like cream and ginger, and her hair looked soft, and she bit her cuticles just like he did, and she stood the wrong way on mall escalators so that the world seemed to get farther away, and when she took bites of the pretzel Vladimir could see the pink muscle of her tongue, and she had big boobs that she tried to cover up (if he hadn't already fallen in love with her, he might have crassly referred to them as a sneak rack), and while she didn't laugh at Vladimir's jokes she at least knew they *were* jokes, and on the surface of her chin a pimple had formed, the pus of which was rising volcanically, and she told Vladimir that she was really, *really* looking forward to popping it. There are young men who did not find these habits and admissions attractive in the opposite sex, but in one afternoon at the Queens Center Mall Vladimir discovered he was not of their number.

He walked her home, and when they got to her door she put a hand on the side of his face, as if the city had gone suddenly dark and she needed to make sure he was still there, in front of her. "I like you," she said.

"I like you, too."

Come on, you idiot. Kiss her.

He didn't. He went home, loving her and hating himself. The next day they saw a movie together. The day after that, they went to a pool hall on Northern Boulevard. The day after that, she couldn't go out because she flunked an algebra test, so they talked for three hours on the phone. In the following days they went back to the mall, saw another movie, ate slices of pizza, sat on a bench in Travers Park with a clear view of the handball courts. And still they had not kissed. Every unconsummated minute brought Vicki and Vladimir closer to Friendship Status. At home, Vladimir stared at himself in the mirror, wondering if he should shave his widow's peak like Misha did, if maybe that would make him irresistible to Vicki, because clearly Vladimir stood incapable of making that first open-mouthed move himself, because he was a spineless, dickless, ass-licking loser. On Thursday—June 13, 2002—Vladimir, again, walked Vicki to her door, and again failed to kiss her. This time, however, she didn't go inside. Instead, they turned back around and she walked him to the train station, where she

passed through the turnstiles—like him, she had a student Metro-Card, so the swipe was free, but still!—and she stood with him on the platform, keeping him company as he waited for his train home.

They didn't say much. Under the ground, through their rubber-soled shoes, they began to feel the first soft rumblings of an oncoming train. Vladimir stepped up to the cautionary yellow line, leaned out over the tracks, and peered into the mouth of the tunnel. The rumbling grew louder. On the tracks, newspaper sheets and magazine pages twitched nervously. The air changed. Still no actual, physical train, but across the walls bloomed a heraldic light.

Vladimir decided he'd rather be the kind of guy who tries to kiss the girl and strikes out than the kind of guy who doesn't try at all. Wetting his lips, he turned to Vicki, who had already opened her mouth.

She tasted like she smelled, like ginger and cream. He clicked against the ridge of her teeth. He felt the slick underside of her tongue. Halfway through, Vladimir and Vicki remembered to close their eyes. It was the first French kiss for either of them, and not knowing when there'd be a second, they felt reluctant to stop. Eventually, however, they ran out of oxygen.

The train had come, the E express. The doors had opened, the commuters had stepped off.

"So," Vladimir said. Down by his hips, his hands opened and closed, grabbing at nothing. "I guess I'll see you."

She smiled and ran up the stairs.

By any objective criterion, it wasn't the world's greatest kiss. But don't tell Vladimir that. Or do. Tell him that kissing, like most things, only gets better with practice. Tell him that and see what happens. Because as the E express lurched toward Manhattan, Vladimir could barely keep his feet on the ground. If he was to jump—just a little hop, that's all—Vladimir would've smashed through the ceiling of the train car, through the tunnels, past the rats, past the mole men and Morlocks, up and into the East River that separates Queens from Manhattan, and once in that murky black-green water, he would've whooped it up, scissor-kicking his legs, using his hands to high-five the steroidal fins of radioactive fish.

He wanted to tell his brother so bad. Despite all of Misha's money, they still shared a room, and only two, maybe three feet of space separated their twin beds. That night, with the lights turned off, Vladimir

tried to find the courage to tell his brother that only a few hours previous he went underground and stood on a subway platform, and while trains whistled behind his back, he kissed a girl for the very first time. But Vladimir felt afraid. He worried Misha might find the confession too intimate, too feminine; he worried Misha might think it took Vladimir too long to nab his first kiss; he worried Misha might ask the color of Vicki's skin. Because while she wasn't Black, she was black, and Vladimir knew that would disappoint. And if Misha asked, Vladimir couldn't lie. He could steal from his brother and think the occasional evil thought about him, but he couldn't lie to him, not even in the dark. Nor could he disappoint him. So he didn't say anything. He went to bed burdened. He didn't tell his tale and somehow that made the kiss less real.

But Vladimir tells Misha now. He lies in a different bed, a hospital bed, with injuries consistent with blunt force trauma, as if Vladimir had been in an automobile accident or beaten with a pipe: cracked ribs, unfairly on both sides of the cage; a bruised sternum; a shattered bone in his left hand from trying to defend himself; and, worst of all, a broken jaw the doctors had to wire shut. He'll have to eat smoothies for months, but at least he can still talk. In a voice that sounds strange to him—slower, deeper, more distant—Vladimir tells his brother everything: about the kiss, the E-beeper, the Air Jordans, the cloudy features of their mother. Talking with a wired jaw doesn't hurt so bad, but crying does, and his whole body shakes from the effort of trying to stop.

Misha climbs into bed with him. A ponytailed nurse appears in the door, but Misha waves her away. He puts his arms around his brother's body. He collects the hospital gown, that flimsy thing, in his fists. He wants to spoon Vladimir. He wants to feel the delicate wings of his shoulder blades. But there are doctor's orders. With broken ribs, Vladimir must lie flat on his back.

"Shh," Misha says. "I love you. Okay? You're my brother. I love you."

Later in life, when Vladimir thinks of his brother—which will be *every single day*—he will often think of this moment. He will be pouring a cup of bitter coffee in the faculty lounge and all of a sudden he'll feel the ghost arms of his brother take hold of his body.

"You can never do anything wrong," Misha says. "Do you understand? We'll invite this girl over for dinner. Would you like that?"

"I won't be able to kiss her anymore," he says. Because he can barely open his mouth, the words come out muffled. "She won't even *want* to kiss me like this."

To keep himself from squeezing tighter, Misha lets go. His hands—still damp from a recent scrubbing—hover above Vladimir's body, unsure of where to touch down. Where do you put them? When your brother's ribs are broken and his chest is bruised, when he can hardly breathe, when his jaw is wired shut and his hand bandaged, where do you put *your* hands? What can you do that won't make the pain worse? Misha rubs the inside of Vladimir's elbow. He pours all his love into this one spot on his brother's body, and for everything else, for the rest of the world and the people in it, he feels only an unspeakable rage.

10

The Department of Worry

Alfredo and Tariq push through the bowling alley's heavy glass doors, and an air pocket pushes back, as if the building doesn't want them here. That's fine. Alfredo doesn't want to be here either. The carpet smells like cigarettes and chicken grease. Balls strike pins with the thunderous monotony of a roadside chain gang pulverizing rocks. And these balls don't glow in the dark, as they would at a schmancy Manhattan bowling alley. There is no dark here. Every bulb in every socket burns brightly, giving off the creepy orange gleam of fast-food heat lamps, and at each lane, under the pressure of these orange lights, the same painful tableau is enacted: men, women, and children, whether they're here on a second date or for a league game or a birthday party, whether they've picked up a strike or a gutter or some quantity of pins between the two, all the bowlers having bowled their balls and registered their scores, turn around now and make the exceedingly awkward walk back to their parties. The bowlers seem to wither under the scrutiny of observation. They have been watched, their roll judged, and now, not knowing what to do with their hands or where to put their eyes, not knowing how to act, these bowlers perform, and, of course, they perform disingenuously. They shrug. They pump fists. Overwhelmed with panic, they convert their thumbs and index fingers into pistols, take aim, and fire, *kapow kapow,* some of these

poor unfortunate souls going so far as to raise their fingertips to their lips and blow out invisible wisps of smoke. Alfredo, painfully self-conscious himself, hates to see others collapsing under the strain of painful self-consciousness. This is what happens, he thinks, when management leaves on the lights.

Tariq points to a lane in the back. "There's Baka," he says.

Like Alfredo, Baka is a self-conscious paranoiac, but unlike Alfredo, he wasn't born that way. An athletic child, Baka dominated Elmjack baseball. He stole bases standing up, spiraled footballs at eleven, drove his mother crazy with in-house ball playing and kitchen wind sprints and room-to-room dribbling, employed a patient, monotonous handball style, forcing no issues, striking no killers, simply keeping the ball in play from baseline to baseline until lung-scorched opponents gave up midpoint to bend over and take hold of their knees. And then at fifteen years old, he was diagnosed with Cushing's syndrome. A rare endocrine disorder, it caused his adrenal fight-or-flight mechanism to behave erratically. Even worse for young Baka, the Cushing's inflated his body to 250 pounds. Although increasingly unlikely, an athletic career remained technically, theoretically possible. At sixteen, he weighed more than 300 pounds. At twenty-eight, he no longer bothers with scales. Baka is centrally obese, which is to say the Cushing's has expanded his trunk and face while sparing his limbs. Which is to say he looks like a big black lion. He sweats too much. He bruises easily. Fatty pads layer the back of his neck, giving him a buffalo hump. And as is understandable for a man who once hoped to play center field for the Mets but can now no longer fit in the stadium seats, Baka has taken on an air of cynicism. He knows that bad things—missed beanballs, double-crossing business partners, terrorist attacks, nonhereditary endocrine disorders—suddenly poof into existence. And so he acts accordingly. To minimize risk, he doesn't go to drug dealers' houses, nor does he have drug dealers come to his. Instead, he prefers to meet in large public spaces, and because his competitive spirit remains, those large public spaces tend to be pool halls, pubs with dartboards, arcades with skee ball, bowling alleys like Whitestone Lanes. A couple of years ago, in the dimly lit parking lot out front, an upper-level drug dealer from the Bronx got himself shot in the head; Baka may or may not have been the executioner, but the very possibility tightens Alfredo's scrotum.

"Pretend you don't see him," Alfredo says.

"Yeah right," Tariq says. "Look at the size of him."

A young black kid, the latest protégé, rests a hand on Baka's considerable shoulder. They stare at Alfredo, and Alfredo stares back. He crinkles his eyes. He squints past them, watches an attendant scuttle out to the no-man's-land of the pins, watches a curly haired white girl bounce a ball off the bumpers. With his head moving like a sprinkler, Alfredo scans the lanes to Baka's right, lane 37, lane 38, lane 39, all the way to the end of the bowling alley. When he finishes, he turns and gives Tariq a big vaudeville shrug.

"You don't see him? He's right over—"

"Hold up," Alfredo says, flipping open his cell phone. He lowers his brother's arm. "Don't look at him. Look at me."

"You're *calling* him?"

"Not really." Alfredo keeps the phone on his ear for as long as it would take another phone to ring a few times and click into voice mail. "I don't want him to know we've seen him already. So I'm pretending to call him."

"Put your finger in your other ear," Tariq says. "It'll look more authentic that way."

After Alfredo hangs up the phone, he leads his brother to the shoe rental counter, where a white guy stands sentry on an elevated platform like a pharmacist. Alfredo asks him how much it costs to rent a locker.

"Fifty dollars for the year."

"Well, come on now," Alfredo says. He has a whopping two hundred dollars—the entirety of his life savings—at the bottom of his sock, but he ain't about to blow a fourth of it on a bowling alley locker. "How much for a one-day rental?" he asks. To keep himself sharp, Alfredo does the math himself: if the rate remained constant, a locker should cost a little less than fourteen pennies a day.

"We don't rent lockers by the day," the man says. He avoids eye contact, as if the news he's delivering is too terrible to bear. He picks up a shoe and sprays disinfectant into its insides. "We only have yearly rentals, I'm afraid. And that's fifty dollars. Like I was telling you."

"Where they at then? I wanna check them out before I throw down fifty dollars."

The man leans his head out over the counter, revealing a scalp

freshly mobilized with hair plugs. Each troop of implanted hair stands at attention, as if these were the first awkward days of boot camp. He points to a row of lockers that are close to Baka's lane but, thankfully, not too close.

As they make their way toward the lockers, Alfredo whips a white envelope out of his pocket. He flourishes it, as a magician might flourish a tricolored hanky. At a waist-level locker, he kneels down and his head dips close to his brother's body. Tariq smells clean, overwhelmingly so. Before they left, he took a "quick shower" that turned into a ninety-minute shower, where, judging by the smell of him, he must've used a full bar of soap. Plus a couple spritzes of Alfredo's cologne. Which is kind of flattering actually. When he asked to borrow a shirt, an XL Mecca tee, Alfredo was happy to lend it. He kneels down by the lockers, smelling his brother, looking at his shirt, and Alfredo feels a surge of love rise into his chest. He didn't invite this feeling, and yet here it is, flooding him. He pushes the envelope through a slit on the locker door.

"How you gonna get it back out?" Tariq says.

"I'm not really worried about it," Alfredo says. "It's empty." They're walking back to the shoe rental counter. "I owe Baka five hundred bucks, but it ain't like I've got that kind of money."

Tariq stops walking. "You don't have five hundred bucks?"

"No, no, no, no, no. What I mean is that I'm not gonna hand over that kind of money to a fat fuck like Baka just because he asked me to. But I think he might start some shit—"

"Because of the money you owe him."

"Over some other shit actually. But if he thinks I've got his cash in one of them lockers, then that'll check him. Know what I mean? He won't start any shit till he gets his money."

"Oh," Tariq says, nodding his head. "Well, I hope you got a Plan B."

Alfredo tells the white guy behind the counter that he ain't interested in them raggedy-ass lockers, but he would like to rent some bowling shoes. He requests a pair of size tens (he's actually a size nine, but he doesn't like anyone to know that, not even a potentially sympathetic stranger with hair plugs), and as is New York bowling alley policy, the man asks for Alfredo's Timberlands. He needs to keep them behind the counter as collateral against theft.

"You're kidding," Alfredo says. The bowling shoes sport a dizzying

design of red leather squares alternating with tan leather squares. The heels are frayed, the laces blackened with dirt. Even the insoles have gone missing. Nothing will separate Alfredo's feet from fungus but the thin cotton of his athletic socks. So as to ensure he won't steal these ridiculous bowling shoes, Alfredo has to relinquish his prized pair of Timberland boots.

"Well, I guess we only need to hold on to one," the man says. He offers a boot back, which Alfredo gladly accepts. "And you, sir? What size do you need?"

"I ain't wearing them shoes," Tariq says.

The man looks down at Tariq's prison-issue Converses. "I'm sorry, sir. But I'm afraid you can't bowl in sneakers."

"What do you mean, you're 'afraid'?" Tariq says. "Seriously. Explain that to me. You're afraid of what?" When the man doesn't say anything, when he just turns around and sticks Alfredo's boot in the cubbyhole, Tariq says, "You think you're a big deal? Standing up on your platform?"

Alfredo pulls his brother away. He wants Baka to see Tariq while he's like this, combustible. Alfredo figures that at some point in the last two and a half years, Tariq took down the pictures of Isabel he had taped to his cell's wall, and while Alfredo doesn't fool himself into thinking Tariq removed those photos calmly—he imagines Tariq vented his spleen on some poor inmate, as he vented his spleen just now on that poor shoe-rental guy—but after some quiet, religious reflection, it's possible Tariq decided that blood is indeed thicker than water. Right? There's *gotta* be something to that effect in the Qur'an. But Alfredo doubts there's anything in that holy book protecting overweight drug dealers.

As they approach Baka, Alfredo throws up his hand as if seeing him for the first time. Out of the corner of his mouth, he tells Tariq, "Try to look intimidating."

"Ah," he says. "I'm the Plan B."

When they get within earshot, Baka says, "Maybe we oughtta get you a new pair of glasses." He lounges in a leather booth skirting the perimeter of the lane. As befits his standing as a gentleman of leisure, he wears a tracksuit, and as befits the tracksuit wearer, his default mode is ball busting. "If you need new glasses—which, let me tell you, you obviously do—I can hook you up. I know a lady, works at an

optomalamadingdong shop. She can get you a sick discount. Little Puerto Rican lady. Tell her I sent you when you go. Drop my name."

"I tried calling you," Alfredo says.

"Negatory. Didn't get a call."

"Let me see your phone."

"You don't believe me?" Baka says. Tariq has taken a seat next to Baka on the booth, and Baka has to turn his body to talk to him. "I'd know, right? Believe me—when your brother calls, it's like an event around here. I write it down in my diary. Like a lunar eclipse, you know what I'm saying? Does not happen every day, am I right? Most definitely does not happen *twice* a day. Unless he needs something. Then, yeah, sure—I'll get a call. But he never calls just for friendship. And if I call *him*? Start leaving messages, which I never like to do? And then these messages start getting more and more frantic as I get more and more crazed? Forget it. I might as well be the girl with acne on the night of the prom. I start to get offended, if you know what I mean."

"Maybe he's trying to offend you," Tariq says.

"Maybe he is." Baka shakes his head mournfully. "It occurs to me. In my darker moments. The worst is when I worry that something's happened to him. Pierre here—have you met Pierre?" He gestures to the young black kid sitting in a chair with his back to them. The kid scratches his neck and enters names on the lane's computer keypad; either maliciously or not, he's spelled "Alfredo" as "Alfraido." "Pierre," Baka says, "tells me I've got a catastrophic imagination. You've heard of this? Catastrophic imagination? Me either. Which is cause for alarm, right? Because I start worrying where Pierre's heard this shit. In a fucking book? Impossible. And then, Jesus, don't get me started—I get to worrying if Pierre is smarter than I am. Which is a scary thought. Just wait till you talk to him. I'm up nights. I mean, I'm up nights anyway, but I'm bugging out over this, and the point is that all this bugging out over catastrophic imaginations is I guess a pretty good indicator that I actually *have* a catastrophic imagination, and so when I call and call and don't hear from your brother, I start to think, Aw Christ, oh no, maybe the big Dito got himself hurt somehow."

"Why would you think that?" Alfredo says.

"How *you* doing, by the way?" Baka asks Tariq. "Good to be home? Good to have you back, let me say that much. You look good. Hitting the weights, that's obvious. Let me tell you something—you go to

prison strong, you come home stronger. It's like a supervillain factory, am I right? Of course I wouldn't know. Anyway, you look good. Other than the cheek, which is infected by the way. That's some shit I do know about. Pierre, baby. Get over here. You're being very, very rude."

With his wiry arms and bony hands, Pierre looks a bit like a young Curtis Hughes. If Alfredo had to bet, he'd put the kid at sixteen years old. Maybe even younger. He's much taller than Alfredo, and by the looks of his oversized feet, he's only going to get bigger. He probably wakes up every morning with stretch marks on his shoulders and new coils of hair on his chest, probably outgrows his clothes every three months. Which is why he's got to invest in shirts like the one he's got on: a long white tee that comes to an end a few inches above his knees. Across the chest is a picture of Al Pacino, a Technicolor still frame from *Scarface*. Alfredo's never seen the movie—who's got the time?— but he's watched enough rap videos and heard more than enough impressions to be at least familiar with the scene on the shirt. An orange tulip of gunfire blossoms from the tip of an enormous gun, and Pacino, like Baka, tenders introductions: *Say hello to my little friend.* Alfredo and Pierre slap palms.

"I don't think I've ever met a black guy named Pierre before," Alfredo says.

Pierre inflates his chest. "Funny story, actually—"

"What is *that*?" Alfredo says. He leans in close to look at Pierre's neck, where a red constellation of bumps blotches the skin. Like fingers, the bumps reach down the collar of his shirt. "What the fuck is wrong with your neck?"

"My neck?"

"Poison ivy," Baka says, sounding impatient. "We gonna bullshit all night or are we gonna talk business?"

"We do need to talk some business," Tariq says.

"Poison ivy?" Alfredo says.

"Yeah, me and my boys? We was doing some graffiti shit over by the Maple Grove Cemetery, and we got into some bushes and whatnot, tagging this big—"

"Are you kidding me?" Alfredo says. "That shit is contagious."

Pierre shakes his head. "I looked it up online. They said it wasn't." He looks to Baka for support. "Right? The Internet? They said it wasn't catching."

Alfredo wipes his hand against the front of his shirt. "It's contagious, man. That's what poison ivy *does*."

"Don't worry," Pierre says.

The kid, obviously, has no idea who he's talking to. For the purposes of spatial efficiency, Alfredo's neurological Department of Regret splits an office with the interrelated Department of Worry. They've got separate desks and filing cabinets but share the same frosted glass door. Many of Regret's overcaffeinated staffers work freelance in Worry, almost all of them preferring the latter job as it requires the use of more creative faculties. They wear green visors and chew unlit cigars—there is no smoking in the brain, for obvious reasons—and they draft worries on triplicate forms, each worry, like each correct response on *Jeopardy!* phrased in the form of a question. For instance: What's the incubation time on poison ivy? What are the dangers of exposing a pregnant woman to it? Did Pierre kill Curtis Hughes? Did he use a metal bat or a tire iron to compensate for the Alphabet Brother's knockout fists? Did Curtis, at any point, think Pierre kinda looked like a younger version of himself, or do people not recognize that kind of thing?

"The Internet said I'd be fine as long as I took a bath every day in tomato juice."

"That's for skunks," Alfredo says.

"What is?" Pierre says.

"Baths in tomato juice."

"Why would a skunk take a bath in tomato juice?"

"See?" Baka says. "This is the guy who comes to me with 'catastrophic imagination.' Can you imagine?"

"We need four ounces of cocaine," Tariq says. He sits hunched over on the edge of the booth. Between his knees, his hands dangle in a way Alfredo finds disconcertingly nonthreatening. "Nothing stepped on," Tariq says. "No filler. We want it by Tuesday at the latest. And we won't pay more than seven hundred an ounce. Which is what? Twenty-eight hundred dollars? I get that math right, Alfredo?"

No, Alfredo thinks. He sits in the swivel chair next to the computer keypad, away from the men in the booth. No, that math is not right. Well, okay, yes, the *math* is right, but the numbers are ludicrous. An ounce at seven hundred would be a pure gram cost of twenty-five, which is maybe what it costs off the boat when the shit comes into the

country, but to demand those prices now, from Baka, in a bowling alley in Flushing? And what would he even do with that much coke? Cook it in Mama's cast-iron frying pan, smooth out the bubbles with Mama's butter knife, store it in Mama's freezer till it hardened into crack rocks? Type in an ounce on a pusherman's calculator and you get 168 rocks. Four ounces then makes 672. Sell that on the street for ten dollars a rock (*well . . .* let's say fifteen a rock, considering Alfredo's salesmanship), and you've got $10,080, or a profit of over seven G's, which is probably how Tariq arrived at the original number, saying to himself, *Boy, I'd sure like to make seven thousand dollars—how do I do that?* Unless, of course, seven hundred an ounce was a reasonable price before Tariq went away, in which case Alfredo completely missed out on the porous-bordered heyday of drug dealing. If he were three years older and if he had the stones to sling rocks, Alfredo and Isabel would have their own apartment by now, with a flat-screen TV and a Sub-Zero refrigerator.

From his sitting position, Baka lightly kicks the boot in Alfredo's hand. "You're clutching that thing like a teddy bear," Baka says. "You didn't want to let the nice shoe rental guy hold on to it?"

"You kidding? I'm not gonna give that high school dropout *both* my boots."

"Aren't you a high school dropout?" Baka says.

"Yeah. And I'd steal somebody's boots."

"He didn't hear me?" Tariq asks Alfredo. Tariq won't even look at Baka. "He didn't hear me ask him for four ounces?"

"Maybe he's trying to offend you," Alfredo says.

Baka smiles as he wags his finger in Alfredo's face. With his free hand he waves over the waitress. She is a big-bottomed, middle-aged Latina. Alfredo's never seen her before, which isn't surprising considering Alfredo's never seen any of the waitresses here more than once. Whitestone Lanes employs one server at a time, converting them into perpetual motion machines, bouncing them from one end of the bowling alley to the other, age accelerating their weary bodies. Alfredo imagines that when this particular waitress came to her job interview she was a long-legged teenaged bombshell—almost as pretty as his Isabel—and she got hired on the spot. That was probably a week ago. Within the hour she'll have gray hair and arthritic knees.

Baka orders a strawberry milk. Pierre gets nothing—he's wandered

off toward the ball rack—and Tariq doesn't get anything either, which surprises Alfredo, considering Tariq didn't eat any dinner. It's like he doesn't even know the waitress is here. As he stares down at his hands, his lips move silently.

"What can I get you, sweetie?" the waitress says, and it takes Alfredo a moment to realize she's talking to him. He orders a beer, and she asks for some ID.

"I'll have a Coke," he says. She slips the nibbled pencil behind her ear and hustles away, toward another party in a different lane.

"So what's the story?" Pierre says. He hugs a giant black ball to his chest, his arms quivering with the effort. "We bowling, or what?"

"I don't think so," Baka says. His voice softens. "I don't know if the big bad Batista brothers have come here to play games."

"Are you serious? I already put everyone's names on the computer!"

"I know," Baka says. "I know. But how about you go and bowl for everyone. Yeah? Take our turns for us. See who wins."

The three of them watch Pierre slink away to the lip of the lane. He spreads his feet wide and cradles the ball between his legs, as if it were an elephantine testicle. He pitches it down the lane, and the ball breaks left, dropping heavily into the gutter. The pins stand erect, unimpressed. Not that Pierre seems to care. He races back to the ball return machine. He scratches his neck as he stares into the machine's black mouth, waiting for it to belch back what's rightfully his.

"We don't need to go through you," Tariq is telling Baka. "If you can't pull down that much weight, we'll go to somebody else. We came to you first as a favor."

"And I'm very, very flattered." Baka pats Tariq's knee. "Nice jeans. Expensive jeans."

"Maybe we've come into some dough," Alfredo says. He lets his eyes drift toward the lockers.

"Great," Baka says. "You can pay me the money you owe me." He squeezes Tariq's shoulder, and Tariq winces under the contact. "What'd you guys do?" Baka says. "Take out an advance on your gambling winnings tonight? That's a bad habit, let me tell you."

"What gambling winnings?" Tariq says.

"The dogfight," Baka says. He sounds surprised. "The party in your honor."

"Right, right," Tariq says. "The party."

"See?" Baka says. "You know everything. You're so fucking smart."

Tariq mutters under his breath, something about insolence or indolence. Something about—Alfredo can't be quite sure about this—rending the earth asunder.

"I'm not so sure the party's still on," Alfredo says.

Baka says, "The Alphabet Brothers—or at least the two that are still alive—they seem to think it's still on." He straightens the cuffs of his tracksuit. "I called them to offer condolences. You called them, right? To pay respects? No? Well that's not very nice, Fredo. Funeral's gonna be at Conway on Northern. Hope to see you there, God willing." He smiles at Tariq. "Or Allah willing, am I right? Anyway, the ABC bros told me they're still coming tonight. Apparently their dog was really Curtis's dog, first and foremost. He was the one who fed it and picked up its shit. So they're putting the pooch in the ring as a tribute to Curtis. I don't really get it. My opinion? I think they're grieving in an unhealthy way. They tell me they've got some aggression to work out."

"What's that supposed to mean?" Alfredo says. "They said that about me?"

Baka's cracked lips smile. "What do you mean?"

Alfredo looks to his brother for help, but Tariq is staring off into space. Alfredo closes his eyes. He needs a quiet room. He needs to crawl into this ball return machine and follow its underground tunnels to the magmatic center of the earth. Once there, he can prop his feet up on some stalagmites and figure this whole thing out.

The waitress puts a beer in Alfredo's hand. Stubborn ice crystals cling to the bottle's neck; the label has already started to peel off. Alfredo takes a long sip. The beer tastes cold and necessary. He wants to thank the woman who brought it, but having already dropped off the check and Baka's strawberry milk, she's disappeared.

"That was nice of her," Alfredo says.

"That *was*," Baka says. He takes the straw out of his milk glass and flicks it onto the ground. "People take a liking to you, Fredo. You ask Pierre what the fuck's wrong with his neck, and he doesn't even get mad. Tries to tell you a story. You steal your brother's girlfriend, knock her up, and he doesn't even look angry. Well, he looks a little angry, but he always looks like that. Oh, he's looking *real* angry now. Yikes. What's the matter? You didn't know about Dito and Isabel? Course you did. You know everything." Baka bends to his milk glass and slurps

pink foam off the top. He tells Alfredo, "That waitress could've lost her job giving you that beer. But she *liked* you for some reason. You've got a way, I guess. Now here I am. About to do you a very, very foolish favor myself. I got you a present, a beautiful snub-nose thirty-eight revolver that'll fit right in your waistband. A beautiful pistol. And you *gotta* take it. I already lost the receipt."

Alfredo never intended to be the kind of person who wants, much less needs, a gun. He looks over at Pierre, who bowls with perfect form: bent forward at the waist, left arm horizontal to his body, right leg tucked, head straight, fingers outstretched. The ball spins down the lane and knocks down all the pins but one. Up on the TV screen, an arrow points to Pierre's name. When bowling for himself, Pierre knocks down nines; when bowling for anyone else, he throws gutters. In a contest in which he's the only participant, Pierre cheats. He's the kind of guy, Alfredo realizes, who'd bring a bat to a fistfight.

"What do I need a gun for?" Alfredo says.

"Why does anyone need a gun? Self-defense!" Baka spreads his legs wide apart, settling into his story. "The kid you put in the hospital yesterday? His brother calls me up. Asks me who I sell drugs to in East Elmhurst. I say, 'Why?' He says, 'I'm looking for two black kids and a Puerto Rican.' I say, 'Jesus, you're kidding. That's everybody.' He says, 'One black kid hits like a motherfucker, the other one wears a Spider-Man hat.' You notice how this guy fixates on the black people? I'd get upset—well, that's not true. I *do* get upset, but what are you gonna do? I tell him one of the kids has gotta be a Hughes brother. And the other one is Winston, no doubt about it. I tell him Winston's Haitian, not African American. But he doesn't care. He wants to know about the Boricuan now. I tell him, 'If Winston was there, the Puerto Rican's gotta be Alfredo Batista. He's a nice guy.' See? I put in a good word for you. Well, maybe I didn't. Who can remember? So then the guy says—"

"This is the chemist we're talking about?"

"Chemist?" Baka says.

"Winston told me the kid's brother was a chemist."

"Winston told you?" Baka says.

Oh God. Winston? Winston thinks the expressions are "nip it in the butt" and "one foul swoop" and "play it by year." He says "eck cetera." He once bet Alfredo money that the arcade prodigy in "Pinball

178

Wizard" is a deaf, dumb, and black kid. He dropped out of high school in the eleventh grade, in the middle of midterms, when he opened up his exam booklet and discovered, with a sunken stomach, that he stayed up the night before studying the wrong subject. He told Alfredo that Boris was a chemist, that there was nothing to worry about, and Alfredo believed him because he wanted to believe him.

"Who," Alfredo asks, "is Vladimir's brother?"

"Mike Shifrin," Baka says triumphantly. "He's a drug dealer."

"I don't know who that is."

"Well, when he woke up yesterday he'd never heard of you either. What a difference a day makes, huh?"

"So call him up," Alfredo says. "Call him up and tell him you won't sell him any more drugs unless he backs off and leaves me alone."

"I don't sell him drugs."

"He's got your logo on his X."

"I got his logo on *my* X," Baka says. "I buy drugs from *him*. Actually, I buy drugs from a guy in Chinatown, and he buys drugs from Mike Shifrin. This guy's a Russian gangster. The real deal boss hog."

"This isn't fair," Alfredo says. He turns to Tariq. "I only hit the kid one time. I was getting the drugs for you. To give to you. I didn't even hit him that hard."

"Where's the gun at?" Tariq says.

"Queensbridge," Baka says. "The Ravenswood Houses. Pierre will drive you there. The both of you. Take you ten, fifteen minutes."

Alfredo peels the label off his beer bottle. "I don't want to go to Queensbridge."

"Oh, don't worry about that," Baka says. A foamy pink mustache lies slithered above his upper lip. "Queensbridge ain't as bad as the rappers make it seem."

"You know where this Shifrin guy lives?" Tariq asks.

"I'll find out. But first things first. Go to Ravenswood and pick up the pistol. Afterwards, Pierre—who's a very responsible driver, by the way—will drive you home. Save you a bus ride." He turns his round, leonine face toward Alfredo. "I don't give a shit that Curtis got merked. He was always too . . . brutish. But you? I *like* you, Fredo. You dance around shit. You crack jokes. You know how to flirt with my ass, which I've always appreciated. Know what I mean?"

Alfredo doesn't know anything. Maybe Pierre will drive him and his

brother to Ravenswood, and they'll park in front of a hydrant and run into the projects, and when the elevators don't work, because they never work, the three of them will take the stairs, and it'll be there, in a stairwell that smells like urine, that Pierre will open up their throats with a box cutter. Or maybe they never even get to the car in the first place. Maybe Pierre kills them in the dimly lit parking lot of White-stone Lanes, and somebody reads about them in the paper and says what Alfredo said when he read about that poor kid from the Bronx: *Oh shit, Whitestone Lanes—I've been there!* Or maybe—who knows?— Baka isn't setting him up. Maybe they really will go get a gun. But that won't have anything to do with Alfredo being likable. If Alfredo kills Mike Shifrin, then a vacancy becomes available, and Baka gets to creep up the drug-dealing ladder. And if that's what Baka wants, then maybe he made all this shit up. Maybe it's just a story he told. *But that can't be right,* Alfredo thinks. Mike Shifrin killing Curtis Hughes and then coming after Alfredo has gotta be true. In a weird way, Alfredo wants it to be true. It confirms his original theory, corresponds exactly to his worldview: there are boogeymen out there, lurking in shadows, plotting attacks.

If he gets killed, Isabel will never ever forgive him.

"What about the money?" Alfredo says. He's torn the beer label to bits. Little white pieces congregate on his T-shirt; the glue sticks to his fingers. "What about the five hundred I owe you? I've got an envelope."

"An envelope," Baka says, smiling.

"Yeah. I got your money in an envelope. Right over there. In one of them lockers. But listen, I'm not gonna give it to you unless you talk to this Shifrin guy. Okay? You gotta talk to this Shifrin guy, because if I get killed, how you gonna get your money, you see what I'm saying?"

"Sunken costs," Baka says. "I just won't send flowers to your funeral."

"But the envelope," Alfredo says.

"What about it?" Baka says. "What am I gonna do with an envelope? My African pen pals don't write back to me anymore. I pay all my bills online. The jerk-offs at the post office, they raise the price of stamps three fucking times a month. An envelope? Please, Fredo. That's the last thing I need. Hey, Pierre, you don't look so good. Too much bowling?"

Pierre has wandered over. Having finished all forty frames, his arm

hangs off his body as if wilted. He steals a big swallow of Baka's straw-berry milk, drinks straight from the glass.

"What about the coke?" Tariq says.

"Ah," Baka says. "The coke." He puts his arm around Tariq's shoul-ders. "Forget about the insulting prices. Insulting prices can be negoti-ated. Forget about the fact that I think your business partner is going to be dead by Monday. I'm sorry. I'm not rooting for it, but come on, let's be real. Forget that I don't even think you *have* the three thousand dollars. Let me be real, my man. I ain't getting you your coke because I think you're going to be back in jail before I turn my fat ass around, and as a general rule I don't sell drugs to gangsters on their way to jail. But hey, listen—thanks for thinking of me. It's always nice to be con-sidered. Now go to that big charitable drug dealer who can get you ounces at seven hundo, and go with my blessing, papi chulo. Thanks for coming down. Sorry you didn't get to bowl. Pierre? Baby? Do me a favor and drive these assholes to Ravenswood."

Pierre lifts the strawberry milk to his mouth, seemingly intending to drain it as payment for his services, when the shadow of a large black bowling ball crosses his face and the glass shatters in his hand. He drops down to his knees. Both hands cover his mouth, as if stifling a terrible secret. Blood seeps through the fingers.

The bowling ball dangles from Tariq's hand. A small cut has opened up underneath his eye, where a shard of glass must have ricocheted and caught him in the face. The red blood trembles. Tariq drops the bowling ball—it crushes the straw Baka flicked away earlier—and dabs at his cut with the tip of his pinky.

Pierre's cries are muffled, unintelligible. It's possible his lips have come loose from his face. Alfredo turns away, looks instead at the air vent on the ball return machine. He passes his hand over the slats. The air feels nice, but he wishes it was cooler.

"What are you gonna do now?" Baka says. He sounds as exhausted as his mother must have sounded when she came home from a double shift and found her house a mess, the vases broken, rugs trampled, her only son covered in infield mud. Still sitting in his big leather booth, he hasn't even made a move to help Pierre. "Where you think you gonna hide?"

Tariq pushes his face close to Baka, and the big man flinches. The Cushing's may have damaged his fight-or-flight response, but appar-

ently his body can still react instinctively when faced with a more dangerous predator. Tariq's mouth hangs open. His eyes are gleaming. He waits for Baka to say something else—but for once, he stays quiet. With a disappointed hitch in his shoulders, Tariq walks away.

Alfredo chases after him, just as, it seems, he's always chased after him. They pass lanes full of people. They pass the shoe rental guy, who has no problem making eye contact now. With a phone pressed to his ear, he glares at them, as if memorizing their eye color, their heights, their distinguishing characteristics. Alfredo glares back. He doesn't care about this guy—it's only the waitress he wants to avoid. He'd hate for her to regret her kindness toward him.

As soon as they get outside, Alfredo realizes he left his Timberlands behind. In these red and tan bowling shoes, he feels pounds and pounds lighter. He feels faster. And a good thing, too. Tariq dashes through the parking lot, his prison-built chest hardly heaving, and Alfredo struggles to keep up. While he runs, he peers into the windows of parked cars. He doesn't know what Mike Shifrin looks like, but he imagines an older version of Vladimir, a pale white face, a round head, a bottle of expensive vodka in the passenger seat.

"Hurry up," Tariq says.

When they reach the sidewalk, Alfredo feels as if he's burst through a forest, through dark trees and into a clearing. The lights are brighter. Tariq raises his arm, and the air all around him feels charged, pregnant with the threat of rain. Across the street, a squirrel runs by with half a hot dog bun in its mouth.

"Come *on*," Tariq says. A gypsy cab has pulled over to the curb and it sits palsied at Tariq's feet like a giant nervous panther. "Let's go. Get in."

"What are we gonna do?" Alfredo whispers.

"I don't know," Tariq says. He slaps Alfredo hard between the shoulder blades. "But I'm sure you'll figure something out."

The brothers slide into the backseat. Over a dashboard-mounted walkie-talkie, a faraway dispatcher barks orders in a crackly, unintelligible Spanish. Or at least it sounds like Spanish, which is odd considering the driver has a turban wrapped around his head. Scented cardboard Christmas trees—each of them arctic blue—hang from the rearview mirror. They've all got the plastic wrappers still on them, some of these wrappers barely opened, others dangling from midtier

branches, as if the scented trees were exotic women in various states of undress.

"Where to?" the driver says.

Alfredo wonders if this guy is the father of the two little Indian girls in the park yesterday, the ones who walked with a swagger and had Mister Softee's schedule memorized. Alfredo tells the driver Jackson Heights, looking for some thrill of homecoming in the man's eyes. The cab takes off into the street.

"You thought Baka was setting us up?" Alfredo says.

"I don't know. But if he didn't want to fuck you up before, he'll want to fuck you up now."

"Oh great. Thanks."

"You're welcome," Tariq says. He reaches over and picks off the beer-label bits stuck to Alfredo's shirt. "It's important to know who your enemies are, Dito. If this Shifrin dude's big-time, you'll want him to act soon, while he's still mad enough to come solo. And now you know Baka will bring him to you."

"He doesn't know where we live," Alfredo says.

"But he knows where you'll be tonight, yeah?"

The cab lurches down the Whitestone Expressway. With the Mets game long over, traffic is only half bad. Up ahead a smattering of bleary red brake lights are glowing. The driver speeds up, cuts off a rival yellow cab, and both men lean into their horns.

Alfredo puts the E-beeper in his brother's hands. He tells Tariq that when you slide off the top, rows of pills suddenly materialize. *Welcome home*, Alfredo says without actually saying it. *Welcome home. This is my present to you.*

"How much does this sell for?" Tariq says.

Alfredo rounds up: "Fifteen hundo."

"That ain't enough," Tariq says and shoves the beeper into his pocket.

Alfredo doesn't know what he expected, but, well—he thought he might feel relief to relinquish an object that's brought him only bad luck. Or he thought he might take a gift giver's satisfaction in bestowing a present. At the very least, he looked forward to demonstrating the beeper's ingenuity, and by extension his own ingenuity in figuring it out. With all these pleasures denied to him, Alfredo stares out his window. There are two stickers stuck to the glass, one with the name of

the cab company, Mexicana, and the other with a warning: For Your Own Safety You Are Being Videotaped. Alfredo cracks the window open, lets the air outside toughen his face.

The Department of Worry crams his pneumatic tubes with questions. Fifteen hundred dollars ain't enough for what? If Alfredo is killed, will the mere sight of his dry-bristled toothbrush in the bathroom send Isabel into hysterics? Who will get rid of the tighty-whities under the sofa? The department comes up with many possible afterlives, but the one most frequently imagined is a small room without windows or doors, a black box where darkness fills your mouth like sand. Or maybe he gets to stay on as a ghost. He wonders if, years from now, he'll be hovering in the corner of a dorm room on the night Christian Louis gets too wasted and confesses to his roommates that all he has of his father are a couple of stories his mother told him and a few cheap Happy Meal toys he collected.

Alfredo turns to his brother, to ask him about the Muslim conception of the afterlife, but Tariq's eyes are closed. His breathing has deepened. Air whistles out his nose. Alfredo doesn't even know how this is possible. Less than five minutes ago, Tariq smashed a milk glass into Pierre's face, officially turning Baka against Alfredo. And now? Now his head sags into his chest. While Alfredo panics, while his stomach acid gurgles, Tariq catches up on some Z's.

"You're asleep?" When his brother doesn't answer, Alfredo says, "You gotta be fucking kidding me."

He wants to go home. He wants to fall into Isabel's arms and catch up on some Z's himself, sleep till all the world's vendettas are forgotten, till the ozone layer disappears and the earth explodes. Of course, at some point during that snooze, Izzy's water will break and Christian Louis will insist on his debut. But until then . . . Alfredo asks the driver if he can maybe go a little faster. I'm in a bit of a rush, Alfredo explains. The driver grips the wheel with both hands. He leans forward, his eyes framed in the rearview mirror. Alfredo isn't sure if he's somehow offended the man, or maybe he hasn't been heard. He's about to repeat himself when the car's sudden, extra acceleration throws him against the back of his seat. Wind howls into the cab, over the top of Alfredo's cracked-open window. With the exception of the ghetto car, Alfredo's never driven in his life, never had to worry about staying in his lane or keeping his eye on the road, and so, when in a car passing other cars,

he is free to stare out his window at all the people in all those other cars, who always seem to be moving backward, getting sucked into the past. He likes to catch them in some sealed-off moment of privacy— picking their noses, bobbing their heads to songs he can't hear. But when Alfredo looks out his window now, he can't see anyone clearly. Just a few blurry figures stooped behind a few blurry wheels. The cab is moving way too fast. With yet one more pleasure denied to him, Alfredo turns to his brother, who's still sleeping. A snore ripples out from the bottom of his throat. *What a bunch of bullshit*, Alfredo thinks. He picks at the stickers stuck to his window. *Videotaped? For my safety?* It doesn't even make sense, and Alfredo is starting to get a little tired, a little skeptical, of all these people claiming they got his best interests in mind.

By busting up Pierre, Tariq turned potential allies into definite ene- mies. *You're welcome,* he said. *It's important to know who your enemies are.* He provoked Baka so that he'll crash the dogfight and bring Mike Shifrin with him. *Here, tie this bull's-eye round your neck. Now you'll know for sure which way the bullets will be zinging.*

Alfredo realizes he's working with two possibilities here. Either his brother is a fool with a poorly conceived plan, or his brother is both smarter and more dangerous than he anticipated. Alfredo wishes he could come up with some rival explanations. Maybe if he were sit- ting someplace dark and quiet and isolated, where headaches aren't invited, he'd be able to think of something else, but right now this is all he's got: Tariq's plan only makes sense if its intent is not to protect Alfredo, but to nudge him into the crosshairs.

Alfredo—who constantly fights back exhaustion, whose job keeps him up nights, whose filing cabinet keeps him up past that, who gets three or four hours before the sun shoots through the blinds, before Isabel wakes him up for a prenatal appointment, before his father wakes him up for a favor, before his mother wakes him up with a grievance, before Winston wakes him up with a request to meet him at the park—watches Tariq sleep the sleep of the wicked. His eyes remain shut and his lips parted. With his head tucked into his chest, a small indent is made visible at the base of his neck. A little recess, deep enough for a thimbleful of water. A soft and familiar pocket. If given one thousand photographs of the backs of one thousand necks, Alfredo would be able to pick out his brother's every single time. The

skin around the indent seems to swell with pride. Red tiny bumps—presumably from the teeth of a barber's razor—encircle it, encroaching upon it dangerously.

"You know," Alfredo says out loud, "I'm not so sure you're as dumb as you seem."

Tariq's eyes snap open. Without emotion, as if reading lines off a cue card, he says, "We ain't never backed down from thugs and bitches. And you ain't gonna start now."

"Right," Alfredo says.

Contrary to street gossip, Alfredo never dropped a dime on the Virgil's robbers. Why would he have? To get rid of his brother? To get closer to Isabel? Come on! Before Tariq went upstate, Alfredo hardly even knew Isabel. He'd seen her around, of course, poised on the brick incline of the handball courts like some kind of talent scout, buying movie magazines at Max's candy store, gently stripping away the aluminum foil on a gyro as she waited for the traffic light to turn green, standing behind the blue police barricade at the Sunnyside Puerto Rican parade—but these moments only became charged by hindsight, reassembled *after* they'd fallen in love. Prior to Tariq's incarceration, Alfredo and Isabel had never even spoken, other than half-muttered hellos when they passed each other in the street. She was his brother's girlfriend. What could they possibly have to talk about? Besides, her physical appearance elicited a feeling previously unfamiliar to Alfredo: she made him feel shy.

And then, late one night, a month into Tariq's Fishkill sentence, she appeared, trudging through snow toward the candy store, toward Winston and Alfredo. She wore boots and mittens and a bubble jacket zipped up to her chin. A scarf completely covered the lower half of her face, and it seemed to Alfredo that this wasn't only protection from the cold, but a kind of disguise, as if she preferred to wander the streets incognito. But who could she fool? The eyes above that scarf could only be Isabel's. Her hair, exposed and dark, glittered with snowflakes.

Winston and Alfredo stood together under Max's red and gold awning. According to procedure, Winston should've been across the street, guarding the stash, but it was too cold a night to be all alone in the Alleyway, too cold to be outside at all, selling drugs *or* buying them. And yet there they were, in matching wool knit caps that Alfredo

had bought for them. They stomped their feet and breathed out smoke and watched Isabel come toward them through the snow.

She said something—it sounded like *hzgnoe*—and both Winston and Alfredo leaned forward and asked her to repeat herself. With obvious reluctance she pulled the scarf away from her mouth. What she had said, she explained, was hello.

"Oh," Alfredo said. "Hello."

"Hello," she said again. "I don't think we've met," she told Winston, as she extended her hand toward him. "I'm Isabel."

"Oh, I know that," he said. He grabbed her hand, not shaking it, just holding it, and while Alfredo looked on, frantically flipping through his conversational Rolodex, Winston *continued* to hold on to her hand, obviously reluctant to give it back. Tremendously stoned, he dropped his voice to a Casanova bass and said, "Let's stay like this forever."

"Sure is cold!" Alfredo said. It was the best he could do.

"It is," she said, pulling her hand free. "It is unbelievably cold."

"Freezing!" Alfredo said.

Winston tapped the bridge of his nose. "When it gets cold like this?" he said. "Oh my God, my nose hairs go buck wild. I can feel like each little hair up there. It's like they've gone stiff. Like they've turned into icicles. It weirds me out, but at the same time I kinda like it. This ever happen to you?"

"So," Isabel said, turning to Alfredo. "You talk to your brother lately?"

Ah. The reason for her visit. Alfredo had been worried she'd heard the neighborhood rumors and had come down here to jab her finger into his chest, to accuse him of doing her man dirty for financial gain. And so when it became clear that she only wanted to pump Alfredo for some Jose-related info, he felt relieved, although it was a relief tinged with disappointment. In the subsequent years, he's tried to pinpoint the source of that disappointment, and the safest explanation he can come up with is who the hell would want to talk to a beautiful woman about some other man? But that's what he did. He told Isabel that his mother had gone up to Fishkill, took the train and everything, but Jose asked her never to come back. Alfredo didn't describe Lizette's reaction to this, that when she got home she locked herself in the bathroom, nor did he share with Isabel his own reaction, that he thought it

selfish, not to mention cruel, but that he was, as always, trying to extend to Jose the benefit of the doubt, that maybe his brother was embarrassed and didn't want their mother seeing him behind Plexiglas, in those orange jumpsuits or whatever they've got on up there.

"Have *you* heard from him?" he asked her, although her presence here made it obvious that she had not.

"My mother the puta did something to our phone," she said. "It can't get collect calls or something."

"That sucks," Alfredo said.

"Yeah, right? It won't even give you the *option* of accepting collect calls. So like if he's trying to get ahold of me, I wouldn't even know."

"Was he trying to call you before your mother fucked with the phone?" When she didn't answer, Alfredo knew he should probably stay quiet, but he's always had trouble keeping his mouth shut, just as he's always had trouble resisting the urge to press his fingertips against walls with wet paint signs. "He's sent you some letters though, right?"

Her face darkened. "Jose didn't talk about you much," she said. "The only thing I remember him telling me is a story about how your father took you two on the subway for a funeral scam. And you started crying real bad."

"Oh yeah, you didn't know? I'm a real wuss."

"Getting colder out here," Winston said. He jerked a thumb over his shoulder toward the candy store. "I think I'm going to go inside. Where it's warmer? And, you know—"

"Less awkward?" Isabel said.

"Exactly."

Before the door closed shut behind him, a little heat from inside the store trickled out onto the sidewalk. A sign—ATM Available Inside—hung off the awning, and Alfredo slapped at it to give his hand something to do.

"I should probably get going," she said.

"I'll walk you home."

"And disappoint all your customers?" she said, laughing. "No, that's okay. I live right up the block."

"My father tells me that like fifty percent of your body heat comes off the top of your head. I don't know if it's true or not. But you know. That's what I've been told," and he handed her his wool knit cap.

188

Maybe 50 percent was an overestimate, a typical Jose Sr. exaggeration, but *man:* without his hat, Alfredo felt his body heat plummet. And he wasn't going to get any warmer either. Isabel looked at the cap in her hands as if it embarrassed her, and Alfredo's ears turned red, thinking he'd done something else he shouldn't have done. Later, he'd find out that she simply didn't have much experience receiving small kindnesses. "You don't have to take it," he said. "If you don't want to."

She dipped her nose to the wool and gave it a whiff. "You don't smell alike," she said. "You and your brother."

"No?"

"No. You're a little bit funkier." She slipped the cap over her head. It fit so snugly that she seemed to have a little difficulty tucking her ears under the wool. She smiled. As if she were at the supermarket, in the produce section, prodding a melon, she brought her mittened hands to his temples and gave him a squeeze. "You've got a really small head," she told him.

"Thank you."

"Sorry," she said, still smiling, looking not sorry at all.

She walked away from him, toward home, through the sidewalk's thin blanket of snow. She stepped in the footprints she'd made coming here, as if she were playing a game, or as if she wanted to leave behind as little evidence of herself as possible. When she got to the end of the block, she turned around and waved, and Alfredo's hand—without his permission, acting on its own—went up in the air and waved back.

The following night temperatures had dropped even further, and once again—procedure be damned—Winston refused to sit by himself in the Alleyway. If he was going to freeze to death, he at least wanted some company, someone he could talk to through their respective blocks of ice. And so he and Alfredo were together, in the exact same spot (outside the bodega), doing the exact same thing (selling drugs to nonexistent customers), when Isabel came around the corner again.

Under his breath, Winston said, "Don't do anything I wouldn't do." And then he disappeared. The bastard. Alfredo tried to grab him—*come on!*—but Winston wiggled away, hid himself inside the candy store. Abandoned, Alfredo watched Isabel approach.

From a distance of three or four feet, she tossed him his hat, which he fumbled, too eager as always. When he stooped to pick it up, he saw

that the cap looked cleaner, brighter, as if the time spent on Isabel's head had been restorative, a much-needed vacation.

As she had done the previous night, he brought the hat to his nose and gave it a whiff. "You washed it," he said.

"I just smell like that, actually."

"Really?"

"Nah, I washed it." Like Alfredo, she seemed to have a tendency to laugh at her own jokes. "Thanks for letting me borrow it," she said. "It was really nice of you. *Really* nice."

"Well, when I offered it to you I didn't think you were actually going to take it."

Instead of laughing like she was supposed to—it wasn't *her* joke, after all—she asked Alfredo if he liked dioramas, and Alfredo responded, naturally, by asking, "Dioramas?"

"I'm going to the Museum of Natural History tomorrow," she said. "In Manhattan? They've got these huge dioramas with antelopes and cavemen. Stuff like that. They got dinosaurs, too. The bones. I don't know. I thought if you like that kind of thing, you'd maybe wanna come with me."

"You have a boyfriend," he said.

"I'm not asking you out on a date, you dick." She pulled the hat out of his hands and put it on her head. "Don't you have any like female *friends*?"

"No."

He didn't really understand why she'd want to hang out with him—he still doesn't—but what he told himself at the time was that despite his slight edge in the funkiness department, he reminded her of Jose. That's all. With her boyfriend locked up, she settled for palling around with the next best thing: his little bro. The comparison flattered Alfredo. And the idea of a female friend actually sounded kind of nice. Maybe she'd help him pick out more flattering pairs of jeans, maybe she'd drag him out of the borough every now and again for some culture and shit, foreign films and art openings and diorama museums and opera boxes with them little mini binoculars on a stick.

Early the next morning, he picked her up at her place, and together they rode the E train, then the C, to Eighty-first Street. They wandered through the Museum of Natural History until he complained of

sore feet—*big wuss, remember?*—and then they ate bowls of chicken noodle soup in the fourth-floor cafeteria, where between slurps they agreed that the very best thing they saw that day was a ninety-four-foot-long replica of a blue whale, suspended from ceiling wires in the Hall of Ocean Life. They imagined what it would be like to be swimming next to one of those blubbery monsters, with its mouth gaping open, threatening to swallow them whole.

Over the next couple of weeks, with increasing frequency, Isabel and Alfredo went back into Manhattan, which seemed so very far away. They went everywhere. To Times Square and Union Square, Chelsea, Bryant Park, that roller rink the Guggenheim. They got hot chocolate at City Bakery. They sat in the lobby of the Pierre Hotel, where they pretended they were waiting for some glamorous friend. They went to FAO Schwarz, so Isabel could dance on the giant floor piano like Tom Hanks in *Big*, but the line was too long so they walked through Central Park instead. She even brought him to the video store where she worked, although they didn't go inside because what was there to see? On their first few expeditions they talked about Jose, and when they weren't doing that they tried to out-funny each other, top each other's jokes—but eventually, as Alfredo and Isabel grew more comfortable, those impulses faded. He told her about his considerable collection of phobias, and she told him about her history with her mother the puta and Raul the Cubano. When they discussed the future they agreed that they both felt ready for the ground to shudder under their feet, for life to bring them something different, some kind of dramatic upheaval, not yet realizing that this was their something different, their dramatic upheaval.

On a Saturday night in late February, Isabel and Alfredo—as friends, as friends!—went to Greenwich Village, where he'd made reservations at an impressively schmancy jazz club. For an hour and a half they sat in mandatory silence, drank seven-dollar screwdrivers (at least no one carded them), and listened to the supposedly world-famous Darren Gelato Trio. It was incredibly boring. At intermission, with the check on their table, Isabel pulled Alfredo outside for a cigarette. *You smoke?* he asked. *Not exactly,* she told him. Searching her purse for a phantom pack of cigarettes, she led Alfredo past the bouncers, ambled to the end of the block, turned the corner, and ran.

Alfredo chased after her. She'd never run out on a check before, not once, never done anything like it in her whole entire life. Drunk on adrenaline, she flew down the sidewalk. Tightness spread through Alfredo's chest. He heard the buzzing in his ears. Four vodka OJs and ninety minutes of jazz—all of it stolen. He knew that if he kept running, he'd collapse, right there on Sixth Avenue. "Hold on," he said, clutching her coat.

She turned around, steeled herself with a quick breath, and leaned toward him, her mouth parting softly. He thought she was trying to tell him something. So as to hear her better, he turned his ear to her face and she missed his lips, kissed him accidentally at the corner of his mouth. Miserably embarrassed, he tried to explain. *I thought you had something to tell me. I thought you were saying something!* She asked him to please stop squirming. She grabbed his chin and kissed him again—thank God—caught him this time flush on the mouth. When she pulled away, her eyes were wide open. She blushed, because it was her turn to be embarrassed.

"I'm sorry," she said. "It's just that, oh I don't know. I'm sorry. Is that okay? It's just that I *wanted* to, I guess. Is that okay? What I just did?"

He looked down to see his hands on her hips. His mind stammered. He pulled her toward him and together they fell backward against the fence of the West Fourth Street basketball courts. The chain links caught them, kept them up on their feet. She straightened the glasses on his face. Then she kissed him again, kissed his mouth, kissed his neck, slipped her thigh between his legs. Because she wanted to. He slid his hand into her coat sleeve, to feel the warmth of her skin. She laughed. She was wearing his wool cap, and he pulled it down over her eyes—confirmation, she later told him, that he was the right man for her. He felt calm. He felt happy as her kisses traveled up the side of his neck. Around the corner from the jazz club, only a few yards away from the mountainous bouncers, with that unpaid check still on the table, Isabel brought her mouth to Alfredo's ear and whispered, "What if we get caught?"

So there you go. Alfredo didn't initiate that first kiss and he never sold out his brother to the police, but he's initiated countless kisses since, and as he sits next to Tariq in the backseat of this cab, Alfredo decides

that he's going to sell him out tonight. Didn't drop any dimes two and a half years ago, but he's going to drop one now.

"Listen," he says, as the cab speeds toward the Northern Boulevard exit. "I got some shit to take care of. You mind if I drop you off at home?"

Tariq stares straight ahead, still and quiet, with his hands folded peacefully in his lap. Alfredo doesn't know how to read that. He hates the idea of leaving his brother in the same apartment as Isabel, but it's not like they'll be alone—both Mama and Papi will be there—and besides, you can't rat someone out while they're hanging off your elbow. Right? Since Tariq converted potential allies Baka and Pierre into definite enemies, then Alfredo—who feels as if he's gotten along just fine in this life doing whatever his brother wouldn't do—needs to convert some potential enemies into definite allies. Needs to invite some cruel motherfuckers of his own: the police. He plans to go down to the Dunkin' Donuts on Seventieth and Northern and wait for the Anti-Crime cops to show up, as they do every night, two or three times a shift. He'll ask them if they'd like to crash a dogfight. If they'd like to put their cuffs on his brother, the ex-con, the man on parole.

The cab exits the expressway and accelerates through Corona. With a string of green lights ahead, Alfredo and Tariq are getting closer to Jackson Heights, closer to home. Outside the window, the Langston Hughes Library gives way to a liquor store, which gives way to an Argentinean steakhouse, which gives way to a parking meter with a red canvas bag wrapped around its face.

Alfredo feels itchy all over, and he wonders if he's caught the poison ivy, or if this is just his mind attacking his body.

"You'll be okay?" he asks. "With getting dropped off at home?"

Tariq continues to stare straight ahead. "Where *you* going?" he asks.

"I gotta grab a cup of coffee with somebody," Alfredo says, which is both a lie and not a lie, one of his specialties. "I'm gonna be mad quick." He reaches over and taps the face of Tariq's digital watch. Alfredo wants this emphasized. How fast he's going to be. "Back before you know it," he says.

"You think you can fool me?" Tariq says. "Coffee?" His grin extends into the scar on his cheek so that it becomes one long lopsided smile. "You got a girl, Dito? A little something on the side?"

"See?" Alfredo says, scratching his neck. "That's what I'm talking

about. Right there. Maybe you didn't hear me before, because you were sleeping and all that. But I was saying that I didn't think you were as dumb as you seem. And now lookit: you got me nailed."

"You are, aren't you? You're going to see a girl. You little shit." He laughs. "I'm not as dumb as I seem, huh? You know what, Dito? I'm not so sure that's a compliment."

"It's comments like that," Alfredo says, "that prove my point exactly."

11

The Door Factory

Tariq knows that in a certain kind of book—not the Book, of course, but a pretend book, a make-believe book—a man in his spot would have to deal with moats and drawbridges and arrows and catapulted boulders and cauldrons of black tar and devils and demons and dragons and dwarves and bearded ogres and trickster brothers and who knows what else. This man, the hero of that make-believe book, would be standing out in the open air, just as Tariq is standing out in the open air, and he would look upon a large fortress-like structure, just as Tariq is looking up at his parents' apartment building, and blood would rush to the crown of that hero's head, just as Tariq's blood rushes, surges, leaving him dizzied. When the cab dropped him off, his brother gave him a set of house keys and told him, again, that he'd be right back. Sure, sure. Right back. See you in a jiff. These keys weigh heavy in his hand. The building pulls him toward it.

Not yet. Be patient. There are still moves to be made.

He walks down to a corner of Northern Boulevard previously populated with newspaper machines, all of them lined up like a squat robot army. Not anymore. People were apparently paying for one paper, opening the latch, and thieving them all. Just cause they could. And so

publishers, mindful of profits, took their machines off the corner. Besides the stench of garbage, the only thing left here are the free papers: the penny-savers, the *Queens Tribune,* the *Queens Gazette,* the job-hunting circulars. It doesn't look like a robot army no more. It looks like a bunch of cheap plastic row houses, with all the tenants inside calling out to Tariq desperately. *Take one! Grab one! Free! Free!!*

He goes to the end of the line, to a little green house with little attic windows jutting out of its roof. The door swings up. He finds inside two neat stacks of paperback books, which are all the same issue of *Apartment Finder,* June 2002. A sticker on the inside of the house— he's shoved his head all the way in, drawn by the plastic smell—says Warning: Destruction of This Property Will Result in Civil Fine or Imprisonment.

Okay, whatever. He sticks one of the books in his back pocket, where it crinkles his parole paperwork. He'd like to take all the books and toss them down the gutter, to disadvantage the apartment-hunting competition, but these little green houses are probably all over Queens. To make a significant dent, he'd have to go to each and every one, and really—who's got that kind of time?

Eight hours since Tariq bolted that Charleston Chew in the Macy's dressing room, and since then he's had nothing to eat. No pizza at Gianni's, none of Mama's spicy chicken, not even a burger at White-stone Lanes. And now it seems too late. He's missed out on his chance. While incarcerated, he'd often stay up two nights in a row, reading in the sliver with his cheek against the bars, and on the third night, although bone-tired, he'd feel too jittered for sleep. He feels like that now. Too hungry to eat. Standing outside the Laundromat, across from Papi's old store, Tariq wonders if his stomach has left him, trans-planted itself into one of the bodies nearby, into the Chinese delivery-man who pedals past him, reeking of lo mein, or maybe into any one of the ants at his feet, disappearing down a sandy hole between side-walk panels.

This is as it should be. The straight path is paved with hunger. Muhammad, peace be upon Him, fasted in the caves of Mount Hira and returned home the Prophet. Deprived of food himself, Tariq feels only a pulsing pain behind his eyeballs, and although he can live with

pain—and with scars on his face and specks of glass under his eye, and with betrayal and insult and disrespect, and with backbiters and maligners and jinn-possessed demons—he worries that this dull hunger will prevent his thoughts from proceeding in orderly ranks.

The sign on the Laundromat's door reads Change Is for Customers Only and it takes Tariq too long to understand they mean change as in quarters and dimes. As if embarrassed for him, his stomach grumbles noisily. Inside the Laundromat, a bald-headed black guy, one of those customers with the right to receive change, looks up at Tariq pushing through the door. The guy sits in a chair next to a washing machine, with his feet rudely propped up on another chair. He's working on a laptop. A real pro—his mother must be awfully proud, Tariq thinks—he doesn't need to look down when he types. Allowing him to stare at Tariq. And why? Because of these pathetic Converses? Because Tariq's walked in here without a laundry basket? Meanwhile, these Rocawear jeans alone cost ten times more than everything this black guy's wearing put together. And yet, unable to help himself, unable to summon the requisite pride, Tariq punks out and looks down at the floor. He doesn't know why. He feels an uncomfortable tingling, the same tingling one of them ants must feel when crouched under a magnifying glass.

Still tingling, he hurries over to the magazine rack, where he grabs a circular called *Rentals*, a circular called *Rent 411*, and, thickest of all, a circular called *The Real Estate Book*. He feels the guy's eyes on the back of his head. He hears his fingers striking the keyboard. He punishes that laptop, as if he were writing down everything Tariq's doing, narrating all of his movements.

When Tariq stops, the man stops, and he doesn't start typing again until Tariq walks past him, carrying the three rental magazines over to the bulletin board. Because everyone in this Laundromat conspires to annoy him, a fat Ecuadorian woman sits directly under the board. The TV above the dryers plays a telenovela, which the woman watches with her mouth hanging open and with her fingers absently worrying the beads of her necklace. Tariq has to lean over her—his crotch inches from her ear—in order to read the business cards thumbtacked to the board. Psychics next to personal injury lawyers next to massage specialists next to computer repairmen. A homemade flyer advertises babysitting services. The nanny's phone number is repeated on little

strips of paper, which dangle off the flyer like piano keys. Another flyer offers a reward for a lost dog, a floppy-eared beagle. Tariq leans over farther, brings his face closer to the cork of the board. *Classic 2 Bdrm for Rent.* Now we're talking. A two-bedroom is exactly what he's looking for—it'd be nice to have an office for his studies, with a little sewing machine set up in the corner for Isabel—but he doesn't take the flyer's dangling piano key because he knows "classic" is just a fancier word for old.

More apartment listings hang off the board, but in order to see them he'd have to sit on this woman's head. The guy stops typing. Waits for Tariq to make the next move. With all these dryers going, with all this static electricity in the air, the Laundromat smells like the first few minutes after a lightning storm. Tariq clears his throat to see if the guy will start typing again, maybe even write that down—*The monster clears his throat*—but instead the woman looks up at him. She flinches when she sees him leaning over her. He never meant to frighten her, but come on lady, who asked you to sit directly under the fucking bulletin board? Now that he's here, now that she's staring at his scar, he has to do *something* to justify his presence and so he reaches out blindly and rips a random piano key off the bulletin board. He's still muttering apologies when the Laundromat door closes behind him.

Because the frustration never ends, the crumpled piano key in his fist turns out to have nothing at all to do with apartment rentals. It says,

Meth Study
Queens College

Under that it asks him to call a 718 telephone number. Yeah right. He tears it up and chucks the bits of paper into the street.

He knows exactly where he is—he's escorted his mother to this Laundromat thousands of times; he used to *live* in that bodega right across the street—and yet he feels lost, as if he's only been told about this place, as if all his memories belong to somebody else. Apparently he exudes this confusion. A homeless man hustles over, eager to pounce.

Normally an expert at identifying the ethnicities of other men—

credit Queens, credit prison—Tariq can't tell if this guy is Indian or Pakistani or Bangladeshi or something else altogether. Despite the heat, the man wears a thick sweatshirt, as gray and dirty as his beard. Powerful drugs, or withdrawal from powerful drugs, cause his left leg to tremble. Head bowed, he asks for some spare change.

"Haven't you heard?" Tariq says. "Change is for customers only."

"What?"

Tariq reminds himself, not for the first time, that he should leave the joke-telling to others. He rolls up all the rental magazines, and the man takes a step backward, as if he were a spider about to be swatted. Tariq shoves the magazines into his back pocket. Both pockets are embarrassingly full now, a pair of unsightly bulges stretching out his Rocawear jeans. He expects the homeless guy to make some sort of crack, call him a peckerwood or something, and when he doesn't, Tariq gives him his last three dollars.

"Good luck, my brother," Tariq says happily, for as everyone knows the upper hand is better than the lower hand. "Peace be upon you."

Rather than dwell any further on his own benevolence, he walks away from the man and all of his thank-yous. It feels good to be moving. Up in the sky, the sun's purple light still lingers. Things are as they should be. Having given that man the last of his money, Tariq feels as if he's reclaimed his neighborhood. He could stroll through these streets indefinitely, humming a wordless tune, his hands in his pockets, but the Casio F-91W tells him he better hurry up. Let's see a little urgency in that gait. You're losing time you can never get back. Or as the Book says:

The Hour has come and split is the moon.

He breaks out into a jog. Keeps his head down, watches sidewalk panels disappear beneath his feet. Watch out, people! Get out the way! It felt good to be moving, but my oh my, it feels even better to run.

Three deadbolts protect his parents' door. He tries a square key, but it won't fit in any of the locks. He tries a different square key. He tries squat keys and round keys and skinny keys, but none of them fit, no matter how hard he pushes. Desperate, he tries a mailbox key. His

heart quickens when an extra-long key fits into the middle lock, but of course of course of *course* that key refuses to turn. He tries an eye-balled comparison between the teeth of the keys and the mouths of the locks, but it's hopeless, he can't see that well and the hallway lights are dim and there are just too many fucking keys, a massive jumble of keys, a janitor's wet dream of keys, keys his brother probably found on the street and stuck in his pocket, keys to their old apartment behind Papi's bodega, keys that lack any known function, unlocking doors that probably don't even exist anymore. This is just like him, Tariq thinks. His brother keeps keys past their usefulness because he wants to seem like a *romantic,* a man who stays up all night blinking back nostalgia. A thick metal hoop spears the keys, and dangling off that hoop is a cheap plastic bottle opener. The engraving on that cheap plastic bottle opener reads World's Greatest Dad.

Halfway through, Tariq loses track of which keys he's tried and which ones he hasn't, and so he has to start over. Black spots of mildew blemish the walls. One more thing that up in Fishkill, dreaming of his return, he failed to imagine.

The possibility occurs to him that no matter how badly he wants them to, none of these keys will open any of these locks. His brother may have intentionally given him a fake set as a joke, an attempt to humiliate him, to have him impotently scratching at locks, to make him ring the bell or knock on the door like an outsider, a Jehovah's Witness or a traveling salesman, a man with his hat in his hand and his dick tucked between his legs.

On the other side of the door, the TV plays loudly. Tariq thinks he hears laughter. And not the TV laughter of a simulated studio audience, but real laughter from real people *inside the living room.* Breathless, he presses his face to the door. His dog is whimpering, and yes, someone inside is definitely laughing. Truly right here, home and yet not home, he feels closing in upon him painful torment: fetters and fire and food that chokes. He bends one of the keys in half, which isn't easy, which leaves a ridged imprint on the meat of his thumb. Hands shaking, he reaches inside of himself, grabs hold of the Book:

Your Lord has neither left you, nor despises you. What is to come is better for you than what has gone before; for your Lord will certainly give you, and you will be content. Did He not find you an

orphan and take care of you? Did He not find you perplexed, and
show you the way? Did He not find you poor and enrich you?

So of course there are locks. Of course there are obstacles. Tariq knows
he's been put on a straight path, but not necessarily an easy one. With
the steady, guiding hand of Allah, the Most Merciful, the Most Com-
passionate, he tries again, one by one, and this time into the right locks
he drives the right keys. Orphans, all of them, they slide into their
chambers with the ripple of homecoming.

When he walks into the apartment, Isabel and Papi turn their plastic, mock-innocent faces toward him. They sit close to each other:
Isabel on the sofa with her feet tucked under her thighs, and Papi in
his wheelchair with a blanket covering his lap. Between them, on the
floor, sits an air mattress, shiny and inflated and looking as if it would
be easily punctured. Get this: Papi turns away from Tariq and directs
his attention back to the television. Apparently Tariq's return to this
apartment has become another boring, taken-for-granted, humdrum
affair. Apparently he can't compete with the TV screen, where a white
woman, her voice unnaturally amplified, shills September 11 com-
memorative coins: *We will never forget. Proud to be an American. A*
necessary addition to any patriotic collection.

At least the dog welcomes him. Still chained to the leg of the sofa, he
lunges to get at Tariq, and every time he lunges he gags on the spikes of
his pinch collar. Determined, smart, quick to adapt, he abandons the
lunging and instead takes small steps, one paw after another, with the
history of his breed defined in the muscles of his neck. The sofa inches
forward. He's dragging it across the carpet, and Isabel, who had been
sitting Indian-style on the cushions, sends her feet to the floor. The
dog leans into his collar. If Isabel stood up, the sofa would surely shoot
toward Tariq, but if she continues to sit, with her feet rooted to the
ground—and no reason to think that she won't—the dog will strangle
himself. This is a train for which Isabel's already paid her fare. This is a
test between her and the dog, and Tariq watches impassively, not
knowing whom to root for. The dog's legs are shaking. His tongue falls
out of his mouth.

"Where's Alfredo?" Isabel says. "Is he okay? Did something happen
to him?"

Despite his struggle, the dog doesn't even bark. Of all the things

Tariq admires about this animal, this is at the top of the list. He's all bite. Tariq goes to him and unclips the leash from his collar. *Thank you, thank you.* The dog jumps on him, hugs on him, almost knocking him over, his paws scrambling across Tariq's chest. Tariq plays their game where he blows into his marbled eyes, and the dog squirms away, pretending to be annoyed.

"Your mother don't want him off the leash," Papi says.

"Oh yeah?" Tariq says. He forces the dog's mouth closed, so he can't drool on his jeans or lick at his cheek. "And where *is* Mama?"

"In bed. Comatose. She tried to stay up till you got home, to tell you something . . ." He snaps his fingers. "What was she gonna tell him?" he asks Isabel.

She shakes her head, as if she cannot recall. But there's no way, Tariq thinks. There is no way she forgot.

To help himself remember, Papi closes his eyes and tilts back his head. A loose purse of skin hangs from his neck. Something evil, Tariq thinks, has drawn his father's gray cheeks into his face. It's as if Papi's been using one of those breathing machines, one of those clear plastic jockstraps that cover the nose and the lips. Except instead of providing oxygen, this cruel machine pulls it out. And now Papi looks like this, someone who's given up, who's already half gone, one paralyzed foot in the Cedar Grove Cemetery. The Book says:

> *If one or both of them grow old in your company, do not say fie to them, nor reprove them, but say gentle words to them and look after them with kindness and love, and say: "O Lord, have mercy on them as they nourished me when I was small."*

Yeah well, Tariq's first objection is that the whole nourishment part of this sura may not apply in his particular case. Second of all, Papi did not grow old in Tariq's presence. This happened during Tariq's incarceration. This happened, he is sure, *because* of his incarceration.

"I remember now," Papi says.

"Did you hear me outside the door?"

"Your mother wanted me to remind—"

"Did you hear me? Outside the door?"

Jose looks over at Isabel, and Tariq is careful to notice if anything

rises on his face—if his eyebrows arch, or if his flaky, dehydrated lips curl into a smirk. "What do you mean?" he asks.

"Did you hear me when I was out in the hall? Struggling with the locks."

"I guess."

"You're not sure?"

"We figured you were maybe a little—you know."

"No, Papi. I don't know. Can you please explain it to me?"

"I don't know, Junior. A little buzzed maybe? First day back, maybe you and Dito get a little drunk. Smoke a spliff or something." He draws a hit from an invisible joint, his pinky raised in the air. "Come home a little stoned and maybe you have some trouble opening the door. I don't know. We didn't really think about it, tell you the truth."

"You didn't really think about it? Don't look at her. Look at me. You didn't—"

"What right do you have, talking to me like this?"

"Please don't interrupt me when I'm speaking." Tariq forces the dog's head down into the carpet. "You say you weren't really thinking about me outside the door, fumbling with the locks like an *idiot*. But then what were you thinking about? What were you *laughing* about, Papi?"

"Laughing?" he says. He smoothes out the wrinkles on his lap, a clear giveaway. "What's the matter with you? You wanted me to get up? Unlock the door for you?"

"Here's the thing," Tariq says. He tries not to smile when he sees how closely Isabel is watching him. She sits on her hands, as if perfectly composed, but he's willing to bet dollars to donuts that if he put his ear to her breast he'd hear her heart wildly thumping. "Here's the thing," he says again, stepping closer to his father. "How would you feel if I laughed in the face of your pathetic moments? When you need help coming in and out of the bathtub. Or when you've pissed your pants in the middle of the day and don't even know it?"

"This subject is closed," Jose says. He points the remote at the television and raises its volume. "Your mother wanted me to remind you to call your parole officer. Before it's too late."

Tariq's on him before he even has a chance. He forces his hands behind Jose's knees and under his tailbone, and hoists him out of

the wheelchair. The old man weightlessly floats into Tariq's arms, as easily as cream rises in coffee. And then he starts fighting. He punches Tariq's ear, his face, his back, the cluster of muscles between his shoulder blades. *Put me down,* he says. *Put me down right now!* Imagine that. Granting this old man's request. How easily these thin legs would shatter. Tariq is laughing. He tosses him up in the air, as one might do with a baby. They are swirled together, father and son. Jose is still fighting and Tariq is still laughing. To protect the gash on his cheek, he sticks his face in Jose's armpit, which smells like sofrito. He carries him toward the back of the apartment. Tariq can't see where he's going—his face stays buried in Jose's armpit—but he doesn't need to see where he's going. This is his house. He knows where the parrots hang low and where sock-snagging nailheads stick out of the carpet. As they go through the kitchen, Tariq tilts his father's helpless body and walks sideways like a crab, so that Jose's dangling legs don't get clipped on a doorway.

Isabel says nothing. *I'm the main event,* Tariq thinks. *I'm the chaos she needs.* Like the perfect audience member, she sits still and silent in the dark.

He throws his father onto the bed, and Jose lands as a pile of shirts might land—with a soft thud, in a twisted heap. Grease-stained pillows bounce to the floor. The mattress springs creak. Rising up onto his elbows, Jose shows his son the face of an old man, red and swollen and accusatory. This face demands to know what right Tariq has. What right? What right? Tariq could ask him to elaborate, but he's too disgusted. He cuts straight to his father's lies.

"Where's Mama?"

Jose's lost his voice. The words come out thin and black, barely even whispered: "What right do you have?"

Oh please. Tariq gets down on the carpet and slides a hand under his father's dresser. The wood feels bumpy, as if infected with disease. Something contagious. Years ago, when Tariq was just a kid, he'd root around inside the dresser drawers for whatever his little hands could find: loose change, cough drops, porno mags, airplane bottles of Bacardi, an inexplicable yarmulke, condoms that he'd blow up like balloons. This time, however, Tariq searches for something specific: a

package he'd duct-taped to the bottom of the dresser. It should be right in the middle. A clear plastic baggie, it is full, or at least it should be full, with $930, his share of the Virgil's money.

When he can't find it, he crawls across the floor and checks under his mother's dresser. No money there either, and he isn't surprised. Nothing's safe around this family. He stands up slowly, brushes the dirt and dust off his hands. His father's thin chest trembles.

In the hallway outside his parents' bedroom, Tariq bumps into Isabel. He thought she would've waited for him in the living room, but of course not. She *had* to follow him here. Had to see what he might do next. Smiling, he moves toward her, and she backs away into the wall.

"What's the matter with you?" she says.

"I don't know," he says, still smiling. "What's the matter with me?"

"He's your *father*."

"He's a liar. Did you know that? He said my mother had gone to bed when—"

"She sleeps in your old room."

"Please don't interrupt me when I'm speaking," he says. He looks down at her stomach, which presses against the zippered fly of his crotch. Oh, he wishes their positions were reversed, that it was him backed up against the wall, supported, unable to crumple to the ground. Isabel smells faintly sour, like milk on the day it expires. He'd like to wash the smell off of her. Shampoo her hair, lather her back. When he brings his face closer to hers, she turns her head and looks blankly out the kitchen window. The purple dusk that lingered throughout the early evening has been swallowed, devoured by darkness. Wise of him to have waited, to have delayed, for as the Book says:

Surely in the watches of the night the soul is most receptive and words more telling.

Twenty-nine months of imagined scenarios, and not a single one took place here, in this darkened hallway, with these familial pictures on the walls, with Isabel wearing his little brother's Fatima T-shirt. Can't complain, though. You tussle with what is, and you do the very best that you can.

"I got these for you," he says as he digs into his pockets. "I went down to the corner. And to the Laundromat, too."

He pushes the magazines into her hands, giving them to her one at a time, so as to prolong this moment for as long as he can. He watches her face. The book, *Apartment Finder,* he saves for last, sliding it over the top. He pats his pockets. That's it. That's everything. If not for that fat Ecuadorian bitch, he would've had more, dozens more, flyers and piano keys, a thick catalog of choices that would overflow Isabel's arms and cascade to the floor.

"If you look right here you'll see that the magazine's pages are color coded according to neighborhood. If I was you, Izzy, that's where I'd start. Choose a place to live first, and then go on from there. There's no place that's off-limits, okay? Don't worry about prices." He doesn't tell her that he didn't find the Virgil's money, or that he failed to get the grams of coke from Baka—those are his problems, not hers. "I like Astoria," he says. "And I'd recommend a two-bedroom apartment. It'd be nice, that extra room. But all the final decisions are entirely up to you."

He can tell by her face that he's not explaining himself very well.

"Here's the thing about that second bedroom," he says. "We could put a sewing machine in there for you. And I'd like to use it as an office. I'd like to learn Arabic, you know? So I can read the Qur'an the way it's meant to be read. I bet that's something you never thought I'd want to do. Am I right? Never in a million years, right? But that's what I'm telling you. I'm different now. It's like I've got words overflowing my head." He looks away, suddenly embarrassed. "I'm going to need that office," he says. "There are things I've got planned. Impressive things."

"Did something happen to Alfredo?"

Tariq would sigh if he had the energy. "At least ask it right," he says. "Don't ask if something happened to Alfredo. Ask if I happened to Alfredo. You see what I mean? Ask if he's not here with you because of something I did to him."

She's crying now and it makes him want to slap her face. "Did you hurt him?" she says.

"Who?"

"Alfredo."

"Try again. Do it right."

"Did you hurt Alfredo?"

"No I did not. But thank you for asking me so directly."

The dog follows Tariq into the bathroom. Not exactly his first choice—he'd rather have Isabel behind him, with a big fluffy towel wrapped around her body—but hey, whatever, it's nice to have the company. The dog's paws click on the tiles as he makes his way toward the toilet bowl. It sounds like a typewriter without paper, the keys striking an empty roll. He looks over at Tariq—*what kind of rules are we dealing with here?*—before plunging his face into the toilet and drinking its water. Tariq thinks he should probably yell at the dog, but the little beast is probably mad thirsty, and besides, Tariq's got his own problems to manage. He stares at his cheek in the mirror. What a mess. With a wad of wetted toilet paper, he dabs at the little eggies of pus embedded around the gash. Maybe if Isabel doesn't get too close, she won't see anything . . . but that's ridiculous and he knows it. Girl's a first-class noticer, just like himself.

Blood dribbles out of his nose. It's all this stress. He's been bugging out over appearances, over money, over trying to set everything up perfectly, trying to make all the right moves, and it's too much, he wants to scream, he wants to smash his face against the mirror. He grips the handles of the sink. Leaves little comets of blood all over the family's face towel. *Don't worry,* he tells himself. *Calm down. So you got blood on the towel? So what? Mama does laundry on the regs and it's not like you got hepatitis or HIV or some other junkyard shit. Right, doggy?*

The dog doesn't answer. Like a little explorer, he steps into the bathtub. His paws go *click, clack. Click, clack.*

Tariq walks out of the bathroom and into an apartment blazing with light. Every switch has been flipped, every lamp turned on. Bulbs shine in the kitchen and in the hallway and especially in the living room, where he finds Isabel haloed, scrutinizing a cordless phone. She's stopped crying and it looks to him as if her face has taken on an erotic intensity.

"You sweet little innocent girl," he says. He sits down next to her

on the couch, takes her flaccid hand in his. As he stares at her fingers, he imagines a world without razor blades, a world where Isabel would surely be the hairiest woman alive. He used to hound her about it all the time, teasing her until she started shaving her legs every day and waxing her forearms and upper lip and privates. She'd even Bic her fingers, so that when he held her hand he'd feel between her knuckles a dark gunpowder of stubble. Now, however, that powder explodes out of the skin. It feels wonderfully soft under his thumb, and for the life of him he can't understand why he ever asked her to shave.

"His phone's going straight to voice mail," she says. She won't look at him. The rental magazines lie next to her on the sofa in a humiliatingly small pile. "If you know where he is—"

"He went to go see a girl," Tariq says. "You happy now? That's all I know."

"Just tell me the truth. Please. I promise I won't be mad at you."

"Does this kind of thing happen a lot? Does he usually not come home until late at night?"

She pulls her hand away from him.

"Here's my question," Tariq says. "If he's working all the time—look at me. If he's working all the time, then where's all the money? You know what I mean, Izzy? Where's the *money* at? Why you two still living with my parents?"

"He has to take care of your father," she says.

"Or does my father take care of you? Is he the babysitter? Does he stay up with you all night till your hardworking man comes home? Come *on*. This has to have occurred to you. If it was just the two of you in your own apartment, you'd be staying up all night by yourself. Without any distractions. And then maybe you'd get to wondering what that boyfriend of yours is up to. Maybe you'd open your *eyes.*"

The dog totters into the living room with his head slumped, as if he were ashamed to be interrupting them. And rightfully so! Tariq flies off the couch and backs the whimpering dog into the kitchen. While he's up, he decides to turn off all these romance-murdering lights. It's been a long time since he's been able to do this. Because of him, because of his hand on a switch, Con Edison's power meters are quivering. In control, reluctant to stop, he flips the switch in the kitchen on

and off. Up on the ceiling, his mother's decorative light covering, an insect crematorium, glows and then darkens.

On his way out of the kitchen he turns off the hallway light and then all the lamps in the living room so that only the television's bluey glow remains. While he was gone, Isabel maxed out the volume and changed the channel to a sports highlight show, a program she apparently thought might interest him. He turns it off.

"What happened to Winston?" he asks. He's whispering; under this burden of darkness he feels chastised into lowering his voice. "Did he go home?"

"Yes."

"Did you ask him to stick around? Were you worried I might come home alone?"

"What do you want me to say?"

"Why didn't you go somewhere? You gotta have someplace you could've gone. The movie theater, maybe? See? I remember. You could've gone to the movie theater, but you know what I think? I think maybe you wanted to be here when I came home. Maybe you knew I'd be showing up all by my lonesome."

"No," she says. "I never thought you'd be alone."

"Well, guess what?"

He kneels down on the carpet in front of her. She lifts her chin, stares into the empty space above his head. She can't see, he realizes. She can't see a thing and maybe she thinks he can't either, but he can, he can, his eyes have been institutionally adjusted to the dark. He sees everything: the outline of her jaw, the bulge of her stomach, her thighs pressed together, her hands bunching the fabric of her sweatpants. Her breath thickens as he peels off her socks. Innocent girl. She smells like the soil that anchors a potted plant. He grabs her sweatpants by the waist, and because she's still holding on, bunching the fabric, when he pulls them off, her body comes toward him. Her face hovers above his. Her legs feel cold and rough. His hands find the lanyards of brutalized skin, where the kitchen knife tore up her calves. You see? There are no secrets. His hands creep up, toward her thighs. Bruises dapple the skin. So fast, as always. Back in the day, he'd pull off her pants in the backseat of his van and he'd see his blue thumbprints all over her body and he'd be amazed, proud of his passion, that this was something he did just by squeezing and grabbing and pinching.

When he pulls down her white cotton panties, he finds underneath them another pair of white cotton panties. *Isabel*, he thinks. *You are an odd bird.* He pulls down the second pair, halfway expecting a third, but instead he uncovers the rich dark thicket of her pubic hair. No shaving here, it seems. But that's fine with him. That's even better. He leaves both pairs of panties tangled around her knees. He drinks the air coming out of her mouth.

She goes limp on the couch. Her bones have turned to soup and in order to reanimate her, to bring her back into her body, Tariq sticks her hand down the front of his pants. She screams. Her neck tightens as she calls out for help, bellows the name of his mother. *Lizette! Lizette!* He covers her mouth with his hand. He wants to tell her that Love will deliver her this instant from herself, and he wishes she'd understand that he *is* Love, her custodian and witness, sending his soul forward in order to save her from all of this, from his brother, from his parents, from this apartment strung with parrots and given to wickedness, from a life of mediocrity, bewilderment, the fire that is closed in, the spider's flimsiest of houses, the crack of doom, the stone-hurling wind. She bites the fleshy web of his palm, but he can always push down harder. The wings of her nostrils expand. A violent trembling swims to the surface of her face.

Outside the window, cars wash by, their headlights bleaching the walls. Tariq lifts his hand and Isabel calls out for Lizette. And so it's here we go again. One more time. His hand reclamped on her mouth.

He tells her to unbutton his jeans. He wishes he had a belt she could unbuckle, just to delay delay delay, but that's life. Fishkill didn't give him a belt, and besides, he's running out of time. He reaches into his pocket and pulls out the beeper. He tries to slide off its plastic top, but he can't manage it with only one free hand. For leverage, he pins the beeper under his chin and yanks on it. But it won't budge. He tries using his teeth, which doesn't work either. Isabel's fingers hang limp at his waist. He bangs the beeper against the carpeted floor, and then against the sofa's metal leg. He's banging and banging, a steel driver swinging his hammer, and a loud crash comes out of the kitchen—it sounds like pots getting thrown to the floor—and Tariq wonders if he's made this happen, if his banging in the living room created this unseen clattering in the kitchen.

The beeper cracks open. Little round pills spill across the carpet. He

picks one up and wants Isabel to swallow it, but that requires taking his hand off her mouth, which gives her another opportunity to cry for help, but he tells her that if she does, he's going to drag her naked out of this apartment and throw her down four fucking flights of stairs.

Eyes narrowed, her face takes on a desperate, animalistic craving. He slips the pill between her lips, but she spits it back out at him. Her nails dig into his neck. Bewildered, waiting for Love to deliver him this instant from himself, he hits her in the mouth. Blood seeps between her teeth, fills the fold of her fat lower lip. This too she spits out. She sprays her blood all over the crotch of his jeans.

He rips open the front of her shirt, something he never wanted to do. Her breasts hang out, heavy and dark-nippled. Faint blue veins striate the skin. Below these breasts bulges a monstrous stomach, its button popped out like the knob to a door. And for the child behind this door, floating upside down in foul, contaminated juices, the Book says:

He is fully knowledgeable of you as He produced you from the earth, and since you were a foetus in your mother's womb. So do not assert your goodness.

Tariq pushes down on her stomach. He has the sense that someone is watching him, but of course someone is watching him. Someone is always watching. He's crying. He can't believe it. Sobs clog his airway. He chews on the collar of his shirt. He gives up. He hates everything. Okay? He hates *everything.*

"You don't want to hurt me here," she says, trying to push his hands off her stomach. Tears leak out of her eyes, as if she just walked into a howling February wind. But her voice is steady. "Do you understand? You don't want to hurt me here."

He pushes down harder on her stomach. If he tried to penetrate her now, with this wilted dick of his, the head and shaft would double back on itself and flop down uselessly between his legs.

"You don't want to hurt him," she says. She whispers this, hisses it into his ear with the spirit of dizziness. "You want to hurt me. You want to hit my face. Do you understand? You want to make me as ugly as you are."

"Stop it."

"You're a faggot," she says. "You hear me? You're a pathetic faggot. Look at you. Look at how ugly you are. Who cut your cheek open? Your boyfriend? Your boyfriend cut your cheek open, you little fag?"

It takes three blows in the exact same spot—the bulging cheekbone, just below her right eye—before she cries out in pain. He backs away, trips over the air mattress. Something stirs inside of him. He takes a handful of pills off the carpet and gnashes them between his teeth. He watches her breathe.

She doesn't call out for help, but Jose does. Behind his closed door, spread out on the bed, or maybe crawling across the floor, burning his elbows on the carpet, Jose screams out the name of his wife.

He hurries to the bathroom—the apartment's smallest, calmest place—and on his way there, passing through the kitchen, he finds the trash can turned over. The black garbage bag has been ripped open, its contents spilled out across the floor. The dog gnaws on a chicken carcass. Tariq tries to pet him, but he moves away angrily. Too busy, too hungry. As the dog rips meat from bone, the carcass's jellied husk slides across the tiles.

The bathroom smells terrible. Tariq thinks that it's him, something foul and terrible oozing out of his body, but when he pulls back the shower curtain, he sees that the dog took a shit in the tub. One more mess to clean up. He pumps liquid hand soap on the pile of shit. While the bath runs, he sits on the edge of the tub and listens to the water rushing out of the faucet. He reads the label on the hand soap. *Lavender Blossom. Delicately scented. List of ingredients. Directions for use.* When he finishes reading the label, he starts over and reads it again.

When he gets out of the bathroom, he sees his mother standing at the kitchen counter. Keeping her back to him, she drops frozen sofrito cubes into a small pink hand towel. Down by her feet, the dog chews on a chicken bone in the midst of an entire day's worth of garbage: yellow grains of rice, batteries, a shampoo bottle, cucumber peels, coffee grounds, a water-damaged issue of *Entertainment Weekly*, a moldy tomato, bread crusts, crumpled Lotto tickets, sections of the *Post*, a

dented can of Goya beans, a near-full package of Oreo cookies. A brown liquid oozes out of the garbage bag and streams across the linoleum.

"I'm sorry, Mama. I'll fix this."

She twists off the top of the hand towel. With its belly sagged down with cubes, it looks like a pink Chinese dumpling. She carries it into what is now considered her room, where Isabel lies on the bottom bunk, her hair on the pillow, her face turned to the wall. She doesn't roll over when Lizette hands her the towel. Lizette whispers something in Spanish—something Tariq can't quite hear—and pulls the covers over Isabel's shoulders.

When his mother comes back out into the hallway, she seems to have trouble looking at him. She squints. Her sleep mask hangs from a ribbon around her neck. He wants to tell her, again, that he's sorry. He wants to ask her about mops and brooms and vacuums and paper towels and spray bottles of disinfectant.

"The dog's gonna choke on that bone," she says. "It'll shatter and get stuck in his throat."

She goes back into her room, closing the door behind her. Somewhere in this world there is a factory, Tariq thinks, and this factory only makes doors designed to be slammed in his face. The phone is ringing.

An hour later. Maybe more. The phone is ringing. His brother. He tells Tariq to come down to Papi's old store right away. Use the alleyways, he says. Come in through the bodega's back door. He speaks rudely, which is just like him. Unappreciative of the danger he's in. Tariq hangs up.

The phone is ringing. It rings and rings

and rings and rings. He snaps off the antenna. He pulls the cord from the wall.

12

Dogfight

Alfredo runs upstairs into the candy store, cops three cigars, runs back down into the basement, and, with a nervous grin, distributes those cigars, as if this were a dress rehearsal for Christian Louis's world premiere. Here. Take one. Take one. The cigars—cheap, thin, black—are called Dutch Masters and they should only cost $1.25, *maybe* $1.50, but Max, who's in an incredibly pissy mood tonight, has been selling them for two fucking dollars apiece. And Alfredo's been buying them anyway. What else is he gonna do? Dutch Masters come with an extra layer of skin, a tobacco leaf rolled around the stogie, which makes them harder to roll, which makes them the preferred apparatus of the weed-smoking connoisseurs down in this basement. He hands the cigars to K-Lo, Jossie, and Timmy P., the three nimble-fingered experts. Each one sticks the entire Dutch in his mouth and coats it with saliva, gets that tobacco dermis moist and removable. If Dutch Masters came with balls, these dudes would be fondling them, but no one makes that easy comparison, or at least no one says it out loud, because these dudes—like the Rembrandts and Vermeers from whom the cigar gets its name—are *artistes.* (Fancy-pants pronunciation preferred.) Besides, there ain't no reason to be thinking dirty thoughts. No reason to get all negative. There's weed to be smoked! Each expert peels off his tobacco leaf and hands it to somebody else—

Marc Franschetta, Jeff Hernandez, Billy Fitzgerald—apprentices who cup the leaf in their hands and breathe on it heavily, keeping it soft and pliable for the rewrap. Next up: splitting the stogies' spines. Penknives work nicely here, as do the tips of scissors, but K-Lo, Jossie, and Timmy P. all use their extra-long pinky nails. Tobacco guts get dumped onto the floor, which, Alfredo thinks, Max ain't gonna appreciate. Weed is broken up. Stems and seeds removed. Each expert stuffs their Dutch full of herb, rolls it tight, and—yo, let me get that skin back—wraps it back up. Now here's the hard part. K-Lo, Jossie, and Timmy P. start saying, *No, no, no, no* and *Hold up, hold up* because the men down here—Rick Sprinkle who sells perfume knockoffs on the street, Paulie Guns who sells heroin, Sean Lau who escorts escorts, Virgin Light whose real name no one remembers, Rhino who's recently come into some opium, Forest Hills David, Soft-Core Jonas, Lee who came all the way out here from Staten Island, Winston, Alex Hughes, Bam-Bam Hughes, the ghost of Curtis Hughes, even the apprentices Marc, Jeff, and Billy—all converge on the Dutch Masters. But the Dutches ain't ready. Still moist, if prematurely smoked, they would droop like wet noodles. Back up, people. Back up. Everybody's gonna have to be patient, an attribute—a virtue, if you ask Alfredo—that's been in short supply thus far.

"Yo, Alfredo. Where's this dog of yours at?"

"Yo, Alfredo. Where's your brother at?"

"Yo, Alfredo. What the fuck is up with them corny-ass shoes?"

Alex and Bam-Bam Hughes haven't punched Alfredo in the face yet, which he thinks is a pretty good indication that they either don't hold him responsible for Curtis's death or that Baka didn't tell them about the Vladimir mugging. Because when it comes to punching people in the face, Alex and Bam-Bam are not the type to bide their time. They huddle in the center of the basement, near the makeshift ring, arguing over which one of them should drag Diana upstairs. They worry that once the Dutches get sparked, the pooch might get blazed. It's not like anyone would slip a stogie between her drool-slicked jaws, but she could catch a contact high, could start giggling and craving Cheetos, rendered useless for her upcoming dogfight. A German shepherd with steeple-shaped ears, she needs to get taken out of stupefaction's way, and yet neither brother wants to miss his chance to get stupefied. They got brain cells to kill, shit to forget.

How do brothers fairly decide who has to go and who gets to stay? They start with the primary stratagem of intrafraternal diplomacy: rock-paper-scissors. When that doesn't work—each brother keeps throwing down rock—they turn to the primary creed of potheads around the world: *Ah, fuck it.* They'll both stay down here and get blazed. It'll be fine. They figure if there's one dog alive who's built up an immunity to THC, it's gotta be Diana.

Neck extended, snout in the air, she paces inside her ring like an uppity movie star, reluctant to sign autographs. The men down here watch her indifferently. Almost everyone plans to bet on Alfredo's dog because pit bulls carry more gangster cachet than German shepherds, because Diana seems too snooty for dogfighting, because, primarily, Alfredo's dog hasn't shown up yet and imaginations grow fat on the unseen. The guys down here have endowed the pit bull with four rows of fangs, a set of titanium nuts, a two-pack-a-day smoking habit, a rap sheet going back to juvie, a tail shaped like a swastika. Diana's tail? You kidding? It's fuzzy and droops off her ass. The bottom of it drags across the floor as she sniffs the cardboard boxes demarcating the ring's boundaries. Stacked waist high, the boxes are full of Max Marshmallow's heavier inventory bottles of laundry detergent, cans of Goya beans—and Diana presses her nose to the cardboard, as if she can smell the frijoles negros inside.

Dry at last, the Dutch Masters get sparked. Paulie Guns pulls out a Zippo, for which he gets roundly mocked. You out of your mind, Paulie? The butane contaminates the flavor. Even the apprentices know that much. Three Dutches make their way through three separate ciphers. They pull beautifully. With a Dutch pinched between his fingers, Rick Sprinkle talks and talks and talks about some calling card scam until his boy Rhino yells at him to stop sleeping on that shit and pass it along. Chastened, Sprinkle takes two extra hits and the tip of his Dutch glows red like a pimple. He passes it on to Soft-Core Jonas, who intentionally coughs out the smoke, hoping to dilate his lungs.

"Don't be blowing that shit at the dog," Bam-Bam warns.

"Where else is it supposed to go?" Jonas says, and it is a fair enough point. Diana's ring is in the middle of a basement without windows or ventilation, and the haze—with no place to go but everywhere—spreads its fuzzy tentacles outward, drops down into all corners, wraps itself around the leg of a rickety card table, fills lungs, fills nostrils,

climbs the stairs into the candy store, and creeps up the rungs of a wooden ladder that leads to a pair of metal grate doors. These doors, the basement's only exit besides the stairs into the store, open up onto the sidewalk for deliveries; scattered around the borough, they are the kind of doors Isabel always makes Alfredo step around when they're walking together down the street.

A Dutch comes his way, but he passes it on, unsampled. Alfredo doesn't need weed softening his synapses, not with all the shit he has to juggle: the mounting impatience in this basement, Max Marshmallow's regret, the Impala full of cops parked across the street and waiting for Alfredo's go-ahead. But he can't give that go-ahead till the guest of honor arrives. And if Tariq doesn't come? If he never shows up? Then Alfredo will have gone to all this trouble, ass-fucked all his friends, for nothing. More important, if Tariq doesn't show up—these questions come straight from the Department of Worry in bold, fourteen-point font—then where the hell is he? And what's he doing? And where's Isabel in all this? It has been over an hour since Alfredo last heard from his brother. Alfredo called and called, and the phone rang and rang, until *something happened,* and all Alfredo could hear was the dead dial tone of his parents' line, a nasal sound, an auditory cousin to the G-flat hum of the Emergency Broadcast System, a sound of panic, of disaster, of terrorist attacks and nightmares come true.

The Dutch returns to Alfredo, smaller than before, and this time he does not pass it along. Not because he wants a toke—it's the last thing he needs—but because he's distracted. His eyes are closed, his ears cocked. He looks at the ceiling, and slowly, one by one, so does everyone else. Footsteps creak on the floorboards above their heads.

"About fucking time," Jossie says. "I'm not trying to wait around here all night."

The footsteps keep creaking. The men follow the sound blindly, their faces upturned toward the ceiling and its pink clouds of foam insulation. Stoned, their mouths hang open, as if they were watching an airplane descend toward LaGuardia.

Alfredo fights his way to the front of the crowd, but just as he feared, just as the pessimists expected, this isn't Tariq plodding down the stairs, but a poorly goateed white kid named AIDS.

When the groan goes up, AIDS puts his hands in the air and says,

"What'd I do?" He wasn't even going to come tonight, thinking his friends don't really like him (his nickname is *AIDS,* for chrissakes), but his mother doesn't want him spending his Saturday nights alone, playing Xbox, eating junk food, and so she hectored him out of the house. *Where are your friends, honey? What are they up to tonight?* When he got to the bodega, the lights were off and the sign in the window turned to CLOSED. He felt relieved to be able to go home, back to his room, back to his *Halo,* but just as he was about to turn around, an old man thrust his puffy-cheeked face out the door and asked what's what. AIDS froze. He assumed there was a secret password that (of course) no one had told him about. When he stammered something about a dogfight, the old man told him to go around to the back of the store. Which was just so cool! AIDS felt like a Prohibition gangster as he hopped over the fence into a dead-grass backyard. The old man swung open the back door and led him through a little railroad apartment and into the bodega and now here he is. Walking into a basement full of disappointment. "What'd I do?" he says. He doesn't know. He never does.

"Yo, Alfredo," says a voice from the haze. "When the fuck's this dog of yours gonna get here?"

Alfredo goes upstairs and buys beer at two times the regular cost. Olde E, Bud Light, Natty Ice, Modelo Especial.

"Thanks," says a different voice from the haze. "But when the fuck's this dog of yours gonna get here?"

He goes back upstairs and buys snacks for the stoned. Drake's cakes, Airheads, plantain chips, quarter waters.

"Thanks, but . . ."

He goes back upstairs—his calves starting to burn—and buys another Dutch, which he brings straight over to Rhino. He asks Rhino if he has any of that rumored opium on him, and if so, would he mind rolling a Dutch and sprinkling some of it over the herb. Opium is a rarity around here and Alfredo hopes the mere sight of it, the mere *smell* of it—in this windowless basement full of young men, cheap beer, and its flatulent aftereffects—will compel people to stick around, as the promise of crème brûlée might keep bored dinner guests in their chairs. Until, of course, the spoon scrapes the bottom of the dish. Until, of course, the O-laced Dutch gets smoked down to the quick.

"Sorry," Rhino says. If he has any opium, it's gonna stay in his

pocket, wrapped up in butcher's paper. "But yo, listen—why don't you just call your brother?"

"The phone's been disconnected."

"Then go fucking get him," Alex says.

Only three blocks separate the Batistas' apartment from Max's candy store, but Alfredo feels reluctant to traverse those streets at night. Look at the grief-puffed eyes of Alex and Bam-Bam Hughes. Check out how high their shoulders are hunched. It's a scary world out there.

"This is a *dogfight*," Alfredo whines. "Shit isn't *supposed* to start on time, know what I mean?"

No one knows what he means. None of the guys down here even *pretend* to have been to a dogfight, except for Jeff Hernandez, who pretends to have been to all sorts of things (he also claims to have invented the "Jingle Bells/Batman Smells" song). Before anyone arrived, Alfredo put a strip of duct tape in the center of the ring, dividing it in two. He isn't sure if that's protocol, but a basketball court has a center line, so maybe a dogfighting pit does too. Who knows? Should the ring be built over a tarp, to keep blood off the floor? What about referees, judges, a bell clapper? Is betting handicapped? Should there be an undercard, a pair of roosters pecking each other to death, a bikini-clad kitten parading a poster board with the number of the round? Nobody knows. But they do know there should be two dogs: it's the without-which-there-ain't-shit of dogfighting. The guys down here don't need rap videos or DMX lyrics to tell them that.

"This is fucking bullshit," says a voice from the haze. It becomes a refrain, a refrain that circles the room twice as fast as any herb-stuffed Dutch. It's fucking bullshit that Alfredo's dog ain't here yet, that they've all been standing for hours, that they work shitty jobs at RadioShack and Foot Locker, that the weekend's already half over, that no one brought cards for Spades, that no one brought dice for Cee-lo, that they still live with their mothers, that going to high school sucked, but not being in high school sucks worse, that the Mets missed Clemens, that the weatherman predicts rain, that there ain't any bitches down here except Diana pacing inside her ring, and, speaking of which, it's fucking bullshit that she's in there at all, getting mad comfortable, chilling in that cardboard arena before the fight starts, which probably gives her like a totally unfair advantage.

"Bullshit," Bam-Bam says.

Winston steps on Rhino's relatively new sneakers. Rhino bought them at a discount from David, who stole them from the Foot Locker he works at in Forest Hills, and now—would you look at this?—they've got a big black scuff on them. When Rhino starts bitching, Winston asks him what does he expect, walking around in white fucking shoes for crying out loud. After he says this, Winston's eyes bug out of his skull a little bit farther than usual, as if his mouthing off has surprised even himself. Maybe, Alfredo thinks, Winston is at long last growing some balls. Maybe with Mike Shifrin somewhere outside this basement Winston has got enough to worry about and doesn't need Rhino and his bitching on top of it—but that's impossible, Alfredo reminds himself, because he never told Winston about Baka's intelligence report. Alfredo didn't want to overburden his friend, didn't want more hair falling out of his head. Whatever the impetus behind Winston's newfound moxie, it doesn't seem to matter to Rhino. He knocks the beer out of Winston's hand, the can sprays what looks like bile all over Billy Fitz's jeans, and so Billy shoves Marc Franschetta, not because Marc did anything, but because Billy's Irish and Marc's Italian (third generation, but still: one keeps a shamrock in his wallet, the other drives a souped-up Camaro), and the both of them are convinced they're supposed to hate each other and administer headlocks whenever the opportunity presents itself, and because the opportunity has officially presented itself, there is more shoving, more screaming, more beers knocked out of more hands, which strikes Alfredo as a very good thing, since a fight—even one between people, not dogs—will at least keep his friends entertained. No such luck, Dito. Max Marshmallow appears on the stairs, wrinkling his nose. He wears his new gray sneakers, a pair of khaki pants clasped, in the manner of all old men, well above his waist, and a linen button-down shirt—Max all pimped out for his return to the world of shady goings-on, a return that has so far been less triumphant than dispiriting.

"I want everybody out of here," he tells Alfredo.

"Don't worry about a thing," Alfredo says. Guilt prevents him from looking Max in the face. Alfredo doesn't know what's going to happen tonight, doesn't know if Baka or Shifrin or Tariq are ever going to show up, but he does know that there are three DTs parked in an Impala across the street and they're busting in here, no matter what.

And once they do, it'll be trouble for Max. *Can't be running dogfights in your basement,* the law books say. Or something like that. He'll probably lose the store *and* the apartment behind it. The couch, the TV, the toilet with the handle that still sticks, the crystal dish overflowing with butterscotch candies—Alfredo worries that it'll all be corded off with yellow tape and then taken away. Auctioned off to law-abiding citizens, to fill the city's pockets. "You gotta trust me," he tells Max's chest. "I've got this all under control."

"Exactly *what* have you got under control?" Max says.

"Maybe I oughta buy some more Dutches off you. Get these guys to mellow out a bit."

"How much money you think I lost from closing the store tonight?" His Adam's apple protrudes violently. "All the shit I coulda sold, but didn't. How much money you think that is?"

"Let's go upstairs," Alfredo says. "You got any of those little apple pies? I'll buy them off you for three dollars apiece."

"I wanted a poker game," Max groans. What he has instead is a mob of thugs who expect violent entertainment and who have so far been denied. Like a leaky gas stove, these young men will be easily ignited. He sees his store, his home, his shingles-scarred body erupting in a giant, orange, billowing ball of fire. If only he would've gotten his poker game! There would've been cigar smoke instead of reefer smoke. He would've been able to kibitz in the purest sense of the word: sit just beyond the green-felt table and, with much tongue clucking and head wagging, offer his expertise on how best to bluff and false bluff, how to tease the pot, look at your cards, stack your chips, and time your bathroom breaks. "This," Max says as a do-ragged kid hocks up a loogie and *spits it onto his floor,* "is not what I had in mind."

"My brother could be upstairs right now," Alfredo says. He imagines Tariq in the fence-enclosed yard behind the store, banging on the screen door as if it were keeping secrets from him. If he gives up, if he goes to the front of the store with the dog on a leash, then he'll be seen by the police, who won't hesitate to nab him right then and there. Which isn't exactly ideal. Alfredo wants his brother cuffed up and sent back to Fishkill, sure, but he wants that shit to go down when he says it can go down. "While you're here messing with me," Alfredo says, "my brother could be upstairs trying to get in."

"I want them going out that way," Max says. He points to the

wooden ladder that leads up to the metal cellar doors. "Right now. Send them out that way. To the street. I don't want these animals tramping through my store. Send them out onto the fucking street."

"Ten minutes," Alfredo says. "Please. Just give me ten minutes. As a favor to our friendship." Max checks his watch, which Alfredo interprets as a positive sign. He knows he needs to talk whiter, show Max that the two of them are on the same side. "I'm asking for ten minutes, that's all, and if my brother isn't here by then, if we're not making money by then, I'll personally kick each of these assholes to the curb."

Across the street, Officer Lopez returns with bounty. Three sodas and three shish kebabs, purchased from the halal vendor around the corner. Whoever goes out and buys the food gets to sit shotgun. These are the rules. But when Lopez pulls on the door handle, it pulls back, locked from the inside. He shifts the food and drinks to one hand. He pulls on the handle again, and again it pulls back. Behind the car's tinted black windows, Sergeant Wright and Officer Hutchison are snickering. They're bullies, these two, and Lopez knows all about bullies. A couple of years earlier, when asked in his academy interview why he wanted to become a police officer, Lopez—who, to his detriment, has always been overly honest (cf. the Unnecessary Marital Confession of 1998)—said he'd been picked on as a kid. Only when the cap came off the interviewer's red pen did Lopez realize how badly he'd answered. Might as well have said, *I have some scores to settle. Can I get a gun now please?* But he managed to recover, talked some bullshit about how he knew what it was like to feel voiceless, what it was like to feel powerless, and what it was like to feel, uh, disenfranchised, a word he remembered from a John Jay criminal justice course. The interviewer recapped his pen. Ruben Lopez became Officer Lopez. And here he is, still surrounded by snickering bullies. But he doesn't need a gun, or even a nightstick, to handle these two, not when he has access to what his communication books call reward power, the ability to confer valued material goods.

He passes to the front of the car, where he will be most visible, and leans against the hood. Hot sauce dribbles down his wrist. On top of each wooden skewer a golden dinner roll sits speared. Lopez decrowns one of the kebabs and tosses the bread into the street. A gift for the

birds when they wake up tomorrow morning. Next he'll throw away the meat, sliding it off the skewer piece by piece. Needless to say, this particular shish kebab—extra hot sauce, extra BBQ sauce, extra lemon juice—belongs to Wright. The passenger's side door swings open.

Inside the car, Lopez distributes the bounty. Because Wright and Hutchison are Coca-Cola enthusiasts, and because Lopez can be a consummate ball-buster himself, he gives them each a can of Sunkist.

"Come on!" Hutchison says through a mouthful of meat. He is the heavier of the two bullies, and the less cruel. "Orange soda?"

"Yeah, sorry about that," Lopez says as he pops the tab on his Coke. "I woulda got you one of these, but the Afghani only had one left."

Orange, incidentally, is the color of the day.

Before the shish kebabs, Lopez, Hutchison, and Wright ate some slices (pepperoni, cheese, Sicilian) at Gianni's, and before the pizza they ate some arepas (cheese, cheese, cheese) from the arepa lady on Roosevelt Avenue, and before the arepas they risked cliché and went to Dunkin' Donuts (large coffee, Boston Kreme; large coffee, jelly; large coffee and that's it, Wright's alcoholism having long ago obliterated his sweet tooth). It was at Dunkin' Donuts that they ran into the skinny little Hispanic runt of a drug dealer from the night before. When he saw them approach, a grin broke across his face and Lopez couldn't shake the feeling that the kid had been there a long time, sitting at a table by the window, nursing a Coolatta and waiting for them to show up.

"Where's Ringo?" the kid said.

While his partners waited on line for coffee, Lopez sat down at the drug dealer's table. The kid carried some serious luggage under his eyes, pouches of skin that looked as if they concealed more pouches of skin, the way good suitcases have secret zippered compartments. Lopez put the kid in his late teens, long overdue for a growth spurt and already unfairly old; he was probably one of those babies who hit the delivery table looking exhausted, knowing full well the best sleep of his life was behind him, left in the womb. His face, shiny with oil, reflected the weak light of the donut shop. His legs shook under the table.

"Nice jersey," the kid said.

Lopez nodded, unsure if the kid was fucking with him. Earlier in the evening, Wright and Hutchison, both of whom wore Piazza jerseys, had taken umbrage with Lopez's outfit: a time-worn blue and

orange Knicks jersey from the mid-1990s. *You ain't wearing a Mets jersey?* they asked. *On today of all days?* Lopez didn't know what to tell them.

"What's the name on the back?" the kid asked.

"Starks."

"That's what I thought," he said. "That's what I was *hoping.* You know, I used to have a Starks poster up in my bedroom. The one where's he dunking on Jordan? A lot of people never forgave him—Starks, I mean—for that game seven in ninety-four. You know the one I'm talking about? Against the Rockets? Where he missed all them shots? But the thing that people forget was that he was so money in game six that we never would've even have gotten—"

"I'm sure," Lopez said, "that you've got other people you can talk basketball with. Right? People who care?"

The kid rolled his eyes. "Friendly as always," he said. "Shouldn't there be four of you? Where's the other guy at? The Habib. He in the car? No offense or nothing, but I wanted to talk to him."

Lopez wished he'd asked, *Talk about what?* But instead, his vanity easily punctured, he said, "You don't wanna talk to me?"

"Well, the Habib last night—he wasn't nice or anything. But he wasn't an asshole, you know?" He let that make its way across the table. He was probably the kind of kid who thought he got away with more than he actually did. Too loved as a child, parents trying to compensate for those heavy black bags under his eyes, no one around to call him on his shit.

"You wanna get paid?" Lopez said. "Is that it? You wanna get on the official CI list? Sing your song for cash?"

"Can you please keep your voice down?" The kid stared out the window into the parking lot. "Forget it. This was a mistake."

"Okay," Lopez said. "Let's start over." He put his hands flat on the table. He'd always been too aggressive, pushed too hard. Before joining the world's greatest police force, Lopez—who, like this kid, is a tad undersized—spent his mornings sucking down protein shakes, his Tuesday and Thursday nights in kung fu classes, his Saturdays out at a range on Long Island, firing thousands of rounds of ammo. Since becoming a police officer, however, faced with the day-to-day realities of the job, dismayed by the frequency (one might call it the eagerness) with which he unholstered his firearm, Lopez ditched the Wing Chun

and the target practice, met secretly with a department-sanctioned therapist, and, just as secretly, started reading communication books. (His favorite—*People Skills: How to Assert Yourself, Listen to Others, and Resolve Conflicts*—is sitting at the bottom of his gym bag, the book's cover wrapped up in brown paper.) He hoped the therapy and textbooks would make him a better, less gun-happy police officer, and not only has that proved true, but they've steadily strengthened his marriage as well. Sitting across from the drug dealer, Lopez tried what the textbooks call a reflective listening exercise. "Let me get this straight," he said, his voice stripped of all its hard, constabulary edges. "What I heard you say is that you've got something you want to talk to one of us about. Did I get that right?"

The kid scratched nervously at some dried-up custard on the tabletop. "I've gotten myself into trouble."

"What kind of trouble?"

"The bad kind."

"Yeah, well," Lopez said. "That's the kind I see the most of."

"I'm fucked, man. Jesus fucking Christ, I am *fucked*," and his hand flew to his forehead, his stomach, lengthwise across his chest, all four corners of the cross. He groaned, desperate and angry, as if he'd been up all night whipping his own back. Lopez sat up in his seat. He'd originally assumed the kid wanted to rat on somebody—most likely a rival drug dealer—but now things were looking significantly more promising. The kid didn't look like he was about to drop a dime on somebody else; he looked like he was about to drop a dime on *himself*. He had a confession to make. While the kid scratched at the tabletop, Lopez could almost see the Hughes homicide shimmering under the surface, golden scaled, ready to bite. Could almost see his long-coveted promotion to detective, his wife pouring him a congratulatory glass of Guinness when he got home, his mother's face when he called to tell her the news, the guys in the locker room whispering amongst themselves: *You hear? Lopez collared the Hughes homicide. Lopez? Yeah, brought the guy in all by himself.* There it was, right in front of him, legs jiggling under the tabletop. Did the kid look like a killer? With the exception of his two young daughters, everyone as far as Lopez was concerned looked like a killer. If he just sat here, let silence work its interrogative magic, kept his line still in the water, then the kid would

come swimming toward him. Lopez put on his most neutral, most nonjudgmental face. A face designed to take on your burdens. To absolve all your sins. The kid frowned, as if he already had Lopez's hook caught fast in his mouth.

"The comedian drug dealer!" shouted Officer Hutchison. He stood over them, his round stomach hanging over the table's edge. "How long has it been? A whole day, maybe? Where's your boyfriend? He got you running errands? Jesus, kid, not to be critical or anything, but you look like shit. You're getting enough sleep, I hope."

Sergeant Wright, the skinnier and the meaner of the two bullies, sat down next to Lopez. He gave him a large coffee and a Boston Kreme, angling for shotgun privileges. Then he looked at the drug dealer and blew him a kiss.

Hutchison pointed under the table. "What the hell you got on your feet, kid?"

"Bowling shoes," Wright said without even having to look. Lopez dipped his head under the table to confirm; he hated that Wright had noticed this before he had.

"Bowling shoes?" Hutchison said.

"Don't you know anything about fashion?" Wright said. "Red pleather is the new shits."

"Let me ask you something," Hutchison said, but the drug dealer wouldn't even look at him. "Come Christmastime, my kid's gonna be begging me for a two-hundred-dollar pair of bowling shoes. But by then they'll be outta style, am I right? Save me some grief here. Six months down the line, what's gonna be the *new* shits? And don't tell me cowboy boots. I'd think you were messing with me."

"Kid tells me he's gotten into some kind of trouble," Lopez said.

"Tell him to call the police," Hutchison said. He took a bite of his donut, and like pus inside a zit, red jelly squirted all over his hand. "Number's nine-one-one. Think you can remember that?"

For the first time, the kid looked up at Hutchison. "You didn't want to get a whole box of donuts? Is that because you guys are undercover?"

"The comedian." Hutchison smiled. After he licked powdered sugar off his fingers, he took the kid's Coolatta and threw it in the trash.

Wright grabbed the baton. "If you're not eating or drinking any-

thing," he said. "If you're just sitting here, at an empty table, staring out the window—"

"Then that's loitering," Hutchison said, sounding almost sorry. "And loitering—"

"Is against the law," the kid said. He pushed himself out of his chair. "I get it. I understand."

Lopez followed him to the door. "Just tell me if this has anything to do with the Hughes homicide," he said softly. He felt the line about to snap, his future promotion about to dive back under the sea. "Just nod yes or no."

"This was a dumb idea," the kid said without turning around. "I didn't want to talk to *any* of you. I wanted to talk to the Habib."

Officer Ramsaran—the quartet's fourth, their Habib, their Ringo as the kid would have it—had taken the night off. He called the precinct, cashing in his emergency day, and then he called Lopez, providing the details. He'd been robbed. A humiliating experience for anyone, it is particularly hard on an officer of the law. *I would love to have caught 'em doing it,* he'd said, his voice shaking. He was taking the e-day, he explained, because he wanted to do some investigating himself, without departmental distractions or guidelines. He was going to ask the neighbors if they saw anything, ask pet store owners if they had any new customers, post some flyers on lampposts that would most likely be ripped off by tomorrow morning. *I'll do whatever you need,* Lopez promised. A Gulf War veteran with twelve years in the department, Officer Ramsaran was the kind of cop Lopez wanted to become: competent, well respected, an overall nice guy who was willing—and here's the big thing—to get ugly when he had to. Take for example an incident last year when, due to a contract dispute, the union delegate told all the men on the ground to go on strike. Nothing formal. No picket lines or hand-printed placards. Violent crimes were to be stopped— the union didn't want to *invite* chaos into the city—but the delegates did call for a moratorium on summons writing. There was to be no police work that generated revenue for the city. At least not until the contract dispute got settled. But an Egyptian officer named Kandil crossed that informal line and gave a woman a disorderly conduct ticket for calling him a pig. Everyone deferred to Ramsaran, Kandil's best friend on the force. And what did he do? In one heaping armful, he took everything out of Kandil's locker—sneakers, jeans, CD player,

family photographs, a gym bag that may have concealed some secret book wrapped up in brown paper—and he dumped it all into the hallway. It couldn't have been easy for Ramsaran—he didn't seem too happy doing it—but like Lopez tells his daughters when they complain about brushing their teeth or doing their arithmetic homework, *Hey, that's life. A series of crap you have to do, even if,* especially *if, you don't want to. That's what it's all about.* So if Ramsaran wanted Lopez to ask some questions, keep his ears open, turn over some rocks—then Lopez was going to do it. Even if it meant establishing a line of inquiry away from the Hughes homicide and toward a low-grade larceny. Even if it would never lead to a promotion, that much-coveted gold star pinned to the inside of his wallet.

"Hey, kid," Lopez said in the Dunkin' Donuts parking lot. "You know anything about a stolen pit bull?"

Lopez, Wright, and Hutchison are all plainclothes patrolmen who belong to the NYPD's Anti-Crime Unit, the department's version of chemotherapy, poisons injected onto diseased streets in order to kill deadlier, more dangerous poisons. They have the simplest job description—drive around and harass—and it's this watery vagueness that Lopez will miss least about the job if he ever makes detective. (*When* he makes detective. Power of positive thinking, Lopez.) Detectives have specific problems to solve, files to open and files to close; Anti-Crime drives the same streets night after night, harasses the same people, eats the same greasy food from the same greasy places. The lack of a concrete agenda can drive a man mad—it's driving Lopez mad—but it can also have its uses. With nothing to do, they can do anything they want. They can sit in a car outside a bodega and tear lamb meat off skewers and wait and wait and wait and wait and wait and wait for a skinny Puerto Rican to come out into the street with the thumbs-up, the green light, the A-okay.

"He ain't coming," Wright says.

"He's coming," Lopez says.

Originally the kid said he'd call them when Ramsaran's dog showed up. He said he didn't know where the dog was currently, but he knew where the dog would be: in the basement of a bodega in East Elmhurst. If they waited there, parked across the street, the kid would

call them as soon as the dog—and the thug who stole that dog—arrived. When he asked for the number to one of their cell phones, Hutchison laughed out loud. *Sure. You got a pen? My number's 1-917-GO-FUCKYOURSELF.* The new plan: as soon as the dog shows up, the kid will come out to the car, like a dinette waitress on roller skates, and deliver the message in person. Then Lopez & Co. swoop in and take back the pit bull. There's a couple of ways to go about this. They apply for a warrant, wait a couple of days, get it, storm into an empty bodega, make zero arrests, retrieve zero dogs, and finally explain to Ramsaran that they failed to retrieve his pit bull (which, most likely, would be dead by then) because they failed to react quickly enough; or they call up a judge, apply for an emergency warrant, drive over to the courthouse in Kew Gardens, pick up the warrant, drive back to East Elmhurst, storm into the bodega, make some arrests if anyone's still there, and scoop Ramsaran's dead dog off the ground; or they just go in and grab the motherfucker. After delivering the message, the kid's supposed to leave the door open. Because God forbid they're ever separated, Hutchison and Wright go in together. They enter through the front—under the pretense of grabbing a cup of coffee, because you don't need a warrant for *that,* do you?—and once inside the store, they hear some ruckus down in the basement and they decide to investigate. Lopez, working alone, will go around to the back and seal off the exit in case someone tries to sneak out the dogs. They'll even make some arrests for the overtime. And if they can't get prosecutions—any public defender able to find his own dick would use it to piss all over their probable cause and get the arrests thrown out of court—then so what? They will have pushed some ass-holes through the system. They will have harassed. They will have rescued the dog, which they will then deliver to a grateful Ramsaran, who doesn't even know they're out here, who will be so overwhelmed, so impressed, that—and this is Lopez's secret plan—when Ramsaran gets promoted to some elite investigative task force, he'll hand-select Lopez to be his partner. Why not? Why can't he think that way? Why can't he let his imagination go wherever it wants? All he's doing is sitting here and staring out the window and waiting for a fucking drug dealer, the world's scrawniest bouncer to lift the velvet rope and invite them inside.

"You know there ain't no way he's coming," Hutchison says. His skewer picked clean, he javelins it out the window. "You know we're just sitting here with our thumbs up our asses."

From the backseat Wright says, "He likes sitting with his thumb up his ass."

"Is it true?" Hutchison says.

"Hey, Lopez," Wright says. "Let me ask you something. You shave that space in the middle of your mustache? Or is that natural? How's that work, cause I've always been curious."

Lopez stares out the window, as if it renders him invisible. If he doesn't look at them, they can't see him. The bodega across the street is disconcertingly dark. Bodegas aren't *supposed* to be dark, Lopez thinks—not in this neighborhood, not at this time of night. He doesn't like it any more than he likes opening up his fridge at home and having the interior lightbulb stay dim. He blames the kid for some reason, as if the bodega's darkness were his fault, just as he always blames his wife for leaving the refrigerator door open too long. He adjusts his passenger-side mirror. Two figures have appeared in the glass: one a man-sized white guy, the other black and as big as a house. *They are closer than they appear,* the mirror warns.

"Hey, Lopez," Hutchison says. "You wanna stop them? Let's stop them. Ten bucks says they've got guns."

Wright sticks his head into the front seat, his face a few inches from Lopez's. "Let me guess," he says. "You think they're smuggling Chihuahuas in their pants. Is that right? For the big bad dogfight?"

"We gonna stop these guys, or what?" Hutchison says.

Lopez knows that both Hutchison and Wright have already assumed this night is going nowhere—no dog, no arrests, no overtime, no fun—and so they've put all quarterbacking responsibilities on him. The decisions are his to make, the fuckups will be his to bear. That way, when they go back to the 115th Precinct having done nothing all night but sit on their asses in a car without air-conditioning, Hutchison and Wright will be able to direct the full force of their prodigious ball-busting powers onto only one set of nuts.

At the entrance to the bodega, the two guys split up. The white guy continues down the block, while the big black guy goes around, as the others had done before him, to the back of the store. Neither holds

much interest for Lopez, because neither drags Ramsaran's dog on a leash.

"I'm almost sure those guys had guns," Hutchison says.

"Just so I got this straight," Wright says. "We're trying *not* to make collars tonight?"

"I want an empanada," Hutchison says. "Does anyone else want an empanada?"

"Hey, Lopez," Wright says. He rattles the headrest in front of him. Anti-Crime cops are not designed to be this still for this long. "Are you sleeping up there? Have you fallen *asleep*?"

"I'm awake," Lopez says.

"Oh thank God," Wright says. "Can you run the plan past me again? Because I'm confused. We wait here all night, yeah? That's the plan? We wait here and do nothing? Jesus fucking Christ, Lopez. Give up. Your little spic friend ain't coming back out."

"He'll come," Lopez says. He presses his tongue against the roof of his mouth to keep his teeth from grinding. "Any minute now."

The men in Max Marshmallow's basement look up. They hear a creaking, a groaning, the floorboards' lament, and like the basement dwellers in Samson's palace, each of these men fears the ceiling will come crashing down on top of their heads. Eyeballs nervously check exits. K-Lo, nearest the ladder, rests an uneasy hand on a rung. If anything happens, he'll climb up to the metal cellar doors, push them open, and escape out onto the sidewalk. Jossie and Paulie Guns and Virgin Light all retreat from the center of the basement and press their backs against the walls. The more paranoid—Alfredo among them—foresee rubble and rescue workers. The more dimwitted—Soft-Core Jonas among them—assume the sagging weight belongs to the Batistas' dog, a gargantuan, three-headed beast. Only Diana seems unaffected. As the ceiling groans, she paces inside her ring, her ears pressed neatly to the top of her head. She knows that whoever's coming down these stairs ain't got no quarrel with her.

"Look at all these beautiful faces," Baka says. He fills the stairway, poses as if someone were taking his picture. "What's going on? The big dogfight hasn't started yet? I'm not too late?"

"Not at all," Alfredo says as he picks his way through the people in front of him. This is his party and no matter who crashes the gate, he will act the gracious host. He wishes he had a Dutch to give him, fresh off the welcome wagon. He wishes Baka had a coat he could take and hang up on two hangers. "You're here just on time. We waited for you, matter of fact."

"How you doing? You doing good? Hanging in there?" Hands in pockets, Baka looks over Alfredo's head, scanning the room. "Where's your brother at?"

"You come all by yourself?" Alfredo says.

"You mean did I bring Pierre? Pierre of the busted grill? He's at home, thanks for asking. He's recuperating. He got himself hit—did I tell you this yet?—he got himself hit in the mouth with a bowling ball."

"Well," Alfredo says, "those things do happen." With a possessive, guiding hand, he steers Baka ringside, toward the cardboard boxes. A VIP view for a VIP guest. Not that there's much to see. A basement full of goons, smoking Dutches, drinking beers, eating candy bars, quoting from *The Big Lebowski*, and arguing, always arguing, about whatever binary they can think of: McDonald's/Burger King, Nas/Jay-Z, Shaq/Kobe, Marty/Dceve, Ron Jeremy/Peter North, the handball courts on Eighty-fifth vs. the handball courts at Travers Park. Alfredo looks around. K-Lo still lingers by the ladder, Sean Lau by the stairs. Lee, who came all the way out here from Staten Island, stands alone with his arms crossed in front of his chest. Rick Sprinkle tells a story no one is listening to; Forest Hills David picks up an empty shoebox off the card table and stares into it with a professional interest; Jonas looks like he's asleep on his feet. The only one who actually seems to be enjoying himself is Winston. The perfect cocktail party host, he works the room with a smile on his face, moving from clique to clique, making sure the awkward have fresh cans of beer to stare into. Since getting his own can knocked out of his hand, Winston has gotten another, which he seems to be spitting into instead of drinking from, as if every sip were being shown to Alfredo in reverse. That's weird. Alfredo looks into the ring to see if the dog is walking backward, growing younger—but nope, not at all. She's moving toward Baka. She trots over to his corner of the ring, where she deigns to sniff the fingers of his out-

stretched hand. Without a functioning adrenal system, Baka doesn't emit any fraidy-cat pheromones; there's no fear wafting off his considerable body, nothing that might antagonize the dog.

"A beautiful animal," Baka says, and Diana dips her head with false modesty.

"She sure is," Alfredo says. He watches jealously as Baka scratches behind her ears.

"And where's the pit bull at?" Baka says. "Or did this fine bitch eat him already?"

"Ha ha. No, no. Not yet, at least. The other dog's with my brother."

"Ah," Baka says. He frowns, looking more like a lion than ever. "And this is where I ask you again, like a fool, 'Where's your brother àt?' And then you say, 'He's with the other dog.' And then I say, because I'm still such a fool, 'Okay, where's the dog at?' And then you say . . ."

Alfredo is deciding how hard to laugh at this when he hears someone coming down the stairs behind him. He spins around, goes up on his tiptoes. But it's only Max, easing himself down by the handrail. Alfredo feels strangely disappointed. With Baka having just shown up, Alfredo hoped Mike Shifrin might follow, poisoned dagger in hand; it would confirm the ingenuity of his brother's plan, and by extension, just like the E-beeper, Alfredo's ingenuity in figuring it out. Fuck it. If Shifrin isn't going to show up on his own, then Alfredo will make him appear.

"Ha ha," Alfredo says as Baka continues to outline the Möbius strip of their hypothetical conversation. "You know what? Lemme borrow your phone and I'll call my brother up. See where he's at."

"What's wrong with *your* phone?"

"Juiceless," he says, patting his pocket. "I forgot to charge it last night."

Baka glowers at Alfredo, as if annoyed that he can't think of a good enough reason to turn down so simple a request. "Hurry that shit up," he says, handing Alfredo the phone. "I'm running low on minutes."

Alfredo hits the big green Talk button, and up pops a list of Baka's most recent outgoing calls. The screen is labeled History, as if this were a prime source document, yellowed at the edges. There are some names scattered in there—Amery, Jim, Pierre, Zach—but Alfredo isn't interested in any of them. Paranoid Baka would never enter a business associate's name into his cell, just as Paranoid Alfredo never saved

Baka's name to his own contact list. He scrolls through the list, looking for untagged numbers. Working quickly, he keeps the phone close to his chest, as if it were a half-decent poker hand. When he sees a number he likes the looks of—it's got a preponderance of fours, his father's lucky number—he dials it, knowing the call will never go through. Like a Podunk town in the Bible Belt, Baka's phone has no bars. The basement is a receptionless dead zone, but Alfredo presses the phone to his ear anyway. He's a pro at this by now. When, just as expected, the call fails to connect, Alfredo clicks the cell shut and hands it back to Baka.

"No dice?" Baka says.

"No service." Alfredo shrugs, as if to indicate he doesn't hold this against him. "You want something to drink? A Yoo-hoo or something?"

Instead of answering, Baka looks over Alfredo's shoulder, where a rumpus begins to take shape. Max Marshmallow is clawing at Forest Hills David's elbow, while David, his face contorted by a helpless smile, tries pulling his arm away. A marshmallow falls out of Max's mouth. It sits sticky and gooey on the basement floor, a white dented pillow. Mouth open, breathing heavy, Max grabs at David's wrist, and again David yanks his arm free. They play this game—clutch, release, clutch, release—all the way over to Alfredo.

"Yo, Dito," David says. "Tell this geezer to watch his hands."

"I caught him," Max says, his face red and pulsing. "I caught him. Going through boxes. Stealing."

"Check my pockets," David says. He spreads his arms out wide, pinned to the cross. "Check my fucking pockets *right now*."

Thanks, but no thanks. Alfredo has already gotten into enough trouble going through other people's pockets—or unclipping beepers from belts as the case may be. He looks instead for Sean Lau, the escort's escort. He's probably got a hooker in the backseat of his car right now, and Alfredo wants to broker a deal. If he buys Max a handjob—he'll have to throw in a free Viagra, too—then maybe the old man will leave him alone for a few minutes. But Alfredo doesn't see Sean anywhere. He's gone back to work, it seems, snuck away without tendering regrets. Which is bad news for Alfredo's party. Like a barfly stumbling out of the men's room with toilet paper stuck to his shoe, Sean Lau has broken the seal. If anyone saw him go—*That dude's get-*

ting out of here, he's giving up on the dogfight?—then his exit will only be the first of many.

"You're out of time," Max says. He taps the face of his wristwatch. "Ten minutes later and I've got punk kids going through my merchandise."

"Man, fuck you," David says.

Max sighs, low and long-suffering. With only one marshmallow embedded in his cheek, his face seems lopsided, like a stroke victim's. He is an old man, and Alfredo, fifty years his junior, is jealous. Jealous of the wrinkles and liver spots, the red-rimmed eyes, the purple veins on the tops of his hands, the set of falsies he soaks in warm water at night. Oh, Alfredo thinks, to live so long that teeth turn to powder in your mouth!

Lee, who came all the way out here from Staten Island, claps Alfredo on the back and snaps him out of his reverie. "I think I'm gonna take off," Lee says.

"What? Already? Shit hasn't even started yet."

Lee shrugs, too polite to say he did not drag his ass all the way out to Queens to smoke Dutches and listen to Rick Sprinkle's stories. He came out here for the novelty of a dogfight, and that shit is looking increasingly improbable. If he leaves now and if he catches an E train right away, then he *might* make the 2:30 ferry back to Shaolin, *might* get home and be in bed before the sun comes up—Lee already swearing an oath, as many have sworn before, that never again will he make the trek out to Queens.

"Good," Max says. "Get out. Take your friends. You hear that, everybody? Dogfight's canceled!"

"Max," Alfredo says. "Please."

"Please my ass," Max whispers. "Don't make a jerk out of me. This is my store we're talking about. I *live* here. Understand what I mean? I'll call the police if I have to."

Alfredo wants to grab Max by the shoulders and scream in his face. Forget about yourself for a second. Consider Winston's safety. Consider Isabel, Christian Louis, the dry-bristled toothbrush waiting for me at home. Alfredo wants to duct-tape Max's mouth so he'll stop talking and Diana's mouth so she can't hurt anyone and the Hughes brothers' eyes so Alfredo doesn't have to look into them, and with any

leftover tape he wants to bind Lee's feet to keep him here, down in this basement, where Alfredo will whisper promises in his pink little ear. Sean left and now you're gonna leave and then everyone else is gonna leave, but you can't go, okay? I'm going to need you to listen to me very carefully: I'll do whatever it takes. Whatever it takes to keep you people down here. I'll tell jokes. I'll swallow fire. I'll spin plates, walk on my hands, juggle bowls full of goldfish.

"Just hold up," he tells Lee. "Stick around for a minute. I'll make this right."

As the weathermen predicted, the rain arrives. Fat drops *ping-ping* the metal cellar doors. Alfredo takes off his shirt and tosses it to the floor, as if this were a bathroom shower, not a meteorological one. With his jeans slung low, two inches of his lucky boxer shorts are visible. Made out of silk, with little teddy bears on them, the boxers were a gift from Isabel, paid for with her video store wages. Alfredo worries that these cuddly bears—especially the one in a bow tie, licking an ice cream cone—will draw some *ho snaps!* from the eighteen thugs, criminals, and tough guys crowding Max Marshmallow's basement, but on that score Alfredo is safe. No one looks at his boxers. They look instead at his bare-chested physique.

"Goddamn, Alfredo," Baka says. "You one outrageously skinny motherfucker." At three-hundred-plus pounds, Baka might be a less than credible source, but his judgment represents the consensus. Most of the guys down here have never seen Alfredo with his shirt off, and for those who have, like Winston, it's been a long, long time—circa tenth grade P.E. class. No one expected his ribs to jut out as much as they do. Nobody imagined his shoulders would be so narrow. "Do me a favor and turn sideways," Baka says. "I wanna see if you disappear."

"Yeah, yeah," Alfredo says.

The guys down here want to know if he's half Puerto Rican, half Ethiopian, if his nipples touch, if he needs to run around in the shower to get wet, if there's just one stripe on his pajamas, one belt loop on his pants. People do not usually play this game with Alfredo. He is too good at it, quick to snap back and unafraid of close-to-the-bone meanness. But tonight he ain't interested.

"Everyone get comfortable," Alfredo says. He walks over to the makeshift ring, where Diana lies flat and still on the floor, the base-

ment's cool cement under her belly. Sweat rolls down the bars of Alfredo's rib cage. He steps over a cardboard box, puts a tentative foot inside the ring. "I'm going to fight this dog."

"You're going to fight *our* dog?" Alex says.

Alfredo shrugs. "If that's okay with you."

Bam-Bam's eyebrows reach toward his hairline. On behalf of his brothers, both the living and the dead, he says, "Sure. Knock yourself out."

Diana stands up on wobbly legs. She yawns, and with her mouth swung open and her tongue uncurled, Alfredo can see deep inside her mouth, the dark corners, the fleshy punching bag at the back of her throat. He wishes he had his skull-crushing Timberlands instead of these tractionless bowling shoes. If he slips—it'll probably be on some blood, probably his own—he'll need to tuck his body into the fetal position, cover his neck with his fists, and wait for someone, anyone, to reach in and save him. Instead of looking at Alfredo, Diana watches the stairs, the way a jump shooter won't look at the hoop until the very last moment. Her ears pitch straight up into the air. Her body goes rigid, the tail hooked over her back like a scorpion's. Alfredo wants to call a time-out. He wants to step out of the ring, open up betting, buy himself a few extra minutes. He takes a peek behind him, plotting a possible escape route, and the dog charges. As she gallops toward him, he folds his body inward. He closes his eyes, covers his crotch with his hands, but Diana has already sailed past him. She claws at a cardboard box. She barks, again and again, and each time her head snaps forward and spit flies out of her mouth. The box tears open. Soup cans spill out all over Alfredo's shoes, a chicken noodle jailbreak. Diana retreats, then charges again, throws her irate body against another column of boxes. Her fangs are bared. She wants out of this ring; sensing this, everyone backs away, except for Alfredo, who stands paralyzed right next to her, close enough to feel the heat of her breath. His hands still cover his crotch. Through the fabric of his jeans, he pinches the head of his penis, to remind himself that it's still there. Diana's barking grows louder. She screams, *I'm down here you cunt, waiting for you, waiting all fucking night.*

Her challenge goes answered. No trick of acoustics. No thin echo down here. When Diana barks, she gets barks in return.

Tariq walks down the stairs, a leash snapped taut in his hand. Fight-

ing his way out of that leash is a dog, a pit bull, his eyes hot and enraged.

Lee slides his MetroCard back into his wallet.

Normally in an interrogation, or at least in the interrogations Alfredo's seen in the movies Isabel makes him watch, a long metal table separates the interrogator from the interrogee. Both parties sit in chairs, so that the interrogator, when frustrated, has something to throw against the wall. These chairs are usually cold and gray, in spirit if not in actuality. The room comes equipped with either a one-way mirror, streaked with grime, or a video camera, easily unplugged. These are the basics. Bonus features include blindfolds, polygraph needles, bright lights, tanks full of water, pinky-slicing shears, dental equipment, threats to one's family, interrogees dangling out of open windows, and games of Russian roulette in which the bullet has been discreetly palmed. Unfortunately for Alfredo, this basement has no chairs, no windows, no lie detector, no mirror, either one-way or two, and, for obvious reasons, he can't threaten Tariq's family. Alfredo can only ask questions, and hope to receive truthful answers.

"Where the fuck you been?"

The dog whips his head back and forth, those creepy human eyes of his straining to get out. Tariq holds him by the collar, even sits on his back as if riding a mythological beast, but the dog pulls him forward anyway. They inch closer to Alfredo, closer to the German shepherd on the other side of the room.

"Man oh man," Tariq says, admiring his dog. "Look at how strong he is."

"Where," Alfredo says, "have you been?"

"I'm sorry," Tariq says. "I can't hear you. Can you come a little closer?"

Alfredo stays where he's at. He shouts to be heard over the barking.

"Oh," Tariq says. "I got you now. Where have I *been*? I been at home. With the fam. Right where you left me."

"You been at home," Alfredo says. "This whole time."

"This whole time."

"And what have you been doing?"

"Praying!" he says, as if to say, *What else would I be doing?* His pupils

are dilated, as wide and dark as dirty old pennies. "I've been behind on my prayers today. All this running around."

"You start praying before or after you took some of that Ecstasy I gave you?"

"After," Tariq says. His face beams. "You are a terrific noticer, Dito. You are, excluding myself, the third-best noticer I know. Allah, of course, is the first. I took the drugs and *then* I prayed. Yes. Correct." He wraps a hand around the dog's mouth, and with only the German shepherd barking now, it becomes much easier for Alfredo to hear his brother. "It's against the rules. Drugs. It is strictly forbidden. The Book calls them intoxicants. The Book says they are a loathsome evil of Satan's doing."

"I bet," Alfredo says. "Did anyone outside see you come in here?"

"I used the alleyways to get to the back of the store. Just as you commanded. I found the key in the same spot Papi used to leave it in. Taped to the bottom of that potted plant. So his whores could sneak themselves in. You were probably too young for all that." He wears a faraway smile, as if recalling a party Alfredo hadn't been invited to. "Now let me ask *you* a question, Dito. How come you ain't wearing a shirt?"

Alfredo looks down at his chest, sees himself as his brother must see him. His ribs protrude as if he'd recently swallowed an open umbrella. His nipples are pink and embarrassingly small, set too close together on a chest that would belong more rightly to a prepubescent boy. There is no hair save for a thin trail that leads out of his boxer shorts and up to his belly button, an innie, unlike Isabel's, whom he desperately wants to ask about—*Is she okay? Was she asleep when you left?*—but he's afraid to say her name aloud. It'd give Tariq permission to say it, and the name would curdle in his mouth. Alfredo crosses his arms over his chest, to cover his exposed nipples, and maybe the dog interprets this as a sign of aggression, or maybe the dog's just mean, but either way, he throws Tariq off his back and flies at Alfredo's waist. Tariq pulls on the leash. The dog's teeth click against Alfredo's belt buckle.

"Look at how *strong* he is," Tariq says as he reels the dog in. "You gotta crouch down," he tells Alfredo. "You gotta get on his level. Show him your palms." Tariq cups his hands together, as if he were accepting

communion. Whole inches of the leash slacken. "Show a dog you've got no way to defend yourself and he'll love you forever."

"How much X did you take?"

"I been praying all night. Know what I figured out? Only Allah is perfect. Me? It's like I'm fighting on a crooked path, trying to get better, purer, but I just don't know . . . It's hard to explain." The leash bites into his hand, cutting off blood flow. His fingertips whiten. "It's like I'm either a work in progress, or it's already over for me. Like not in this lifetime. You know? Like maybe I'm broken. Maybe there's something wrong with me that can't get fixed. Maybe I *can't* get better."

"What did you do?"

"Crouch down," Tariq says. "Show this pup your palms and let's see how he reacts."

Baka approaches the brothers hunched over, legs splayed apart, fingers twitching above his hips as if he were a Wild West gunfighter. "Put 'em up," he orders Tariq. "Put 'em up, put 'em up—you dirty, dirty rat."

"You bring the Russian with you?" Tariq says.

"See?" Baka says. "This is what I'm talking about. No, 'Hey, Baka, my man! How's it hanging? How's tricks? That a real nice outfit you got on. Where I get me one of those?' Pleasantries, Jose, Tariq—whatever the fuck your name is. Pleasantries keep the world spinning. Separates us from animals." He pinches the nylon sleeve of his tracksuit. "Sports Authority, by the way. I buy them in bulk. Let me know if you want one. Hey, speaking of animals, and correct me if I'm wrong here, but I thought Muslims weren't allowed to keep dogs as pets."

"I don't know anything about that," Tariq says quickly. He seizes the dog's collar, as if to keep his hands from shaking to pieces. "I follow the Book, and the Book doesn't say anything about that."

"Whatever," Baka says. He turns to Alfredo. "Your clown posse is getting restless. They want to lay down some bets."

"There's nothing in the Book forbidding dogs," Tariq says. He runs his hands down the pit bull's front legs. "You think you know, but you don't know. I know. There's nothing about that at all."

"I'm not talking to you anymore," Baka says. "*Books?* Who gives a shit about books?" He pulls a money clip out of his pocket and waves

it under Alfredo's nose. "I'm talking about *bets,* Fredo. I've got some gambling to do. But if you delay this shit any further, people are either gonna leave or burn this place to the ground."

Alfredo can go to the police right now. *Stay right here,* he could tell everyone. *Be back in a hot minute.* He'll go up the stairs Tariq just came down. He'll take a deep breath, push through the front door, and run, head down, fists pumping like a good leadoff hitter, intent on beating the throw. In these lighter red and tan bowling shoes, he might get to the Impala before Mike Shifrin gets to him. If Shifrin is even out there. If the fucking cops are still out there! And if they are, if they haven't given up on him yet, then he'll stick his head through the Impala's open window and deliver the news. *The dog's here and he's all yours. Godspeed. Don't forget to make your arrests.* Maybe he'll ask one of the cops, the Hispanic one probably, to escort him back home. And then—if the cop wouldn't mind—to come back tomorrow and make sure he's okay. Hey, why stop there? Why not hire the cop as a twenty-four-hour bodyguard? He'll run alongside Alfredo's cabs, jump in front of the occasional bullet. While Alfredo can't actually pay this cop a salary, he'll at least buy him some official-looking sunglasses, some dark suits from the Salvation Army, maybe even one of those earpieces with the fusilli wiring. If they're not too expensive. Oh man, if he only had money. He wouldn't owe Winston anything, he wouldn't owe Baka anything, he wouldn't live with his parents, he wouldn't have stolen fifty-two pills of Ecstasy because he would've just gone out and *bought* fifty-two pills of Ecstasy. If he only had money, he wouldn't have kicked anyone in the throat. Curtis would be alive. And Alfredo would be home, in bed with Isabel, playing I Wish. It isn't fair. He brought out two hundred dollars tonight, but after all the marked-up Dutches and beers and candy bars and Drake's cakes and Little Debbies and plantain chips, he's only got a hundo left. And it's still more than he ever has on his person. And it's *still* less than what everyone else has got. In the pockets of the fuckers around him, Alfredo can see some fat-ass wallets. Where he can't see wallets, he assumes they've got money clips like Baka's, overburdened with bills. How is that fair? The cash in this basement could buy Christian Louis a birthday cake every year of his life, with enough left over for one big blowout bash: a rented-out movie theater, a rented-out roller skating rink, a party with a magician, a party with a clown, a party at McDonald's with their big-

ass ball pit, a trip to a petting zoo where a soft-tongued llama would lick grains out of Christian Louis's delighted little hand. Now we're talking. Worse comes to worst, at least there'd be that. Something happens to Alfredo, at least the little man would have cakes to tear into on his birthday.

Baka snaps his fingers in Alfredo's face. "Where'd you go?" he says. "Who am I supposed to talk to when you check out like that?" He tilts his head toward Tariq. "*Him?*"

Tariq smiles peacefully, and Alfredo knows that if Baka says one more word, Tariq will let go of the leash and that'll be it: pandemonium. Marc and Billy pushing each other over spilled beer and scuffed sneakers is one thing, but if Baka and Tariq go at each other? Forget about it. Alfredo needs to keep this place under *some* measure of control. If shit blows up, everyone will spill out of here, Tariq will never get arrested, the Mike Shifrin problem will go unsolved, and Alfredo will be right where he started. No way, man. Can't happen. He leads Baka away from his brother. They walk over to the card table with the shoebox on it, where Alfredo goes up on his tiptoes and sticks his hand into the haze.

"Single file, everybody. Let's get this shit started. Single file, please. *Single* file. Break out that cash mo, people. Make your wagers. Place your bets."

AIDS, the first man in line, bets twenty on the pit bull. When Alfredo tries to bully him into betting some real money, AIDS spreads open his wallet: ragged, empty, not even a cartoon moth. Because he never knows when to quit, he turns the wallet over and gives it a shake, and all his plastic cards—his Visa card, his Blockbuster card, his Queensboro Public Library card—slip out of their sleeves and fall to the floor. Alfredo places the poor kid's twenty in the shoebox. Next in line, Rick Sprinkle and Timmy P. step over AIDS to bet seventy-five dollars each on the pit bull. Rhino lays down a hundred.

"Ain't you gonna write that down?" he says.

"I don't have to," Alfredo says.

Max hovers behind him, his urge to kibitz stifled for way too long. "Write it down," he says.

"I got it all up here," Alfredo says, tapping his temple. "Locked away in the vault."

"Write it down," Max says.

While Winston goes upstairs to fetch paper and pen, Billy Fitzgerald bets this month's allowance ($140) on the pit bull. Marc bets $145 on Diana. Billy ups his bet to $150. Like an auctioneer, Alfredo points a finger at Marc, but that's all the money he's willing to wager. Billy puffs out his chest, already victorious. Paulie Guns bets last night's drug dealing profits ($64, most of that in five-dollar bills) on the Batistas' dog. *Gotta go with pit bulls,* he explains. Those with legal jobs—David, Foot Locker employee; Jossie, RadioShack employee; Virgin Light, barback at a gay nightclub in Manhattan; and Jonas, men's room attendant at Carnegie Hall—bet chunks of their paycheck, or, in Jonas's case, the $40 in tips dropped into his wicker basket last night. No one knows what Jeff Hernandez does for a living—he claims to be a theater actor, of all things—but he puts $200 on the pit bull. Alex and Bam-Bam bet $300 on their own dog. Wowser! Alfredo makes a show of counting out their money. K-Lo throws a fifty-dollar bill into the shoebox and then runs back to his perch by the ladder. Tariq doesn't bet. Neither does Max. But Baka does. Last on line, he puts $150 on the Batista brothers' dog.

"I thought for sure you'd bet against us," Alfredo says.

"So did I," Baka says.

Winston has yet to return with a pad of paper. Not that Alfredo needs it. Working from memory, he recites each wager aloud and receives head nods and *uh-huhs* and *that's rights* in return. When he's finished, he kicks off his bowling shoe and removes $100 from the bottom of his sock. He drops the money in the box. Purely for the sake of appearances. It's gotta seem like he's betting, right? Also for the sake of appearances—since he already knows the total—he counts up all the cash.

The men down in this basement bet $1,784. That's all together. They bet $1,064 on the pit bull, $720 on Diana. As per gambling custom, the house keeps 10 percent. Alfredo counts out $178 and lays it in Max Marshmallow's palm. (*You're kidding me,* Max says.) Alfredo tells the crowd there will be no handicapping, no odds. Wagers are straight up. If you put $100 into the shoebox and your dog wins, you win $190. There's your 10 percent. Here's the irony, which Alfredo keeps to himself: if Diana, the nominative underdog, wins the fight, then the house makes $310, the difference between what was bet (minus 10 percent)

on Diana vs. what was bet (minus 10 percent) on the pit bull. If the pit bull, the nominative favorite, wins the fight, then the house *loses* $310 because they won't have enough cash in the box to pay out the winners. The money in Max's palm will get taken away. And that still won't cover it all. They'll be $132 short, but really they'll be only $42 short because it's not like Alfredo would collect on his winnings. But still: they'll have to go into Max's old-fashioned cash register and pull out a couple of twenties, essentially taxing the guy for the pleasure of watching people hock up loogies on his basement floor. Like so much else, it doesn't seem fair. But then again, it ain't gonna happen. Diana can't win this dogfight because Alfredo has no intention of ever letting it begin.

"I'm going upstairs," he announces. With the shoebox tucked under his arm, he gives Max what is meant to be a reassuring nod. "I gotta lock up the cash."

Even though AIDS has the least amount of money in the box, he is, of course, the first to object. "Hold on," he says. "*Where* you going?"

"For the duration of the dogfight," Alfredo says, as if reading off a rule book no one else has access to, "the wagered money is supposed to be locked up in a safe place. This is procedure."

"Yeah," AIDS says, stroking his theoretical goatee. "But *why?*"

"Why the fuck you think people lock up money?" Alfredo says. He hopes that if he punishes AIDS enough, then no one else will question him. "I know you don't know shit about nothing, AIDS, but this is procedure. This ain't no dogfighting video game, okay? We lock up the money so we can all enjoy the fight without worrying about somebody sneaking off with the cash."

"Come on," Rick Sprinkle says. "You think someone down here would steal the money?"

Max says, "I'd be surprised if someone *didn't* try to steal the money."

"Is that supposed to be directed at me?" David asks.

Alfredo turns to Max. "You got a safe up there I can use?"

"You know I don't have a safe," Max says.

"Okay. I'll lock it up in the cash register."

"This is ridiculous," Bam-Bam says. "Nobody's gonna steal the money."

"Spoken like a true criminal," Alfredo says.

Baka laughs. He's been watching all this with a smile on his face, as if he were eager to see how it'll all play out. In a gesture halfway between admiration and affection, he wags his finger at Alfredo.

"I'm tired," Alfredo says, and it feels like the first true thing to come out of his mouth in hours. "I'm going up now. Any of you badasses and tough guys wanna keep an eye on me, then please—follow me up. Be my fucking guest." And with that, he heads for the stairs.

He finds Winston in an aisle stocked full of disposable goods: paper plates, plastic cups, paper towels, paper napkins, rolls of toilet paper individually priced. Winston is shaking his head, as if overwhelmed by the number of choices. He holds a can of beer in his hand. A small blue pencil—the kind used to fill out Lotto cards—hangs from his lips. He looks lost, an oversized child trapped in the dark. When he sees Alfredo, he opens his mouth to speak and the pencil falls to the floor.

"I can't find a pad of paper *anywhere*," he cries.

He stoops over to pick up the pencil, and Alfredo grabs him, pulls him toward the front of the store. Winston doesn't protest. As always, he's along for the ride. The two of them move quickly down the darkened aisles. Alfredo knows he's pushing his luck here—he could get Tariq arrested *right now*—but there is almost eighteen hundred dollars in this shoebox and that is too much cash to ignore. He carries it cradled like a baby. As he runs, the bills bounce off the sides of the box, in tune with the thumping in his chest. Cold fingers of sweat tighten across his scalp. His lungs shrivel like fists. As if he's been submerged underwater and is just now breaking the surface, air jumps down his throat, quicker and quicker. He's got to get rid of this shoebox. He puts it up on the counter, next to Max's cash register, and wouldn't you know: his chest unclenches. Able to breathe normally, unburdened of all that cash, he glides to the front door, where, under the eaves of his hands, he peers out into the street, looking for Russian gangsters and Chevy Impalas. The rain falls sideways like flashing needles of light.

"Unbelievable," Winston says, breathing heavily. The top of his beer can has been pushed into itself, making the hole much wider, a mouth caught in mid-yawn. Into this hole, Winston spits a ribbon of brown goo. "A big store like this, and not one goddamned pad of paper."

"What are you doing?"

"You mean this?" He pulls down his lower lip to reveal, tucked into the fold, a black-brown knot of chewing tobacco. His teeth are already stained. "It's called dipping."

"I know what it's called," Alfredo says, although, in truth, he did not. "You play the ukulele now, too?"

"I like it," he says. "It makes me feel mad dizzy."

Alfredo watches Winston drop another ribbon into the can, amazed that they've been here long enough for his best friend to cultivate brand-new addictions.

"Can I borrow your phone?" Alfredo asks. "Mine's dead."

"Seriously," Winston says. "What would you do without me?"

He tosses Alfredo his phone, and because Alfredo is worried about other things—because he's not thinking about catching it—he catches it. He flips it open and sees that Winston's usual background image, an orange-duned desert, has been replaced by a generic picture of an open highway. This annoys Alfredo. He doesn't give a shit about highways or deserts, but he finds it unbelievable that while he was plotting to keep them alive, Winston was sucking down pharmaceutical cocktails, experimenting with this dipping garbage, fiddling with his cell phone's preset wallpaper images. *Seriously? Does anyone out there have any fucking idea of the pressure I'm under?* With his jaw clenched, he scrolls through Winston's phone, past Contacts, past Settings and Tools until he gets to Messaging. He selects Compose New Message, and his thumbs go to work on the keypad.

> *my phone's out of service.*
> *alfredo got bit by a dog. he'll*
> *be coming out the back of*
> *the store. hurry! xo, baka*

The *xo* might be too much—hugs and kisses? really?—but Alfredo can think of no other way to approximate Baka's verbal flamboyance. He closes his eyes, sees the black backdrop of his lids. Summoned, the untagged numbers in Baka's call history float down. Green sevens locking into place next to orange fours. Alfredo enters all the numbers in the text message's address book. In a moment, in pockets scattered around New York City, phones are going to start ringing and beeping and vibrating. Baka's business associates—people Alfredo's never

met—are going to read a message he wrote, a message they won't understand from a number they don't recognize. That's okay. Alfredo is tossing a fistful of darts and needs only one bull's-eye. The odds seem decent to good. But those tireless fucks in the Department of Worry want to know what if Mike Shifrin's phone doesn't have text messaging capabilities. Oh please. Alfredo tears that particular thought down the middle and feeds both halves to the shredder. What kind of twenty-first-century drug dealer can't receive texts? He hits Send.

"What shitty weather, huh?" Winston says, looking out the front door. His breath leaves circles of fog on the glass. "Least it held off for the Mets game, I guess."

Alfredo takes the shoebox off the counter and brings it to Winston as fast as he can. He trades him, as they used to trade Marvel cards: the box for the beer can.

"Wait here five minutes," Alfredo says. "Then go across the street. Run across the street, actually." Five minutes should give Mike Shifrin, if he's even out there, enough time to check his phone, read a text message, cross the street, turn the corner, duck into the alley, and head toward the back of the candy store. Five minutes should be *plenty* of time. "Go over to that parked Impala," Alfredo says, tapping a finger on the glass of the door. "There are three DTs inside. Tell them the dog's here. Okay? And that they should make moves ASAP. Tell them to go around to the back of the store. The *back* of the store. You got it? Okay? Repeat all that back to me."

"There are three DTs across the street?" Winston says.

"They're here for my brother."

"Oh," Winston says. For the first time he looks down at the box in his hands. "Wow. Okay. And you want me to give them this money?"

Alfredo's head sags. It is only by an extraordinary effort of will that he keeps it from falling off his neck and rolling, eyes open, down Max Marshmallow's shiny linoleum floor.

"I want you to wait here for five minutes," Alfredo says. "Tell the police to come to the back of the store. The back. Then I want you to take that money and run home. Hide it under your bed." He tries to smile. "Stash it next to your dirty DVDs."

"This is our friends' money."

"What's the matter?" His hand sinks into the soft dough of Winston's shoulder. "You don't trust me?"

"I don't want to get into trouble."

"Winston, you'll be in trouble if you stay."

"That's not what I mean." He stares into the shoebox, frowning. "I *can't* hold this down. You know what I mean? I'll spend it all on drugs."

"You're quitting tomorrow," Alfredo says gently.

"I'll kill myself. I appreciate your faith in me. I really do. But you give me this money and I will die. Straight up. I'll spend every cent. I'll keep going till my heart bursts."

"All I need you to do is hold it down for twenty-four hours," Alfredo says. He considers the last twenty-four hours, how much can change in so short a time. "If you haven't heard from me by tomorrow, go over to my parents' place. Give the whole box to Isabel."

Max calls out Alfredo's name. He moves toward them through the dark, his voice terribly frayed, warbled at the edges.

"Change of plans," Alfredo whispers. He stands so close to Winston that the shoebox is pressed against both of their stomachs. "Tell the DTs the dog ain't here yet. *They* need to wait five minutes. Understand what I mean? Go now and tell them. They wait five minutes and then they come around to the back."

That should still work. As long as the cops catch Shifrin in the yard, Alfredo should be okay. If Shifrin has a gun on him—and why wouldn't he, if he's the O.G. Baka claims?—then he'll get collared on illegal possession of a firearm. Three and a half years, minimum. One problem solved. Then the cops go down into the basement and arrest everyone else, including Alfredo. Cost of doing business, as Baka might say. Everyone will spend a night, maybe two, in lockup, and then they'll all be back on the street. Except Tariq, who will have violated his parole—*I will not behave in such manner as to violate the provisions of any law to which I am subject, which provide for a penalty of imprisonment.* Problem number two: solved. Of course there might be complications—Max might lose his store, Shifrin might open fire on the police, Alex and Bam-Bam might miss Curtis's funeral, Jose Sr. might not get a Father's Day present—but no plan is perfect. This is as good as Alfredo can do. By Monday night at the latest, he'll be home with Isabel, kissing her ears, telling her, *I got rid of him, I took care of it,*

I did it all for you. Plus they'll have a nice $1,800 for the Christian Louis birthday fund.

"Please don't make me do this," Winston says.

"Hello?" Max cries out. "Alfredo?"

"Coming!" Alfredo says. He takes off Winston's cap and puts it on his own head. The Saturday night outfit he never expected to wear: stolen bowling shoes, yesterday's jeans, silk teddy bear boxer shorts, no shirt, a Spider-Man cap that falls down to his eyes. "How do I look?" he asks.

"You look stupid," Winston says. He runs his hand through the alopecia quilt of his scalp, as he does whenever his head is exposed.

"Imagine how stupid *you* look in this thing."

When Winston reaches for the hat, Alfredo pulls his head back.

"I need it," Winston says. "It's raining."

"You'll be running so fast, you can't get wet."

"It's my trademark," he says.

"I know, but not tonight, okay?" He turns Winston around so he faces the door. Across the street, there might be a man who wants to kill Winston as badly as he wants to kill Alfredo. In an ideal world, Alfredo gives this man his five minutes to go around to the back of the candy store. But with Max Marshmallow's voice getting closer, coming up the aisle behind them, Alfredo does not have that kind of time. This is not an ideal world. This is this world, and in this world Alfredo pushes Winston out the door and into the street.

"Run," Alfredo whispers.

Maybe Winston can't hear him. He hugs the box to his chest. He pokes his head out from under the awning and looks both ways down the street. Toward Manhattan, toward Flushing. Alfredo punches the glass door with the side of his fist, and Winston takes off. Or at least tries to. He runs with the out-of-water coordination of a seal, the shoebox tucked under his jiggling fin. From high school, from P.E. classes, from relay races demarcated by orange cones, Alfredo knows what's coming and already he feels a bodily unease. Winston runs into the street. With the rain coming down hard, he splashes through puddles, his head on a swivel. He looks discombobulated, as if he's been dropped off in a foreign country hostile to his own. He snags his foot on an invisible tripwire, and his free arm shoots out for balance. Here

we go. Tangled feet. Windmilling arms. Alfredo presses his face to the door, the glass cool against his forehead. He watches Winston crash into Marc Franschetta's souped-up Camaro, parked three cars behind the DT's Impala. The alarm goes off. The *honk-honk-honk, oo-woo-oo-woo* that Alfredo, and every other New Yorker, knows by heart. The Camaro's blue headlights flash in rhythm to the alarm, the car a dance party all to itself. Alfredo can't be sure about this—it's hard to see— but it looks like the cops have slumped down in their seats, as if they were uncomfortable being on the other end of these lights and this siren. Despite his fall, Winston has held on to the box. But he looks terribly vulnerable out there, marooned in the middle of the street.

"Alfredo!" Max calls out.

Alfredo turns away from the door and meets Max halfway down the beer aisle, where forties and six-packs sit befogged in humming, buzzing refrigerators. The fridges are backlit, the beers individually glowing. It is the only light in the store—except for the red eye of the smoke detector—and both Max and Alfredo draw near it.

"Let me hold on to the key," Max says.

"The key?"

"The key," Max says. In his agitation, he grabs hold of the closest thing—the refrigerator door handle—for support. "The little yellow register key on the counter. Next to the till."

"Right," Alfredo says.

"Well, let me get it."

Alfredo wants to press his face against this old man's chest. Even with his shirt off, bare-chested, exposed, Alfredo feels comfortable in front of Max. He is a good twenty years older than Jose Sr., but in a different life, a life in which Alfredo was born Jewish and white in, say, 1962, then this old geezer could've been Alfredo's father. Alfredo's name would be Saul, or something like that. He'd live in an alternate New York, where the Mets beat the Yankees in 2000, where Estes plunked Clemens, where the Twin Towers still stand, if not both then maybe one. As Alfredo nears the crisis of his life, he can't help but think of these hypothetical worlds, existing somewhere in some corner of the universe. He never kicked Vladimir in the throat. Jose Sr. never sold the store. Alfredo never brought this trouble into Max's basement.

"If you leave now, you can say we broke in. You can say you never knew anything, you were never even here. I'll back that up."

"You made a jerk out of me," Max says, his mouth emptied out. Alfredo imagines he swallowed the last marshmallow, and it slid all gooey down his old turkey throat. "You made a jerk out of me in my own store."

"You wanted to play gangster," Alfredo says softly.

"Excuse me?"

"You wanted to play gangster," Alfredo says, the reservoir of his sympathy containing only so much. "You wanted to play gangster—this is what you get."

"I'll call the police if I have to."

Alfredo puts the beer can in one of Max's hands, the Spider-Man cap in the other. "I'd let you use my phone," he says, stepping around him. "But the battery's dead."

Misha Shifrin jogs toward the back of the bodega. He is smiling, pleased to have all this rain pouring out of the sky. Water splatters the pavement, drips off the brim of his hat. Black, straight-billed, the hat belongs to Vladimir, and Misha wears it tonight, as he did last night, for good luck. As he nears the fence-enclosed yard, he pulls on a pair of rubber gloves. He isn't worried about leaving behind fingerprints—the rain will wash everything away—no, what Misha's worried about is gunpowder particles staining his hands. The police can test for that kind of thing, and while there's some debate as to whether or not it's admissible, it is certainly incriminating. With the gloves snapped tight around his wrists, Misha hops over the fence. Lands in the yard with a muddy squish.

The moon reveals only half its face. It hangs suspended at last quarter, and in its weak light the grass looks more yellow than green, dying if not already dead. Misha squats down in a corner of the yard, where a garden hose lies snaked between paint cans. There are no trees. No room for ball playing. A chipped ceramic pot has filled up with water. This is, he thinks, as good a place as any. From his corner of the yard, he watches the door, his grip tight on a Baby Glock 26.

He squats there long enough for his calves to cramp and for his brown leather oxfords to sink into the mud. Five hundred dollars these

shoes cost him. He put them on this morning without thinking, distracted by phone calls and emails and the *Today* show and the kettle screaming on the stovetop. When he shifts his weight, the ground sucks at his feet. He'll have to incinerate the shoes when he gets home, along with the gloves. Unbelievable. Five hundred fucking dollars. He fishes a protein bar from his pants pocket, and, reluctant to loosen his grip on the gun, he opens the packaging with his teeth. A bit of wrapper comes loose in his mouth and he spits it into the grass. The protein bar smells like peanut butter and maple syrup and disappears in three bites. He smacks his lips. He is thirsty now but not at all tempted to open his mouth and let the rain fall onto his tongue. Too much acidic content. Particulates. Carcinogens. Toothy tumors eager to congregate on the underside of his lungs.

With his free hand, he searches the grass in front of him. Looking for that tiny bit of wrapper. Stupid. He imagines police investigators finding it, looking up dental records, matching the marks on the wrapper to the teeth in his head. Not that he has any dental records in the States—but still, it isn't worth the risk to leave the wrapper behind, just as it wasn't worth the risk for that gorilla Baka to have sent him a text message. An electronic record of conspiracy. Stored forever in some AT&T supercomputer. Misha considers it his own fault for dealing with those kinds of people in the first place.

Less than a block away, a car alarm goes off. Misha keeps his head down. Tries to make himself as small as possible. With that car alarm blaring, lights might turn on in the houses around him. Faces might come to windows. Someone—unlikely, but possible—might call the police. Misha takes his hand off the gun, tries to wipe his gloves dry against the front of his pants. He considers getting out of here right now, taking a cab to the Okeanos bathhouse in Midtown, trying again tomorrow—but there will always be car alarms, Misha, there will always be bad, sinking feelings, and as your deadbeat alky father used to say, *Kto ne riskuyet tot ne pyot shampanskoe,* or, poorly translated, *Who doesn't make risks doesn't drink the champagne.*

The car alarm changes registers, the horn blaring now, *ank-ank-ank-ank,* growing louder, more insistent, and maybe that's why Misha doesn't hear the Spanish kid running up the alleyway until it's almost too late.

The kid vaults over the fence. Where Misha had landed on both

feet, the kid slips. He falls hard to the ground. Mud splatters his cheap-looking Knicks jersey.

Misha comes out of his crouch. He needs to get close. He'll have one shot before neighbors reach for phones, and then he'll have to take off running. He got lucky with the rain, but he can't expect a peal of thunder to cover the gunshot. The kid is rubbing his hip where he fell. He looks surprised to see Misha coming toward him, just as Vlad must've looked surprised when this coward kicked him in the throat. Misha stands over him, close enough to read the name on his jersey—"Starks"—and now that he's this close, he realizes that the kid is not a kid at all, but a grown man, which is surprising, sure, but it'll make all of this easier. Misha raises his gun, ready to blow the jaw off this cocksucker's face.

Misha is shot through the chest. His mouth fills up with something warm and watery and without taste. He hears more gunshots. Maybe two. Maybe one plus its echo. He doesn't remember firing. The gun is still in his hand, he thinks, but he can't be sure because he can't lift his head off the ground to check. His feet feel like wax. Rain strikes the rusted-over lids of paint cans, and it sounds like a wooden finger tapping on wood. Drenched, the hat constricts around his head. He wants to wiggle out from under it, but he can't get anything to move. He wants to spit out whatever liquid is filling his mouth, but he can't remember how.

Earlier. Alfredo is walking down the stairs, having just given Max the Spider-Man hat and the beer can. He takes the steps one at a time, his hand on the wooden railing. The basement's light swallows him up to his waist. He needs to delay this dogfight till the DTs show up, which—knuckles rapping on the railing—should just be a little bit longer. This is what he'll do: he'll tell the goons down in the basement that before the fight can begin, the dogs need to be wiped down with towels and water. To make sure their coats haven't been covered in poisons. *Procedure*, he'll say. Hey—that's not bad. That should work. Alfredo is feeling good, feeling the intoxicating brew of manipulating all the players, but when he comes off the last step and enters the basement, his stomach lurches. Of course. How foolish of him. No one ever waits. No one's ever patient. The show has started without him.

Inside the ring, the older brothers—Alex Hughes, Tariq Batista—heat up their dogs. The soup cans have been collected and stacked neatly off to the side. Alex holds Diana by the scruff of her neck. She drags him toward the center line, that silver strip of duct tape, and if his sneakers squeak, it goes unheard, swallowed by the barking of the dogs, which is louder than ever. Too loud, Alfredo thinks. Noise trips up the stairs, up the ladder, slips through the cellar doors and runs down the sidewalk. The cops, if they have ears on their heads, will surely be able to hear the barking. And if not the barking, the cheering. Alfredo needs to stop this. He has a deal with the cops. More important: *this is not part of his plan.* But what can he do? His body won't allow him to step into the ring—all collars and leashes have been removed—and there isn't an inch of space in the crowd in front of him. Alfredo's friends and half friends surround the ring, closing around it like a noose. He goes up on his tiptoes to see his brother gripping the dog by the sleek engine of its neck. Tariq moves his lips quickly and purposefully, as if working some kind of enchantment. Sweat drips from his chin, and Alfredo, unthinkingly sympathetic, wipes at his own. Tariq kisses his dog on the top of his head, between the ears—and like an irritated teenager, the dog struggles to get away. They inch closer to the center line. The pit leans forward on powerful legs, lips peeled back from gums. On the other side of the line, Diana tries to bite at his face. The crowd constricts even tighter, which Alfredo didn't think possible. As he takes a step forward, so do the dogs. Right up to the center line. Their noses almost touching. Alex and Tariq struggle to pull them apart and drag them into their respective corners. It is in this moment, with the magnetism between the animals at its strongest, that the handlers let go.

Afterward, when thinking back on this night, everyone down here will remember the crack of initial contact. The way the dogs, both of them airborne, collided in the center of the ring. The way the bone of one dog's skull smashed into the bone of the other dog's skull.

The pit bull's head hangs at an awkward angle to the rest of his body. As if he wants to get a good look at his tail but can't muster the energy. *This isn't fair,* Alfredo wants to shout. He looks to his brother, who stands outside the ring, one foot on a box, arms folded in front of his chest. *This is not fair!* When the dogs collided in midair, the pit bull snapped something in his spine. Look at his neck. Look at how he can't

defend himself as Diana bites into his face. Blood slides down his freckled nose. Thick black drops drip onto Max's floor. When Alfredo imagined this happening, he imagined the dogs barking and the crowd hushed, but it is the other way around. Everyone is screaming; the dogs are silent. Diana hoists her front legs over the pit bull's head. He escapes the clinch, goes low, his body turned sideways, his ribs protruding, his head dragging across the floor. She goes high, tears a chunk from the tip of his ear. She bites his face again. His lower lip swings loose from his mouth. It looks chewed on. It looks like it's been tied up with butcher string. Diana splits his nose. She mauls his face, which turns pink and red, with a little yellow between the eyes. When he limps away into a corner of the ring, toward Tariq, she follows. Without a yelp or a whimper, he sinks down onto his back. He shows her the white of his stomach, the animal kingdom's universal signal of submission. She bends her face to his stomach and disembowels him.

Tariq turns away from the ring, his face drained of color. He holds the leash in his hands and he's fidgeting with it, wrapping it around one palm and then the other, snapping it tight. His lips are moving. He staggers backward, and Alfredo races toward him. He doesn't know what's happening, but his brother is coming apart in a way Alfredo's never seen before. It seems as if he's stopped breathing, and Alfredo needs to get to him, needs to blow air into his mouth. All bodily instinct, he pushes his way through the crowd, throws his elbows when necessary. Tariq jumps when Alfredo grabs hold of his shoulders. His vacant, dilated eyes stare into Alfredo's face as if he no longer recognizes him.

"This is twisted," Tariq says. "This is all upside down."

Alfredo can barely hear him. The noise has exploded: Diana, victorious, crows inside the ring, while everyone else is pulsing, calling for a mop, a garbage bag, a bucket of soapy water, anything, anything at all to clean up this mess. Tariq's eyelids are fluttering. His knees dip, and Alfredo needs to hold him upright. Tariq is shaking his head, moving his lips, but Alfredo can't hear him. He grabs Tariq by the hand and pulls him through the crowd, toward the stairs, where it is quieter, and while at first Tariq resists, dragging his feet, soon Alfredo is not pulling his brother but getting pushed. Tariq puts his head down and forces Alfredo against the wall.

Tariq grabs him by the waist. He squeezes hard, leaves purple finger

bruises on the skin. Alfredo wants to tell him to stop, you're hurting me, but he's not sure he'd be heard. Tariq whimpers. His head snaps forward, smashes into Alfredo's chin—an accident maybe, but Alfredo's teeth click together so hard his ears pop. Tariq squeezes Alfredo's arms, prods at his torso, and it occurs to Alfredo that his brother's roving hands might be looking for an opening—something like an appendix scar—that he can split open and crawl into. He wants rights of possession, Alfredo thinks. He wants to take up residence. He wants to inhabit a body that never went to prison, never got cut up, never lost a girlfriend or a dog, a body without cause for grief.

"You win," Tariq says. His hands drop down to his sides. "Okay? You win. I give up. I'm crashing. You understand?"

No, Alfredo does not. He does not understand. He tries to push his brother away, but he can't extend his arms. Tariq's in too close. He smells like Barbasol and Irish Spring. He hooks his chin over Alfredo's shoulder, his bald head smooth and cool against Alfredo's cheek. And there it is: the indent on the back of his brother's neck. It opens up right in front of Alfredo, that soft pocket he's always been tempted to fill. Maybe—who knows?—Alfredo has one too. How could he be sure he doesn't? It'd be on the back of his neck, which he can't see on his own, and he never thought to ask anyone else to look out for it. It could be a thing he carries with him all the time, a thing Isabel's noticed but never mentioned.

"The police are coming," Alfredo whispers. He is unsure if what he's doing is right, but he cannot help himself. He clinches his arms behind his brother's back. "Go home, okay? Go upstairs into the store and leave out the front door. You'll be safe, you understand? But you gotta go now. You gotta get out of here."

Blood trickles from Tariq's nose. It is bright red, impressively so. Either he snorted some of that X, or he's getting one of the stress-induced nosebleeds he was prone to as a child. Alfredo tries wiping at the blood with his thumb, but he ends up just smearing it across Tariq's upper lip.

"Pinch your nose," Alfredo says. "Tilt your head back." He wipes his bloody thumb off on Tariq's shirt, before remembering that it's actually his shirt. "Aw, shit."

"What's the matter?"

"Tilt your head back."

257

"What's the matter?"

"It's okay. Tilt your head back. You're bleeding."

"No," Tariq says. "That isn't my blood." He takes a step back and spreads his hands over the front of his jeans, where the denim looks discolored, almost rusted. "You're an excellent noticer, but no, that's not my blood. That's Isabel's."

"Jose," Alfredo says softly.

"She spit onto my crotch. It's her blood. It isn't mine. It isn't mine at all."

Alfredo takes Tariq's shirt in his fists. He tries to push him, but Tariq has him pinned against the wall.

"And it's dark down here," he says. "And you *still* noticed. That's real impressive, Dito."

"Is she alive?" It is the most miserable question he's ever asked. He bites down on the insides of his cheeks, but it doesn't work. He has burst into tears. He is afraid to breathe, afraid that if he opens his mouth any wider he will crack the world in two. "Jose? Is she alive?"

"She's at home," he says. "In bed. With Mama, believe it or not."

"And are they *alive*?"

"You think I'd kill my own mother?" he says. When Alfredo doesn't answer, Tariq's shoulders start trembling. He giggles. His eyes are bright and shining, his mood swinging toward elation. Alfredo understands that this shift in mood has nothing to do with the pills his brother swallowed. It is the violence brewing in his chest. "I don't blame you," Tariq says.

People are looking at them now, if they haven't been already.

"It's a disgusting thought," Tariq says with a smile. "But I don't blame you for thinking it. I hurt everything I love, right? I love Allah, I hurt Him. Took all those pills, that loathsome evil. I love Isabel, and then—"

A strangled, desperate moan sweeps through Alfredo's body. Backed up against the wall, he starts quivering. He hates himself. He needs to get away, run home through the streets. Tears drip off his glasses.

"Stop that," Tariq warns. "Stop crying right now."

Alfredo nods. He tries holding his breath. If he had a shirt on, he could dry his face. Instead, he bites into his cheeks again, harder this time.

"I loved that dog," Tariq says. He inches closer, so that there's no space between them. "I loved that dog and now look at it. Look at this *disaster*." He shakes his head, amused. "It's like you're the only one I haven't hurt. What's that supposed to mean? You're so fucking smart—you tell me. What's it mean? Because *I* don't know. I can't understand it, Dito." He shoves a finger in Alfredo's face. "You're the one who broke the rules."

The blood above Tariq's lip has hardened into a brown crusty streak. His breathing deepens. He is smiling, panting, and for Alfredo the potential advantages of being backed up against this wall—it'd protect his kidneys, keep him up on his feet—have all been obliterated. He needs to get away. But there's no room for Alfredo to make a run for it, just as there's no room for him to rear back and deliver a blow. An elbow to the chin might work, if Alfredo could get enough strength behind it. Or he could use his keys. That might work. He could take one of his keys and have it jutting out of his fist. But he can't imagine himself doing it, not properly, not for real. He feels too weak. Blood surges to his temples.

"Isabel broke the rules, too," Tariq says. "But I had always been prepared to forgive her. That was the plan. The straight path. Isabel I had never intended to punish."

Alfredo sinks his fingers into the warm festering wound on his brother's cheek. He hits bone, hits nerves. Tariq's eyes widen in surprise. Lurching away, he screams. Loud enough to silence the dog in the corner. One long sustained head-clearing bell clap. He is bent over, one hand on his cheek, the other punching his thigh. When he turns back to the wall, Alfredo is gone.

The haze has thickened. By now every one of Alfredo's friends has turned away from the ring, away from the pit bull with its bowels coiled and steaming on the floor. They clot the center of the basement, these men. A dark mass of bodies, they seem to be standing one on top of the other, up to the ceiling and all of them shouting.

Alfredo runs toward them, hoping to disappear. He bangs off one body and into another: a pile of flesh, heavily cologned. Baka. Has to be. Alfredo wants to ask him if he has that .38 on him, tucked into his waistband, but there isn't any time. He hears his brother coming behind him. Of course. They're working on Tariq's terms now. This is what he has always wanted: a fight. Alfredo reaches into his pockets for

his keys, a weapon, pulling out loose change, dimes and nickels, a cell phone that goes skittering across the floor. His brother. His brother has the keys. Alfredo runs toward the pyramid of soup cans stacked neatly to the side of the ring. He grabs one off the top. It fits perfectly, as if made for his hand. When he turns around, he sees his brother sprinting toward him, his powerful arms swinging, his face dark and distorted.

The thing to do is wait. If Alfredo throws the can, he'll miss. He knows that. Impressive velocity, unfortunate aim. The thing to do is wait till Tariq gets close enough and then drive the can down into his face. Open up his forehead. Let the blood run into his eyes. But what Alfredo really wants to do, given the events of the last twenty-four hours, given that *he was the one* who failed Isabel, failed her a thousand times over, failed to not only protect her, his one responsibility in life, but actually facilitated her abuse, dropped Tariq off at home, on the doorstep, instead of at Budd's Bar or Gianni's Pizzeria or BQE Billiards or any one of the dozens of strip clubs on Queens Boulevard, volunteered his keys, neglected to call the house and warn her, left her exposed, shattered the life they imagined for themselves during round after round of late-night I Wish . . . because now nothing can ever be the same, not with this horrible thing between them, her mouth filling up with blood, his brother's hands, Christian Louis cowering in the womb . . . given all that, what Alfredo really wants to do is take this can and smash himself in the face. His arms are shaking. He feels helpless and dizzy, drowning as always under a collision of self-berating thoughts and images and fantasies and reveries, and he needs to stop thinking, yes yes yes, he needs to stop thinking and listen to his body because while Alfredo wants to hurt his brother and hurt himself, all his body wants to do is go home. That's all. Isabel is spitting up blood and Alfredo's body wants to hold a cool glass of water to her lips.

He runs. Turns his back to his brother and runs, a body in motion, in flight. Wind fills his ears. It comes up from nothing, this wind, comes leaping out of the smoke and stale air of the basement. The faster he runs, the louder it howls. He turns toward the mouth of the stairs. Gripping the soup can tightly—it's part of his body now, no time to throw it away—he bounds up the steps three at a time. His brother comes storming behind him. It's Tariq who's howling, not the wind. He sounds close. Sounds exhilarated. Their feet pound the

planks of the stairway, Tariq in sneakers, Alfredo in these horrible trac-tionless bowling shoes.

Three steps from the top, he trips. He braces his fall with his arms out in front of him and the soup can explodes on impact, sprays chicken broth, a mini geyser, into his face. It goes up his nose, into his mouth. His jeans rip open at the knees.

The men down in the basement cry out. Alfredo has fallen and his friends raise a collective groan—*Oh!*—their voices wincing with sym-pathy. But that's all they'll do. Facedown on the stairs, Alfredo knows there ain't nobody coming to save him. The cries of the men down in the basement are shot through with pleasure. These men are specta-tors, not participants, and they have been waiting a long time for this reckoning.

Tariq grabs Alfredo by the ankles and yanks him down the stairs. No place to go, no one to save him. Steps dig into Alfredo's cheek, his ribs, the plastic temple of his eyeglasses. Tariq is humming. His hands radi-ate heat as they rub circles on Alfredo's back, on the hunt for just the right spot. He punches Alfredo hard in the kidney. Stay quiet, stay still. An acknowledgment of pain will only frenzy Tariq, and besides, Alfredo's afraid that if he opens his mouth to cry out, his brother will try to curb him: force him to bite down on a step before kicking in the back of his head. Tariq's breath smells sweet, like chocolate. He hits Alfredo again in the kidney, scoops the air from his chest. Again Alfredo doesn't cry out. He focuses on a cross-grained knot of wood in the step above him. When he's hit a third time, his bladder fills up with blood, he feels a sticky warmth in his crotch, feels all the cords of his neck tightening, but he does not cry out. Tariq's humming grows louder, darker. He grabs hold of Alfredo's hair, hoists him up by the waist of his jeans, and this is the chance. Alfredo kicks out behind him, hits—what? The step underneath him? His brother's knee? He doesn't know. He kicks out and hits something hard and pushes off of it. Tariq's hands claw at his back, at the twin nubs of his shoulder blades, but there's no shirt to grab on to, and Alfredo rises up to his feet, up all the stairs, and he is a body again and he accelerates and he runs runs and oh Alfredo oh Alfredo, you sick bastard, you have gotten away.

Light-headed, giddy with panic, he looks over his shoulder and smiles.

Up in the store now, he flies down an aisle full of cleaning supplies,

the shelves deep with detergent, disinfectants, bottles of bleach, three-packs of sponges. It's dark. Alfredo's shoes slap linoleum—level ground at last, a relief after the trip up the stairs. The men down in the basement can surely hear him rumbling above their heads, but they may as well not exist, there's no sense thinking about them, there's no sense thinking at all. How natural this feels! Running through a darkened store he's known his whole life, his brother behind him. Alfredo craves to turn around again and look over his shoulder, but the heat on his neck tells him he shouldn't.

At the end of this aisle, he will have a choice of two exits. Two different ways out of here. He can either keep going straight, to an employees-only door—which will take him through Max's railroad apartment, to a screen door in the back, to the tiny yard enclosed by a waist-high fence, which Alfredo will have to leap over just to get into an alleyway—or he can make an easy left out of this aisle and head toward the entrance at the front of the bodega. It's no choice at all. The front doors will take him to the street. Three blocks from home. Closer to Isabel.

Alfredo plants a hard foot to the right and turns left. Tariq's momentum carries him forward. Bigger, stronger, he has a harder time slowing down. His body caroms off the beer fridge, spiders the glass. Alfredo considers waving good-bye, a little finger flutter off his hip, but it'd slow him down, the last thing he wants. Gotta get home. Out of the aisle and into a clearing, he dashes toward the front doors. This is it. If he makes it to the street, he'll be gone. Impossible to catch. He'll have backyards, the Alleyway, gypsy cabs, the Q32 bus. At intersections, he'll have his choice of four different directions. And he'll never get tired. Even with his kidney burning, he'll fly all the way home.

Bells jingle as the door opens up. Alfredo is still a few feet away and for a crazy half second he wonders if he's done this with his mind. Maybe he's so in tune with his body, he can manipulate the external world, telepathically swing open doors. No. Two men enter the store on a run, come barreling toward Alfredo and Tariq. With one man right behind the other, they even look like Alfredo and Tariq, except white and taller, with sports jerseys on, blue Mets and black Mets, Piazza and Piazza. The heavier of the two men, the one in the blue jersey, doesn't seem to understand what's happening yet. He runs behind his partner, as Tariq runs behind Alfredo, and realization reaches these

stragglers on a delay. But the skinny white cop sees Alfredo at the same time as Alfredo sees him. Right away. His face tightens. His arm swings up to point a gun at Alfredo's chest.

"Hold it!" he shouts. "Stop right there!"

Both cops are still far enough away that they might not recognize Alfredo as the kid from the donut shop. From across the darkened store, he wants to tell them not to worry, that they're on the same side. But of course they are not on the same side. Alfredo doesn't slow down. He runs right at the skinnier of the two cops, the one whose face is a gun barrel only. A toothless mouth. Alfredo goes low as he turns around, uses his hand on the floor to pivot. Three fingers streaking through dirt, as if he were caught on the base paths, between second and third. If the cops are far enough away that they might not recognize him, then they're far enough away that they might miss. And it's not like they can shoot a suspect in the back, right? As he turns, Tariq wraps an arm around his waist, but Alfredo is too slippery, too fast and too free. He runs away from the cops and away from his brother, toward the employees-only door waiting for him behind the counter. Both policemen now, two voices, shouting, warning. Hold it right there! Stop right there! He runs past the deli case with its tubes of meat. Leaps over a stack of today's papers, tied up in twine, their mastheads removed. He is afraid. He can't swallow. He tastes the broth on his tongue. The section of the counter in front of him works on a hinge, lifts up for easy access. Alfredo slides under it. The doorknob turns nicely in his hand.

When Alfredo accelerates, to tear through Max's railroad apartment, he loses track of the cops. He can't hear them anymore. The may be too slow, way behind, or they may have decided not to chase him, choosing instead to go down the stairs into the basement. But Alfredo *can* hear his brother. Tariq is panting, close behind. The apartment they sprint through is as narrow as a subway car, and dark too, darker than the inside of the store. Both men know where they're going. They've been here before. It is any summer night in the late 1980s and Papi stands behind the counter in the store selling Lotto tickets and Mama pan-fries pork chops in the kitchen and because of some mischief—a water gun filled with urine, a mix-tape deribboned— Jose Jr. chases Alfredito under the plush wings of parrots, through a hallway, into the living room, and now the boys are everywhere at

once, it is 1987, it is 1988, it is 1989, and the two dark-haired brothers are running, are asleep on the sofa bed, are playing War on the carpet, are eating single-sliced cheese straight out of the cellophane, are sitting in front of the television plastering He-Man stickers all over its screen. Alfredo wants to warn them—when Papi sees this he's gonna bring the belt to your asses—but the children have already started to shimmer and fade.

A gunshot deadens the air. Blasts the wind from his ears. Confused, he hears beeping. Two more gunshots, and he can't tell if they're coming from in front or behind, they're so explosively loud. He thinks of Isabel and feels something inside of him plummet. He runs faster, panicked. The door upcoming is actually two doors: a wooden door, interior to the apartment, swung all the way open, and an outer door, a screen door, latched closed to the rain. Is Tariq still behind him? Alfredo is too frightened to look. He can't stop. At the end of the couch, in the dark, Max sits with a cordless phone in his hands. It's the phone that's beeping, left off the hook for too long. Max looks small and afraid. He extends his arms out in front of him, palms up, as if bestowing a gift. Almost too late, Alfredo sees what's coming. With his hands rising instinctively to cover his face, he crashes through the screen door, takes it right off its hinges.

"Gun!" he shouts. His arm has punched through the wire meshing of the door, tearing it into flaps. He falls face forward into the yard, into the mud, and as he falls he shouts, "Gun! Gun!"

When he hits the ground his glasses go flying. Everything fuzzes over, loses edges, definition. Less than five feet away, a blurry-faced police officer, the Latino, kneels next to a body on the ground. The cop looks stricken. He turns to Alfredo with a bovine stare, the skin twitching around his mouth. Mike Shifrin—who else could it be?—lies motionless in the grass. Amazing. That Shifrin is here. That he exists. He must've had the drop on the police officer, must've gotten to the yard first, and yet he's the one on his back, his feet crossed peacefully at the ankles, his white shirt bunched up around blood-blooming holes. And the cop is the one who's still alive. All that academy training. Or maybe his policeman's trigger just squeezes more easily. The air smells of smoke. Shifrin looks like he's been shot three times in the chest, maybe more. It's hard to tell. Alfredo can't see as well as he'd like—the rain doesn't help—but he is thinking quickly and clearly, rejuvenated

from the bodily sprint through the store. Splayed out on the grass, his elbows in the mud, Alfredo feels as if he exists inside of time and it is a small safe world enclosed on all sides.

Tariq comes running through what used to be the back door. When he sees what's in front of him—the dead body, the cop, Alfredo low to the ground—he closes his eyes.

"Gun," Alfredo is shouting. "He has a gun! He has a gun!"

Tariq tries to slow down. Alfredo can see it in the way he tilts his head back, the way his hands lift on their own, which is truly the worst thing he could've done, those hands rising, and with a whipcrack of thunder, the first bullet hits him. It rips through his forearm and enters his shoulder, exploding it into fragments of muscle and bone. He is shot two more times in the chest. It spins him. Turning, he sinks down to one knee and slides forward in a crumple, an ear pressed to the ground.

The cop speaks into the silence that follows. "Where is it?" he says. He comes out of his crouch and runs over to Tariq's body. "I don't see it. Where is it?"

Alfredo doesn't know how to answer. He sits in the grass, his head bent, and he paws at the ground in front of him, searching for his eyeglasses. An earthworm gropes blindly out of the soil. It is light red and shiny, almost translucent, and when it slithers across Alfredo's knuckles, he recoils. He feels sick.

"Where is it?" the cop cries. There is blood in his voice, the threat of more violence. "Where the fuck is the gun?"

When Alfredo doesn't say anything, the cop slips his boot into Tariq's open hand. Alfredo wants to tell him to stop—*please don't touch him*—but he is afraid to give orders. He feels like he's waking up from a nightmare, but has still not come all the way out. Something else, something bad, is coming. He picks up off the ground a green piece of paper, a flyer of some sort, blown off a windshield and into the yard. Soaked all the way through, the paper's numbers and letters run together. Nothing makes sense. Rain drums into his eyes. It falls heavily, this rain. Makes music against the busted screen door, fills the open mouth of Mike Shifrin. A gun lies in the grass, close to Shifrin's body. If it's a snub-nosed .38, Alfredo can't tell. He can't see that far, nor does he know what a .38 looks like. The cop seems distracted. He stares into the house, ready—as Alfredo is—for the next bad thing.

The other two cops must be all the way downstairs by now, trying to convince a basement of angry young men to press their palms to the walls. The gun winks at Alfredo. He could crawl squishing through the mud, could grab it so easily. He could make sure. He allows himself to look over at Tariq, who kneels slumped over in the grass, his legs twisted under him, that ear to the ground as if he were straining to hear whispered, underworld voices.

"Don't," the cop says. The pistol he points at Alfredo shakes in his adrenaline-surged hand. "Don't you fucking move."

"No," Alfredo says. His own hands, clenched into fists, hang uselessly at his sides. "Please, no."

With his gun straight out in front of him, the cop circles behind Alfredo. He kicks him hard between the shoulder blades. Alfredo falls forward. Mud fills his ear. The cop digs his knees into Alfredo's back, presses down on his already battered kidney.

"Your friend's dog died," Alfredo says. Facedown in the mud, he doesn't know if he can be heard, but he wants all the facts known. "I'm sorry. I'm sorry about that dog. I never meant for that to happen."

His arms are pulled behind him. With a *click-click-click,* the cop cuffs Alfredo's hands behind his back. Alfredo prays. He prays that Isabel's mouth will heal, that Christian Louis will never know. That his parents, after hearing the news, will not close their hearts to him. The mud gives way under Tariq's head and he slides all the way down onto his stomach, revealing for a flashing moment the indent at the base of his neck. He is dead, and Alfredo has no words of his own to meet that. Silently, to himself, with his thin wrists cuffed so tightly that metal digs into bone, Alfredo recites the Lord's Prayer. He gets halfway through before stopping at daily bread. He does not ask to be forgiven. Why bother? Alfredo's hunger for forgiveness exceeds the world's capacity to dole it out.

Part Three

13

From the New York City Department of Records

1. FULL NAME OF CHILD	First Name **Christian**		Middle Name **Louis**		Last Name **Batista**

3. SEX **male**	3a. NUMBER DELIVERED of this pregnancy **1** 3b. If more than one, number of this child in order of delivery	4a. DATE OF CHILD'S BIRTH (Month) (Day) (Year) **August 14, 2002**	4b. HOUR **7:07 PM**

5a. PLACE OF BIRTH	5a. NEW YORK CITY BOROUGH OF **Queens**	5b. Name of Facility (if not in institution, street address) **Elmhurst Hospital Center**	5c. TYPE OF PLACE **Hospital**

6a. MOTHER'S FULL MAIDEN NAME **Isabel Maritza Guerrero**	6b. MOTHER'S DATE OF BIRTH (Month) (Day) (Year) **October 18, 1982**	6c. MOTHER'S BIRTHPLACE City & State or foreign country **Queens, NY**

7. MOTHER'S USUAL RESIDENCE a. State b. County **NY** **Queens**	7c. City, town, or location **Corona**	7d. Street and house number Zip **34-51 107th Street 11368**	7e. Inside city limits of 7c **Yes**

8a. FATHER'S FULL NAME **Alfredo Victor Batista**	8b. FATHER'S DATE OF BIRTH (Month) (Day) (Year) **January 14, 1983**	8c. FATHER'S BIRTHPLACE City & State or foreign country **Queens, NY**

9a. NAME OF ATTENDANT AT DELIVERY	9b. I CERTIFY THAT THIS CHILD WAS BORN
V. Mukherjee, M.D.	ALIVE AT THE PLACE, DATE, AND TIME GIVEN

information added or amended	
	Signed ~~Bridget Goodman~~
_____	Name of
(Reason)	Signer **Bridget Goodman**
	Address **79-01 Broadway, Elmhurst, NY 11373**
_____ _____	
(Date) (City Registrar)	Date Signed *August 18, 2002*

VITAL RECORDS   DEPARTMENT OF HEALTH AND MENTAL HYGIENE   THE CITY OF NEW YORK

14

The Birthday Party

Isabel opens the cupboard and checks on the one. To make sure it's still there. For what must be the zillionth time today. She checks on the one compulsively, the way a traveler checks pockets and fanny packs, searching for the four familiar corners of a passport. As was the case ten minutes ago, the one glitters in its packaging, hidden behind the pancake mix. It hasn't moved. Despite the sweltering conditions inside the apartment, it hasn't melted. It is a good one. Sturdy base, long Victorian neck, little black wick poking out the top. The one looks as if it's been dipped in vanilla frosting and dotted with rainbow sprinkles. It looks edible, dangerously so. After Isabel sets it on fire, she'll have to make sure Christian Louis doesn't grab it and stick it in his mouth. God knows, he'll try.

When Isabel bought the one, the lady behind the cash register said, "Oh Lord, how exciting. Can you believe how fast time flies?"

Isabel asked Alfredo that very question this morning. She was lying on the air mattress with the baby—check that: with the toddler—while Alfredo stood in front of the mirror, getting ready for work.

"Can you believe how fast time flies?"

By way of answer, Alfredo slapped the wall behind her head. His hand came away with blood on it, the wall smeared with a red crescent moon.

"Don't do that ish on the walls," Isabel said.

"You wanna get bit up by mosquitoes all day, be my f-ing guest."

Christian Louis grabbed hold of Isabel's hair and stuck the ends in his mouth. On his cheek, a wine stain birthmark seemed to pulse with redness, as it always does in the early mornings. "A year already," Isabel said, looking at her son. "I can't believe it. Can you believe it?"

"No," Alfredo said. He folded his lime-green tie and buried it in his pocket. It was a clip-on, part of his everyday uniform, and Alfredo would rather have cut off his hands than be seen wearing it on the subway. He adjusted the cuffs of his shirt, hitched up his polyester pants. "I can't. I can't believe it."

"You look nice," Isabel said.

While she looks at the one, Christian Louis tries to get under the sink. He slides his head between his mama's legs and rattles the cupboard doors, the handles of which are bound by duct tape. When Isabel needs to get at her poisonous cleaning supplies—which is always, what with Christian Louis's table manners and Alfredo's mosquito vendetta—she has to slit the tape with a knife and then rebind it, every single time. Which is not *that* big a deal. The vice president said go out and cop mad duct tape, and so they bought plenty of rolls. They got duct tape coming out their asses. They got duct tape covering the baseboard power outlets. They used to have duct tape sealing the windows shut, a necessity with a moves-making baby in a sixth-floor studio, but it got too f-ing hot to be keeping the windows closed—ninety-one miserable degrees— and so Isabel went out and bought those heavy-duty black metal safety bars. Charged them to the card and installed them herself.

While Christian Louis wiggles between her ankles, Isabel slips the one behind the pancake mix. She could check in the freezer to see if the ice cream cake (Oreo crumb!) is still there, but it doesn't seem necessary. Where's a cake gonna go? She slides Christian Louis across the kitchen floor and deposits him in front of a different cupboard, one without any poisons. But because the handles aren't bound, he expresses little interest. He's like his father in this way: if it ain't forbidden, he ain't interested. He sits still in front of the cupboard, a skeptical expression on his face. But Mama knows best. When she bends over and opens the doors, revealing its bounty, he laughs. He's a great one for laughing. He reaches into the cupboard and pulls down all the

pots and pans. She puts a wooden spoon on the floor in front of him, and he picks it up, because he can do this now. *He can pick things up.* And holy ish, can he make noise. Spoon in hand, pots in front of him, he goes to work, bang-bang-banging away.

If Alfredo were home, he'd say, "Little man's gonna be a drummer like that guy in the Roots. Gonna make us a *fortune.*"

While her baby bangs pots, Isabel sits down in the kitchen chair and blows balloons. They smell nasty, like unlubricated condoms, and after the first dozen she goes a little cross-eyed. The tip of her finger turns purple from tying off the ends. Sweat blots the back of her tank top, but that might have less to do with the effort of balloon blowing and more to do with the throat-tightening humidity inside this apartment. Feeling light-headed, she tosses a balloon toward the drummer boy, and it bounces off his face. He laughs. She tosses another, and this time he swings at it with the spoon. He doesn't make contact—*sawing and a miss!*—but if Alfredo were here, he'd compliment the effort, say something like, "Little man's gonna be a slugger like Piazza. Gonna make us mad millions." And Isabel would say, as she always does, "Little man's gonna be whatever he wants."

One hopes.

She rubs a balloon against the top of his head. His soft dark hair sticks up like he just stuck a fork in an electric outlet. Scratch that. Too frightening an image. His soft dark hair sticks up as if he were . . . as if he were . . . as if he were the world's smallest mad scientist. How would she feel about that? Being the ma dukes of a future corpse reanimator? Sounds great. He could bring her back to life after she dies. They could go on teleportation trips together, celebrate his hundredth birthday on Jupiter. She presses the balloon to the wall, where it clings in place. She wishes she could explain how static electricity works—she'll look it up on one of the library computers—but the lack of an explanation doesn't seem to matter to Christian Louis, future scientist, future target of torch-wielding mobs. He stares at the balloon and slaps his forehead. Still laughing, beyond delighted, he grabs another balloon and sticks the tied-off end in his mouth.

Isabel jumps out of her chair and yanks the balloon away. She remembers something her mother the puta once told her about a cousin, a little girl back in Puerto Rico who swallowed a deflated balloon, choked on it, and died. Isabel's heart is racing. Christian Louis

watches her carry the balloon away from him, his arms straining, his fists grasping at air. If there's one thing she's learned in this past year it's that her baby boy is surprisingly difficult to break, and yet, *better safe than sorry,* the motto of mamas the world over. With a needle plucked from a tomato pincushion, she pops the balloon. It makes a loud, sudden sound, louder than Christian Louis's drumming. Eyebrows crossed, he opens his mouth as if to deliver a particularly abusive diatribe, and then he bursts into tears.

Two dozen more balloons lie scattered around the apartment, the party's first awkward guests. She pinches off each of their necks, slides her needle through. There are no bangs this time, no pops. Air trickles out of the balloons in a slow, painless hiss. She quarantines them all in the sink, where the sight of their wizened husks has her chewing her lip. Great. *Now* what is she supposed to do for decorations? Tomorrow the well-meaning, one-upping Abuela Lizette gets her shot—she's probably already rented out a declawed bear who brings his own unicycle—but tonight is for the three of them, Alfredo, Isabel, and Christian Louis, their own party in their own home, with balloons, there are supposed to be *balloons,* and an Oreo crumb ice cream cake, and a super elegant birthday candle. The one! Isabel checks on it to make sure it's still there—okay, okay, to make herself feel better—and there it is, tucked behind the pancake mix. It is a good one, but it is not the only game in town. As Christian Louis had done earlier, Isabel eyeballs the cupboard under the sink. When they moved into this Corona apartment she bought close to fifty candles—pillar candles, floating candles, tea-light candles, votive candles, lavender-scented heart-shaped candles—and she keeps them under the sink, behind duct-taped handles, saving them for a day that never seems to come, a day when she can slip into a warm bath for an hour, close her eyes, masturbate, and relax. She wants to hold all these candles in her arms, wants to hear their whispered promises.

Christian Louis is still crying. He reaches out for his mother, the balloon popper, the betrayer, and she lifts him up off the kitchen floor. She bounces him in her arms. She is a plane hitting turbulence, and he her only passenger. She flies him to the closet, where behind the door, wrapped up, waits his first birthday present. It is a Fisher-Price musical learning table, but she doesn't tell him that. It's a surprise.

"*Seventy* bucks," Alfredo had said when he saw the receipt. "For a table? Our parents never bought us anything that cost *seventy* bucks."

"Exactly," Isabel had said.

The table is an interactive toy, she explained. It helps kids learn their numbers and ABCs. It has fifteen sing-along songs—nursery rhymes and lullabies—and Isabel feels confident she'll know every single one.

"Does it come with volume control?" Alfredo had asked.

She could check right now, but the table's already been gift-wrapped. She yanks open the closet door, asking the baby in her arms if he can say *birthday present, birthday present.* Before he can gurgle out an answer, she slams the door shut. He gets a peek, that's it. When the sneaky little bastard reaches for the doorknob, she whirls him away.

She's going to tell Alfredo tonight. She'll wait till after the birthday cake, after Christian Louis has opened his present. She'll wait for the very peak of Alfredo's happiness, and then she will pounce. Her timing needs to be perfect, as it must be whenever she does anything: initiate sex, bring up their credit card bill, open her mouth at all. He's been poisonously moody these last few months. Last few months? He's been moody since last June. Worse than moody—she could live with moody—he's been withdrawn. He works as an elevator boy in a deluxe Manhattan apartment building, shepherding the rich from the lobby to their apartments, and from their apartments to the lobby, a never-ending north-south circuit; his boss, Ms. Webb, tells him he'd get promoted to doorman (an escalation in salary and, it seems, in masculinity) if he'd only engage the residents in some chit-chat as they rise and descend, if he'd talk to them about, oh you know, the weather, the Yankees, the latest Broadway shows. *But I don't feel like talking,* he complains to Isabel. *I understand,* she says. *I do. But maybe it's time to reopen that big fat mouth of yours and start yapping again.*

He usually shrugs when she says this. Or closes the bathroom door on her. Or rolls over in bed. Or crushes a blood-fat mosquito against the wall.

So tonight she'll have to wait till his shell shows a crack. Maybe he'll say a joke or laugh at one of hers. Maybe he'll smear ice cream cake on Christian Louis's nose. Sing the itsy-bitsy spider. Look at Isabel kindly, ignoring for once the thin white scar engraved under her eye. He'll be smiling at her with unguarded, soft-faced affection, and right then, in

that moment, she'll drop the news. Another one's coming, she'll say. We're pregnant again.

At around 3:30 in the afternoon, Alfredo staggers into the apartment. Legs quivering, he bangs into the doorframe. His keys slip out of his hand. He is home an hour later than expected, which would normally elicit from Isabel a certain set of questions, but she finds herself distracted by the sweat pouring off his reddened face. He carries—or attempts to carry—an enormous cardboard box. A stack of today's mail slides across the top of the box, and when Alfredo's knees buckle, an envelope corner stabs him in the throat.

"Oh my God," Isabel says. She holds Christian Louis's hands in the air, while he, with the grace of a stringed puppet, puts one foot in front of the other. He tries to get at his father, and Isabel follows. "Tell me that's not a birthday present," she says.

"It's not a birthday present," he says.

"Well, what the H is it?"

"What's H mean?"

"*Hell,*" she whispers.

"We can't say 'hell' in front of him?" he asks, setting the box down on the floor. "It's in the Bible."

"Alfredo," she says. "What's in the box?"

Seemingly too eager to go looking for the scissors, Alfredo uses his keys to slit the packing tape. When he gets the cardboard flaps open, he gives a chunk of Styrofoam to Christian Louis, who sticks it right in his mouth. Alfredo reaches into the box and pulls out—tada!—another box. This second box doesn't look like it conceals more boxes. It is a self-contained animal, made out of plastic and metal, with a three-pronged plug for a tail and a pair of accordion wings.

"An air conditioner?" Isabel says.

"An air conditioner," Alfredo says triumphantly. "I figure, what kind of environment do mosquitoes love the most? Hot and humid, yeah? I figure, where does heat go in a six-story apartment building? To the top, right? To *our* floor."

Isabel checks the box for dents, to see if it fell off the back of a truck.

"How much?" she says.

"Don't worry about it."

"I worry about it. How much? Where'd you get the money?"

"It was mad cheap. It's *August*. Ain't no one buying air conditioners in *August*."

"Well," she says, pulling the Styrofoam out of Christian Louis's mouth, "I hope you got a real smart place to put it, because it ain't fitting in them windows."

Alfredo looks up at the windows, tilts his head to the side.

"It'll fit," he says.

He grabs a magazine from the stack of today's mail and carries it with him to the futon. Leaving behind him, in his wake, bits of cardboard and torn-up tape and plastic wrapping and Styrofoam blocks and Styrofoam crumbs and the air conditioner itself, all over Isabel's floor, expecting, as he always expects, someone else to clean up his messes. Christian Louis, whose disloyalty knows no bounds, toddles over to his father. Alfredo picks him up, holds him in his lap with an arm wrapped around his belly, with a soft and easy tenderness. For not the first time in this past year, Isabel feels jealous of her own son. The baby books warned her that this happens to *fathers*—they look at the nine-month tenancy, they look at the breastfeeding, they look at the close bond between mama and child, and the resentment wheels start a-churning—but Isabel didn't read anything about *mothers* envying their children. You kidding? Good luck trying to find "maternal resentment" in a baby book index. But why shouldn't she feel jealous? When Alfredo holds Isabel it is stiffly, at a distance, as if he had a cold he didn't want to give her.

She has repeatedly told him—most often in bed, in the dark, when it is easiest for her to say these kinds of things—that she does not blame him for the incident, for what happened to her. The man who was responsible was responsible. She cannot say it any clearer than that. But there are moments, moments like right now, when Christian Louis is literally out of her hands and her mind can go to work on attacking itself, and she starts wondering if she's got it all backward. What if Alfredo isn't worried about Isabel blaming him? What if it's the other way around? His brother is dead and he blames *her*. What can she say to that?

In his father's lap, Christian Louis rips pages out of the magazine. Alfredo looks on indulgently, which annoys not only Isabel, but also, it seems, the white guy on the cover, a cartoon soldier whose face is

frozen in teeth-gritted frustration. A video game character probably. The magazine is called *GamePro,* and according to Alfredo he needs to subscribe because there isn't anyplace in Corona where a guy can just walk in and buy a magazine. He didn't explain, however, why a guy who doesn't own, much less play, a single video game would want the magazine in the first place. But Isabel has some ideas.

Alfredo wrestles a torn-out page from Christian Louis and holds it above his head. The baby—sorry, the toddler—strains to get at it. Forget the Fisher-Price musical learning table, forget the Styrofoam. This page is the only thing he wants. He climbs Alfredo's chest, grabs at his hair, but Papi lifts the page higher. He's reading it, and Isabel figures it must be the one page in the magazine devoted to tournament news. Alfredo, she assumes, is looking for Winston's name. For reasons mysterious to her, Winston and Alfredo haven't talked in over a year. When male best friends break up—is there a better way to put it?—it's either over a woman, which can't be the case here since Isabel would be that woman and God knows Winston's terrified of her, or it's over money, a more likely explanation. But not necessarily the correct one. Maybe Alfredo just got tired of trying to convince Winston to quit drugs. Maybe Winston is a pair of concrete boots, and Alfredo felt he had to leave him behind when he left his old lifestyle behind. Maybe Alfredo couldn't look at Winston without feeling corrosively guilty. (Maybe Isabel is projecting here.) She doesn't know. She doesn't know what happened between those two, just as she doesn't know how much the air conditioner cost, or where he bought it, or how he carried it home, or where he got the money to pay for it. She does know, however, that the more she asks, the less likely he'll be to provide answers. She watches him crumple the magazine page and toss it onto the floor.

"And who's cleaning that up?" she says.

"Give me a minute."

"And the box in the middle of my floor? Maybe you haven't heard, but I've got a birthday party to throw."

"Where's the balloons at?" he says, grinning. "I thought there was supposed to be balloons."

"Are you crazy?" she asks. "Don't you know they're a choking hazard? I had a cousin once who—"

"No balloons?" Alfredo says. "No balloons on his *birthday*?" He

spins Christian Louis around, so that he faces his mother. "Lookit," Alfredo says. "Lookit how sad he is not to have any balloons."

Spit bubbles up between his lips. He reaches toward her—that's right, that's right, he ain't playing Daddy's dirty little games—and Isabel tries to take him away, tries to lift him into the air, but Alfredo has hold of his foot.

"Where's the screwdriver at?" he says. "I'm gonna take the bars out of one of them windows and put in the AC."

"It's not gonna fit."

"It'll fit."

It fits. While Alfredo muscles it into the window frame, Isabel worries the AC's droopy ass will slip out of his hands and pancake some poor soul on the street. But he read the instructions for once. As he puts in the mounting brackets, he almost looks like he knows what he's doing. He uses the window to anchor the unit, and while that doesn't exactly seem sturdy enough, Isabel is past the point of doubting his competence. Isabel, as a matter of fact, is officially impressed. Alfredo spreads the accordion wings an inch in each direction—this is a *tight* fit—and secures them to the window frame. He takes a step back and slaps the top of the AC. It doesn't budge.

"Not bad, huh?"

"Not bad," she says.

"Don't go all gushy on me," he says, and his thin lips smile. Because she hasn't asked in a while, because it seems as if she's no longer interested, he says, "I charged it to the Visa."

"Okay," she says. With the monthly bills getting fatter and fatter, she and Alfredo had agreed to put a freeze on their credit card spending, but she chooses not to reprimand him here because (1) that he paid with the card means that he did not pay with cash, which means that he did not go out and do something stupid to get that cash; (2) Isabel has made some recent credit card purchases of her own, including, but not limited to, the birthday balloons that are currently hiding at the bottom of the trash can, the birthday cake, the birthday candle, and the musical table birthday present; (3) as he paces in front of his successfully installed air conditioner, Alfredo looks happier than he has in weeks, maybe months, and Isabel needs his good mood to snowball.

"Well what you waiting for?" she says. "Plug it in."

The machine grumbles to life. Isabel and Alfredo lean toward it, as if welcoming a friendly visitor into their home. In his mama's arms, Christian Louis struggles to get at this strange new beast, to touch its buttons and flashing green lights, to slide his fingers into its upturned vents.

"Shouldn't the air be cooler?" she says.

"It needs to warm up."

"It needs to warm up to get cold?"

Alfredo hooks the hem of his work shirt over the vents. The air impregnates him, swells his shirt so that the buttons seem to be straining. He chuckles, a deep *ho ho ho,* as if this is what's expected of all men who've been suddenly, stupendously potbellied.

"Get out the way," Isabel says. "You're blocking the air."

"Thought it wasn't cool enough for you."

"Move it," she says.

Alfredo comes close to her, to steal Christian Louis's nose. "Can you say no more mosquitoes?" he asks. "Can you say no more sweaty balls?"

This is the moment to be terrific, she thinks. With the AC humming. With Christian Louis straining between them, in Mama's arms but reaching for the thumb in Papi's fist. This is the moment to tell him everything. May not get a better chance all night.

"It isn't very cold though, is it?" he says.

"It's fine," she says. Like any longtime couple, in order to practice their craft they sometimes switch positions in an argument. "It just needs time," she says.

"Maybe something's wrong with the filter."

"It's fine," she says. "Leave it alone."

Stooped over, squinting, he hits some of the beep-beep buttons on the AC's console.

"It's *fine,*" she says.

He adjusts the temperature. He switches the settings from cool to fan to money saver, and back again to cool. The AC groans with impatience. Alfredo turns it off, stares at it with his hands on his hips. He gives it a light slap, a warning to get its act together, and when he turns it back on, the AC sputters, clears its throat, and then shuts down completely. Just like that. At the same time, the living room light goes out. At the same time, the kitchen light goes out. At the exact same time—

when the AC shuts down, and when the kitchen and living room lights go out—the refrigerator stops humming. And the coffeemaker clicks off. And the microwave clock goes dark. And the sound of all the power in the apartment going dead seems somehow louder than the sound of all the power in the apartment alive.

"Goddamnit," Alfredo says.

"I told—"

"Don't," he says. He closes his eyes. "Don't say a word."

What do they do first? They do what everyone does first. They try flipping the light switches. With blank expressions on their faces, they flip the switches up and down, well past the point of where it might actually start working. They go hunting for the circuit breaker box—why is it so f-ing hard to locate the circuit breaker in a *studio apartment?*—and, oh hello, they find it in the cupboard with the pancake mix and the number one birthday candle. How about that? The main circuit breaker is big and black and serious-looking, the mother of all light switches, and it turns over with a satisfyingly loud click. But it doesn't do any good. The power stays off. They open the fridge and immediately regret opening the fridge, allowing all that cool fog to escape. They take the AC's fat-headed plug and slide its three prongs into a surge protector, then they take that surge protector and plug it into the wall. They try turning on the AC. Nothing. They try flipping the light switches again.

Outside, cars are honking their horns. Alfredo opens a window and hot air jumps into the apartment. The honking grows louder, angrier. The building across the street is dark, each of its apartments without light, but that might not mean anything. It's early still, not even five o'clock, and most people haven't come home from work yet. To get a better look out the window, Alfredo leans forward and bangs his head.

"I can't fucking—"

"Hey!" Isabel tilts her chin toward Christian Louis, who sits on the carpet and plays with the Styrofoam. "Language please."

"I can't get my f-ing head," Alfredo says, "through that f-ing window with them bars in the way."

"Well," Isabel says. "That's kind of the idea."

He presses his cheek against the bars. "I think I can maybe see the

street corner. Wow. I think the traffic lights are out. This is crazy. Hey—you wanna go outside?"

She comes up behind him, puts her chin on his shoulder. "What if it's terrorists?" she says.

"In *Queens*?"

With Isabel still hovering over his shoulder, Alfredo tries calling his parents. The cell phone screen flashes Connecting . . . Connecting . . . Connecting, a promise it eventually breaks with Signal Lost. Alfredo redials and gets the same runaround. A call continuously pushed up a mountain, a signal that's never found. When Alfredo tries again without success, Isabel volunteers her own phone. It was a gift from Alfredo, given to her last June after the incident, and it has only five numbers saved in its memory: Alfredo's (duh); the video store where she still works part-time; Pizza Sam's; Peking Kitchen; and the Batista residence, which Alfredo is dialing right now, and which, in a moment of bored rebellion, Isabel labeled "Babysitters R Us." When the words flash across the screen, Alfredo smirks.

The call goes through. Sort of. It seems to connect—Isabel thinks she might even hear a ring—but then an automated female voice tells them that the network is busy. Whatever that means. Sounding almost bored, almost distracted, as if she were washing her robot hair, the automated voice tells Alfredo to call back later.

He taps the phone against his chin, stares distantly over the top of Isabel's head. She knows that look. He has officially checked out, transported himself into some past or future self. He walks into the kitchen, and, as Christian Louis had done hours earlier, he rattles the doors to the cupboard under the sink. He asks where the scissors are, so he can cut the duct tape on the handles, and it unfortunately falls to Isabel to tell him that the good scissors are, well, they're inside the cupboard under the sink.

"Where are the *bad* scissors?" Alfredo says. "Or do I not want to know?"

"You can use a knife," she says.

"That's why all the knives are dull?"

"The knives aren't dull," she says. "What you want in there anyway?"

A direct question. How foolish of her. She sits on the futon, watches Alfredo saw at the duct tape with his massive wad of house keys. He has his back to her, his shoulders hunched near his ears, and while Isabel can't see his face, she's pretty sure his tongue is clamped down

between his teeth. He throws open the cupboard doors. He pulls out all the candles—all the pillars and floaters and votives and tea-lights—and stuffs them into a blue plastic grocery bag.

"What the fuck?" she says.

"Language!" he says, sounding delighted to have scored so easy a point.

"Those are mine," she says.

"Don't worry," he says without turning around. "I'm gonna leave some here."

"Those are my candles."

"Don't be selfish, all right? I'm taking them to my parents. Remember them? You used to live in their house for a year?"

"You can't be serious," she says. "You're *leaving*?"

"My parents are old, Izzy. The power has gone out. I'm going to go over to their apartment, see if they're okay." He fills a second bag with Isabel's candles. "I'm not being a bad guy here."

She picks Christian Louis up off the floor and pulls him into her lap. "We're coming with you."

"You can't, I'll be going way too fast." He snaps his fingers. "I'm going to *run* over there."

"But it'll be dark soon."

"Exactly," he says. "Exactly my point."

"But," she says, and Christian Louis grabs at her mouth, as if he wants to shut her up, keep her from saying something she can't take back. She bites down on his fingers, softly, then not so softly. "We have to sing 'Happy Birthday,' " she says. "We have to open presents. We have to eat the cake before it melts."

Alfredo comes out of the kitchen to stand over them. His stomach grumbles; the bags hang heavy in his hands. Isabel won't say anything, and he won't look at her. He stares down at the carpet, afraid, she thinks, to see the chastising scar zigzagged under her eye. In the movie version of her life . . . no, no, no, no, no, no, no . . . she promised herself that she'd leave that line of thinking behind. She doesn't live up on the screen, she lives in *this life*, in a hot, powerless studio apartment in Corona, Queens. She seizes Christian Louis's wrists. She can't have him reaching toward his father. Alfredo needs to know he's leaving not two people but one unit, united against him. She jiggles the baby on her knee. She shoves her nose in his hair, smells the sweet soft crown of his head. Baby powder. Ripe apricots. No-tears shampoo. When Alfredo

walks away, the glass of the votive candles clinks together, as if they were toasting to someone's health, as if they were wishing the world's travelers a hearty bon voyage.

"Be right back," Alfredo says, but Isabel's heard that shit before.

At first Alfredo thought it might only be his block that lost power—wouldn't that be just his luck?—but as he walks through Corona he sees one defunct traffic light after another. The one-family homes are dark. The three-family homes are dark. The churrascarias, the botánicas, the farmacias, the eyebrow threaders, the pizza parlors, the liquor stores, the auto body shops, the Seoul Glass Emporium—they've all gone dark. In every storefront window, neon signs have turned gray, veins without blood. The whole neighborhood's been knocked out. Who knows? Maybe the whole borough. Alfredo feels surrounded not by buildings but by the molted skin of buildings. Queens, for the first time in his life, looks exhausted.

He stops at the corner of Northern and Junction boulevards. His arms are tired. His boxers stick to his thighs. It is here, at this intersection, that his new home, Corona, becomes his old home, Jackson Heights. Out in the street, halfway between those two worlds, a silver-haired black guy directs traffic. He wears an ill-fitting marine uniform and blows on a cheap plastic whistle. Instead of a baton, he wields an empty water bottle, and yet the cars respond, braking when he tells them to brake, speeding up when he lets them. He blows his whistle at Alfredo, invites him across the street.

Without any red lights, Alfredo could drive for miles and miles, his foot on the gas the entire time. He could drive clean out of New York and into a new life in a new state, a state with electricity. Not that he has a car. Or even knows how to drive.

As he crosses the street, he gets close enough to the ex-marine to see the gravy spotting his sleeve. He asks the guy what's going on—*What's the story?*—and the guy's answer is simple.

"End of the world."

Alfredo walks into Jackson Heights. The people he passes—the dog walkers, the butchers outside their shops, the Dominican dudes on milk crates—they all smile and nod, as if to say, *Here we go again.* For a little under two years, they've been waiting for something like this.

And now that it's here, in the form of a blackout, snipping their reading lamps, cutting off their telenovelas and subway lines, New Yorkers resort to one of their oldest fail-safes: aggressive indifference. A shrug of the shoulders. A smile and a nod. When the apocalypse arrives, when a door opens in the sky and God's throne appears sparkling like jasper, and the seven angels blow seven trumpets, and fire devours the armies of Satan, the good people of New York will stick their heads out their windows and say, *Eh*.

"You better drink plenty of water," an old white lady tells him. She's coming out of the supermarket, pushing her own cart, smelling strongly of vinegar. She wraps her dry hand around his wrist. "This kind of heat?" she says, shaking her head sadly. "You better stay *hydrated*."

"Do you know what's going on?" he asks.

"What's going on?" she says.

"No, I'm asking. What's going on? What happened to the power?"

"I haven't got the foggiest," she says. She jerks her head behind her, toward Manhattan. "But I know it's out. Everywhere. Even in the City. And you better drink plenty of water."

"I will," Alfredo says. "I promise." He loves this old lady a little bit, wants to escort her home, make sure she gets there in one piece, but he knows if he offered, he'd just end up spooking her. He keeps walking. He thinks of that poor bastard Brian Schwartz, the college boy whose shift started when Alfredo's ended. If that old lady is right, if the power went out in Manhattan, then Brian's probably stuck in the elevator, his hands pressed to the walls. Man oh man, like being buried alive.

Alfredo misses his brother. It sneaks up on him sometimes, all the time, Brian Schwartz in an elevator, Jose Batista Jr., in the Cavalry Cemetery, and the grief of it, the weight of it, sits on Alfredo's chest like a brick. He can't stop it from coming. Despite everything, Alfredo misses his brother and he does not know what kind of man that makes him.

But, strangely, the farther he walks into his old neighborhood, their old neighborhood, the less he thinks about it. He knows of course that thinking about not thinking about it is a kind of thinking about it, but Jackson Heights, even blacked out, hums with distractions.

Up ahead, a mob of purple-shirted day campers encircle a fire hydrant. It is the most tempting hydrant for miles around. Without any arms, without even the thalidomide stumps of your average fireplug, the hydrant looks particularly defenseless, naked almost, and yet it is kept

safe, perpetually closed, unfairly benefiting from the Mafioso-like protection of a red-bricked firehouse one block away. The children's shirts are soaked through from some earlier, easier escapade. Their hair is wet, their sneakers squishy. One of the boys crouches down in front of the hydrant and fondles its lone breast. If he has a wrench, Alfredo can't see it. But maybe kids these days don't need the brute instruments of Alfredo's youth. Maybe this kid has charm, maybe he can sweet-talk the water out of the pump. The boy is watched, but everyone on this block, on all these blocks, is watched. Behind him, in sidewalk beach chairs outside a travel agency, dark-skinned men mumble words of encouragement. It feels good, Alfredo thinks, to be back in Jackson Heights. Purple, shiny, huddled close together, the children look like a cluster of grapes, and rather than puncture their group, Alfredo steps into the street and goes around. In a parked car, with the windows rolled up, an Indian family of four shares a bucket of fried chicken. You won't see that in Corona. Things seem more alive here, more colorful. Although that might not be fair. It's possible that Alfredo, in his new neighborhood, hasn't been looking hard enough. He hasn't been to the Lemon Ice King of Corona, for instance, hasn't even gone to Flushing Meadows Park to check out the Unisphere. But are the pigeons' eyes in Corona this red? Does the Corona air smell of baked bread, of melted cheese?

Alfredo finds himself, midreverie, on a problematic stretch of sidewalk. Set halfway down this row of stores, like a decaying tooth, lurks Gianni's Pizza. At this time of day, it's probably full of Alfredo's old friends, some of whom spent time with him in lockup last June before the PDs got everyone's cases thrown out of court. *Warrantless search, Your Honor!* Alfredo wants to see those guys, and he doesn't want to see those guys. As he slows down, he catches his reflection in a ninety-nine-cent store. He hates turning around in the middle of the street— it always makes him feel like an asshole—but what else can he do? For the benefit of those who might be looking, he comes to a complete stop, makes a *tsk* sound and throws his head back with exaggerated frustration, as if he forgot to turn the oven off, the iron off, as if he left an important piece of classified microfilm in the wrong titanium suitcase. He spins around on his heel. Goes the way he came. As he passes the Indian family, he keeps his head down, makes a left on Northern

Boulevard. By doing so, he travels, as he always meant to travel, in the opposite direction of his parents' place.

He sets up shop in front of the Alleyway. The Laundromat has closed its doors for the night, but the nail salon stays open. Whether this is the Rapture or Osama bin Laden, some ladies still be needing their manis and pedis. Across the street the Koreans who bought the candy store struggle to pull down their security gate. Worried about looters, and rightfully so. Alfredo, who is feeling good, happy to be here, hollers at the Koreans. Tells them the security gate is electricity powered and won't be budging anytime soon. They throw their hands up, as if swatting at flies, and then go back to pulling on their gate. Whatever. That's their business. They're trying to close, but Alfredo's just getting started. Opportunity's knocked. Alfredo spreads the candles in a half circle around his feet, as if he were warding off evil spirits. He positions pillars with pillars, votives with votives. Like the Statue of Liberty, he hoists a torch in the air.

"Get 'em while you still can, folks. Gonna be dark for a hot minute. Get your candles. Blackout special. Five-dollar candles. Get your candles here. Bring home some light. To your husbands and wives. Five dollars a candle. Five dollars apiece. Buy four, get one free. Five dollars, five dollars, five dollars. Need all the light you can get, folks. Gonna get bad tonight. Terrorists coming to kill us. What do you say? Five dollars. Get your light right here. Queens prices. Can't beat 'em. Five dollars apiece. Get your light. Gonna need some light. Selling it here. Stay out of the dark. Everybody needs some light. Five dollars apiece. Talking about light, folks. Light for sale. Light!"

A few hours later, with the sun turning orange behind her head, Isabel finally tracks down her man. She shifts the baby in her arms, checks his diaper for softness. When Alfredo sees them walking toward him, he laces his hands behind his head, probably thinking it makes him look casual, like an awfully cool dude lounging on a beach blanket, but really he looks like a man preparing himself to be arrested.

"How much for the whole thing?" Isabel says.

"That's a lot of candles," he says.

"I thought maybe I'd get a family discount." Christian Louis yanks

on her ponytail, as if he were ringing a bell. "I thought maybe since they were my fucking candles—"

"Hey!" Alfredo says, and tilts his head toward the baby.

"Are you serious?" she says. "Are you *seriously* telling me what I can and cannot say?"

Alfredo watches a taper candle roll away from him, all on its own, and get stuck in the space between sidewalk panels.

"You see my parents?" he says.

She did. She tried waiting at home, lasted a full ninety minutes, but when the apartment shadows thickened, she scooped up Christian Louis and bolted out the door. When they got to Babysitters R Us, Lizette clapped her hands together, squealed with abuela delight. She had birthday presents, she had noisemakers, she had party hats, she had some nice ripe bananas she could fry up . . . but what she did not have, what she hadn't even seen today, was a five-foot six-inch flat-assed Puerto Rican pendejo. To get out of the house, Isabel practically had to peel Lizette's fingers off Christian Louis. She begged them not to go. Talked about the blackout of seventy-seven. Said it wasn't safe for a mother and her young child to be out on the streets when the sun went down. But Isabel—how stupid of her—thought Alfredo might be in some kind of trouble.

"I want to say I'm surprised," she says. "I want to *be* surprised. But you know what?"

"I was gonna replace all the candles I sold," he says. He sounds excited. "But that's not all I was gonna do. I was gonna buy Christian Louis a chair for his new table. The sickest chair they had. I was gonna take you out for a romantic dinner, just me and you. Do it right, you know. Get us back on track. I was gonna pay off some of the Visa bill."

"And how many candles you sell so far?"

He shrugs, deflated. "It's not the busiest block."

"Maybe you're not the best salesman," she says.

Christian Louis turns red. His birthmark glows. He's been up for too long, overstimulated, feeding off Mama's fury, and now he squirms in her arms, moments away from a crankfest explosion. She didn't bring the stroller because she wanted Christian Louis up against her chest, wanted to feel, through his skin, the thump-thump of his heartbeat. She's regretting her sentimentality. She gives him her house keys, which

he sticks under his tongue. Happy birthday! Face soured, he chucks the keys into the street, and then, of course, unavoidably: the wrath.

"Shh," Alfredo says. He comes closer to rub Christian Louis's back. "You see him toss them keys?" Alfredo asks softly. "Little man's gonna be a strikeout king."

"You can't be leaving us anymore," she says. The baby still wails between them, mouth open, his enraged face tilted toward the red-slatted rooftops. Birds bend the branches of a tree. They perch themselves on streetlamps and telephone poles, under air conditioners and awnings, their bright avian eyes turned to the street. "You hear me?" Isabel says.

"I'm out here for *us,*" Alfredo says.

"You want to do us a favor? Stop leaving."

"A guy came up to me," Alfredo says, looking her in the face. "White guy. I tried to sell him a candle, and he called me a piece of trash. Got in my space. Said I was exploiting something or another, you know? I thought he was going to kill me. A big guy. Then I thought that maybe he'd been sent to kill me, you know? Someone my brother knew. Someone Shifrin knew. I think about this shit all the time. This guy's in my face and I'm like this is it. Here we go."

"And did he?"

"Did he kill me?" Alfredo says. He looks down at his work shoes, his work pants, his work shirt, as if he wants to make certain before he answers. "No," he says.

"There you are," Isabel says.

"Here I am."

"So I'm pregnant," she says. She looks up at the sky. "You think we'll see stars tonight?"

Alfredo leans against the brick wall behind him. He doesn't collapse against the wall or fall against it as if he'd been punched in the chest. He does it calmly, bends his body to the bricks. He puts his hands deep down into his pockets.

"I think it's a boy," she says. She's not certain. This new baby hasn't started whispering secrets in her ear yet, but she feels inside of her a decidedly masculine presence. She imagines him—a quarter of an inch long, half the size of her pinky nail—stretching his legs out in front of him, hands plunged in pockets, trying to look casual as the uterine walls around him expand. "You want a little brother?" she asks Christian Louis. "You want a little bro to boss around?"

"I don't think I can handle this," Alfredo says.

She misunderstands him. When Alfredo says he can't handle this, he means he feels unqualified to handle this in a moral sense. He considers himself a corrupt human being—the things he's done, the things he thinks—a man unfit to raise one boy, much less two. In the last year, each folder in his intracranial filing cabinet has been tagged with the ass-reaming rebuke *And you're supposed to be a father?* He can't face more stickers on his files, stickers emblazoned with this unborn baby's name.

But Isabel thinks he's talking about money. She thinks he means they can't raise two children on his elevator boy's salary. And so when he says he can't handle this, she says, "Sure we can." She has him hold the baby, positions his arms so that they provide an acceptable sling of support. She asks, "How much you selling these candles for?"

"Five dollars," he says.

She rolls her eyes. She stoops over to pick up her house keys and the candle that fell between sidewalk panels.

"I'm keeping this one," she says, and slips the candle into her back pocket. "This one came to me."

Christian Louis seizes his father's finger and clamps down hard. Isabel turns away from them. She walks to the lip of the curb, where the sidewalk meets the street. People come and go, fanning themselves with takeout menus. Right around here, just up the block in fact, her mother the puta is probably in her recliner, halfway through a pre-evening nap, a white tube sock draped over her eyes. In just a moment Isabel will start hawking candles—the finest candles in Queens—for the low low blackout special price of ten bucks apiece. And eventually, when night falls and the streets darken, her voice will begin to falter. And when that happens, Alfredo will put their child in her arms, and the two of them will stand close together and take turns calling out prices. But first, before all that, while her voice is still strong, Isabel is going to scream. Her mother is sleeping and Isabel wants to wake that bitch up. She wants to see pigeons scatter and curtains flutter, wants glass to break, wants to drown out her baby's crying, wants to knock butterflies out of the air and ice cream out of cones and buttons off of shirts, wants ears to bleed and buildings to crumble, wants to feel the tingle, the rattle, the streets catching fire. Get ready. She takes a deep breath, cups her hands to her mouth.